Tangled Threads

Born in Gainsborough, Lincolnshire, Margaret Dickinson moved to the coast at the age of seven and so began her love for the sea and the Lincolnshire landscape.

Her ambition to be a writer began early and she had her first novel published at the age of twenty-five. This was followed by twenty-seven further titles including *Plough the Furrow*, *Sow the Seed* and *Reap the Harvest*, which make up her Lincolnshire Fleethaven trilogy. Many of her novels are set in the heart of her home county, but in *Tangled Threads* and *Twisted Strands* the stories include not only Lincolnshire but also the framework knitting and lace industries of Nottingham. Her 2012 and 2013 novels, *Jenny's War* and *The Clippie Girls,* were both top twenty bestsellers and her 2014 novel, *Fairfield Hall*, went to number nine on the *Sunday Times* bestseller list.

Margaret Dickinson

Tangled Threads

PAN BOOKS

First published 2002 by Macmillan

This edition published 2014 by Pan Books
an imprint of Pan Macmillan
20 New Wharf Road, London N1 9RR
Associated companies throughout the world
www.panmacmillan.com

ISBN 978-1-5098-0845-8

Printed and bound by CPI Group (UK) Ltd, Croydon, CR0 4YY

Visit www.panmacmillan.com to read more about all our books
and to buy them. You will also find features, author interviews and
news of any author events, and you can sign up for e-newsletters
so that you're always first to hear about our new releases.

For Dennis

Acknowledgements

The area to the west of Grantham around Barrowby and Casthorpe, the village of Ruddington and, of course, Nottingham are the places of inspiration for the settings in this novel although the story and all the characters are entirely fictitious. The siting of a factory and warehouse on Canal Street in Nottingham and the homes of all the characters within the city in 1900 are also my own invention.

I am deeply grateful to Mr Jack Smirfitt, Miller and all their colleagues at the Ruddington Framework Knitters' Museum for all their wonderful help. I also wish to thank the staff at the Lace Market Centre, Nottingham, for answering my questions and, in particular, Peter Mee, a former twist-hand in the lace industry, who so kindly and generously shared his knowledge and experience with me.

My love and thanks as always to my family and friends for their constant support and encouragement especially those who read and comment on the script in its early stages; my sister and brother-in-law, Robena and Fred Hill; my brother and sister-in-law, David and Una Dickinson; my friends Linda and Terry Allaway and Pauline Griggs. Thank you all so much.

One

1900

'I saw you with him near Bernby Covert,' Jimmy Hard-castle teased his sister when he brought the cows into the byre for evening milking. 'Wait 'til I tell our mam.' He paused for greater effect and then added, 'and Dad.'

Eveleen grabbed hold of him, her fingers digging into his skinny arm. 'Don't you dare,' she hissed.

Jimmy laughed disdainfully as he twisted free of her grasp. 'Stephen Dunsmore'll never marry the likes of you. Oh, he might get you into trouble, but then he'd be off like a rabbit with a ferret on its tail.'

Eveleen's eyes narrowed. 'What about you getting some poor girl into trouble? I've heard about you chasing after Alice Parks. I don't think Mam'll be best pleased to hear about that either.'

'She wouldn't believe you.'

The brother and sister glared at each other. They were remarkably alike. Seeing them together for the first time, strangers could be forgiven for mistaking them for twins. They were equal in height, even though Jimmy, at sixteen, was a year younger than his sister. They had the same dark brown eyes and the same well-shaped nose that on Eveleen was maybe just a fraction too large for true beauty. Their mouths were wide and generous and usually stretched in ready laughter. They even had the same

1

curly hair, a rich chestnut colour, but while Jimmy's was cut short, Eveleen's was a cloud of tangled curls about her face. Though she brushed it one hundred times every night in front of the speckled mirror in the privacy of her bedroom, she could never quite tame it into neatness.

'But I have got nice eyes,' she would murmur. Eveleen's soft and gentle eyes, fringed with long dark lashes, belied a mischievous spirit which her mother, however hard she tried, could not quite quell.

'Besides,' Jimmy went on, 'if anyone said I'd fathered a child—' he stepped back out of her reach as he added, 'I'd say it wasn't mine.'

Eveleen gasped. 'You wouldn't!'

''Course I would. It's what all the lads'd do. Ted told me.'

Ted Morton was twenty and, in Eveleen's opinion, not a good influence on her brother. Ted flirted with her, but Eveleen kept him at arm's length. Literally, for he had never been able even to steal a kiss. She never gave him the chance though she always managed to answer his saucy comments with good-humoured teasing. She had no wish to fall out with Ted. They had grown up together and their fathers, living and working on the same farm estate, were good friends. But Ted Morton was not for her.

Now Stephen Dunsmore, she was thinking, he's a different matter. Her knees trembled at the mere thought of him.

Jimmy's voice broke into her daydreaming. 'It's different for a girl. If you got in the family way, Mam'd go daft. 'Specially if it was with *him*. You know what she's like about "knowing our place".' The youth gave a fair impression of their mother's prim tones. 'And she

2

wouldn't think you walking out with our employer's son was "seemly".'

'Why ever not?' Eveleen flashed back. 'Stephen's father and our dad used to work side by side in the fields and their fathers before them.'

'I know all about Dad's tales,' Jimmy mocked. 'But now we work *for* 'em, not *with* 'em.' There was resentment in Jimmy's tone and it deepened as he went on. 'You don't see Mr Dunsmore getting his hands dirty nowadays and as for Master Stephen, all he's good for is riding about the estate all day in his posh clothes handing out his orders. I bet he doesn't even know *how* to milk a cow. He's never had to work from morning 'til night like our dad.'

To that, Eveleen had no reply. What Jimmy said was true. Ernest Dunsmore, his wife and their son Stephen lived in a large mansion, Fairfield House, just across the fields from the Hardcastles' home. They had live-in servants and all the men employed on their farm lived in tied farmhouses or cottages. And yet Eveleen had always thought of Stephen as one of them. As a young boy, home for the holidays from boarding school, on warm summer evenings he had joined the games of the children living on his family's farmland. In the field behind the big house leading down to the beck he had run races with them and played tiggy-off-ground, leaping onto tree stumps or hanging from the branches of trees to avoid being caught and tigged. Then, as the balmy evenings had shadowed into dusk and the younger children had been called in, he had held Eveleen's hand and walked her home.

But now they were grown and when they met he held her in his arms and kissed her. He did not walk her home any more in case they were seen. By mutual, silent consent, their recent meetings had been secret.

Until this moment.

'We were only talking,' she said now to Jimmy, mentally crossing her fingers.

'Oh aye?' Jimmy sneered. 'Why were you hiding in the trees then?' He shoved his hands in his pockets and walked away, a swagger in his step. He called back over his shoulder. 'You wait 'til I tell 'em at suppertime.'

His shrill, nonchalant whistling echoed round the yard as he walked towards the barn.

Eveleen stared after him. There was nothing she could do. If Jimmy carried out his threat then she was going to be in trouble.

Two

At the supper table, Eveleen pushed the food around her plate. Her appetite had deserted her. Was Jimmy really going to carry out his threat?

'What's the matter, love?' Walter Hardcastle asked his daughter. 'Aren't you hungry?'

At their father's tender concern for her, Eveleen saw the spark of jealousy in her brother's eyes and before she could answer, Jimmy said, 'She's in love. That's what's up with her.'

Mary, coming in from the scullery carrying a plate of buttered plum bread, heard only her son's remark. 'What's that? Some girl got her eye on you, Jimmy?' She sat down next to him and nudged him playfully. 'Well, I'm not surprised. A handsome young man like you. She'll be a lucky girl to get you for a husband.'

Eveleen, despite her growing fear, exchanged a glance with her father and they both had to control their laughter as they saw the horrified expression on Jimmy's face. 'Married? Me?' he spluttered.

'Give the lad time, Mary,' Walter said.

Mary smiled at her son, reached out and smoothed back the hair from his forehead. 'I'm only teasing, love. I don't want to lose you yet a while.'

Playing up to her as always, Jimmy said artfully, 'I'll never find anyone who can cook as good as you, Mam.'

'Oh, go on with you,' Mary said, but her cheeks were

pink with pleasure. It was only as she turned to her daughter that her tone sharpened. 'Eveleen, eat your supper.'

Beneath the table, Eveleen swung her foot to kick his shins, but Jimmy kept his feet tucked under his chair. He said no more and, as the meal ended and she began to clear away the dishes, Eveleen thought she had escaped.

With the sigh of a weary man at the end of a long working day, Walter Hardcastle lowered himself into the wooden chair at the side of the range. He leaned his head against the back of the chair and closed his eyes. Eveleen watched him for a moment, concern in her dark eyes.

Her father was a tall, thin man with a slight stoop. At forty-three his once dark hair was prematurely grey and deep lines gouged his weather-beaten face. He had removed his heavy boots but still wore the striped shirt, black trousers and waistcoat that were his working clothes. As he warmed his aching feet against the fender, he gave another sigh, but this time it was one of contentment.

Eveleen smiled fondly and quietly began to stack the dishes.

Mary fussed around her husband, setting his pipe and tobacco tin within easy reach before she took off the long white apron she had worn all day and sat down opposite him. Then she picked up her pillow lace and bent her head over her work.

Mary looked much younger than Walter although only three years separated them. Her brown hair, pulled back into a neat bun, had only wisps of grey at the temples. The blue and black striped blouse fitted her still slim figure, assisted to even greater shapeliness by her tightly laced corset, and her neat waist was accentuated by a wide belt fastened with silver clips. But there were lines of strain around her blue eyes and her mouth was often pursed with disapproval. Eveleen, carrying the dishes out into the scullery, knew she was often the focus of this disapproval.

As she passed Jimmy, still hovering near the door, Eveleen hissed, 'Well, go if you're going.'

Jimmy glanced at her out of the corner of his eye. 'When I'm good an' ready.'

'Jimmy,' came Mary's voice. 'Close the door, dear. There's a draught round my feet.'

'I'm off out, Mam. To Ted's.' He knew there would be no objection to him visiting the Mortons just down the lane.

Mary glanced at the clock on the mantelpiece above the range. 'Half an hour, then.' She smiled indulgently at him. 'Make sure you're home by ten.'

Jimmy would take no notice. Eveleen knew she would hear him creeping up the stairs at midnight or later, but she would not tell tales of him. She was holding her breath now, willing him to say no more and go. But her brother was not so loyal.

'I reckon Master Stephen is sweet on our Eveleen,' he said into the comfortable peace of the room. 'Can't think why. I've seen better clothes on that scarecrow Ted's put up in Ten Acre Field.'

Mary's fingers were suspended, momentarily idle, above the pillow lace. Eveleen held her breath as her mother glanced at her. Mary's mouth was suddenly tight.

Eveleen laughed nervously and said quickly, 'He's teasing, Mam.'

'I hope so.' The creases between Mary's eyebrows deepened.

'So why's this part of the farm suddenly needing a great deal of Master Stephen's attention these days?' Jimmy asked.

'Could be he's keeping an eye on you,' Eveleen countered. 'Just making sure you're not slipping off to flirt with one of the milkmaids. Alice, for instance.'

'You're the only milkmaid in our crewyard,' Jimmy pointed out. 'And it's not me doing the flirting.'

'Thanks, Jimmy,' Eveleen muttered. He had deliberately ensnared her in a web of trouble.

'I'm off,' Jimmy said airily. 'I'll let you know, Evie, if he's lurking about the cowhouse waiting to catch sight of you.' Then he was gone, slamming the door behind him. They heard his whistling fade as he walked across the yard and out into the lane.

Walter opened his eyes and lifted his head. 'Dun't that lad know how to shut a door quietly?' he murmured, but without real irritation. He began to close his eyes and lean back again, but Mary had no intention now of letting him rest.

'Did you hear what Jimmy said?' she demanded and then snapped at Eveleen. 'And just you put those plates down, miss, and come back here. I want an explanation.'

Eveleen set the plates near the sink in the scullery and, taking a deep breath, returned to the kitchen.

She heard her father's deep sigh as he said, 'What's the matter now?'

'Jimmy says Master Stephen's sweet on Eveleen.' The words were repeated scathingly, as if such a thing could not, should not, be possible. 'I won't have it, Walter. I won't have her getting ideas above herself. It'll all end in tears.' Mary leant towards him, her gaze holding his as she added meaningfully, 'You know it will.'

Walter leant forward in his chair, his kindly, concerned

glance upon his daughter. 'Has Stephen Dunsmore been bothering you, Eveleen?'

Now Eveleen could laugh with ease and say, 'Of course he hasn't, Dad. Master Stephen's too nice to do that.' She ran her tongue around her lips that were suddenly dry as she said carefully, 'But I can hardly ignore him if he – if he wants to – to talk to me, can I? We've been friends for years. Remember how he used to play with us when we were kids?'

'Only because there were no other children from his own class nearby.'

'Oh come now, Mary love,' Walter remonstrated gently. 'The Dunsmores aren't snobs. You can't accuse them of that. Why, the old man used to work alongside us in the fields. That was Stephen's grandfather, of course. George. I was only a lad then. Miles and miles he'd walk behind the two shire horses at ploughing time.'

'That's as maybe,' Mary snapped, for once impatient with Walter's reminiscing. 'But now his son and grandson ride around the estate on a horse instead of walking behind it.'

Walter shrugged, his kindly, placid nature ready to accept change without a trace of bitterness. 'Ernest worked hard as a lad, I'll say that for him, but they've done well for themselves, Mary, that's all. They've a big estate to run now.'

'And you really think that the Dunsmores would allow their son to court the daughter of their gathman?' Mary asked.

Eveleen felt her father's gaze upon her. He smiled. 'Why ever not? She'd make a grand wife for him. Stephen's a fine young man.'

Mary leaned forward. 'I shouldn't think for a moment that marriage is what the "fine young man" has in mind.'

9

Now Walter swivelled his gaze to meet his wife's angry eyes. The smile left his face and he frowned, concerned now at Mary's insinuations. He glanced worriedly back to his daughter. 'Eveleen, has Stephen suggested anything – anything that's not – not . . .' he seemed to be struggling to find the right word, 'proper.'

Mary too was watching her, awaiting her answer. Eveleen trembled at the memory of Stephen's kisses beneath the shadows of the trees in Bernby Covert. The way he held her close and murmured in her ear. 'Oh, Eveleen, how I want you.'

She ran her tongue around her lips once more but was thankful that she was able to meet their eyes steadily and say, quite truthfully, 'No, Dad, he hasn't.'

'Well, mind you never give him the chance,' Mary snapped.

'Eveleen won't – what I mean is – she's . . .' Walter began.

A long look passed between her mother and father, a look of mutual understanding and something even more. Memories, perhaps, that their daughter could not share.

Walter reached across the hearth to touch his wife's hand in a tender gesture. 'She'll be all right, love. Eveleen will be all right.'

For a moment Mary held his gaze, then she nodded and lowered her head over her work again, but not before Eveleen had seen unshed tears glistening in her mother's eyes.

Three

Pear Tree Farm, the Hardcastles' home, was larger than the cottages occupied by the other workers on the estate. It had a large crewyard and cowhouse, two barns, a henhouse and two pigsties. The weekly wash was done in the washhouse attached to the end of the house where a brick copper built into the corner boiled the clothes, and where Eveleen laboured over the rinsing tub and the mangle. The back door of the house itself opened into the scullery and then into the kitchen where the family ate their meals and sat at night near the range which provided heat and hot water and cooked their food. In this one room Mary cooked and baked and ironed. In the centre of the room was a plain wooden table and to one side stood a dresser holding the pots and pans they used every day. In the drawers Mary kept her lace-edged table linen. Down two steps out of the kitchen, the pantry shelves were lined with bottled fruit, home-made jams, chutneys and pickles, and from hooks in the ceiling hung cured hams wrapped in muslin.

In the far corner of the kitchen, a door led into a small hallway and then into Mary's best room – the parlour – only used on Sundays and at Christmas. This room, by any farm labourer's standards, was grand. The walls were papered with heavily patterned green paper and pictures adorned each wall. In a corner cupboard was Mary's prize possession, a willow-patterned tea service. Above the fireplace was a mantelpiece draped in green fabric to blend with the wallpaper and above that an oval mirror with an elaborately carved wooden frame. A dining table covered with a plush green cloth and four chairs stood in the centre of the room. From the hallway between the two rooms, the staircase led up to the master bedroom, a second smaller room that was Eveleen's and, beyond that, a long, narrow room with a sloping ceiling where Jimmy slept.

Only Eveleen ever heard her brother creeping up the stairs late at night and tiptoeing through her room to reach his own.

Not knowing what had transpired, it was ironic that Stephen chose the very next morning to visit Pear Tree Farm quite openly. Eveleen was in the warm barn, gently turning the eggs in the incubator. Dust floated in the shaft of sunlight slanting through a hole in the rafters and the rays highlighted her chestnut hair with golden tints.

'What a pretty picture,' he said softly. Though she jumped at the sound of his voice from the doorway and her fingers trembled, Eveleen managed to carry on moistening the eggs, inspecting each one for the first sign of a hairline crack that would herald the arrival of a fluffy yellow chick. She closed the incubator carefully, checked that the paraffin lamp at the side was still alight and turned to face him.

'Master Stephen,' she said, managing to keep her voice level though her heart leapt at the sight of him. She felt dishevelled in her plain brown skirt, cream blouse and rough hessian apron. She tried to smooth the wild halo of her unruly curls, mortified to think that there might be wisps of straw tangled in her tresses. If only she could have been dressed in her best blue dress and new bonnet, with a parasol to protect her face from the sun. That was the sort of girl Stephen Dunsmore would court, she thought, not some poorly clad milkmaid employed on his father's farm.

And yet he was here, smiling down at her as he leaned nonchalantly against the door jamb, idly slapping his riding crop against his soft leather boot.

'So formal, Miss Hardcastle,' he teased, but his eyes caressed her.

Eveleen thought him the most handsome man she knew. Gently curved eyebrows above blue eyes, a long straight nose, high cheekbones and a chin that was delicately rounded. The early morning sun behind him glinted on his fair hair, the white collar of his shirt gleamed against his lightly tanned skin and the tightly fitting riding jacket outlined strong shoulders. Whenever she saw him, Eveleen would feel the breath leave her body and her limbs tremble.

She glanced out of the barn door but the yard was deserted, except for his horse tethered at the gate. Then, drawing back into the shadows, she whispered, 'They know. Jimmy saw us yesterday in Bernby Covert.'

Stephen's laugh was unconcerned. 'So?'

'He told Mam and Dad at suppertime last night.'

Stephen's left eyebrow arched a fraction. He lifted his riding crop and tapped the ivory handle thoughtfully against his lips. 'Did he, indeed? That was very foolish of him, wasn't it? I think you'd better warn your dear brother not to tell tales in future.'

'Warn him?'

For a brief moment, his blue eyes were steely. 'If he values his job.'

13

Eveleen's dark brown eyes widened in alarm. 'Oh, you wouldn't?'

Then he was laughing as if it had all been a joke. 'Of course I wouldn't, darling. But Jimmy doesn't know that, does he? And we'll just have to be more discreet, won't we?'

Relief flooded through her. He wanted to go on seeing her. He did love her as much as she loved him.

He was reaching out towards her, his fingers almost touching her hair when, from the back door of the farmhouse, her mother's voice floated across the yard. 'Eveleen? Eveleen, where are you?'

Stephen let his hand fall and pulled a wry expression. Standing aside for her to pass he murmured, 'You'd better go.'

As she hurried across the yard, Eveleen was acutely conscious of his gaze following her and knew that her mother had seen him too.

It was not until suppertime that Mary chose to mention Stephen Dunsmore's visit.

'He was here this morning,' she informed her husband in front of both Eveleen and Jimmy. 'And she's been less than useless ever since.'

His fork suspended halfway to his mouth, Walter glanced at Eveleen. Slowly, the fork continued its progress then, chewing the mouthful, he appeared to be thinking.

'And?' he said at last.

'He was in the barn with her. Goodness knows how long he'd been there. I only saw him when I called her in to help me fold the sheets.'

'I told you so,' Jimmy put in smugly, but for once his mother took no notice of him.

'Have you anything you want to tell us, Eveleen?' Walter asked, his face sombre.

Her heart hammering inside her chest, Eveleen swallowed painfully. 'No, Dad,' she whispered. 'There's nothing to tell. Honestly.' It was the truth, at least about their meeting that morning.

Walter pushed his plate away, his supper only half eaten, as if his appetite had suddenly deserted him.

Eveleen dropped her gaze, avoiding his. She could no longer meet those loving, anxious eyes knowing how she was deceiving him.

Mary stood up and crashed the plates together, scraping off Walter's uneaten food on to the topmost plate with swift, angry movements.

Then she leant across the table and wagged her finger in Eveleen's face. 'You'd better come to your senses, miss, and be quick about it. You've been in a dream all day ever since he was here. You burnt a hole in a sheet doing the ironing. Then I found you sitting idly on the hearthrug gazing into space when you should have been polishing the fender. Now you can take these plates into the scullery and wash them. Don't forget to put the meat away in the meat-safe and then you'd better get yourself to bed. You've an early start in the morning if you're going to the fat stock market with your father.' She put her hand on her husband's shoulder and her tone softened as she added, 'And you'd better go to your bed, too, Walter dear. You're looking tired.'

Already Jimmy was sidling towards the door to escape before Mary could send him to bed too.

'I think I will, love.' Walter heaved himself up from his chair and, wishing each member of his family goodnight, he hauled himself up the narrow stairs to the bedroom above.

As she washed and dried the dishes and put everything away, Eveleen's pulse quickened. Stephen often went to the cattle market. Perhaps they would see him. Tomorrow she would wear her best bonnet to ride in the pony and trap to Grantham.

As she returned to the kitchen to say goodnight it was as if her mother, sitting once more with her pillow lace, had read her thoughts.

'And don't you be thinking you can wear your Sunday best tomorrow,' Mary said.

Thankful that the comment made no direct accusations, Eveleen was emboldened to protest. 'But, Mam, I can't go to town in my working clothes. What would people think?'

'Of course I don't mean you should go looking like a ragamuffin.' Mary Hardcastle bristled with indignation. 'But your second-best dress and shawl will be quite serviceable.' She pursed her mouth primly. 'I don't want anyone to think you're getting ideas above your station.'

A spark of rebellion made Eveleen ask, 'And what is my "station", Mam? Because I'd really like to know.'

'Eveleen! Don't you dare to answer me back. Now, get to bed and I'll have to decide whether I even let you go tomorrow.'

'But, Mam—'

'Not another word.' Mary flapped her hand, dismissing her daughter.

Eveleen bit her lip to still an angry response. Her mother knew full well that one of the harshest punishments she could inflict upon her daughter was to stop her weekly trip into town with her father. Silently she left the kitchen to the sound of her mother's mutterings about ungrateful children and climbed the stairs.

Sleep deserted her. She didn't like upsetting her mother, but sometimes retorts sprang to her lips and were out of her mouth before she could stop them. In the darkness Eveleen sighed. It was her biggest failing, she knew. But her mother was a difficult and complex woman to understand. Even Mary herself did not seem to know exactly what it was she wanted in life, so how were her children expected to know. At times she would be exhorting them to work harder, to "make something of themselves"; at others she was castigating them for "getting above themselves" and warning them that they should "know their place".

Now their father . . . Eveleen smiled to herself at the mere thought of him. He was easy to understand. Straightforward, placid, loving, and generous as far as his meagre wage would allow him to be. His generosity of spirit went much further than monetary gifts. More than anything, he gave of himself. He gave time and patience to his children. He always had done so, as far back as Eveleen could remember, even helping her as a small child to learn to read, though hardly a scholar himself. He would painstakingly write the letters of the alphabet on to her slate with a piece of white chalk and point to each one, guiding her hand as she traced the outlines of the letters herself.

Even then her mother had grumbled. 'An education's wasted on a girl. What she needs to learn is how to cook and wash and sew and look after a family. What good's fancy learning going to be for her?'

But Walter Hardcastle only smiled indulgently at his wife and said gently, 'You're right, of course, my dear. Eveleen must learn all those things and who better to teach her than you.' Then he would pause and add quietly, but with a firmness that even his wife could not ignore, 'But it will do her no harm to learn her letters and go to school. One day, it might come in useful.'

Despite a restless night, Eveleen was up first the following morning. The fire in the range had been stoked up and the breakfast laid before even her father appeared. When her mother came down, Eveleen went back upstairs to her bedroom to wash in the china bowl and to put on her pink dress with a high neckline and leg o' mutton sleeves. Today Jimmy would cope with the early morning milking, so Eveleen made her bed and then laid out the only two bonnets she possessed. Biting her lip, she stood looking down at them. The newest, the one she had only had since the previous Easter, was by far the prettiest, but it was her best one. The older one was becoming shabby, although her mother declared there was plenty of wear left in it yet.

Deciding suddenly, Eveleen snatched up her best bonnet and pushed the other one back into the wardrobe. She would have to get past her mother without Mary seeing it. She crept down the stairs and into the kitchen. Her mother, clearing away the breakfast things, looked up.

'Look sharp, Eveleen, your father's waiting for you in the yard.'

Hiding the bonnet beneath the cream shawl she carried, Eveleen hurried forward to kiss her mother's cheek and then flew out of the house. Picking up her skirts she ran across the yard and climbed into the pony and trap borrowed each market day from the big house.

Only when they were safely out of the gate and a short distance down the lane did Eveleen breathe a sigh of satisfaction and put on her bonnet.

'Oho,' Walter Hardcastle chuckled. 'I wondered why you came out of the house at a gallop. Now I know.'

Eveleen laughed aloud and then tucked her arm through her father's. 'But you won't tell her, Dad, will you?'

''Course not, love. Our secret, eh?'

Eveleen hugged his arm to her side, her love for him spilling over as they laughed together.

Then Eveleen lifted her face and breathed in the sharp air. An early morning frost silvered the ground and turned trees and hedges into gossamer threads as delicate as her mother's pillow lace. A mist hung over the land and shrouded the trees. But the sun, rising palely before them, would soon warm the earth, melt away the frost and disperse the mist. It was going to be a lovely day.

And today she might see Stephen.

Four

The village of Bernby lay on a hill to the west of Grantham. Even further west, down the steep, narrow lane twisting beneath the overhanging trees of Bernby Covert and over the footbridge across the bubbling beck, lay the Dunsmores' 700-acre farm and the homes of their employees.

George Dunsmore had been born in Pear Tree Farm and at the age of twenty had inherited the house, forty acres of arable land and a herd of cows. But George was ambitious. He chose as his wife a girl from good farming stock and together they determined to build a future, not only for themselves, but also for the next generation.

Ann Dunsmore bore five children but only three lived to adulthood. George Dunsmore focused his hopes and dreams upon his only surviving son, Ernest. With Ernest's birth in 1855, George added more acreage to his farm and built a grand mansion, Fairfield House, just across the fields behind his former home.

Ben Hardcastle had worked on the land from the age of twelve and at fifteen had been the first farm labourer George Dunsmore employed. They worked shoulder to shoulder, just the two of them, from dawn to dusk and beyond. A year after George's son's birth, Ben married Emily and George offered them the tied dwelling, Pear Tree Farm. Soon George employed other men on his expanding farm, but he made Ben his head stockman and

Ben Hardcastle was always the man the others looked up to.

George Dunsmore was a lucky man. By the time he died in 1890 at the age of sixty-five, he had lived long enough to see his ambitions realized and he died happy in the certain knowledge that his son would continue his life's work. By that time, the farm had already grown to five hundred acres and he had seen Ernest marry and present him with a grandson, Stephen, who would one day inherit all that George had striven for.

The Hardcastles had not been quite so fortunate. A year after their marriage Emily gave birth to a son, Walter, but that same night his birth had caused her death. Within a year, however, Ben married a kindly woman who, unable to have children of her own, had lavished affection on her stepson. Neither Ben nor his son Walter had been ambitious and were content to live on in Pear Tree Farm and work for the enterprising Dunsmores. As the years passed and the estate grew, the Hardcastles, while being liked and respected, no longer held the unofficial position of the boss's right-hand man and confidant. A farm bailiff, Josiah Jackson, now administered the day-to-day running of the estate and while Walter carried on his father's work as gathman, he no longer held a privileged position.

'That Josiah Jackson would turn us out of our home, if he could,' Mary would often say, only to be placated by her gentle, unassuming husband.

'Oh come now, Mary love, I'm sure that isn't so.'

Mary would shake her head and smile and say, 'Oh, Walter, what am I going to do with you? Sometimes, I think you're just too good to be true. You don't see wrong in anyone, do you?' And she would pass the back of his chair and plant a kiss on his thinning hair. Walter would only chuckle and his eyes would twinkle. 'Well, I've my stepmother to thank for that, love,' he would say.

'She was a lovely woman,' Walter, speaking of Elizabeth, his stepmother, would tell Eveleen often. 'It's my only real sorrow in life that neither my dad nor my stepmother lived to see you and Jimmy. How she would have loved you,' he would murmur, reaching out to touch his daughter's wild halo of hair.

Then Eveleen would hug her father. 'I wish I'd known her too, Dad, and your father.'

'He was a nice man, such a kind man.' Her father's voice would soften as he remembered. 'Such a shame he died earlier than he should have done. He was only in his forties. I – I found him you know. Collapsed in the field next to our house. A heart attack, the doctor said. No one could have done anything, even if we'd been with him when it happened.'

Eveleen would always shudder when her father recounted this tragedy. She could feel her father's sadness and share his helplessness. The poor man, dying alone in the middle of a field and no one even there to hold his hand.

'What happened to your stepmother?' Eveleen knew the answer, but also knew instinctively that her question helped her father to talk about it. It did him good to talk about one of the saddest days in his life.

'She was distraught, devastated by my father's death. Couldn't come to terms with it at all. She blamed hersen, although that was nonsense, of course. The doctor – everyone – tried to reassure her but she wouldn't listen. She just went downhill afterwards. So fast. I wouldn't have believed it if I hadn't seen it with me own eyes that anyone could go from being a happy, laughing, healthy woman to skin and bone in a few weeks. She didn't live many months after he went.'

Sorrow and guilt were in her father's voice. 'It wasn't your fault. You mustn't feel responsible, Dad,' Eveleen would try to reassure him, but her father's answer was always the same. 'But I do, love. I do. I can't help thinking that if only I'd looked after her better . . .'

Now, sitting together in the trap bowling their way to market, Eveleen asked, 'Dad, how did you and Mam meet? I know you lived alone in our house after your parents died, but you've never told me how you met our mam.'

Joining the lane at the end of the track leading from their home, Walter turned to the left and then after a quarter of a mile or so took another left turn. They passed the wrought-iron gates leading into the sweeping drive of Fairfield House. Eveleen risked a glance and found she was holding her breath, but there was no sign of Stephen.

The pony trotted on, splashing through the ford beside the footbridge across the beck and labouring up the hill towards Bernby Covert. The road passed beneath the trees, cold where the sun had not yet penetrated the shadows, and on towards Bernby village and then Grantham. Eveleen loved these trips with her father, loved having him all to herself for a few precious hours. They talked about all sorts of things and she soaked up his knowledge, his wisdom and revelled in his obvious love for his family.

But now he was not answering her immediately. He was sitting, holding the reins lightly in his hands and staring straight ahead.

'Dad?' Eveleen prompted.

With her arm still through his, she felt, rather than heard, his heavy sigh. His words came hesitantly, reluctantly. 'She came to work for the Dunsmores one potato-picking time.' Walter cleared his throat and seemed to be choosing his words very carefully. 'The work was very hard for her. Not – not what she had been used to. She was – er – ill and, because I was living on my own, I took her in and looked after her. Mrs Dunsmore – the old lady that is – heard about it and said it wasn't seemly.'

Father and daughter exchanged a knowing smile. It was the sort of phrase that Mary herself now used constantly.

'So you married her?'

'Not straight away.' Again, Eveleen could detect that Walter was being careful to select his words. 'Mr Ernest had been married just over a year and his wife had just had Master Stephen and she needed help about the place. In the house and with the dairy work. So when ya mam felt well again, she went to live in for a while at Fairfield House.'

Eveleen could not keep the surprise from her tone. 'Mrs Rachel used to work?'

Her father's expression lightened a little as he said, 'Oh yes. I remember the time when they were first married, Mr Ernest still used to plough fields himself and his bride, Rachel, used to help milk the cows. That was when the old man, Mr George, was still alive. After he died, it began to change and now, of course, like your mam always says . . .' without a trace of resentment or envy in his tone, Walter said, laughingly, 'the Dunsmores can afford to employ others to do all the work while the master and his son ride around the estate on their horses instead of walking mile after mile behind them.'

'But where did Mam come from? Did her family live near here?'

'No – no, she came from a little village just south of Nottingham.'

'Nottingham!' Eveleen could not keep the surprise from her tone, and yet this revelation did answer a question that had been in her mind as she had been growing up but had never been voiced. Aloud she murmured, 'So that's why she talks different to you.'

Walter Hardcastle spoke with the broad Lincolnshire dialect of the area, but Mary's speech was different.

Walter was chuckling softly to himself. 'I'm sure your mother would be delighted to hear you say that. She has tried so hard to erase dialect of any sort from her own way of speaking. And from you and Jimmy. 'Fraid she hasn't managed it with me, though, much to her disappointment.'

They travelled for a few moments before Eveleen took a deep breath and asked, 'Did you know her family?'

There was a long silence and when her father did answer he was now noticeably hesitant. 'Eveleen, love, it's not for me to tell you. If your mother wants you to know, she will tell you in her own good time.'

For a moment Eveleen held her breath, restraining the tumult of questions that threatened to spill out. Then she released her breath slowly, but her mind was racing. So, there was some mystery surrounding her mother's early life. Her mother never mentioned her family and Eveleen did not know if she had grandparents, aunts, uncles, or even cousins. Whatever could have happened to make Mary lose contact with her family so completely?

She risked one more tentative question. 'Are her

25

parents still alive? Have I got a grandpa and granny somewhere?'

There was genuine sadness in Walter's tone. 'I don't know, love.' Then, more firmly, he added, 'Please, Eveleen, don't ask me any more.'

The remainder of the journey passed without either of them speaking. A shadow had passed across their day.

They came to Westgate in the town close to the cattle market.

'It's busy today,' Walter remarked. 'I'll have to leave the trap here.' They climbed down. 'You can go and look around the shops, Eveleen. Don't get lost.'

They smiled at each other and the constraint that had been briefly between them fled. Eveleen laughed. She knew this part of Grantham almost as well as the lanes around her own home.

'I won't, Dad. Besides, I've a list of things to buy for Mam. I'm not going to have much time for dawdling.'

'Well, enjoy yarsen, lass. You don't get into town very much. Now,' his attention turned to his work, 'I must find Master Stephen. We're here to buy a bull today. Mr Ernest wants to start breeding shorthorns, so I must be sure to find him a good one.'

'You will,' Eveleen said, confident in her father's knowledge of cattle. Walter was reputed to be the best cowman in the area and while the modest man would never speak of it himself, the knowledge filled Eveleen with pride. 'If I see Stephen, I'll tell him you're looking for him.'

At the mere mention of his name, her foolish heart began to beat a little faster and she could feel the colour creeping up her neck. She turned away before her father

should see the sparkle in her eyes and her smile of anti-
cipation.

She wove her way through the throng, nodding and
smiling at acquaintances and then she was brought to a
sudden halt by the tall, lanky figure barring her path.

'If it isn't the lovely Eveleen in her best Sunday
bonnet.'

She smiled up at the young man. 'Hello, Ted. What
brings you to town on market day?'

'All the pretty girls, of course. But there's none as
pretty as you, Evie.' Before she could protest, he had
grabbed hold of her hand and pulled it through his arm.
'When are you going to start walking out with me
properly?'

Eveleen looked up at him, threw back her head and
laughed aloud. 'When the sun shines on both sides of the
hedge at once,' she teased.

Ted pretended to be heartbroken and pressed his hand
against his chest. 'Oh, I'll die of love for you,' he clowned.
Then, dropping to one knee, he clasped both his hands
together in supplication as if proposing.

His tomfoolery caused a ripple of laughter among the
passers-by and Eveleen had to wipe tears of merriment
from her eyes. 'Get up, you idiot. What will people
think?'

'I don't care,' he proclaimed loudly, with feigned
passion. 'You're breaking my heart, Eveleen Hardcastle.'

A voice spoke behind her. A voice that made her legs
tremble and her heart feel as if it was doing somersaults.
As she turned to face him, Eveleen caught her breath. On
Stephen's face there was an unmistakable look of jealousy
as he glanced away from her to glare at the young man
who was scrambling hastily to his feet and, for once,
looking embarrassed himself.

'Sorry, Master Stephen. Only having a bit of fun with Evie.'

'I see,' Stephen said slowly. 'And have you been given time off from work to "have a bit of fun" with Miss Hardcastle?'

'Oh – er – well, sir.' Ted was fumbling now. He, like his father Bill Morton, worked for the Dunsmores.

Smoothly, Eveleen intervened. While she had no time for Ted as a prospective suitor, she did not want to see him in trouble. 'You were looking for my father, weren't you, Ted?' she asked, and Ted, quick on the uptake, glanced at her gratefully as she went on, 'He's gone to look over the bulls. You'll find him there.'

'Thanks, Evie.' Ted pulled off his cap, gave an awkward gesture, something between a nod and a bow, to Stephen Dunsmore and hurried away, pulling his cap back on his head as he went.

Eveleen turned back to smile up at Stephen. Now she could say quite truthfully, 'And my father was hoping to meet up with you, too.'

Stephen looked down at her, but there was no responding smile. His eyes still glittered with angry resentment. 'Was he?' He raised his hat and bowed his head in a tiny, stiff movement that implied condescension rather than courtesy. 'Then I had better find him. I'll bid you good-day, Miss Hardcastle.'

'Stephen—' she began, reaching out trembling fingers towards him. But he turned and was gone, striding away from her through the crowds that seemed to part for him as if recognizing his position of authority.

Eveleen watched him go, her heart heavy with disappointment.

Five

Eveleen's mind was not on the shopping list her mother has given her. She had been to Boot's Cash Chemist in Market Place and to Mr Crow's, the linen draper's shop, on High Street. Coming out, she paused to consult her list, but her eyes hardly focused on Mary's spidery handwriting. All she could see was Stephen's angry face.

There had been no hint of friendliness towards her. He had not even smiled at her. He had acted as if they were strangers.

Eveleen sighed. Her joy in the day's outing was spoilt and now she was hungry and thirsty too, but she could imagine her mother's tirade if she were to spend precious housekeeping money on the luxury of a cup of tea and a bun.

She folded the piece of paper in her hand and was about to set off in search of the next item on the list when she felt someone grip her elbow and a voice say in her ear, 'Here you are. I've been looking all over for you. You've led me a merry dance.'

Eveleen twisted round and looked up into Stephen's face. He was smiling down at her now and his earlier hostility had evaporated.

'I – I thought you didn't want to be with me,' she murmured.

Stephen released her arm and glanced up and down the street. 'Of course I want to be with you, but we must be careful.' Then, almost as a hasty afterthought, he added, 'I don't want you to be in more trouble with your parents.'

Again he glanced to right and left and then he crooked his arm and offered it for her to take. Self-consciously, Eveleen wiped her trembling hand down the skirt of her dress before putting it on his arm.

'You're looking very pretty today,' he said as they walked along together. 'But I expect young Morton has already told you that.' Again, there was jealousy in the words and in his tone.

Eveleen's heart leapt at the thought that he minded about Ted Morton. Yet she did not want him to think there was anything between them. 'Ted and I have grown up together. We're more like brother and sister than – than anything.'

Stephen smiled at her as he leant towards her, his mouth close to her ear and said softly, 'I'm very glad to hear it. Now, we'll go in here and I'll buy you a drink.' He nodded towards the dim interior of the Horse and Jockey public house.

'Oh, I couldn't. I – I . . .' she said in a squeak. She could almost hear her mother's voice saying, "It wouldn't be seemly, Eveleen. You should know your place."

'It's just a drink. I'm sure it's hours since you had breakfast. I know it is since I had mine. Come, I won't take no for an answer.'

Eveleen glanced around, her pulse racing with excitement and sudden daring. Her father was busy over at the cattle market, engaged in business for his employer. It would be hours yet before he was ready to go home. Eveleen felt a spark of defiance. Why shouldn't she? If he didn't think it was proper, then Stephen wouldn't be asking her, she reasoned. Where was the harm?

She pulled in a deep breath and felt suddenly calmer.

'Thank you, Master Stephen,' she said politely and, to her surprise, found that her voice was strong and steady now. 'I'd be delighted.'

Inside it was dark but certainly not dismal for a bright log fire burned in the grate and the small round tables were polished until they gleamed. Farmers, leaning against the bar and sitting at the tables, glanced at her curiously for a moment and then looked away.

Stephen ushered her into a chair in the farthest corner of the room from the entrance and went to the bar. He had not asked her what she would like to drink but returned with a pale, frothy liquid in a tall glass for her and a tankard of beer for himself. When Eveleen took a sip she found it rather bitter, but at this moment, in Stephen's company, water from the beck would have tasted like nectar to her.

He sat down beside her and, beneath the table, reached for her hand, holding it between both his own. 'Oh, Eveleen, you don't know how I long to have you to myself. Do you know that I ride past your home every day just in the hope of seeing you?'

'Really?' Eveleen felt a thrill run through her and then her sense of humour rose to the surface and she laughed. 'My mother would say, "Haven't you anything better to do with your time?"'

He glanced over his shoulder, but there was no one else nearby. With a courtly gesture, Stephen raised her fingers to his lips. 'I can't think of any better way to spend my time,' he murmured.

He took a long drink, almost emptying the tankard. 'Another?' he asked her.

Eveleen smiled and shook her head. 'No – no, thank you.' She had drunk only half the contents of the glass and already she felt strangely light-headed.

As Stephen went to the bar again she noticed another young man enter.

'Dunsmore, old chap,' he boomed in greeting, slapping Stephen on the back. 'What are you drinking?'

Stephen smiled but shook his head and leaned closer to speak into the newcomer's ear. The young man, dressed in plus fours, turned and looked directly at Eveleen. His loud guffaw echoed around the bar above the buzz of conversation, causing some of the other men to glance again in her direction. Then, as Eveleen saw him nudge Stephen and wink, she felt the colour begin to rise in her face. Her glance flickered around the room and she saw to her utter dismay and confusion what she had not noticed when she had come in. She had been so overwhelmed by Stephen's attention and the excitement of being with him, she had failed to realize that she was the only woman in the public bar of the Horse and Jockey.

'You're late home, Walter. Is everything all right?'

Mary appeared out of the back door of the house as her husband manoeuvred the trap into the yard. Drawing to a halt, Walter climbed down and then held out his hand to help his daughter alight, laughing as he did so. 'It's thanks to this little minx if we are late, Mary. She says you gave her so much shopping to do, I was hanging about for her for over half an hour after I'd finished my bit of business in the market.'

Mary's eyebrows drew together in a frown as she looked keenly at her daughter. 'I didn't give you that much,' she began and then, before Eveleen could think of a reply, Mary pointed to her head. 'And what, miss, do you think you're doing wearing your best Sunday bonnet? I told you to wear your second-best dress and bonnet.'

In her excitement at being with Stephen and then the flurry of being late back to meet her father, Eveleen had completely forgotten that she had deliberately disobeyed her mother.

'I'm sorry, Mam,' she began, 'but my other bonnet is beginning to look shabby and—'

'Don't scold the girl, Mary,' her father interrupted, coming to her rescue. 'Where's the harm?'

'She deliberately disobeyed me,' Mary insisted.

Walter tried to adopt a disapproving expression but his eyes twinkled. 'You shouldn't have done that, Eveleen. Now say you're sorry to your mother and we'll say no more about it.'

'I'm sorry, Mam.'

'Very well, then.' Mary was a little mollified. 'But don't let it happen again or I shall stop you going into town.'

As they began to unload the packages from the back of the trap, Jimmy sauntered into the yard. With a calculated air of innocence, he said, 'Ted says to thank you for saving his bacon with Master Stephen.' Then he glanced slyly towards their mother.

'What's this about Master Stephen?' Mary missed nothing, as Jimmy had known full well.

Eveleen glared at her brother, but was obliged to explain at least part of it. 'I was talking to Ted in the market place. He was acting the fool as he always does, but meant no harm. Master Stephen came up to us and asked him straight out if he had permission to be off work.' She shrugged. 'All I could think of was to say that Ted was meeting Dad.' She looked to her father, hoping he would feel able to back up her story. 'So I told him where to find you.' Mentally she was crossing her fingers that no one had seen her in the Horse and Jockey.

With gentle remonstration, Walter said, 'I can understand why you said it, but it wasn't entirely true, was it, Eveleen?'

Eveleen bit her lip. 'No, Dad. I'm sorry.'

She seemed to be saying nothing but 'I'm sorry'.

'And then what?' Mary was not about to let the matter drop.

Eveleen trembled but managed to say calmly, 'I went and did your shopping and then – and then I happened to meet Master Stephen again. Completely by accident. Honestly, Mam.'

Mary's face was like an ominous thundercloud. 'And?'

Now she was floundering. 'Well – we just talked.'

'Ted saw you with him,' Jimmy said, and as he turned and began to move away, he threw the words back over his shoulder. 'Coming out of the Horse and Jockey in High Street.'

'He – what?' The scandalized expression on her mother's face would have reduced Eveleen to helpless laughter had she not realized that now she was in deep trouble.

'Do you mean to tell me, miss, that you actually went into a public house?'

Eveleen nodded. Mary moved towards her menacingly. 'Do you know,' she said with dreadful emphasis on every word, 'what sort of women go into those places?'

'But I was with Stephen. I thought—'

Without warning, Mary Hardcastle's hand met her daughter's cheek with a resounding slap that echoed around the yard. 'You little trollop! Have you remembered nothing I've taught you, girl? Haven't I always told

34

you to remember your place? What will people think of you if they saw you with him and in a public house too?'

The memory of the stranger's laughter and his suggestive nudge made Eveleen wince. Now she realized what he, and probably all the other men there too, had been thinking about her.

Mary lunged at Eveleen as if to strike her again, but Walter caught hold of his wife. 'Now, now, there's no need for that. Let's talk about this.'

Mary struggled against her husband's grip. 'You keep out of this, Walter. This has nothing to do with you. You wouldn't understand.' Her words were scathing as she added, 'Being a man.'

Calmly, Walter said, 'Of course I understand and it has everything to do with me. She's my daughter too and don't you think a father understands better than anyone what young men are like?' Even in the midst of the quarrel, he smiled a little as he added, 'I was young once, you know.'

The fight seemed to drain out of Mary and she sagged against him. 'Oh, Walter, you were always good and kind and considerate. You would never have taken advantage of any girl.'

Walter allowed himself a grimace. 'Now you're making me sound very dull, Mary.'

'No, no,' she insisted at once, twisting round in his arms to face him and reaching up to touch his face in a tender gesture. 'You know I didn't mean that.'

'No, no, of course you didn't.' Above Mary's head, he glanced at Eveleen. 'But have you thought, Mary love, that it's perhaps my fault if Eveleen is so trusting of all young men?'

'Of course it isn't your fault,' Mary snapped, her anger rising once more. 'Haven't I dinned it into her until I'm dizzy that she should look to her own kind for a husband, not be setting her cap at the gentry? Someone like Stephen Dunsmore is only amusing himself with the likes of her. Taking her into a pub with no thought for her reputation. That tells you a lot, doesn't it?'

Doubt and anxiety crossed Walter's face, but then he said, 'He's only young too, Mary. Mebbe he just didn't think.'

'Didn't think about *her*, you mean. She's just a plaything to him. Nothing more. He'll likely seduce her and bring shame on this family and care not a jot when he does it.' Without allowing Walter time to protest any further, Mary turned back to Eveleen. 'You're not to meet him again. I forbid it. And if I catch you with him, I'll – I'll send you away. Yes, yes, that's what I'll do, I'll send you away from here. Now get to your bed. No supper for you. If you've been drinking with the gentry you've no need of my supper.'

Eveleen glanced at her father, seeking his support, but for once Walter avoided meeting her gaze. Tears smarted behind her eyes and she bit down hard on her lower lip to stop it trembling. Then she turned and fled into the house and up the stairs to her room. Tearing the offending bonnet from her head she sat down before the mirror and in the half-light she stared at her reflection. Her brown eyes were large and round with distress, her cheeks pink, her bosom heaving and her hair flying wild and loose around her shoulders, and she was trembling all over.

Then she buried her face in her hands and sobbed.

Six

Eveleen kept to her room for the remainder of the evening and for the second night running she slept fitfully. By the morning, however, she had come to a decision.

Whatever her mother said, she would not stop meeting Stephen. She was falling in love with him and she did not want to stop herself if there was the slightest chance that he could possibly care for her.

As she dressed, shivering in the sharp early morning air, Eveleen's resolve hardened. She would do her work, she would be dutiful to her parents in every other way, but in this one thing she would not obey them.

Downstairs Eveleen stoked up the fire, set the kettle on the hob and laid the table for breakfast before she went out into the cowhouse to milk the first of the cows her father would already have brought to the crewyard.

As she was finishing milking the last cow, a shadow appeared in the doorway and she heard Jimmy's voice. 'By heck, you're for it now, aren't ya?' There was glee in his voice. 'You ought to have had more sense. And if I catch him round here—'

A sudden spurt of anger made Eveleen stand up quickly. 'Oh aye, Jimmy Hardcastle, and just what do you think you're going to do, eh? Have fisticuffs with the master's son so that you lose your job?'

'Wouldn't bother me. I'd go to sea. Just like I've always wanted.' He glared at her defiantly.

'Then what about our dad? Think about him. Do you want him to lose his job an' all?'

The lad thrust his hands into his pockets and shrugged. ''Course not,' he said, but his tone was nonchalant as if he didn't really care one way or the other.

'And we'd lose our home, don't forget. Have you thought about that?' Eveleen persisted.

'Have *you* thought about what *you're* doing?' he answered her back. 'You could be making as much trouble for us all as anyone.'

Eveleen stared at him, suddenly unsure. 'How do you mean?'

'Stephen's got a hold over you, ain't he? If you don't do what he wants, he can have us all put out of a job. And,' he added pointedly, 'as you've just said, out of our home an' all.'

'Stephen's not like that. He wouldn't do anything so – so . . .'

Jimmy shrugged again as he turned away. 'You think not. He's a man, our Evie, ain't he?'

Eveleen stood still, watching her brother cross the yard, whistling as he went.

'He's not like that,' she murmured to herself. 'I just know he's not.'

Late in the afternoon, Eveleen ran up the hill towards Bernby Covert where she could see him waiting for her.

'There you are.' The delight was evident in his tone as he dismounted and came towards her, his hands out-stretched to take hers into his own.

She threw herself against him. 'Stephen,' she began, breathless from running. She felt the familiar lurch of pleasure at the sight of him, at being near him. 'Stephen,' she said again, savouring the name. Then she tilted back her head and looked up into his eyes. 'They know about our meeting yesterday. About the Horse and Jockey – everything.'

His mouth tightened as he muttered, 'Damnation take the fellow.' He looked down at her. 'I presume it was young Morton?'

Eveleen realized suddenly that although she was standing very close to him and clutching at him, he was now making no effort to hold her. She let her arms fall and took a step away from him.

'Sort of,' she said guardedly, anxious that he should not blame Ted. 'Ted told my brother that – that he had seen us together. But he wouldn't see any harm in that. He wouldn't know.'

'Mm. I'm not so sure.'

'Ted doesn't know about us. Only my family.' Before she had stopped to think what she was saying, the words spilled out. 'It's my precious brother we've to thank for that.'

Stephen raised his eyebrows sardonically and drawled, 'Is it indeed? Then we'll have to do something about him, won't we?'

She moved closer again and put her hands, palms flat, against his chest. 'Don't let's waste time thinking about him. I can't stay long.'

As he pulled her beneath the shadows of the trees and into his arms they both heard the sound of a twig snapping. Stephen stared beyond her, over her shoulder, and then he thrust her away from him and plunged towards where the trees grew closely together and the undergrowth was thick. A moment later, Eveleen was horrified to see him hauling her brother out from among the bushes by the scruff of his neck.

Stephen was taller and broader than the younger boy, but Jimmy was wiry and strong. He kicked and hit out at his captor until Stephen, with a cry of pain, was forced to let go of him. But as Jimmy made to escape, Eveleen grabbed him. 'Oh no you don't. Just what do you think you're doing, spying on us?'

Jimmy's face was ugly as he faced her. 'Wait till I tell our dad about this. Just wait till he hears about his precious, darling daughter. You'll not be his favourite for much longer.'

Despite her anger, Eveleen was filled with a sudden sadness. 'This hasn't anything to do with me and Stephen, has it? You're just jealous of me.'

'Huh! I couldn't care less.' Jimmy's tone was deliberately offhand, but Eveleen could see the hurt in his eyes.

As her grip loosened, Jimmy pulled himself free and began to run. Only then did Stephen shout after him, 'You're sacked, Hardcastle.'

Jimmy stopped, turned to face them and shook his fist at Eveleen. 'See? I told you so. See what you've done now?'

Then he was gone, crashing through the undergrowth.

Eveleen turned to Stephen and wound her arms about him, burying her face against him. 'Please don't sack him. Oh please say you didn't mean it.'

He was breathing hard, his chest rising and falling against her cheek. Then he bent his head and began to kiss her hair, her forehead, the tip of her nose and finally her mouth, murmuring as he did so, 'That all – depends on – how nice – you are to me.'

As his mouth came down hard upon hers and he pressed her to the ground, it was not only the sudden breeze rustling through the trees that chilled her heart.

*

'Jimmy? Jimmy, are you in here?' As soon as she arrived back at the farm, Eveleen went in search of her brother. As her eyes became accustomed to the dim interior of the barn, she could see him sitting on a mound of hay, staring into space, a resentful expression on his face.

'Shouldn't you be fetching the cows in?'

'He can fetch 'em himself,' Jimmy muttered.

'Who? Dad?'

'No. 'Im. If he's sacked me, I aren't doing another thing.'

Eveleen crossed the dirt floor and sat down beside him. 'He hasn't sacked you. He was just angry.'

'Oh aye. Persuade him to change his mind, did you? What did you have to do? Lift your skirts for him?'

'No, I didn't,' Eveleen said hotly. 'Don't you dare think such a thing about me.'

'Pull the other one, Evie. You must have done something. Something,' he added maliciously, 'that Dad wouldn't like to hear about.'

Eveleen stared at him through the gloom. Then slowly and deliberately she said, 'As long as you promise not to tell Mam and Dad, you can keep your job.'

'Oho, blackmail now, is it?' Then, surprisingly, he laughed and there was even a note of grudging admiration in his tone. 'Well, I'll say this for you, our Evie. From being a right goody-goody, you're certainly learning fast.'

He stood up and, dusting the bits of hay from his clothes, he glanced down at her. 'Not sure I want his precious job, anyway.' He sniffed. 'I'll be going to sea soon.'

As he left the barn, Eveleen could not stop the words escaping her lips as she called after him. 'And what would Mam do then, without her precious baby boy?'

41

At once she was ashamed of her own resentment of the closeness between her mother and brother. 'I'm as bad as he is,' she told herself sharply.

Then she hauled herself up and went to start the evening milking.

Later, with their day's work finished and about to go into the house for supper, Eveleen put her hand on her father's arm.

'Dad,' she asked quietly. 'Why is Mam so upset about me and Stephen?'

In the dim interior of the cowshed, she could not see Walter's features clearly enough to read their expression.

'Eveleen, there are things I cannot tell you – it would be breaking a confidence if I did. But you must believe me if I tell you that your mother has good reason to want to – to protect you. She doesn't want to see you hurt.'

Eveleen's sharp mind was running riot and then, with sudden clarity, she began to understand. 'She was hurt like that, wasn't she? Was it before she met you? Was it?'

'Don't ask me, love. And please . . .' He took her hand and gripped it now. 'Please – never, ever, ask your mother.'

'Is that why she's estranged from her family? Did they throw her out?''

'Eveleen,' her father's voice was firm now. 'I've told you – don't ask me, because I'm not going to tell you. I've said too much already.'

But Eveleen could guess enough to understand now. He had not denied her speculation, and if she had been far from the truth, he would have done so.

In a small voice she asked, 'Dad, what do you say about me meeting Stephen?'

'Oh, love, I don't know. I really don't. He seems a nice enough young man, but I can understand your mother's fears. She's afraid, him being our employer – or at least the son of our employer – that he's only – what is it they say?' Despite the gravity of their conversation, there was suddenly a hint of mirth in his tone. 'He's only trifling with your affections.'

Eveleen laughed. 'That's rather a grand expression for the likes of us, Dad.'

'Well, that's the trouble, lass. It is the "likes of us" and the "likes of him" that's the problem. The two don't mix.' His voice was wistful for a moment as he added, 'Not now.'

'Are *you* forbidding me to see him too?'

'I can't exactly do that, can I? You're bound to run into him and he's every right to come here whenever he wants.'

'That's the bit that really worries me, Dad. They could turn us all out of our home if – if . . .' She hesitated to tell him what had happened earlier in the woods when Stephen's threat had sounded so real.

'Don't you worry your head about that,' Walter was saying. 'His father's not likely to give me the sack just because my daughter won't let herself be seduced by his son.' Then his tone was completely serious as he added, 'You won't, will you?'

'No,' Eveleen said firmly. 'Oh no, I won't let that happen.' But she could say no more. She could not give her father the promise he really wanted to hear.

She would not promise to stop seeing Stephen.

Seven

As the spring began to give way to early summer, the two young lovers continued to meet in secrecy, snatching brief moments together whenever and wherever they could.

Taking the cows back to the meadow behind the house after milking one evening, Eveleen heard, through the dusk, the call of an owl from Bernby Covert. It was his signal. He was there, waiting for her.

She took off her boots and stockings and paddled through the beck to race across the next field, up the hill towards the trees and into his arms.

'I can't stay long,' she said breathlessly while he rained kisses on her upturned face. 'It'll soon be our suppertime. They'll miss me. Or worse still, come looking for me.'

'How I long to put you on my horse and ride off into the night with you, my lovely Eveleen,' he murmured against her hair.

She shivered and though it was more with excitement than cold, Stephen wrapped his arms around her.

'The beck was icy cold,' she said. 'It was snowing today. Did you see it? There were snowflakes floating on the breeze. They melted as soon as they touched the ground, but who would have thought it? Snow, in the middle of May.'

He was kissing her again and she forgot the cold. She forgot everything except his lips against hers and the feel of his arms around her.

'Oh, Stephen,' she breathed. 'I do love you so.'

'My lovely Eveleen,' he whispered, his words a caress.

'I must go,' she said at last, pushing against him, but he held her fast and buried his face in her neck.

'No, no, just a little longer,' he pleaded. 'Make up some excuse. Say you were at the Mortons' place.' His grip tightened on her. 'I'm sure your dear mama wouldn't object to you being in young Morton's company.'

Eveleen gasped at his glib invention and her tone was sharper than she meant it to be as she said, 'I'm deceiving them enough without telling more lies.'

'Don't be such a prude, Eveleen. I thought you had more daring than that.'

'Daring's got nothing to do with it. I don't like deceiving my parents at all and lying to them only makes it worse.'

He released her. 'Then you'd better go,' he drawled. 'I don't want to be guilty of your consigning your soul to eternal damnation.'

She began to tremble and now it had nothing to do with the cold. Was he telling her it was over? Was it to finish so soon? All through some silly quarrel?

She put her arms around his waist and snuggled her head to his chest. 'Please don't let's quarrel. We have such a short time together. It's so precious.'

He seemed to hesitate for a moment, to hold back, but then, as he groaned deep in his throat and his arms came about her again, she knew that he could not resist her nearness. It was heady to think she had such power over him.

'I do love you so,' she murmured again, 'but where is it all going to end?'

He did not answer but his eager mouth was searching for hers. The present was enough, she supposed, as she surrendered to the passion of his kiss. The future would take care of itself.

A while later, as she emerged from the woods, Eveleen heard her father's voice calling her name in the distance.

'Oh no,' she breathed. Picking up her skirts, she began to run.

At the beck she pulled off her footwear again and stepped into the water, gasping at the cold. Scrambling up the bank, she called out, 'I'm here, Dad. Over here.'

As she paused to pull on her boots, his shape loomed up in the darkness. 'Eveleen, whatever are you doing?'

The words were slipping off her tongue before she could stop them. 'Looking for Buttercup. She strayed across the beck.'

'Buttercup did? You do surprise me. She's never done that before. I didn't think she liked water. Where is she now?'

'Back with the others, I think.' Eveleen gestured vaguely in the direction she thought the cows would be.

'Come along, then. Let's get you home and into the warm. It's no weather for going paddling, even if it is the middle of May. I don't want you taking cold, love. Here, have my jacket.'

His consideration was almost her undoing. In that moment she hated herself for deceiving him.

As they entered the house with Walter still fussing over her, Eveleen was aware of her mother's suspicious glance. Mary was not so easily fooled.

Eight

The long, hot days of summer blurred into each other as Eveleen sped through her chores, living only for the blissful moments she spent in Stephen's arms.

But, of course, it could not last.

'What's all this?' Walter, weary from a long day's harvesting, pointed to the supper table where only three places were laid. Already Jimmy was seated at the table, leaving only two chairs unoccupied.

Mary Hardcastle banged a stack of plates on to the table with a vehemence that threatened to break them. 'She's still meeting him. Creeping away to that old barn in Long Meadow. Jimmy's seen them. He's just told me. It's been going on all summer. So, as far as I'm concerned, Walter, I have no daughter. For two pins, I'd turn her out.' She leant across the table towards him, her face twisted with anger. 'But I suppose you wouldn't allow that, would you?'

'Mary, love—' he began, but his wife was not prepared to listen. She jabbed her finger towards Eveleen. 'You're blind where that girl's concerned, aren't you? But I'm not.'

At last even Walter was provoked into saying sternly, 'That's enough, Mary.'

Eveleen felt guilt surge through her. Never had she seen her parents quarrel like this. Normally, they were such a loving couple. Indeed, until recently they had all seemed such a loving family. 'Mam, Dad. Please, I—'

Mary whirled around on her. 'Don't you dare to call me that, girl. Not ever again. You can leave this house for all I care.' Her lip curled. 'If I had my way, you'd be gone already.'

Mother and daughter stared at each other, the older woman with a look almost akin to hatred. Horrified, Eveleen felt the colour drain from her face. For a moment the room seemed to spin around her.

'You'd better go to bed, Eveleen,' Walter said harshly. He rubbed his hand across his eyes as if he were weary of the whole unpleasant business.

Eveleen stumbled towards the door leading to the stairs. As she went, she was aware of her brother's gaze following her, a smirk of satisfaction on his face.

Mary was not able to turn her daughter out of the house for her husband would not allow it. But the woman refused to speak to Eveleen and acted as if the girl were not even there. She never served her any food at meal-times and Eveleen's clothes remained unwashed, unless she washed them herself, for her mother would not include them in the weekly wash. All the things that her mother had always done for her were now left untouched. It was as if Eveleen were no longer a part of the family.

Jimmy revelled in seeing his sister out of favour, not only with Mary but with their father too.

'Who's this, then?' he would say as he sat down at the supper table. But his jesting only heightened the tension, for Mary would smile at him and say, 'I can't think who you mean. I see no one else here. At least, no one worth talking about.'

Mother and son would smile at each other. Walter would sigh and shake his head sadly that Jimmy relished stirring up even more trouble. And worse still, that Mary should egg him on.

If Eveleen had believed that her brother would heed her warnings and threats, she was sadly disillusioned. He delighted in giving nightly reports across the supper table. 'I saw her with him today. Down by the bridge,' he would say, or, 'Where were you all afternoon, then? As if we didn't know.'

'Eat your supper, Jimmy, and be quiet,' Walter would say, an unusual sharpness in his voice, but Jimmy, though saying no more, would glance from his mother to his sister and back again, an evil grin on his face.

At last, after supper one evening, Walter got up from the table and stood over them. 'This can't go on, Mary. I don't like the atmosphere in this house. We used to be a happy, united family. And look at us now.'

Eveleen glanced up at her father. He looked so tired beneath his weather-beaten features, but it was the sadness in his eyes that touched her the most.

'And who's to blame for that?' Mary said.

'You all are,' Walter said, his voice rising in anger.

Eveleen and even Jimmy were shocked now. They could not remember their father ever raising his voice to any one of them. 'You, Mary, for not listening to the girl when she wants to tell you what's going on. Wants to confide in you. Needs her mother's guidance.'

Mary, too, was on her feet now, leaning across the table shouting at her husband. 'I've given her a mother's guidance, but she ignores it.'

'No, you haven't, Mary. You've not talked it out with her, explained to her why you feel the way you do. And you, Eveleen.' He pointed at his daughter. 'For disobeying your mother. You should know her well enough to know that she would not be demanding this of you without a very good reason, even if she does not feel able to explain that reason to you. And as for you.' Now he turned to Jimmy. 'You're just enjoying stoking up the fires, aren't you?'

Eveleen now sprang to her feet. 'Oh, Dad, I'm sorry.' She turned to her mother. 'Mam, please—'

'He'll get you with child and then cast you off.' Mary was hysterical now, the words pouring from her mouth in a torrent. 'Leave you to face the shame alone. He won't care whether your family stands by you or not. He'll not care if you have to live rough. In the woods, in a barn, any shelter you can find. He'll not care if you give birth alone in a dirty, stinking ditch at the side of a field when you're tatie picking, trying to earn pennies to keep yourself and your child alive. Only you won't keep it alive. It'll die. There in the ditch and mebbe you along with it.'

Tears were coursing down Mary's face as she painted the tragic picture. A picture, Eveleen realized, that had a dreadful ring of truth about it. She watched as Walter put his arms around his wife and drew her close, resting his cheek against her hair while Mary sobbed against his chest.

'There, there, Mary love. Don't fret.' Above his wife's head, Walter's sorrowful eyes met Eveleen's. Then he asked the question he had to ask, even though he feared the answer. 'Has he – have you let him – touch you?' His tone was stern as he added, 'The truth now.'

She shook her head firmly. 'No, Dad. I haven't. Not the way you mean.'

He stared at her for a long moment, as if trying to read from her expression if she was now telling him the truth. 'No more lies, Eveleen,' he said.

Eveleen bit her lip, not trusting herself to speak. As

she shook her head, she saw his shoulders relax. This time, he did believe her.

Walter led his wife to her chair by the fire. 'Sit there, love, and Eveleen will make you a cup of tea.' He straightened up and turned to Jimmy. 'And as for you, young man, you're going nowhere tonight. You can clear away the supper dishes and wash up.'

Jimmy's face was a picture. 'That's women's work. I aren't washing up.'

'You'll do as I say,' Walter said calmly, but there was a hint of steel in his tone.

Muttering under his breath, Jimmy began to stack the plates, crashing them together as if he would like to break every one to save him the trouble of having to wash them.

'Be careful, else I'll be taking the cost of any breakages out of your wages,' Walter frowned.

Eveleen busied herself making tea for her mother. As she stood over her, holding out the cup and saucer, Mary looked up at her. All the anger and the hysteria had drained out of her now and just a dreadful sadness seemed to have settled upon her. 'So now you know the whole shameful tale. I hope you're satisfied.'

'Oh, Mam,' Eveleen cried with tears in her eyes, 'I'm so sorry. If only you'd said. If only you'd explained, I—'

'It wouldn't have made any difference. You'd have still done exactly what you wanted. You're headstrong and disobedient.' As she took the proffered cup of tea, Mary shook her head sadly. 'Stubborn and wilful . . .' she murmured and a tiny smile touched her mouth. 'Just like I was at your age.'

*

Later, when the supper dishes were washed and put away and Jimmy had stamped angrily up the stairs to his room, Walter followed him wearily to his own bed. Walter hated quarrels and the trouble Eveleen had caused had left him looking white and strained.

Now only mother and daughter sat opposite each other in front of the fire.

'Nothing can come of it, love,' Mary said, surprisingly gentle now. 'Stephen Dunsmore will never marry you. His family wouldn't let him, even if he wanted to.'

'Don't you think he – he would stand up against them? After all, it's his life.'

Mary sighed. 'The Dunsmores now think of themselves as landed gentry. They own a lot of land and Mr Ernest employs other people to do the work while he lives the life of a gentleman farmer. And his wife, Mrs Rachel, she thinks herself a lady now. They won't take kindly to their only son wanting to marry their gathman's daughter. I'm sure they've already got plans for him to make a more suitable marriage.'

'And you think Stephen will – will go along with whatever those plans are?'

Her mother's smile was sad, 'Oh yes, he'll have to. If he wants to inherit the estate.'

'So . . .' Eveleen could not hide the catch in her voice as she said, 'so you think Stephen doesn't really love me.'

Mary reached out and took her daughter's hand. 'I'm sure he does love you, in his own way. But he's only young. Let's see – he's just twenty, isn't he?'

Eveleen stared at her mother. She longed to ask her about her early life, about her family, about what had happened, but she did not dare. This moment between herself and her mother was so precious. She could not bear to break the bond of understanding that was, at last, strengthening between them. Maybe one day . . .

Instead Eveleen said simply, 'Well, I love him.'

Mary's hold on her hand tightened but it was a gesture more of sympathy than joy at her daughter's words.

The silence between them grew but at least now it was no longer the angry silence of the last few weeks. At least now her mother was on her side, even though she could still offer no hope of a happy future for the young lovers.

But you're wrong, Eveleen wanted to cry. You're all wrong. Stephen loves me, I know he does. But the words remained unspoken as they lingered together beside the dying embers in the range.

Nine

The following day, after evening milking, Eveleen paddled through the beck and ran up the hill towards Bernby Covert. Taking the cows back to the meadow, she had heard Stephen's signal from the trees, the soft whoo-whoo of an owl. She felt happier than she had done for weeks for now she had a new resolve, and there would be no reason for their meetings to be secret any more. Tonight, she was going to ask Stephen to speak to her father. If Walter knew that Stephen's intentions were, indeed, honourable – Eveleen chuckled aloud at the prim saying – then perhaps he would be on her side.

Her father was the one person who could persuade Mary. While her mother now no longer treated her as if she did not exist, Mary still said sadly, 'It'll all end in tears. You'd be better off with Ted Morton and that's saying something, because I know what he's like with the girls. But I still say, you'd be better off with him.'

As she neared the trees, Eveleen could see Stephen's horse tethered there. She picked up her skirts and ran the rest of the way, arriving breathless and flushed, to run straight into his arms.

'Oh, Stephen.'

He was holding her and kissing her as if he would never let her go and she returned his kisses with equal ardour.

'Oh darling, darling Eveleen. You're so lovely,' he

murmured against her hair. 'Let me love you. Please, let me love you properly . . .'

Eveleen drew back a little and looked up into his face. Beneath the trees it was shadowy, but she could see enough to see her own love and passion for him mirrored in his face. Oh how she longed to lie with him, to give herself to him. But her mother's warnings were still fresh in her mind and her own instincts were so strong.

'Forgive me, but I can't. You know I can't.'

'You think I wouldn't respect you, wouldn't love you afterwards? Is that it?'

'I wouldn't respect myself. So how could you?'

'Darling, it's not wrong when two people love each other. I swear I'd love you more, not less, knowing you were mine and mine alone. Please, Eveleen.'

He was pulling her closer to him again, holding her tightly, but now she put her palms flat against his chest and pushed him back.

He flung himself away from her angrily. 'You say you love me, but you don't show it.' He grabbed hold of her again and pulled her roughly to him. 'Prove it, Eveleen. Prove how much you love me.'

Eveleen didn't know what to say or do to convince him of her love, short of doing what he asked of her. They were so close that she could feel his breath on her face. His mouth twisted into a sneer. 'I suppose your dear mama has drilled it into you from the time you could walk that you must never let a man have his wicked way with you until you've his ring on your finger. And a *wedding* band at that.'

'This has nothing to do with my mother,' she said hotly. 'This is to do with me. How I feel. I'm – I'm not saying we have to be married first. I'm just saying now is too early. Too soon.' He said nothing so she went on and her tone hardened as she said, 'A few secret meetings in an old barn or in the woods and you expect me to lift my skirts for you.' She was speaking with deliberate crudity, because that was what he was trying to turn their love into: some sordid, clandestine coupling no better than the beast in the field.

He released her. 'You mean,' he said mockingly, 'that if I was to take you out, wine you and dine you, shower you with gifts and take you home to meet my people, then you would?'

'No,' Eveleen said carefully. 'I don't mean that at all. We know each other's "people", as you put it. But this is hardly a proper courtship, is it? Not hiding away as if we're ashamed of our love.' She put her hand on his arm as she went on eagerly. 'Stephen, I want you to speak to my father about us. We can meet openly then. Please, say you will?'

His gaze dropped away from meeting her eyes. He sat down and leant back against a tree, his hands linked behind his head.

'I could,' he said, evenly. 'But I'm going to be busy for a while. I may not be able to see you so much.'

Eveleen felt as if the breath were being squeezed out of her body. She sat beside him. 'Why?'

Stephen sat forward in a quick, eager movement. His face, animated with excitement, was close to hers. 'My father is going to stand for Parliament and he wants me to take on more responsibility for the estate. He's going to be very busy campaigning.'

'But why does that mean we can't meet?'

'I told you. I'll be busy.'

'But you've got Mr Jackson. The estate bailiff. Won't he—'

Stephen dismissed him with a wave of his hand. 'Jackson's all right. But he's still only an employee. It's not the same.'

'Are you . . . ?' Unshed tears caught at her throat. 'Are you telling me it's finished?'

He put his arms about her and pulled her to him. 'Darling, of course not.' He kissed her but beneath his mouth her lips were cold and unresponsive.

'Darling Eveleen.' He kissed her neck and his hands stroked her hair. 'Of course, it's not over. It's only just beginning.'

Won over by his caresses and his whispered endearments, Eveleen wound her arms around his neck.

'Oh, Stephen,' she whispered. 'It's just that I do love you so much.'

Eveleen ran down the hill through the gathering dusk, her heart singing. Stephen loved her, she knew he did. He hadn't actually said it, but she was sure that was because he was shy. She had found it difficult to say "I love you" the first time, but now the words came as effortlessly to her as breathing.

'I love you, Stephen Dunsmore. I'll love you till the day I die,' she shouted to the cattle grazing in the field. They took no notice and Eveleen laughed aloud, throwing back her head and looking up to the stars above that were just beginning to glow. She held up her arms as if to embrace the whole world. 'I love you, Stephen Dunsmore. I love you, love you, love you.'

She sat on the bank of the beck and took off her boots and stockings, drawing in a swift breath as she stepped into the chill water. Reaching the opposite bank, she was about to sit down to dry her feet on her apron and then pull on her stockings once more when she noticed that several of the cows had wandered down to the beck. They were standing grouped in a sorrowful bunch on the edge of the bank. Then she noticed, through the gloom, a dark shape in the middle of the rushing water. Dropping her boots and stockings she ran forward, afraid that one of the beasts had fallen in. But as she neared it, she saw that the mound was far smaller than a cow though larger than any of the rocks and small boulders on the bed of the stream. Eveleen stopped, struck by a shaft of terror.

The shape was that of a person, a man. She leapt forwards, scrambling down the bank and splashing into the cold water once more. The rushing water bubbled its way around the object in its path as Eveleen reached out with a trembling hand. Though she expected it, knew even before she touched it, it was still a shock to feel the rough fabric of her father's jacket.

'Oh, Dad. Dad!' She ran her hand up and her fingers touched his hair. He was lying face downwards in the water. Crying now, she tried to grip his shoulders and heave him upwards, but the inert form slipped from her grasp and splashed back into the beck. She felt cold droplets spatter her face. She took a firmer hold of him this time, turning him over on to his back so that she could grip him beneath his armpits and haul him out of the water. Sobbing, she pulled and heaved his body, made heavier by the water-soaked clothing, on to the bank. Breathless she collapsed beside him and felt for his face. It was as cold as the water in the beck.

'Dad, Dad,' she cried, but knew in her heart already that it was hopeless. She searched for his pulse but her own fingers were stiff with cold, yet trembling with fear.

And then she began to scream for help, the sound piercing the gloom and echoing around the field, but there was no one to hear her cries, no one to come to her aid.

Eveleen buried her face against her father's sodden jacket and wrapped her arms around him, willing the life back into him. But it was the hopeless gesture of a grief-stricken young girl. Tearing sobs wracked her and it was several moments before she was able to force herself to rise and stumble her way across the field towards her home. She reached the gateway leading into the yard and, breathless, fell against it for a moment. At the sound of the back door opening, she looked up to see her mother standing silhouetted in the lamplight.

'Is that you, Walter?' Mary called.

Eveleen straightened up and began to move towards her. 'No, Mam. It's me.'

'Oh, there you are. Where have you been? Worrying your poor father half to death.' In her anxiety, Mary did not seem to be aware of Eveleen's bedraggled state. 'He's gone out looking for you instead of having his supper. He should be sitting in front of the range by now, resting, instead of—' She paused, surprised into silence as Eveleen put her arms around her and buried her face against her shoulder. 'Why, Eveleen, whatever's the matter?'

Before she could answer, her mother's voice hardened as she pushed Eveleen away from her and grasped her shoulders. Shaking her, she said, 'It's him, isn't it? What's he done to you?'

Stupid with grief, Eveleen said, 'Who?'

'Stephen Dunsmore.'

Eveleen shook her head, sending a shower of icy droplets over her mother.

'But you're wet through. Your clothes, your hair—'

'Mam – you don't understand—'

'Oh I think I understand only too well.'

'No, Mam. Listen!' Now it was Eveleen who took hold of her mother's arms. 'It's Dad. I've found him. He – he was in the beck. I – I think he's dead.'

There was a brief, stunned silence as mother and daughter stared at each other in the dim light. Then, sharply, Mary said, 'Don't be ridiculous, Eveleen. Where is he? Let me—'

Eveleen's grip on her mother's arms tightened. 'No, Mam. Don't. Please, don't go down there.'

'Of course, I'm going to him. It's me he'll want to help him. I expect he's twisted his ankle or something, going out in the dark to look for you, you naughty, wilful girl. Look what trouble you've caused now. Get inside and up those stairs this minute. Jimmy!' She raised her voice. 'Jimmy, come and help me. We must go to your father.'

Jimmy came out of the back door. 'I'm off out,' he began, but seeing the state of his sister, he stopped and asked, 'What's up?'

'It's Dad. I found him in the beck.'

'What do you mean?'

Instead of wasting more time explaining further, Eveleen said, 'Jimmy, fetch Bill Morton and *run*.'

Catching her anxiety and distress, for once Jimmy did as she asked him. He was away like the wind, running out of the yard and down the cart track towards the lane leading to Furze Farm, the Mortons' home.

Mary clicked her tongue against her teeth impatiently. 'You needn't have done that, Eveleen. I can go to him.'

'No,' Eveleen said harshly. 'You stay here, Mam. I'll – I'll go back. When Bill comes, send him down to the beck.'

'Perhaps you're right. I'll get some dry clothes ready for your father and a hot bowl of soup.'

Mary went back into the house, leaving Eveleen staring after her, unable to comprehend that her mother was refusing to believe what she was trying to tell her. Then Eveleen turned and ran back to the place where she had found her father.

Ten

Bill and his son, Ted, carried Walter home on a door, with Eveleen and Jimmy walking beside them. They hesitated briefly as they entered the yard and saw Mary waiting. Eveleen ran forward, her boots and skirt still soaking, mud and tears streaking her face.

'Mam, oh, Mam—' she began, reaching out to her mother, but Mary brushed her aside and went towards the two men carrying her husband.

She did not touch him, she did not even begin to cry, but stood there, staring down at him.

Everyone else just stood there too, not knowing what to do or where to take him until Bill said gently, 'Missis?'

Mary sighed heavily and then said flatly, 'Bring him in, Bill. Into the kitchen and on to the table.' She turned and began to lead the way. 'I'll see to him.'

'My Dorothy will come over, if you want, missis.'

Mary shook her head. 'No need, Bill. I'll manage and Eveleen can help me. Now, gently with him. Don't make it worse than it already is.'

Eveleen stared at her mother. What could be worse than what had already happened? Jimmy came to stand beside his sister as they watched the men struggle to manoeuvre their tragic load through the narrow door of the house and into the kitchen.

Bill and his son laid the door across the table and stepped back, pulling their caps from their heads and standing a moment as if silently paying their respects. Then they trooped out, nodding awkwardly to the two youngsters waiting in the yard. When they were gone, Eveleen and Jimmy went into the house.

They watched in amazement as their mother bustled into the scullery to fetch a bowl, soap and flannel. 'He's in a right mess,' she said, almost conversationally, as if her husband had merely fallen in the ditch, dragged himself out and squelched his way home to be met by his wife's berating. 'And you get yourself out of those wet clothes, Eveleen, or you'll catch your death.'

She turned away as if not realizing what she had said. Brother and sister exchanged a horrified glance.

'I don't reckon she's taken it in,' Jimmy murmured, his glance following their mother as she bent to draw hot water into the bowl from the tap at the side of the range. 'She – she's acting like she did when I fell in the dyke that time when I was a kid and came out in black mud from head to foot. I got a right telling off, but she peeled off all me clothes and washed me all the time she was doing it.'

Mary placed the bowl carefully on the table at the side of the still and silent figure. 'Fancy getting yourself in such a mess, Walter,' she said gently as she began to wash his face tenderly. 'There, there, we'll soon have you cleaned up and then you can sit by the fire and have a nice bowl of hot soup. How'd that be, eh?'

Although she clapped her hand to her mouth, Eveleen could not quite stifle the startled cry that escaped her lips.

'She doesn't realize, Evie. She doesn't know.'

Eveleen pulled in a deep shuddering breath, trying to calm her shaking limbs. They both continued to watch their mother as she washed the inert form, murmuring endearments and gentle chastisement in turn.

'I'm off,' Jimmy muttered. 'I can't stand this.' As he made to turn and leave, Eveleen gripped his shoulder.

'Wait,' she hissed. 'We can't leave her like this, we—'

'You can do what you like, our Eveleen. I'm off.'

Mary was crooning, like a mother bathing her baby, smiling and singing to it.

Eveleen took a deep breath and gave Jimmy's shoulder a tiny shake. With a voice that was not quite steady, she said, 'Go and fetch Bill back and ask Dorothy to come too.'

'Right,' Jimmy agreed at once. He turned and fled the house, relieved to have an excuse to get out. But there was no such escape for Eveleen. She moved forward to stand on the other side of the table to her mother.

'Mam,' she began hesitantly.

'Oh, Eveleen, there you are. Help me get these wet clothes off your dad. He'll catch his death, else.'

It was a favourite saying of Mary's and one she had now used twice in the space of a few minutes. Tears sprang to Eveleen's eyes, but she blinked them back furiously. She must be strong. She had to be strong for all their sakes.

'Mam,' she said gently, her voice hoarse with emotion. 'It's – it's no use. Don't you see? He's – he's . . .' She couldn't bring herself to say the words, not even now. 'He's not going to be all right. He's—'

'Don't be so foolish, Eveleen,' Mary answered spiritedly. 'Of course he'll be all right. He's just cold and tired.' She looked down once more at the white face. 'Come along, Walter. Stir yourself. You'll have to help us. Me and Eveleen can't lift you.'

Eveleen moved round the table and put her arm about her mother's shoulders, trying to lead her away now.

'Mam, come away. It's no use. It's – it's too late. He's – he's gone.'

'What on earth are you talking about?' Mary snapped. 'Will you do as I say and help me instead of standing there talking a lot of nonsense?'

Eveleen's voice was a husky croak as she said, 'Mam. He's dead. Dad's dead.'

Beneath her touch, she felt her mother's body go rigid. Mary stared at her daughter and then slowly turned her head to look down at her husband once more. There was a second's silence and then Eveleen jumped physically as her mother let out a heart-rending scream and threw herself across the lifeless body.

She was still trying to prise Mary away when the back door opened and Bill's huge frame stood there. At once he took in the scene, moved forward and lifted Mary bodily. He held her in his strong embrace, stroked her hair and made soothing noises.

Eveleen felt a huge lump in her throat and the tears she had tried to hold back spilled over and ran down her face. To see this big man being so gentle and caring with her distraught mother seemed to emphasize the painful truth as nothing else could have done.

'Bill?' Dorothy stepped into the kitchen and, at her husband's nod towards Eveleen, opened her arms to the girl. With a sob, Eveleen allowed herself to give way to her own grief, leaving, for the moment, Bill to cope with her hysterical mother.

At last they got her calmed down, but it took Bill, Dorothy and Eveleen to coax Mary to sit down by the range.

'Here, Mary dear,' Dorothy said, 'drink this. 'Tis hot sweet tea. Now,' she went on gently, 'Bill and Ted will move poor Walter into your parlour and then I'll see to him. Ted came back with us,' she explained to Eveleen. 'He's waiting in the yard in case we needed him.'

Dorothy was the person the community ran to in times of trouble. A motherly, buxom woman with a round, placid face, she was the unofficial midwife and nurse. She was always there to lay out the dead when a family could not bring themselves to carry out the sad duty.

'Has anyone called Doctor Roper?' Dorothy asked Eveleen. 'I can't do anything until the doctor's seen him.'

'I'm sorry. I didn't think about that. I knew the minute I found him face down in the beck that he – that he . . .' Her voice trailed away and Dorothy put her arm around Eveleen's shoulders.

'It's all right, love. You couldn't be expected to know what needed doing. You leave it to us now. We'll sort everything out for you.' She turned towards her husband. 'Send Ted for Doctor Roper.'

'Jimmy could go,' Eveleen put in.

The two kindly people looked at her. 'He's run off, love. He came to fetch us and then he went off somewhere.'

Anger sparked in Eveleen's dark eyes. 'That's just like him.'

'Don't be too hard on him, dear. He's very young to have to cope with something like this. I know you're only a year older than he is, but you're so much more sensible.' She gave a little gesture with her head towards where Mary still sat huddled in front of the fire. 'You're going to have to be the strong one in this family from now on, love.'

Eveleen felt the burden of responsibility settle like a

heavy weight on her young shoulders. Automatically, she straightened up and lifted her head as she met the woman's sympathetic eyes.

'Yes,' the young girl said solemnly. 'I am, aren't I?'

Eleven

All the legal requirements surrounding a sudden death had been satisfied and the funeral arranged, but still Mary Hardcastle had scarcely moved from her chair in front of the fire. Eveleen had been trying to coax her to undress and go to her bed when Mary hit her and shouted, 'Leave me be. Let me rot. I don't want to live any more.' Then she began to wail. 'What am I going to do without him? Who's going to look after me now?'

Rubbing her arm where Mary had lashed out at her, Eveleen said quietly, 'We'll look after you, Mam. Jimmy and me.'

'You? You, look after me?' Mary's voice was shrill with bitterness. 'You haven't a thought in your head except skipping off to meet that young feller.' She shook her fist at Eveleen, anger rousing her from her apathy for the first time. 'You'll come to a bad end, my girl, you mark my words. Where's Jimmy? I want my Jimmy. He'll look after me. Jimmy'll look after his mam.'

Jimmy would do nothing of the sort, Eveleen thought. There was only one person that Jimmy Hardcastle was ever going to look after. Himself. But aloud she said, 'He's had to go to work, Mam,' as she sat down on the opposite side of the range in the chair that had been her father's.

A wild shriek from her mother made Eveleen jump up again as if she had been burnt.

'Get out of that chair. That's his chair. Don't you dare to sit in it. You aren't fit to sit in his chair.'

Mary struggled to her feet. She swayed a moment and then, regaining her balance, she came, fists flailing, striking Eveleen on the chin and about the head before the girl could even move to defend herself.

Eveleen caught hold of Mary's wrists and held them tightly. From her work about the farm, Eveleen was strong and, once she had a firm grip, she had no trouble in restraining the distraught woman.

'Mam, don't. Look, sit down and I'll make you a nice drink and some dinner.'

Mary thrust her face close to Eveleen's. 'Oh aye. And what'll you put in it, eh? Poison?'

Appalled, Eveleen stared at her. For the past few days Eveleen had had not only to contend with her own grief over her father's death but to be the mainstay in her mother's life. And she had had little or no help from her brother. Early each morning Jimmy left the house and did not return until late at night, leaving Eveleen to cope alone with all the arrangements and with Mary's paralysing distress. She understood the shattering blow her mother had suffered and had been infinitely patient with her. But now, for the first time, Eveleen began to fear for her mother's reason.

She felt Mary's whole body begin to tremble. She loosened her grasp on her mother's wrists so that Mary was able to twist herself free. Eveleen stepped backwards, expecting more blows, but now her mother sank back into her chair. Eveleen too, began to sit down, but realizing she was once more about to sit in her father's chair, drew a chair from the table closer to the hearth and sat down on that.

'Mam,' she began gently. 'You don't know what

you're saying. You can't possibly think I'd ever harm you.'

'Oh no? I'm in the way now, aren't I? A burden.'

'Of course you're not. You'll soon be your old self again and—'

'I'll never be my old self again,' Mary moaned and sank once more into self-pity. 'Not now he's gone. Without Walter, I'm no good.'

Tentatively, fearing to provoke another onslaught, Eveleen reached out and patted her mother's hand where it rested on the chair arm. If her mother was acting like this now, how on earth was she going to behave at the funeral the following day? Eveleen had visions of the hysterical woman throwing herself across the coffin.

Uncannily, Mary seemed to be following Eveleen's train of thought. 'I wish I could die with him.'

'Mam, please,' Eveleen said, feeling utterly helpless. Then making up her mind, she stood up. 'I'm going for Doctor Roper right now.' Perhaps there was some way he could help.

'We can't afford a doctor. We'll be homeless soon enough.'

Eveleen had begun to turn away but now she swung round and stared down at her mother. 'What did you say?'

'I said,' Mary repeated, 'we'll be homeless soon enough.'

Eveleen's legs gave way beneath her and she sank back on to the chair. Her mother's outburst had subsided and now she sounded rational and very serious.

'Whatever do you mean?' Eveleen whispered.

'I mean,' Mary said, 'that now your father's gone, we

shall be turned out of our home. It's only a tied house, Eveleen. Tied to his job.'

'But we still work for Mr Dunsmore. Jimmy and me. And you often help out in the dairy.'

'Huh. Even if he keeps you two, he'll want the house. You and Jimmy'll have to go into lodgings. They'll want this house –' she jabbed her forefinger towards the floor – 'for the man who takes Walter's job.' She sighed heavily, as she added, 'Stands to reason.'

'But it's our home.'

Mary shrugged. 'It has been our home, Eveleen, but the property belongs to Mr Dunsmore and he'll want it vacated. Once the funeral's over, you mark my words, we'll get a visit from Mr Jackson.'

Conjured up at once in Eveleen's mind was a picture of Josiah Jackson, the farm bailiff, a scrawny, ferret-like man with beady eyes and thin, mean lips. She shuddered. Thinking of him, she could begin to believe her mother's words.

She stood up. 'I'll see Stephen. He'll not let us be turned out of our home.'

Mary rested her head against the back of the chair and closed her eyes. Her shoulders began to shake and Eveleen bent down.

'Mam, don't get upset. Stephen's taking on more responsibility around the estate. He told me. He'll help us.' Then with a shock she saw that her mother was not crying, but laughing. But there was no humour in the sound, only bitterness.

Mary opened her eyes and looked up at her. 'Oh Eveleen, if you believe that, then you're more of a naïve fool than even I thought you were.'

*

As Eveleen hurried along the lane towards Bernby village, she muttered to herself. 'She's wrong. I know she's wrong. Stephen wouldn't do that. He'll help us, I know he will.'

She was desperate to find him now, this minute, but knew she must go for the doctor first. Her mother needed help. These irrational outbursts were so unlike her. Eveleen's footsteps slowed of their own volition as the truth slipped into her reasoning. No, she was wrong. Mary Hardcastle had always been unpredictable.

Eveleen felt her face crumple and she pressed the back of her hand to her mouth as the realization came to her. Only her father, her lovely, patient, understanding father, had been able to calm Mary and keep her volatile temperament on an even keel.

And now he was gone.

The girl stood a moment in the lane, missing her father and feeling desperately lonely.

Then she lifted her head. It was up to her now. Up to her to look after her mother and her brother and to hold the family together. She would have to be sensible. She would not be afraid or too proud to ask for help.

She began to walk again. She would do what she had planned. She would see Doctor Roper and ask his advice. And then she would go in search of Stephen.

Her spirits lifted at the mere thought of seeing him again. It seemed an age since he had held her and kissed her and now she needed the comfort of his arms as never before. Her steps quickened and her heart felt lighter than it had done since that dreadful moment when she had found her father face down in the beck.

Stephen, Stephen, her heart sang. He would help her. She must find him.

*

'I'm afraid master Stephen is not available,' the manservant answering the front door at Fairfield House informed her in pompous tones. Then he leant forward and hissed at her. 'And you should have gone round to the back door.'

Eveleen stood her ground. 'Where is he?'

The man, whose name Eveleen knew to be Tomkins, straightened up and adopted his formal manner again. 'I am afraid I am not aware of Master Stephen's whereabouts.' Once more, he dropped the pose. 'And I wouldn't tell the likes of you, if I was.'

'Thanks,' Eveleen said tartly and turned away. She skirted the big house and crossed the yard at the back. Passing through the kitchen gardens she entered the field at the back of the house. Shading her eyes, she scanned the scene before her. Below her to the left, was the beck and beyond it the field leading to Pear Tree Farm. To the right the land rose to Bernby Covert.

Maybe he was there, waiting for her.

Eveleen picked up her skirts and began to run.

She had waited over an hour. The sun had gone and a chill wind rustled through the trees. Eveleen rubbed her arms and emerged from the wood. She would have to go home. She had stayed here too long already.

I should have tried the barn, she thought. Maybe he's there.

She turned and went back through the trees to the road, crossed it into Long Meadow and began to run, stumbling on the uneven ground.

Panting, she arrived at the door, but the only sound that greeted her was the loose board rattling in the breeze. She waited a few minutes and then went back to the road. She crossed the tiny bridge over the beck and turned towards her own home.

'I'll go there this afternoon. Maybe he'll be waiting for me then,' she promised herself.

But Stephen was not at the barn that afternoon either.

After evening milking, Eveleen put on her Sunday best dress and bonnet. She stood in front of her mother, expecting a tirade. Mary, staring into the fire, did not seem to notice and when Eveleen said, 'I won't be long, Mam,' her mother did not even raise her head or speak.

Eveleen sighed inwardly and closed the door quietly. It was starting to rain and by the time she reached Fairfield House, her shawl was soaking and her bonnet ruined. Standing in the warm kitchen, she felt the eyes of the servants on her.

Proudly, she raised her head. 'I wish to speak to Master Stephen, if you please.'

'Not looking like that, you won't.' The manservant she had seen earlier was carrying huge silver salvers into the kitchen, presumably, Eveleen thought, from the dining room after the family's evening meal.

Two maids, scurrying about at the man's bidding, giggled, hiding their smirks behind their hands.

Eveleen shot them a withering glance and said stiffly, 'I can hardly help the weather. My boots, though wet, are clean.' She took a bold step further into the kitchen. 'If you do not show me up, I will ring the bell at the front door again.'

Her glare caught and held the man's eyes.

'Oh very well then. But stay here until I see if he'll see you. Who shall I say it is?'

'You know very well who it is, Mr Tomkins,' Eveleen snapped. 'You've lived here long enough to know everyone on the estate.'

'I,' Tomkins lifted his nose in the air deliberately, 'do not mix with the outdoor servants.'

Adopting a lofty tone herself, Eveleen said, 'Please inform your young master that Miss Eveleen Hardcastle wishes to speak to him.'

As the man gave a sniff of disapproval and left the room, the cook said, 'Sit by the fire, love, and get warm.'

Eveleen smiled at her gratefully.

'I think there's a cuppa left in the pot.' The woman poured out a cup of tea and handed it to Eveleen. 'There, you drink that while you're waiting, 'cos if I know Mr High and Mighty Tomkins, he'll be a while coming back.'

There was a pause before she added. 'I was that sorry to hear about your dad, love. Nice man, he was.'

Eveleen nodded and whispered her thanks. She drank the tea and sat by the crackling fire. By the time Tomkins returned, Eveleen had been waiting so long that her clothes had nearly dried out and she was almost asleep, made drowsy by the heat of the fire on her face.

'Master Stephen has gone out,' he told her shortly.

Slowly, Eveleen rose to her feet. The man was either lying or he had deliberately waited until his young master had left the house.

Eveleen said, 'Thank you,' and then before she could hold her wayward tongue in check, added 'for nothing.'

The man looked her up and down with a sneer on his face, but said no more. As he turned and left the room, Eveleen thanked the cook for the tea and left the house by the back door.

Pausing in the yard she pondered whether to go back

to the barn, but she doubted whether he would be there at this time in the evening. They had hardly ever met after what he called dinner.

I'll see him tomorrow, she promised herself. Tomorrow, he'll come to meet me as usual.

But then she remembered. Tomorrow they would be laying her poor father to rest in Bernby churchyard.

Twelve

Before anyone else was up the following morning, Eveleen left the house, paddled through the beck and ran up the field to the back of Fairfield House.

Already there was movement near the stables and peering round the corner of one of the buildings she saw Ted Morton saddling up the horse that Stephen always rode.

'Ted,' she called softly. 'Ted.'

She saw him look round, puzzled, not knowing where the sound was coming from.

'Ted. Here,' she called a little louder now. 'Over here.'

Now he saw her and, smiling, came towards her. 'Evie. What are you doing here?'

'I'm looking for Stephen. Is he coming out soon? That's his horse you're saddling up, isn't it?'

The look of pleasure that had been on Ted's face when he had first seen her, died. 'I should have guessed it wouldn't be me you were looking for.'

Impulsively, she put out her hand and touched his. 'Oh please don't be like that, Ted. I've enough on my plate without you going mardy on me.'

The young man had the grace to look ashamed. 'Sorry, Evie. Yes, he should be out in a minute.'

'I'll wait here. I won't get in your way.'

'You could never get in my way, Evie,' Ted said softly, but as the back door of the house banged, he moved away and Eveleen saw Stephen, dressed in his riding habit, striding across the yard.

She ran towards him. Startled, he stopped and his tone, as he asked the very same question as Ted had a few moments ago, was harsh. 'What are you doing here?'

'Stephen, I have to talk to you. I tried to see you yesterday, but—'

'I know,' he said, and Eveleen realized that the man-servant had not been to blame. Stephen himself had refused to see her. 'I had to go out.'

No apology. No real explanation. Just the bald truth. If, indeed, it was the truth.

He was speaking again. 'And I can't stop now.'

She caught hold of his arm. 'I must talk to you. My mother's worrying herself silly, saying that we're going to be thrown out of the house now my father – since my father . . .'

She stopped and stared at him, her hand falling away from his arm. Where was the young man who had held her and kissed her and said all those wonderful things to her?

'There's nothing I can do,' Stephen said stiffly, his handsome face a mask of indifference. He was standing only a few inches away from her but the chasm that had now opened up between them felt thousands of feet deep and a world apart.

This was the first time she had seen him since her father's death. Whilst she did not expect him to take her into his arms here in the open yard, with a shock that was like a knife in her heart she realized that he had not even said how sorry he was.

'Wh— what do you mean? Can't you speak to your father? Ask him to let us stay?'

'I told you, my father has handed over the running of the estate to me.'

'Then you tell Mr Jackson.'

'I'm sorry, but you will have to move. The farmhouse you live in . . .' – she could sense that he was choosing his words carefully, minding not to say, 'your home' – 'goes with the position of gathman.'

'But it's our home. And we work for you too. My brother and me. Even my mother helps out with the dairy work.'

'You and your brother are single people. You could lodge with other estate workers.'

'We're a family. We're still a family.'

He was shaking his head. 'The positions you and your brother hold don't warrant a house. Your father's did.'

'You mean – you mean you're really going to turn us out when you know we have nowhere to go?'

Not an eyelid flickered. He didn't even flinch at her bald statement but merely said coldly, 'Naturally we shall try to assist you in finding alternative accommodation. But . . .'

'So that's how it is.' She was too angry to weep. The tears would come later, in the privacy of her bedroom.

Her mother had been right. The Dunsmores wouldn't give a second thought before casting them out of their home. And though it broke Eveleen's heart to admit it, Mary had been right too about the young man standing before her. Stephen Dunsmore didn't love her. Not as she had loved him. Eveleen doubted he even knew the meaning of the word.

Thank God, she thought with fervent reverence, thank the good Lord that I didn't give way to this man's protestations of love. For all her weathervane moods, her mother had been right about that too.

Eveleen turned to leave, feeling physically sick. She glanced back at him, just once, still hoping for a sign that he had some concern, some feeling for her.

A few feet away Ted stood holding Stephen's mount. He could do nothing to help her, Eveleen knew, but the look on the young man's face told her that at this moment Ted would like to throttle the young master.

As for Stephen, he stood in the middle of the yard, idly slapping his riding crop against his boot just watching her go, his face expressionless. He made no move towards her, gave her no words of farewell in what he must realize would be their final parting.

A sob rose in her throat but she held it in check until she had passed through the gate and into the field.

Then she began to run and run as if she couldn't put distance between them fast enough. 'I hate you, Stephen Dunsmore. One day, I'll have my revenge on you.'

Those who could take time from work on the estate attended Walter Hardcastle's funeral.

'They'd all have come if they could have,' Bill Morton told Eveleen. 'But you know what Jackson's like.' He had nodded across to where Josiah Jackson was standing. 'He'd dock their pay if they missed a couple of hours to attend. He's only here because he has to represent the Dunsmore family. But him and ya dad never got on. I think Jackson was jealous of your dad because Walter always got on well with Mr Dunsmore. Him and ya dad went back a long way to when Mr Ernest worked as hard as any of the men he employed.'

Eveleen's mind was working fast. How stupid she

had been. It was Mr Ernest, Stephen's father, she should have gone to see. Maybe he would have been kinder, more understanding. But at Bill's next words, her hopes faded. 'But that was a long time ago. Before he got rich and moved up in the world.' He sighed. 'He seems to have forgotten now how they started.' Then he added resentfully, 'And all those who helped him do it. And now with all this Parliament business.' He put his arm about Eveleen's shoulders. 'Ne'er mind, lass. Least we can sleep in our beds at night with a clear conscience, eh?'

'Not for much longer, Bill,' Eveleen said quietly. 'If what my mother says is right, we'll be out on our ears now the funeral's over.'

To this Bill could say nothing.

Josiah Jackson knocked at the door of their house the following morning.

'I've come to see your mother.'

'She's not well enough to see anyone,' Eveleen informed him and, making no attempt to invite him inside, stood in the doorway with her arms folded. 'You'll have to deal with me.'

The man gave a grunt of disapproval but said, 'Very well then.' He held out a long, brown envelope. 'This is your formal notice to vacate these premises by the end of the month. There are lodgings to be had with other estate workers if you and your brother want to continue working here, but there's no place for your mother. We do not require her services any longer.'

Eveleen snatched the envelope from his bony fingers. 'And where do you suggest my mother goes? The workhouse?'

'If your father did not have the foresight to put a little aside, then I'm afraid she has no alternative.'

'On the measly wages the Dunsmores pay?'

Josiah wagged his forefinger at her. 'You watch your tongue, my girl, or you'll find yourself in the workhouse alongside her.'

'That'd be better than working for the Dunsmores.' The words were out of her mouth before she could stop them. Appalled at her own rash stupidity, Eveleen waited, holding her breath, for the axe to fall. The blow was not many seconds in coming.

'If that's how you feel, then you'd better all go there. You're dismissed, Miss Hardcastle.' The man smiled maliciously. 'You and your brother. All of you. And you can be out of this house by the end of the week.'

He turned and walked swiftly away while Eveleen closed the door and leant against it. Now what had she done?

Thirteen

'It's all your fault, Eveleen,' Mary wailed, rocking backwards and forwards in her chair. 'You and that tongue of yours. How many times have I told you it'll get you into trouble one of these days? And now it's got us all into trouble. The workhouse! What would your poor father say if he was still here?' She covered her face with her apron. 'Oh, what will become of us?'

Eveleen bit back the words, If Dad was still here, we wouldn't be in this mess. Her rash tongue had done quite enough damage for one day.

'If you hadn't been so disobedient,' Mary went on. 'So wayward and caused him all that worry, he'd never have had a heart attack.'

Eveleen felt the colour drain from her face. This was a guilt she had tried to keep buried, tried to put from her own mind, yet now her mother was voicing it aloud.

''Tain't Evie's fault,' Jimmy said as he spooned the last of the apple turnover into his ever-hungry mouth.

Eveleen glanced at her brother. It wasn't often that Jimmy took her side. 'Dad's father died in the same way, didn't he?' he went on. 'Was that Evie's fault too?'

Eveleen held her breath, but Mary was not listening to him. She was too sunk in her despair. 'The workhouse,' she was murmuring. 'He saved me from it once, but now . . .' Her voice faded away and she sat staring into the flames and shaking her head, sad and defeated.

Eveleen took a deep breath and stood up. 'We're not going to the workhouse. None of us. Jimmy and me'll find work. There are other farms, other cottages.'

'You're too young,' Mary was refusing to be hopeful. 'No one'll give you a house any more than the Dunsmores'll let you stay here.'

'Then we'll find work in Grantham and get lodgings or a house to rent. There must be work in the town.'

'It'll be hopeless.' Mary was refusing to be optimistic. 'How are you going to find anything by the end of the week? It'll take us 'til then to pack everything up.' She sighed heavily and added, 'But what's the point of packing up anyway, if we've nowhere to go?'

Eveleen bit her lip. 'Bill said they'd help out if they could. Maybe you could stay with him and Dorothy. We could put our belongings in their barn.'

'And get him the wrong side of Jackson, an' all? Get him the sack too? No, no, your dad wouldn't want us to do that. He thought a lot of Bill Morton. He wouldn't want you to bring trouble on him and his family.'

Eveleen thought back to the previous day as the mourners had all trooped away from the graveside. Out of all those who had come to pay their respects only Bill and Dorothy Morton and their son had remained behind to offer practical help. Eveleen had been surprised and touched by Ted's words. He had taken hold of both her hands and looked at her with serious eyes.

'Evie, if there's anything I can do, anything at all, you will tell me, won't you? I heard what *he* said this morning. I wanted to black his eye.'

Despite the sadness of the occasion, Eveleen felt the urge to smile. 'I know you did. I could see it in your face.' That was nothing, she thought, to what I wanted to do to him. She sighed. 'Thanks, Ted. But I don't think there's anything anyone can do for us without putting themselves at risk, and . . .' – there was a catch in her voice – 'Dad wouldn't have wanted that.'

'I don't reckon your dad would have thought for a minute that the Dunsmores'd do this to you though. But don't forget, if there is anything I can do . . .'

As she had nodded and thanked him, a tiny part of her mind was thinking, the only thing you can do is to marry me and get a cottage where we could all live. But she buried the thought deep. She was prepared to make all manner of sacrifices to look after her mother and Jimmy, to keep what was left of the family together, but that was one thing she would not do. Marry a man she did not love.

And the man she had loved with all her heart had turned his back on her when she had needed him the most.

Now, putting all thoughts of Stephen Dunsmore firmly out of her mind, she said, 'Tomorrow Jimmy and me'll walk into Grantham, Mam.' She wagged her forefinger, half-playfully, half-seriously, at her brother. 'And we're not coming home until one of us has got a job.'

'It's market day,' Jimmy observed. 'We'll go there and ask around.'

Eveleen smiled at him. 'That's a very good idea.'

Mary raised her head and looked across at Jimmy. 'There, you see, Eveleen. I knew Jimmy would look after me. He'll look after us both, won't you, love?'

Eveleen did not know whether to laugh or cry.

It was raining the following morning; a fine, steady drizzle that looked innocent enough but by the time they arrived in Grantham had soaked them. But the two youngsters, so intent on finding work, were oblivious to the cold seeping through to their skins as they wove their way among the farmers milling round the livestock pens in the market.

'There's Ted,' Jimmy said suddenly and darted off.

'Jimmy, don't—' Eveleen began but Jimmy had gone. Sighing she followed him.

'Hello, Evie,' Ted greeted her with a smile, but concern showed in his eyes.

Eveleen greeted him but then said, 'Come on, Jimmy, we must speak to as many farmers as we can.'

'He's just been telling me why you're here,' Ted said. 'Try old man Johnson. He's always looking for someone.'

Jimmy pulled a face. 'Aye, an' we all know why, don't we? He treats his workers that badly, no one'll stay with him long.'

Ted grinned. 'He treats his animals well though. To him, his animals are more important than people.'

'We'll leave him 'til last,' Eveleen said. 'We'll see how desperate we get.'

By mid-afternoon, they were indeed desperate enough to seek out Mr Johnson.

'We've no one else left to ask,' Eveleen said. 'Everyone I've spoken to won't take the three of us together. They'll take you or me or even both of us. But not Mam.'

Jimmy scuffed his foot on the ground and muttered, 'Same here. I could have had three jobs easy. And there was lodgings. Just for me, of course.' He looked up at Eveleen. 'Why don't I take one of 'em? It'd be better than nothing, wouldn't it?'

'We agreed, Jimmy. All or nothing. We stick together.'

'*You* agreed, you mean. I don't remember having much say in the matter.'

'Well, if that's how you feel—'

'Don't start, Evie. It's just that it seems daft to be turning down jobs. Why don't I take one and you and Mam get a little cottage somewhere.' His face brightened suddenly. 'Or I could go to sea, just like I've always wanted. I'd send you money each week.'

Eveleen glanced at him sceptically. 'Aye, an' pigs might fly.' She grasped his arm. 'Come on, let's go and find old man Johnson.'

The old farmer was climbing into his pony and trap as they approached.

'Mr Johnson,' Eveleen called. 'Could you spare us a minute, please?'

'Eh? What?' The man, bent with age and hard work, frowned at them from beneath bushy white eyebrows. 'What d'you want?'

Eveleen licked her lips nervously, while Jimmy stood beside her, silent and morose, his hands shoved deep into his pockets.

'We wondered if you needed help on your farm.'

'I allus need help,' the old man snapped. 'But the beggars allus want paying. They want their keep and paying an' all.' He glowered down at Eveleen as if she were personally responsible. 'You young folks don't know the meaning of hard work. Why, when I were a lad, I had to be up at four every morning . . .'

She stood patiently, listening to the old man's grumbling while Jimmy fidgeted beside her and kicked small stones, sending them rattling along the road.

'All we need is somewhere to live, Mr Johnson. My brother and I could work for you on the farm and my mother can even take a turn in the dairy.'

'Ain't no dairy,' Mr Johnson muttered. 'I keep pigs. And me harvest's all in. Don't need no extra help. Not now.'

'My mother's a good cook,' Eveleen tried again.

'So's me wife. Don't need no cook. And I ain't got no cottage, neither.' He picked up the reins and flicked them. The pony began to move, but Eveleen grasped the side of the trap.

'Please, mister. You knew our dad, didn't you? You know our family. We're good workers. Reliable and—'

She was still hanging on to the trap and moving along with it.

'I heard you'd been turned out of your jobs and your house. If the Dunsmores don't want you, then neither do I. Good day, young woman.'

He raised his whip and brought it down across her hands. More shocked by his unexpected action than by the pain, Eveleen let go at once. As the trap moved away she was left staring after him, rubbing her stinging hands.

Jimmy swore loudly and shook his fist after the old man. 'Keep your job, you miserable old bugger.'

'Come on, Jimmy,' Eveleen said forlornly, noticing for the first time how cold and wet and hungry she was. 'We'd better go home.' Then she added sadly, 'While we've still got one to go to.'

'I'm sorry, Mam. We couldn't find anyone to take the three of us.'

'I didn't think you would.' Mary was sitting exactly as they had left her early that morning. There was no supper set ready and the fire, though not quite out, was very low. Eveleen wondered if Mary had moved from her chair at all during the day.

'I could have got a job,' Jimmy put in and glowered at his sister. 'But Evie says we must stick together.'

Mary leant back and closed her eyes. Wearily she said,

'You'd do better to find yourselves a job and put me in the workhouse.'

'We're doing no such thing,' Eveleen snapped. 'And I don't want to hear another word about the workhouse.' She looked down at her mother, trying to rouse her from her apathy. 'Have you any suggestions, Mam? I mean, sensible ones.'

Slowly Mary raised her gaze to her daughter. 'We'll have to go home.'

Eveleen caught her breath. Had her mother's mind really turned? 'This is our home, Mam, and – and we've got to leave it.'

Mary shook her head. 'No. Back home to Flawford. To my family.'

Mystified, Jimmy gave a wordless shrug. Out of sight of his mother, he tapped the side of his head indicating that he, too, thought she was losing her reason.

Anxious not to upset her further, Eveleen bent closer to Mary. 'Mam,' she began carefully, 'is that where you came from? Flawford?'

Mary nodded.

'And – and have you still got family living there, then?'

'Dunno.'

'But you think you might have?'

'Shouldn't think my parents are still alive, but Harry might be.'

'Who's Harry?' Eveleen asked gently.

'My brother. My brother, Harry. Maybe he's still there. And his wife, Rose.'

Eveleen and Jimmy exchanged a glance. An uncle and an aunt, maybe even cousins, they were both thinking. All this time they had had these relatives, close relatives, and they had never known a thing about them. They had not even known they existed.

'Right then,' Eveleen said firmly, standing up. 'That's where we'll go, Mam. Back to your folks.'

But Mary was shaking her head yet again. 'They'll not want us. They turned me out once, disowned me. What makes you think they'd help us now?'

'They're family, Mam. Your family – and ours. Surely they will help us? Surely your own brother won't turn his back on you?'

'Huh!' Mary at last let out a sound that had some spirit in it. 'He was the worst of the lot of them. Very religious, is our Harry. Hell and damnation, that's where he said I was headed. Aye . . .' Once more she began to sink back into self-pity. 'And if it hadn't been for your dad, that's where I would have ended up.'

'That was years ago. Surely, he won't still feel – well – that way towards you. Not now.'

'Oho, you don't know Harry. He's the "if thy right hand offend thee, cut it off" type. So,' she added simply, 'that's what he did. He cut me off.'

Eveleen took her mother's hand. Softly, she asked, 'Was it so very dreadful? What you did?'

Slowly Mary raised her head and looked straight into Eveleen's eyes. 'Oh yes. It was very dreadful. At least, in his eyes. And in the eyes of the whole community. Everyone shunned me. Everyone.'

Tears spilled down Mary's face and Eveleen patted her hand. 'Don't, Mam. Please don't cry.' Once more she silently gave heartfelt thanks that she had resisted Stephen's pleading and his sweet words. She understood her mother so much better now.

With renewed resolve, Eveleen put her arm about her mother's shoulders and glanced towards Jimmy. 'We're going to take you home, Mam. Back to your family. Surely, after all this time, they will have forgiven you.'

'I doubt it,' Mary murmured.

Well,' Eveleen said, 'whether they want us or not, they're going to get us. Watch out, Flawford, here we come.'

Fourteen

'Have we got everything, Mam?' Eveleen asked, taking a last look around all the rooms. 'Are you sure you've got everything you want? We don't seem to be keeping very much. Our trunks and boxes have only taken up half the length of the dray.'

Her mother stood in front of the cold range. It was the first time that Eveleen could remember not seeing a fire burning in the grate. The whole house seemed chilly because of it. Mary glanced about her. 'I've got everything I *can* take,' she said pointedly. 'It's no good taking a lot of furniture. There'll be nowhere to put it.' Then her face crumpled. 'Oh Evie, I don't want to go. I don't want to leave here. It's the only place I've ever been really happy.'

'Weren't you happy as a child? Before – before your trouble?'

Mary pressed her lips together to stop herself weeping and shook her head. 'My father was a hard man. He ruled us all with a rod of iron, and the men that worked for him, an' all.'

'Worked for him? Your father employed people?'

Mary nodded and said airily, 'Oh yes.'

'What doing? I mean, was he a farmer?'

'No. He was a stockinger.'

'A what?'

'A hosier. He ran a workshop making socks and stockings and other knitted garments.'

Eveleen stared at her mother.

'I 'spect it's all still there,' Mary mused, more to herself now than to her daughter. 'I 'spect Harry's got it all now.' She stood for a moment as if the memories of her childhood were crowding in on her. Then she shook her head again. 'I don't want to go back, Evie. I really don't. I love the countryside. I love Lincolnshire. Even though I wasn't born here, it's my home and I don't want to leave it. Oh, Evie,' Mary held up her arms and wailed, 'I don't want to go.'

'Mam.' Eveleen enfolded the older woman in her embrace. 'We have to go. You know we can't stay here. They won't let us. And we have to go somewhere.'

'But they won't want us either. They'll turn us away and where will we go then? The workhouse?'

'I told you, Mam,' Eveleen tried to make her voice playfully stern. 'You're not to mention that again. I promise you, you'll never have to go into the workhouse. Don't even think it.' She hugged Mary harder, noticing with a pang of regret how thin her mother had become even in the short space of time since Walter's death. 'And one day I'll bring you back to Lincolnshire. I swear to you that I'll bring you back home.'

It was a solemn vow, but the young girl, only seventeen, could not possibly know just how difficult that promise would be to keep.

Together they took a last look around the house. They were having to leave so many of their possessions.

Mary smiled pensively as she ran her fingers along the back of Walter's wooden chair and, seeing her, Eveleen had to swallow the lump that rose in her throat. In the parlour, Mary nodded towards the cabinet where her best china tea service was still displayed on the shelves. 'That was our only wedding present, you know.'

'Who from?'

'Your dad said it was from Mrs Rachel Dunsmore, but I reckon he bought it himself, just to make me think that someone, other than him, thought enough about me to buy us a gift.'

'We ought to take it with us,' Eveleen said, but Mary shook her head firmly. 'No, we've got everything we need. Someone else can have it.'

As Eveleen led her mother towards the door she noticed that Mary took one last lingering look at the sparkling willow-patterned cups, saucers and plates that she had so lovingly washed every week of her married life.

'I just hope someone will take good care of it,' Mary murmured.

Eveleen locked the door and slipped the key beneath the loose brick beside the doorstep. Taking her mother's arm, she led her towards the farm dray. Jimmy was already sitting on the back, swinging his legs and chewing on a piece of straw. Ted was standing awkwardly beside him, kicking aimlessly at loose stones while Bill stood near the two huge black and white shire horses. He had been given time off to drive the family to their new home.

'You'd best be back by the next evening, else it'll be the worse for you,' Eveleen had heard Josiah Jackson telling him.

'I'll do my best,' Bill had replied in his deep, placid tones.

'You'll do better than that, else you'll be following them next week.'

Bill had faced the farm bailiff and said steadily, 'And who would manage the horses, Mr Jackson, if you sack me?' At which the bailiff had thrust his gaunt features close to Bill's face and muttered, 'No one's indispensable, Morton. Just you remember that.'

'Oh I will, Mr Jackson. I certainly will.' Bill kept his tone deferential but his expression implied, No, no one is indispensable, Josiah Jackson. Not even you.

Now the day had come to take the Hardcastle family to their new life. The kindly man feared for them. More than anything he pitied the young girl who seemed to have such a burden of responsibility resting on her young shoulders: a mother who was not quite stable, especially since the death of her husband, and a youth who had the makings of a real rascal. Here, in this community who knew, liked and respected the family, Jimmy might have been kept on the straight and narrow. Lord alone knew what would happen to a lad like him turned loose on city streets.

'Now then, missis,' Bill moved forward to help Mary on to the front of the dray. 'Where is it we're headed? Nottingham, is it?'

Mary did not answer. She was holding a handkerchief to her face and sobbing.

Eveleen glanced helplessly at Bill. Her mother was making as much fuss as if they were indeed heading for the workhouse. The girl forced herself to be patient with the unhappy woman. Mary had suffered a most grievous loss with her husband's death and to be cruelly deprived of the only home where she had been truly happy was a devastating second blow.

Eveleen was suffering too, and not only for the same reasons as her mother. Added to her misery was Stephen's callous rejection of her. She glanced back one last time at the farmhouse. In the pale light of early morning the dwelling looked lifeless and lost as if it, too, did not want to see the Hardcastle family leaving. Her gaze flickered around the yard, taking one last look.

The previous evening she had gone alone to the beck. 'Goodbye, Dad,' she had murmured to the place where she had found him. 'For now. But I'll bring her back to you one day. I promise.'

Then she had lifted her gaze. In the far distance to the left, she could just see the spire of Bernby church where her father now lay, high on the hill overlooking his beloved fields. His grave was beside those of his father, mother and his adored stepmother. Walter was at peace and she knew he would have been content with the resting place they had chosen for him, even though it would not have been his wish to leave his family so soon.

As her gaze came closer to home, to the trees of Bernby Covert, the lump of sorrow and disappointment in her throat had threatened to choke her. Her emotions were in chaos. She loved and hated Stephen Dunsmore all in the same moment. She had turned away to walk slowly back to the farmyard. Already the place had a deserted air. There were no pigs snuffling and grunting in the sties. No hens scratching and complaining in the yard. Even the cows in the neighbouring field had been taken away. Bill had come to the farm early that morning, an embarrassed flush on his ruddy face. 'I'm sorry, Eveleen, but Jackson's ordered me to take all the livestock up to the big house.'

In the strange silence, Eveleen had leaned on the gate and looked towards the western sky to watch the red glow of the sinking sun silhouetting the ramparts of Belvoir Castle on the distant hills. It was a sight she had always loved, one that her beloved father had always relished and they had often stood together on this very spot and watched the glorious sunset of a late summer evening. No wonder, Eveleen thought, that her mother had found refuge in this place and could not bear to leave it.

As the sun sank below the skyline, Eveleen had leant her head on her arm and shed tears for her deep sense of loss and loneliness. When at last she raised her head again, a velvety dusk had fallen. Then she glanced back, just once, to the dark shape of trees and tall chimneys of Fairfield House.

'I've shed my last tears over you, Stephen Dunsmore,' she vowed, but as she turned to go into the house, to spend the last night under the roof that had been her only home, the misery was like a leaden weight inside her.

Now, in the cold light of morning, she took a final look round.

'Evie.' Ted came towards her, his face unusually solemn. 'I just wanted to say – I mean, I know me dad and me mam have said it all – but . . .' He was gauche and clumsy, but Eveleen knew he meant well. 'Don't forget us, will you? And if you need any help, well, just send word and we'll come. Wherever you are, we'll come.'

She was touched by his genuine concern and, impulsively, she put her hands on his shoulders and reached up to plant a kiss on his cheek. She was surprised at the colour that suffused the young man's face. 'Thanks, Ted. I don't know what we'd have done without you all these last few days. And no, I won't forget.' Then she forced a smile and punched him playfully on the shoulder. 'And don't you forget us either, 'cos we'll be back. One day, we're coming back.'

Now Ted grinned. 'You'd better,' he said as he helped her to climb up on to the front of the dray beside his father. Bill took the reins and, as the horse began to move, Ted stood in the centre of the yard waving. But only Jimmy, at the back of the dray, waved goodbye in return. Neither Mary, sobbing into her handkerchief, nor Eveleen, who set her face determinedly to the future, looked back.

As they joined the lane at the end of the track and began to turn right to take them to the main road to Nottingham, Eveleen saw a rider on horseback coming towards them, galloping at speed.

Her heart lifted in joyous relief. Stephen. He was coming to her. He was coming to rescue her family, even at this, the last moment. He hadn't meant to be so cruel. He had been obeying his father's orders. He was coming to her. She put out her hand and murmured, 'Stop, Bill. Please stop a moment.'

Bill pulled on the reins. 'Forgotten summat, lass?'

Eveleen, her gaze still on the galloping figure coming nearer and nearer, shook her head. 'It's him. I knew he didn't mean it. It's him.'

Nearer and nearer he came, riding towards her as if his life depended on it. Nearer and nearer, not slowing, not stopping.

Eveleen gasped as the young man neither slowed his horse's pace nor even glanced in her direction but thundered past the dray and rode on round the bend in the lane. Her gaze followed him until she could no longer see him and the hoof beats were a faint thudding sound that echoed the beating of her heart.

Her shoulders slumped, the last vestige of hope gone. He had not been coming to her. He had not even glanced at her as he had passed by.

She felt Bill's strong arm about her shoulders. 'Come on, lass,' the big man said gently. 'Time to go.'

They set off along the lane once more with Eveleen sitting rigidly on the front of the dray beside Bill, staring straight ahead, neither speaking nor looking about her.

But Mary, sitting the other side of Bill, now twisted and turned in her seat, exclaiming, 'I don't want to leave, Bill. It's such a lovely place. Such a peaceful place. Look how pretty the trees are. They'll be turning such wonderful colours soon, gold and brown. And the beck. Oh, how can I leave the place where my poor Walter died? How can I leave him lying there all alone in the churchyard? I can't bear to go.'

But all Eveleen was seeing was Stephen's face, set in disdainful, callous lines. Then anger came to her rescue. It spurted through her, hardening her resolve. Her eyes were dry and her head rose in defiance as she pulled in a deep, shuddering breath. 'Don't fret, Mam. We'll be back. You mark my words. One day, we'll be back.'

Fifteen

'Where is it we're going exactly?' Bill asked.

They had been travelling the road towards Nottingham all the morning and had stopped to eat the picnic that Dorothy had packed into a hamper and insisted Bill brought.

'They'll not have time to be making sandwiches, poor things,' his wife had said. 'So I've packed enough for all of you.'

Now, opening it, Bill chuckled. As he had suspected, his missis had packed enough to feed an army. 'Well, if we don't reach wherever we're going by nightfall, lass,' Bill said to Eveleen, 'I reckon we've enough food here to last us the week.'

Jimmy tucked in ravenously, but Mary only nibbled at a sandwich and Eveleen chewed the food round and round in her mouth, finding swallowing it difficult for the misery still choking her.

Eveleen glanced at her mother as she answered Bill's question. 'It's a place called Flawford. It's where my mother came from.'

'Oh aye,' Bill nodded. 'Can't say I've heard of it, but then, I've never been far from Bernby.'

Tears flooded Mary's eyes again as she said, 'You're lucky.'

Bill glanced at Eveleen apologetically. Eveleen said, 'Are we on the right road, Mam?'

'I don't know and I don't care,' was all the pitiful woman would say.

They finished eating and climbed back on to the dray. Taking the reins, Bill said quietly to Eveleen, 'We'll go a bit further and then I'll ask someone. Don't bother ya mam.' Beneath his breath he murmured, 'Poor soul.'

The sun was a copper-coloured ball sinking beneath the horizon when Bill, following the directions he had been given by a farmer herding his cows turned off the road skirting the south of the city of Nottingham and took the direction towards Loughborough.

'He said it was about a couple of miles down this road, didn't he, Eveleen?'

Eveleen nodded. 'We take a sharp right turn somewhere down here and then straight across at the crossroads, he said, and we'll come to the village.'

They trundled on with Eveleen leaning forward eagerly to catch the first sight of the place that she hoped would be their home. There were houses ahead.

'Is this it, Mam? Is this Flawford?'

Flatly, Mary said, 'Yes, it is,' but a few minutes later, with surprising sureness, she added, 'Keep straight on, Bill, until I tell you to turn left.'

Eveleen and Bill exchanged a glance.

'You do remember the way then, Mam?'

Mary's mouth was a narrow, compressed line. 'Oh aye,' she said, bitterly. 'I remember all right.' In a lower voice, she added, 'As if I could ever forget.'

The dray rattled on and passers-by stared up at the three people sitting on the front and the boy at the back swinging his legs and munching yet another apple.

'Oh my goodness,' Mary exclaimed suddenly and clapped her hand over her mouth.

'What is it, Mam? What's the matter?'

'That's Georgie Turner as I live and breathe.'

'Who's Georgie Turner?'

'A village lad, that's all. He used to work for my father. I wonder,' she added, musing, 'if he still lives in one of our cottages.'

As she watched her mother's gaze fix upon the man standing at the side of the road, Eveleen pondered. Was that all that Georgie Turner had been or had he been her mother's sweetheart all those years ago?

One wheel ran into a deep rut at the side of the road, causing the passengers to clutch each other in alarm and Jimmy to yell from the rear. 'Eh, look out. You'll have me off the back 'ere. I've dropped me apple, now.'

Bill grinned. 'Sorry, folks.'

They travelled for a short distance and then Mary spoke again. 'Turn left.' A few yards more and then she said, 'Now right into Ranters' Row.'

Eveleen gasped. 'Is that what this street's called?'

For the first time, Mary smiled, but it was a grim smile; a smile that did not reach her eyes. 'No, it's the locals' name for it. Its proper name is Chapel Row. It's a dead end and a bit narrow, but there should be room enough to turn the dray around. Pull up outside that gate, Bill, on the left-hand side.'

Bill drew the dray to a halt, but Mary made no move to climb down.

'Is this it, Mam?'

'Yes,' she said but still she did not move. 'You go, Eveleen.'

'Where do I go? That door there?'

To the side of the gate was a long brick wall with windows and a door in the centre, but Mary was shaking her head, 'No. That's the door to one of the cottages.'

As Eveleen looked mystified, Mary explained briefly,

gesturing towards the building. 'This is a row of four cottages. Two at either end and two in the middle that are back to back. The entrance to the one at this side is off the street.'

Eveleen still hesitated.

'Well, get on with it, if you're going,' Mary snapped. 'Ask for Harry Singleton and tell him who you are.'

'And then?' Eveleen asked.

Mary's only reply was a slight lift of her shoulders as if to say, How should I know?

Eveleen sighed and jumped down. Jimmy joined her and they stood looking up at the tall, solid gate.

'Looks like a prison,' he muttered and stuffed his hands into the pockets of his trousers.

'Take your hands out of your pockets and smarten yourself up a bit,' Eveleen said, pulling his cap straight and smoothing her own wayward hair. 'Now, come on. Let's get it over with.'

They opened the gate and walked through, closing it carefully behind them. They had walked into one corner of a rectangular enclosure. At the end nearest to where they were standing was the line of cottages that her mother had described. Now Eveleen could see the doors leading to the other three homes. The street side of the building had looked austere, but on this side a huge peach tree climbed the walls straddling the whole frontage, the fruit hanging heavily on the branches.

As she saw Jimmy's hand creep upward towards a ripe peach, Eveleen gripped his shoulder. 'Don't you dare,' she hissed.

Jimmy grinned roguishly at her, but dropped his hand away.

A brick path ran in front of the cottages and halfway along it was a pump. From this, another path ran the length of the yard, branching off to the buildings on either side and at the far end. There were patches of garden on either side: a few flowers, but mostly vegetables – carrots, cabbage and lettuce – and, entwined in a wooden frame, a trailing blackberry plant laden with juicy black fruit.

'What's that noise?' Jimmy said. 'It's coming from there.'

Eveleen followed the line of his pointing finger toward the buildings standing on either side of the yard. These were obviously not homes. She took a few steps forward, staring up at the two-storey buildings. On each floor there was one long window, with tiny square panes, running the full length of the wall.

Taking the words from her mouth, Jimmy said, 'Them's funny windows.' Then he paused and sniffed the air. 'Evie, do you smell what I smell?'

For the first time in two weeks her smile was genuine as together they said, 'Pigs!'

The smell, and now they could hear the sound too, of pigs, was coming from the buildings across the end of the yard. They tiptoed along the brick path. Next to the pigsty were communal lavatories, presumably for all the workers as well as for the residents of the cottages, Eveleen thought, and a coal store.

'Why are we creeping about?' Jimmy asked.

'And why are we whispering?' Eveleen giggled.

'Because we feel like a couple of criminals, that's why.'

Closer now they could identify the noise as the clatter of machinery coming from the long buildings.

'It must be the workshops or whatever they call them, where our uncle has his knitting machines.'

As she glanced about her, she saw a girl emerge from a door at one end of the workshops. She had her sleeves rolled up to her elbows and she was drying her hands on a piece of rough towelling. Steam billowed from the door behind her and Eveleen recognized the look of someone on washday. It was a bit late in the day to be washing, Eveleen could not help thinking.

The girl was slim with black hair in one long plait, although strands had escaped and lay plastered against her forehead. Her face was thin with high cheekbones and, at this moment, her cheeks were flushed from the heat of the copper. She stared at the strangers for a moment and then slowly came towards them. Eveleen could see now that her eyes were a deep blue and fringed with black eyelashes. Her eyebrows were neat, arched lines, so well defined it looked as if someone had pencilled them in. 'Are you looking for someone?' Her voice, when she spoke was soft and low.

Eveleen nodded. 'Mr Harry Singleton.'

'That's my father,' the girl said. 'I expect you've come looking for work, have you? Well, I'm sorry, I don't think there are any vacancies at the moment.' She glanced at Jimmy, smiled a little uncertainly and then dropped her gaze shyly.

Eveleen's heart fell. If there was no work for them to help pay for their keep, their uncle was even less likely to take them in.

She took a deep breath and said, 'We do need work, yes, but we've come to see your father because – because he's our uncle. Our mam's outside on the dray. She's – she's his sister.'

The girl's eyes widened as she stared at them. 'His sister? I didn't even know he had a sister.'

So, Eveleen thought grimly, the family rift went so deep that this girl did not even know of their existence. And yet, she reminded herself, until a short time ago, she had not known of hers. She forced herself to smile and say brightly. 'Can we see him?'

'Well,' the girl looked about her uncertainly, 'I don't know. He's working and he doesn't like to be stopped. Not until teatime and that's an hour or so yet. Six o'clock, he'll stop.' The girl bit her lip, hesitating. Then slowly, she said, 'I suppose you could see Gran, if you want.'

'Your gran?' Eveleen thought quickly. 'Is she your father's mother?'

The girl nodded.

'Then she must be my gran too,' Eveleen smiled.

'I suppose so.' For a moment doubt crossed the girl's face, looking as if she felt she had offered more than she should have done. 'I'll go and ask her if you like. Who – who shall I say it is?'

'I'm Eveleen and this is Jimmy. We're Mary's children.'

'And your mam is here too?'

'Yes, she's waiting for me. I think she's a bit nervous.'

The girl stared at her, clearly not understanding. 'I'll – I'll go and tell her. You'd best wait here.'

She was gone for what seemed an age to the youngsters who waited. Workers from the machine shops passed through the yard to the communal lavatory and stared curiously at the strangers. One or two nodded and smiled and one young man winked at Eveleen as he looked her up and down with a bold, appraising glance.

Eveleen sniffed and turned her back. She'd had quite enough of good-looking young men to last her a lifetime.

'Gran says she'll see you, but be careful what you say to her. It's put her in one of her moods.'

So, Eveleen thought, as she and Jimmy followed their cousin, our grandmother has moods too, does she?

The girl led them to the end house and in through a green painted door. The small room was dim, lit only through the one window facing out into the yard. It was hot and stuffy and when her eyes grew accustomed to the light, Eveleen could see that an old woman sat in an armchair close to the range where a fire burnt brightly. As her eyes became accustomed to the gloom she saw that the woman wore a high-necked black dress with leg o' mutton sleeves. At her throat was pinned a cameo brooch and her hair was drawn tightly back beneath a white lace cap. Eveleen didn't think she had ever seen anyone with so many wrinkles on her face. Her mouth was shrunken, the lips almost lost, but her eyes were bright and sharp.

'Come here where I can see you.' The voice was high-pitched yet strong and commanding. Eveleen stepped forward and stood on the hearthrug facing the woman, but Jimmy hung back, hovering near the door, ready to escape.

'You too, boy.'

Reluctantly he came to stand beside his sister and submit himself to the old woman's scrutiny. She squinted up at them. 'My eyes aren't as good as they were.' There was a pause as she took in their appearance. 'You don't look like her. How do I know if you're hers? You could be anybody's. Is she dead? Is that why you've come?'

Eveleen hurried to explain. 'No, no. She's outside on the dray. But she wanted us to come in first to see – to –'

'To see if we'd a welcome for the prodigal, eh?' The old woman gave a toothless grin, but the gesture was without humour. 'We've no fatted calf, but I'll see her. Bring her in, girl.'

Eveleen hurried out expecting to leave Jimmy with the old lady but found him following her closely.

'I aren't staying there with that old witch,' he muttered as they reached the gates.

'Shush,' Eveleen tried to scold him but found herself overcome by a fit of the giggles. 'Someone might hear you and then where would you be?'

'I wouldn't care. I don't reckon much to it here anyway.' He glanced around dismally at the narrow street and the terraced houses.

'It's very different,' Eveleen had to agree, her laughter dying. Then, with stout determination, she said, 'Come on, don't let our mam see you looking so glum. Just think how difficult this must be for her.'

Jimmy's only reply was to pull an unsympathetic face and as they reached the dray he said, 'I'll wait here with Bill. You take Mam in.'

Eveleen held her mother's arm as they went back to the house. She could feel Mary trembling even through the thick clothing they had both worn for the long journey on the front of the dray. As they paused outside the door, she was concerned to see that her mother's face was white and she held one hand to her chest as if her breathing was difficult.

'It's all right, Mam. Don't get upset. If they don't want us, we'll go somewhere else.'

'Oh, Evie,' Mary's voice was unsteady. 'But where?'

To that Eveleen had no answer.

Sixteen

'Hello, Mother.'

They were standing side by side, like two naughty children awaiting their punishment, facing the old woman. Eveleen was aware that the young girl was hovering beyond the door leading further into the house, listening to every word.

'So, Mary Singleton,' Bridget, Mary's mother, demanded. 'What brings you back home after all this time?'

'It's – it's Mary Hardcastle now,' Mary mumbled, her head lowered almost to her chest.

'Oh.' The old woman's tone was laced with sarcasm. 'So you did find some poor deluded feller to marry you then?'

Eveleen felt her mother stiffen and her head came up a fraction. 'He was a good, kind man.'

'Oh aye, good enough to take on another feller's bastard. He must have been a good man to do that.' Her screwed up eyes rested upon Eveleen. 'Is this her? Is this Brinsley Stokes's by-blow?'

Mary shuddered and she stumbled over the words. 'No. No. That – that baby died. This is Walter's child.'

'Walter? Who's Walter?'

'My husband. Walter Hardcastle. I – I met him just after . . .' Her voice trailed away, beaten and defeated.

'You've been a very lucky woman to find someone to take you on. A very lucky woman.' Bridget paused and then asked, 'And where is this paragon of virtue? Where is Walter Hardcastle?'

Now Eveleen felt her mother sway and sag against her, so that she put her arm about Mary to support her. She faced her grandmother squarely and said, 'My father died two weeks ago. The cottage we lived in was tied to the job, so—'

'So you're homeless,' the old woman stated baldly. Her gaze returned to Mary, 'And you thought you'd come running home.'

Eveleen lifted her chin. 'If we're not welcome, we'll go. Right now.'

The old woman's eyes were on the young girl's face, now flushed with indignation. She smiled. 'My, but you've a fiery one here, Mary.' The smiled widened. 'I like a girl with spirit. Maybe we'll let you stay a while after all. I reckon you an' me would get on together all right, lass.'

'We aren't looking for charity,' Eveleen said. 'We'll work. All of us. My mother makes pillow lace and—'

'Oho, so you haven't forgotten everything I taught you then?' Bridget's words were heavy with sarcasm again, and Mary's face, from being deathly white, now flushed with embarrassment.

'No, Mother, I haven't forgotten.'

The old woman sniffed. 'We'll have to see what Harry says, mind you. He's head of the family since your father died.'

Mary asked, 'When – when did that happen?'

'Oh years ago,' Bridget said in a matter-of-fact way. 'Fifteen, maybe. Or is it sixteen now. I forget.'

Eveleen was struck by the lack of emotion shown by her grandmother. There had been no show of feelings on meeting her daughter after more than twenty years and now there was not a shred of sorrow in her tone when speaking of her dead husband. Perhaps it was because the event had happened some time ago, whereas their own loss was so recent that each time she even thought about it Eveleen could feel the prickle of tears and the pain in her throat. But the woman sitting before them seemed hard and unfeeling.

What mother greets her long-lost daughter without even reaching out to touch her or rising from her chair to greet her? But this one had. Unless, of course, the hurt went so deep and the bitterness was still so strong that she could not bring herself to welcome her child back even after all these years.

Eveleen sighed inwardly. Her own mother had been right. Her family did not want them. She tightened her hold around her mother's waist and said, 'Mam, I think we'd better go.'

Before Mary could answer, the old woman said, 'Now then, lass, don't be so hasty. I said we'll ask Harry.' She raised her voice. 'Rebecca, get back in here, girl, 'cos I know you're listening at the keyhole.' There was a slight pause before the girl opened the door and slid back into the room.

'Did you call, Gran?' she said innocently.

'You know very well I did. Fetch your father across here.'

'He won't like being fetched from his work.'

'Tell him I sent you.'

Eveleen hid a smile. Harry might well be the notional head of the family, but it seemed to her that, in practice, it was this spirited old lady who ruled the roost. Despite her astonishment at Bridget's callous greeting, Eveleen

111

could not help have a sliver of admiration for her grand-mother. Now she was turning back to Eveleen. 'And you, girl. What do you say your name is?'

'Eveleen.'

For the first time, real emotion flickered on Bridget's face as she looked back at Mary. 'So, you still thought enough about us to name her after my mother, eh?' Her mouth stretched into a wistful smile. 'Another Irish colleen, eh?'

'Irish?' Eveleen blurted out before she could stop her inquisitive tongue. 'You don't sound Irish.' Eveleen had only ever met an Irishman once; a travelling man who had passed through Bernby, pots and pans rattling on his carrier's cart. There was no hint of his rich brogue in Bridget's speech.

The old woman sniffed. 'You should have heard my father.' Suddenly she lapsed into such a perfect imitation of the Irish brogue that Eveleen laughed aloud. 'His name was Michael O'Hallaran, so it was, and a foiner man you never did see. He could drink anyone under the table, so he could. God love him.'

There was a mischievous sparkle in Bridget's eyes, but then, reverting to her normal speech she said, 'Now, go and fetch the boy back here. We'd best be seeing what we're taking on.'

Eveleen gave her mother's arm a squeeze. 'You'll be all right?'

'Of course, she'll be all right. What do you think I'm going to do to her? Eat her alive?'

Mirth unexpectedly bubbled up inside Eveleen. Her eyes sparkled and her laughter spilled over. Catching her merriment, the old woman cackled with laughter and the tension in the room eased.

'Oh sit down, Mary,' Bridget waved a bony hand towards a chair. 'You make the place look untidy.'

The room, though small and cluttered with a lifetime of belongings, was anything but untidy. Eveleen settled her mother into a chair opposite Bridget. 'I'll get Jimmy,' she said and hurried out of the door and along the path. As she did so, she saw a man emerge from one of the buildings. A big man with broad shoulders and strong limbs who, despite his size, seemed to spring along as he walked. Eveleen faltered a moment and paused to look at him. His gaze met hers and he frowned, his heavy eyebrows meeting across the bridge of his large nose. He had a bushy grey beard and moustache that completely hid his mouth, but his dark eyes were piercing. For a workman he was smartly dressed, Eveleen thought. A white shirt and tie and a dark suit that even had a waistcoat. On his head was a bowler hat. Irrationally at such a moment, Eveleen could not help wondering if he wore his hat when working at his machine. The picture in her mind made her want to laugh, but she kept her face straight as she returned his stare.

Behind the man, taking little running steps to keep up with his huge strides, was Rebecca.

This, thought Eveleen, must be her uncle, Harry Singleton. Now she gave an uncertain smile, but her tentative greeting was answered only by a deepening frown.

Eveleen pulled her shawl more closely about her and hurried away to find Jimmy.

Moments later they returned to the house and walked into a violent family quarrel between Harry and the old woman. Mary was still seated by the fire, saying nothing, and Rebecca was standing nervously behind her grandmother's chair, twisting her fingers together, her dark blue eyes huge in her pale face.

Eveleen looked swiftly towards her mother. Mary's face was ashen and the girl guessed that for her it must seem as if the intervening twenty or so years had never happened. Mary was back with her family, about to be cast out once again.

Eveleen hurried to her side leaving Jimmy standing awkwardly by the door. 'Come on, Mam, we're going. We're not staying here for you to be insulted like this.'

'Insulted, you say?' Harry's deep, booming voice was shouting so loudly that the ornaments on the mantelpiece seemed to dance. 'And didn't she insult the name of Singleton? Bringing disgrace on to this family?'

Eveleen whirled around and faced him, her fists clenched at her sides. 'Maybe in your eyes, she did. But she's suffered for whatever she's done and if my father could forgive her and' – she glanced meaningfully at Bridget – 'take her on, then I would have thought her own family could do as much.'

She dredged around in her memory for something her mother had told her about the man standing in front of her. Then she remembered. Slowly and deliberately she said, 'I understand you're a chapel-goer?' And now, latching on to the words her grandmother had used only minutes earlier, she added, 'Well, we don't expect a fatted calf, but I'd have thought you could have welcomed her back into the family fold.'

'Don't you dare preach to me, girl.' The man shook his fist in her face, but Eveleen stood her ground.

Behind them the old woman was cackling with laughter. 'You've met your match now, Harry. She reminds me of myself when I was young. She even looks like me. And she's got my hair.' The last words were said wistfully, for only wisps of white hair peeped from beneath Bridget's lace cap.

Eveleen was not finished yet. 'And isn't there another parable about the rejoicing in heaven over the sheep that was lost and is found?'

The man grunted. 'I'm pleased to hear you know your Bible but let me tell you, the lost sheep needs to show true repentance of her sins to earn forgiveness.'

Uncle and niece continued to glare at each other until Bridget said sharply, 'For goodness' sake sit down and let's talk this out calmly.' Catching sight of Jimmy skulking in the shadows near the door, the old woman raised her shrill voice and said, 'Come here, boy, let's be having a look at you.'

Jimmy came forward reluctantly and stood before her. Bridget glanced from one to the other of her new-found grandchildren. 'Are you twins? Now I see you properly, you look very alike.'

Jimmy stuffed his hands deep into his pockets and muttered, 'No, she's a year older 'n me.'

Bridget laughed. 'So she thinks she can boss you about, eh?' Then her laughter faded and she nodded thoughtfully, but her steady gaze was still on the youth's face. 'But you'll not be told what to do for much longer, though, will you, boy?'

Listening, Eveleen marvelled at the old woman's shrewdness. Jimmy had never been easy to control, even as a child, and Bridget had summed him up in seconds. For a brief moment, Eveleen wished they were staying here. She knew she would have a strong ally in her grandmother. Yet she could not allow her mother to be treated so shabbily by her family. 'Well, he'll have to do as he's told for a while longer.' She turned to her brother. 'Go and ask Bill to turn the dray round.'

'Now, now, girl, sit down, I said. You too, Harry. Rebecca, make these poor folks a cup of tea. It's the least we can do.'

Eveleen glanced at the girl, who was already scuttling away to do her grandmother's bidding. 'Please could you take some tea out to Bill? We've come a long way.'

Rebecca nodded and disappeared.

'Now then,' Bridget began when everyone was seated. She did not intend to mince her words as she said, 'You hurt us all badly, Mary, but we never wanted you to leave home.'

Eveleen saw her mother glance at Harry, but she lowered her gaze again without saying anything. Bridget too had seen the gesture, but went on, 'To run off without a word to any of us. That was almost worse than getting yourself pregnant with the likes of Brinsley Stokes. Your poor father went to his grave not knowing whether you were alive or dead. That was cruel, Mary. Cruel and thoughtless.'

Mary looked up at last. 'I thought you wanted me gone. You made my life hell on earth after you found out. All of you. Not one of you had a word of understanding for me. Telling me that he wanted nothing more to do with me. That he'd gone away. If only I could have seen him, talked to him, just one more time . . .' Her voice trailed away as Mary relived the misery.

Now Eveleen noticed a quick glance pass between Bridget and her son.

'You think you could have persuaded him to marry you, eh?' Bridget was leaning forward. 'The daughter of a humble stockinger. His sort don't marry the likes of us.'

Eveleen shuddered. The words echoed those her mother had used to her only a few short weeks ago.

'His father could have ruined all of us,' Bridget went on. 'Don't forget, he was the bag man.' The phrase mystified Eveleen, but now was not the time to ask questions.

Bridget went on. 'Your father went to see him.'

Now Mary's head shot up. 'I didn't know that.'

'Well, he did and was told in no uncertain terms that if the lad married you he'd be cut off from his family without a shilling. The Stokeses were well off by our standards even then and now they are partners in a factory in Nottingham.'

'So,' Mary said, not really taking in everything her mother was telling her. She was still lost in her own bitterness. 'Brinsley chose to cut me off instead?'

'He was only eighteen.'

'Nineteen,' Mary said softly.

'Nineteen, then. But he'd still have needed parental consent to marry you. And Herbert Stokes was never going to give that. Never in a million years. Herbert Stokes was determined to rise in the world. And he did, but he didn't want his son to make an unfortunate marriage and hinder his grand plans.' Bridget's voice dropped and she reached across to touch Mary's hand. 'Didn't you love Brinsley enough to want what was right and best for him? Never mind what it did to you? Did you really want to ruin his life, because that's what it would have done?'

Tears spilled over and ran down Mary's cheeks. 'I thought he loved me.'

'I'm sure he did . . .'

Mary finished the rest of Bridget's sentence. 'But not enough.'

Eveleen pursed her lips, forcing herself to remain silent. It was not her place, she knew, to say anything, but she felt revolted at what these people had done. They had obviously made life so unbearable for Mary that she had run away. She had given birth in the dark and the cold in a ditch and it had almost been the death of her. If it hadn't been for the kindly and, to Eveleen's mind, truly Christian Walter Hardcastle, Mary might well have died along with her child.

And yet – Eveleen had to be honest – perhaps they had been right. Perhaps the marriage between two young people of very different backgrounds would not have worked. And Mary had carried those instincts into the upbringing of her own daughter when she had vehemently opposed Eveleen's association with Stephen Dunsmore.

And she had been right. So heartlessly had Stephen – just like Brinsley Stokes before him – proved her mother right.

Seventeen

'So, are we going or staying?' Jimmy piped up. ''Cos Bill says he wants to get unloaded and find himself lodgings afore it gets dark.'

'You're staying,' Bridget said firmly, glancing at Harry as if daring him to defy her. 'And they can live with you, Harry. There's only you and Rebecca in that end house. Plenty of room for three more. And this feller, Bill, whoever he is, he can bed down for the night too.' She turned to Mary and Eveleen. 'I've got lodgers who work for us. This place is full, mi duck, else I'd have you here.'

Suddenly Mary smiled. 'Eh, I haven't been called that for twenty years. Mi duck.' And she actually laughed. 'Now I know I'm home.'

They moved into the end house with Harry Singleton and his daughter, Rebecca, and slipped into a routine remarkably quickly, although the phrase "settled in" hardly applied. Eveleen felt far from comfortable in the strict, dour atmosphere of her uncle's house and Jimmy grew more truculent and difficult with each day. As for Mary, she was a bundle of nerves, jumping every time Harry spoke. Her anxiety to please him was pathetic.

They had been given the attic bedroom. Eveleen and her mother would share the double bed while Jimmy had a straw-filled mattress on the floor under the steeply sloping ceiling.

'Huh,' Mary said as she hauled herself up the steep, narrow stairs. 'My old room back. I haven't even graduated to a proper bedroom.'

'I'll have to tidy it up a bit. We haven't had any lodgers recently,' Rebecca explained apologetically.

They pushed their tin trunks into one corner beside a box of Rebecca's old books and discarded toys. Eveleen picked up a small school slate and touched its cool, black surface, evoking poignant memories of her father. She smiled wistfully, remembering her own childhood as she glanced at the toys: a game of draughts, a set of quoits, the coloured rings piled on to the wooden peg, and a child's cricket bat.

'Don't bother on our account,' Mary said stiffly to Rebecca. 'We won't be staying long.' She went to the marble-topped washstand under the window and laid out her hairbrush and comb. There was a rose-patterned ewer and bowl and beside them, a linen towel edged with lace. Mary picked it up and fingered the lace, examining it closely.

'Fancy,' she murmured, 'this is one of mine.' She replaced the towel and turned to the bed, running her palm across the patchwork quilt. 'And Mother and I made this together when I was about twelve.' She glanced around the room, shaking her head in wonder. 'It's not changed in all this time.'

Secretly Eveleen was quite impressed with the house. It was much smaller than the farmhouse they had lived in, but the parlour of her uncle's house, overlooking the yard, seemed to her to be well furnished. The black-leaded range where all the cooking was done dominated the room. In front of it a pegged rug covered part of the brick floor and to one side was set the master's chair, a high-backed wooden Windsor. To the right of the range, set in the alcove, were cupboards and on the left-hand side, beneath the window, was a table covered with a plush gold-coloured tablecloth. Pictures adorned the walls and one, Eveleen noticed, was a portrait of a sweet-faced woman who looked very much like an older Rebecca. Eveleen presumed it to be her mother.

In the far corner of the room stood an organ and beside it a small table covered with a lace cloth. Standing in the centre was a blue and white bowl holding a fleshy-leafed aspidistra. Beside that was a brass-faced grandfather clock that ticked solemnly and struck loudly every hour.

Behind the parlour, with a window facing out on to the street, was the kitchen. A shallow stone sink drained to an outside gutter, although all the water had to be carried into the house from the pump in the yard and heated on the range. Beneath the stairs leading to the two upper floors was a small pantry.

As they had climbed the narrow stairs on their way to the attic room, Eveleen peeped into the two bedrooms on the first floor.

The largest – obviously her uncle's room – held a wrought-iron double bed. In the far corner was a dressing table and near the door was a washstand with pretty patterned brown and white tiles. At the foot of the bed was a wooden blanket chest. Everywhere there was evidence of the industry in which this family was engaged. The flounces on the bed and the counterpane were lace-edged and, though she could not see them, Eveleen suspected that the pillow cases, and maybe even the sheets too, would be edged with lace.

Rebecca's room was smaller, but furnished in much the same way as her father's, the main difference being that hers was a single bed. They had to pass through her room to reach the one above.

Jimmy winked at the girl and said, 'You'll have to watch out I don't catch you in your nightie.'

Rebecca blushed and dropped her gaze while Eveleen smacked the back of her brother's head.

'Hey, what's that for?'

'You know,' Eveleen warned darkly, but Jimmy only grinned cheekily at her. 'At least,' she went on, 'now we're all going to be in one room, you won't be able to stay out half the night without Mam finding out.'

She kept her voice so low that only he could hear. The look of dismay on Jimmy's face made her want to laugh, but then his mouth twisted as he said, 'Be in bed by ten o'clock every night? Not likely, Evie. Not me.'

'We'll see, won't we?'

'Yeah. We will.'

They glared at each other for a moment in a silent battle of wills, until Eveleen relented a little. This tragic change in their circumstances was just as hard on her young brother as on any of them. She smiled as she whispered, 'Just be thankful you aren't having to share the bed with Mam.'

And suddenly the brother and sister were laughing together.

It wasn't so much the fact of sleeping beside her mother that irritated Eveleen. In truth, in the cold attic, they were warmth for each other. It was not even the woman's snoring which kept the girl awake occasionally that tested Eveleen's patience but rather Mary's constant entreaty every night as they got into bed.

'Oh, Evie, when can we go back? I hate it here. When can we go home?'

Eveleen would say, 'One day, Mam, I promise you. One day I'll take you back home.'

Sometimes, they would lie together talking softly, going over the day's events.

'What happened to Uncle Harry's wife? Do you know?' Eveleen asked her mother on the second night of their residence.

'I asked Mother today. Rose died about six years ago when Rebecca was ten.'

There was silence then Eveleen asked, 'And Rebecca has kept house for him ever since?'

''Spect so.'

'You'd think she'd want to go out to work. Have a little independence of her own, wouldn't you?'

'Independence? With Harry for a father? Oh, Eveleen, you've a lot to learn about your uncle if you think he'd even dream of such a thing.'

'Talking of work, I must start in the morning to look for something. It's good of Uncle Harry to have taken Jimmy on as an apprentice.'

'Where is he? He should be in bed by now. Harry will be locking up in a minute and coming upstairs.'

'Serves him right if he's locked out,' said Eveleen, turning on her side with her back to her mother and preparing for sleep.

'Don't be so hard on Jimmy. He doesn't like it here. I know he doesn't.'

'Well, he doesn't have any choice in the matter. Like I say, he's lucky Uncle Harry's at least giving him a try.' She gave a wry laugh. 'He's only got to fall out of bed into work.'

'Mm.' Her mother's voice was growing sleepy, but just before she fell asleep she said, 'It's not the best job in the

123

world. Those machines are heavy to operate and the work's hard on the eyesight. My poor little Jimmy.'

'It's better than a lot of jobs. He's warm and dry and—' But the only response from Mary was a gentle snore.

The following morning Eveleen made her way down the brick path to the workshops standing at right angles to the row of cottages.

The noise of the machinery deafened her even as she climbed the stairs to the workroom and beneath her feet it felt as if the whole building was shaking. She stood at the top of the stairs looking about her. The machines, closely spaced with the operators sitting back to back, were set in a row down the side of the room beneath the long window that she had noticed from the outside on the day of their arrival. Against the opposite wall, too, there were machines even though the light would not be so good there. On the wall above each machine hung a glass bowl filled with acid to reflect the light on to the knitter's work. No one looked up at her appearance at the top of the stairs; they had not heard her above the clatter, so for some time Eveleen stood watching, fascinated by the rhythmic operation the framework knitters carried out with a series of complicated hand and foot movements. She watched carefully and by the time she turned and went down the stairs again, she believed she could carry out all the movements in their proper sequence.

Maybe Uncle Harry would allow her to learn to operate one of the machines. She would speak to him later. She could see now for herself why it was important not to be disturbed during work. Perhaps, she thought, if the rhythm were interrupted at the wrong moment, the whole piece of knitting could be ruined. And while from a short distance away she had just now watched her uncle at work, he had not looked up once to acknowledge her presence. Perhaps he had not even been aware that she was standing there.

At the bottom of the stairs she almost bumped into a young man about to take the steps two at a time. It was the same one who had winked at her cheekily the previous day.

'Oh, sorry,' he mouthed, catching hold of her as she stumbled against the wall. Even down here conversation was impossible because of the noise from the machines above them and from the lower floor too. Although Eveleen twisted herself free of his grasp and said, 'S'all right,' they continued to stare at each other. She gave a quick nod and stepped to one side to pass by him and out into the yard once more. But the young man moved in front of her. 'Hey!' He had to shout to make himself heard. 'Not so fast.' He stepped outside and when she followed, he asked, 'Are you Eveleen? Old Harry's niece?'

Eveleen raised her eyebrow. My word, she thought. We've only been here a couple of days. News does travel fast. But, of course, it would in such a close, confined community. She nodded and the young man's grin widened.

'Pleased to meet you, miss.' He held out his hand. His grasp, when she put her hand into his, was warm and firm. He wore a shirt with the sleeves rolled up to his elbows, a tie, a waistcoat and trousers. Most of the men, Eveleen noticed, wore some kind of headgear, caps or bowlers, hanging them by their machines while they worked but putting them on immediately they stepped out of the workshop. This young man wore neither and she could see that his straight, light brown hair was cut very short. His hazel eyes were looking into hers and when he smiled the laughter lines around his eyes crinkled mischievously.

He was still holding her hand, so Eveleen pulled herself free of his grasp and again stepped to one side to walk past him, but he side-stepped once more to bar her way. 'My name's Andrew Burns and I work for your uncle, so' – he winked at her – 'we'll be seeing a lot of each other.'

'Unfortunately, Mr Burns,' Eveleen said primly. 'Unfortunately.'

His face fell. 'Aw, don't be like that. All uppity. And there I was thinking how nice yer looked.'

He looked so like a boisterous little puppy that had just been smacked that Eveleen could not stop the smile that twitched at the corner of her mouth. Seeing it, he said triumphantly, 'There! I knew I was right.' Then he leant towards her conspiratorially. 'I know, you don't want to let your uncle see you getting friendly wi' me. That it, eh?' He shook his head and added wisely, 'Well, you're quite right. He's a hard man. Keeps poor little Rebecca on a tight leash. She's hardly allowed out the door let alone allowed to speak to the likes o' me. He'll have trouble with her one day, if he's not careful. She'll break out.'

Eveleen stared at him. For a young man, he had a wise head on his shoulders, she thought.

Was that what had happened to her mother, she wondered, a generation earlier? Had she been kept on such a tight leash that, at last, she had broken loose and run wild and free?

'I must go,' she told Andrew and, lest he should try to stop her, added, firmly, 'Really.'

He stepped aside and gave a mock bow. 'We'll meet again.'

'No doubt we will,' she murmured.

As she walked towards the houses, her back straight, her head held high, she did not look back although she sensed that Andrew was standing watching her.

He did seem nice. Friendly and a bit of a rogue. She allowed him that. But, Eveleen told herself sternly, he's a man and I'm done with young men for good.

Eighteen

With three women in Harry Singleton's house, the chores were shared, but there was other work at which they each took turns. While the larger knitting frames in the workshops were operated by men, smaller stocking- and sock-making machines were part of the furniture in many of the houses in the locality.

'I expect I can still remember how to work a Griswold,' Mary murmured as she watched her niece working.

Rebecca looked up shyly. 'I'm sure you can, Aunt Mary. When I've finished this, would you like to have a go?' She glanced from Mary to Eveleen and back again. 'And you too, Eveleen. There's nothing to it really.'

'It looks easy enough,' Eveleen remarked as she watched her cousin turning the handle of the circular knitting machine, the needles sinking and rising again like a wave to form loop after loop and row upon row of knitting. 'It's very clever, though.'

'Father would be so pleased if all three of us could work the machine.' Rebecca pulled a wry face. 'I've often found it hard to keep up with the amount he wants, what with keeping house for him and the washing and seaming. I used to do the yarn winding, but there are two children in the street house' – she jerked her thumb over her shoulder towards the back-to-back house that faced the street – 'so they do that now. And their mother does a lot of the seaming up. And, of course, we sometimes have lodgers, young men who come to work here and then there's extra cooking and baking.'

Eveleen held up her hands in mock horror. 'Oh stop, stop, Rebecca. You're making me feel tired listening to you. And I thought farm work was hard.'

'It's lucky,' Rebecca went on with a glad smile, 'that the attic room was unoccupied when you arrived.'

'Or there might have been no room at the inn, eh?' Mary murmured and smiled a little sadly.

Rebecca laughed softly. 'I'm sure Gran would have made sure you stayed – somehow. I think she's very happy to see you again.'

Mary glanced at her shrewdly. 'But what about your father?'

Colour crept slowly up the girl's neck and face. Uncomfortably, she looked away. 'I'm sure he is pleased to see you.'

'But?' Mary persisted.

Rebecca shrugged and seemed to be struggling to find the right words. Eveleen, who had been listening to the conversation, came to her rescue. 'Don't ask her awkward questions, Mam,' she laughed, trying to make light of the matter. 'What can you expect him to feel? His home's been invaded by three homeless waifs and you're asking if he's pleased to see us? Come on, don't embarrass Rebecca.'

Her cousin cast Eveleen a grateful glance and, more confident now, said, 'I'm sure everything will be all right.' Then with a spark of mischief added, 'Especially if you can both knit socks on this machine.'

The three women laughed together and a bond between them was formed. From this moment, their lives would be as intertwined as the knitting they created.

With only a little practice, Mary was soon working the Griswold. Eveleen took a little longer to learn to cast on and off.

'It's easy once you get going, but it's very different to milking cows,' she laughed and then could have bitten off the end of her tongue as she saw the homesick look on her mother's face.

Later that same afternoon, Eveleen found Rebecca peering out of the parlour window overlooking the yard.

'Are you watching for your father coming in for his tea?'

The girl shook her head. 'No. He's working late tonight. He has a job to finish. The bag man comes in the morning.'

'Tell me, what is a bag man?'

'He's like a middle man. He brings the yarn from the warehouses in Nottingham and then sells the finished garments for us too.'

'Does your father own all those machines?' Eveleen asked innocently and was surprised when Rebecca burst out laughing.

'Oh no. He'd be a wealthy man if he did, wouldn't he?'

Eveleen was puzzled. 'But he owns all this, doesn't he? The workshops and the houses?'

Now Rebecca nodded. 'Yes. Gran's parents came to England at the time of the potato famine in Ireland. At first they were down south, London, I think, but then they came here. Gran married a local man. He was a framework knitter working in his parents' home. When they married they moved into this cottage and began to build the workshops in the yard and later more cottages. I think all this was once farm land.'

'Really?' Eveleen thought of the street outside and the houses all squashed together. She couldn't imagine it ever having been fields with cows grazing or chickens running about the yard.

'So who does own all the machines?'

Rebecca smiled. 'It's a bit complicated, perhaps, for an outsider to understand.'

But Eveleen was intrigued. It was such a different way of life to what she had been used to. Whilst part of her missed the open fields and the mist rising over the flat land, there was something about this place, this life, that excited her. She wanted to become part of it – at least for the time they were here. One day, she knew, she would have to fulfil her promise and take her family back to Bernby. But in the meantime she wanted to learn about the hosiery industry, to learn the trade that was in her maternal family's blood.

Rebecca glanced out of the window again, but there was no one in the yard so the two girls sat down together.

'Father owns four of the machines and the others are owned by all sorts of people. The knitters own some themselves, those who don't want to work in their own home or build their own workshops. Our bag man owns about half a dozen, I think, and some frames are owned by local people, like Mr Mills, the butcher.'

'The butcher?'

Rebecca laughed. 'He doesn't knit himself, but he owns the machine and rents it out to a framework knitter, see?'

Eveleen was doubtful. 'I think so. But you're right, it does sound complicated.'

Rebecca ticked off the points on her fingers. 'So the man who does the work, the framework knitter or the stockinger, whatever you like to call him, pays rent to the owner of the machine and the owner pays a rent to my father for having the machine in the workshops.'

Eveleen's quick mind was rapidly doing sums. 'So Uncle Harry collects rent from all the machines owned by other people?'

'That's it. Of course there are other expenses the knitters have to pay for.' Again she ticked them off one by one. 'Needles and oil, the seaming – unless their wives or children do it – candles, coal, and then if a machine needs a major repair they have to call in a framesmith—'

'Oh stop,' Eveleen said, 'I'm bankrupt already. However do they make a living?'

'We have a saying round here, "As poor as a stockinger". But we're lucky really. Most of our workers are fit and healthy and my father keeps the rent low deliberately. He says he'd sooner have the machines all working than lying idle because some poor feller can't make enough to pay his way.'

'Sounds reasonable.' Eveleen pondered a moment and then said, 'So the bag man brings the yarn, the local children wind it, the men knit it and then wives and daughters do the seaming up.'

'And the washing. Sometimes the garments get oil on them from the machines.'

Eveleen remembered seeing the girl coming out of the washhouse at the end of one of the workshops on the day of their arrival. So that had been the reason for washing being done at an odd time of the day, she thought.

'Then the bag man fetches the finished garments and takes them to the warehouses, or wherever, in Nottingham,' Eveleen concluded.

Rebecca nodded. 'That's about it, yes. Mind you, there are some ruthless men among the bag men, but my father knows what's what. He goes to Nottingham every so often just to be sure we're all being given a fair price for our work.' She laughed again. 'Even us for our socks on the Griswold.'

Eveleen was quiet for a moment. Her mother's sweetheart had been a bag man, or at least his father had, back then. Had he been a ruthless exploiter of the poor stockingers, she wondered, as well as a heartless deserter of a pregnant young woman?

'Oh, here they come.' Rebecca jumped up from her chair and went to the window again.

Eveleen went to stand beside her. 'Who?'

'The lads from the workshops. They're going to play cricket.'

'Cricket?'

Rebecca turned to look at her. 'I'm sorry, I forgot. I thought your mother might have told you.'

Eveleen shook her head. 'My mother told us nothing about her life here.'

'Because the knitters are sort of self-employed they can vary their hours of working to suit themselves. And sometimes work is slack anyway. So,' Rebecca ended simply, 'they play cricket.'

'And your father doesn't mind?'

'Mind?' Rebecca laughed. 'He's the first to pick up the bat and be shouting for someone to bowl to him.'

'Where do they play?'

'They have matches on the cricket ground down near the railway, but our lads practise here. Look—'

Eveleen peered through the window and saw Andrew Burns carrying a cricket bat and positioning himself in front of the pump.

'They use the pump as the wicket. Oh, Father must have finished work. He's joining in. Now, you watch him bowl. He played for the county a few years ago,' she added proudly.

'Did he really?' Eveleen could not keep the surprise from her voice.

Harry had appeared from the workshop. He had left his jacket behind and though dressed in just trousers, shirt and waistcoat, he still wore his bowler hat. Standing at the far end of the yard near the pigsties, he rubbed the ball down his leg and then ran a few paces along the brick path, brought his arm up behind him and over in an arc. He released the ball and it bounced once before Andrew took a swipe at it, knocking it into the patch of herbs.

Among the young men gathered as fielders, Eveleen saw Jimmy scrambling over the fence to retrieve the ball while Andrew was running the length of the brick path and back again, shouting out the number of runs he was making as he ran. 'Two.'

'Come on, Jimmy. Find that ball.'

'Four.'

'Here, here, throw it here.'

'Five.'

'Run him out.'

The yard was alive with shouting, laughing and the thud of the ball against the bat. The game went on until dusk when one or two lads drifted away to go home. Soon only Harry, Andrew and Jimmy were left playing in the yard.

'Do you think,' Eveleen said to Rebecca, 'they'd let us have a go?'

'Oh no!' Rebecca was shocked. 'Girls don't play cricket.'

'Well, it's high time we did. Come on.'

Eveleen was already at the door, lifting the latch and stepping into the yard, with Rebecca saying fearfully, 'Oh, Evie, I don't think we should—'

But Eveleen was already walking towards the pump and saying, 'Come on, Andrew, let's be having a go.'

The lad's mouth dropped open and he seemed too stunned to make any protest when Eveleen took the bat out of his hand and turned to face her uncle.

Harry hesitated for a moment but then bowled a gentle underarm ball towards Eveleen. She brought the bat back and swiped at the ball. She hit it fair and square in the middle of the bat and the ball skidded along the brick path to be blocked by Harry's boot.

'Right, mi lady,' Harry said, and though she could not see if his mouth was smiling beneath the bushy beard, she could hear the amusement in his voice.

Out here, Eveleen thought, he's like a different man, but then she had to concentrate for Harry had retreated as far back as he could and was beginning his run-up. Now he bowled overarm to her, the ball leaving his hand as fast as any of the balls she had seen him deliver to the boys. The ball came flying towards her, bounced and somehow met the flat of her bat. It flew into the air, sailed above Jimmy's outstretched hand and was heading straight for the windows of the upper storey of one of the workshops.

'Oh no,' Eveleen breathed. 'Now I'm in trouble.'

There was the sound of shattering glass and the dull thud of the ball dropping on to the floor. All eyes were turned up to look at the broken pane and then they saw Wilf Carter's face at the window, shaking his fist.

Eveleen swallowed fearfully as she glanced at her uncle. But to her surprise, and by the look on her face

Rebecca's too, Harry Singleton put his hands on his sides, threw back his head and roared with laughter.

'First team next week, lass,' he spluttered. 'First team next week.'

Nineteen

'Now who can that be when we're just about to sit down to dinner,' Eveleen muttered, exasperated by the knock at the door.

'I don't want to see anyone.' Mary's voice was high-pitched with fear.

Eveleen shot her a glance but said nothing as she opened the door to a middle-aged woman in a black skirt and white blouse with a lace shawl about her shoulders. Her brown hair, liberally streaked with grey, was drawn back into a bun. She was plump and stood with her arms folded beneath the shelf of her bosom. When she smiled, her eyes, full of curiosity, twinkled.

''Hello, mi duck,' she nodded as she greeted Eveleen, but craned her neck, trying to see past the girl and into the room behind her. 'Is she here?'

Eveleen's face cleared. 'Oh, you want Rebecca. I'll just—'

'No, no. It's Mary I've come to see. Mary Singleton. My George said he'd seen 'er riding through the village on a dray.' Her inquisitive eyes grew even brighter. 'Has she come home? Is she here?'

'Well . . .' Eveleen was uncertain. If the woman chose to peer through the window at the side of the door, she would be able to see Mary sitting by the range. Eveleen was still hesitating when her mother spoke resignedly.

'Let her in, Eveleen. I'd better get it over with.' Then

she raised her voice and said, belligerently, 'Come on in, Gracie Allenby – if you must.'

The woman almost pushed her way past Eveleen in her eagerness. 'Well, I never did,' she said as she stood before Mary looking down at her. 'Mary Singleton as I live and breathe.'

'It's Mary Hardcastle now, Gracie.'

'And I'm Gracie Turner.'

Mary looked up with a sudden spark of interest. 'You married George?'

Gracie nodded and added proudly, 'I did and we've 'ad six kids. Eldest is fifteen, youngest is four.' Her tone softened and her eyes were sympathetic as she asked, 'What about you, Mary?' Her glance flickered briefly over Eveleen and then back to Mary's face. 'This your lass, is it?'

Now the hostility in Mary's tone was undisguised. 'What if it is? What's it to you?'

Eveleen held her breath but Grace only laughed and, without being invited, sat down in Harry's chair on the opposite side of the hearth. 'Aw now, Mary, don't be like that. Don't bear grudges, mi duck. Not after all this time.'

Eveleen stood silently watching, ready to intervene if the visitor should distress her mother, but Mary was glowering at Gracie Turner and appeared to be quite able to defend herself. 'Forgive and forget, eh? Well, if you want me to do that, you'd better ask my dear brother to do the same.'

'Oh Harry!' Gracie laughed and dismissed him with a flap of her hand. 'That brother of yours should have been a preacher. In fact, it's always surprised me that he isn't. He'd have made a good one alongside that feller who gave you such a hard time. Jeremiah Tranter. "Tranter the Ranter" we called 'im. D'you remember?'

Eveleen felt the laughter bubbling up inside her, but she was still anxious for her mother.

'As if I could ever forget,' Mary said. 'I'll never set foot inside that chapel again.'

Gracie laughed, a loud infectious sound. 'Don't blame the chapel, mi duck. It was years ago. Times have changed a bit since then. We've got a lovely young feller as our minister on the circuit now.'

Mary eyed her suspiciously. 'Are you trying to tell me that none of the preachers stand up in that pulpit and harangue the congregation for their sinful ways?'

Gracie tried hard, but could not deny it.

'No, I thought not,' Mary said grimly, her mouth pursed. 'And you and all the rest followed suit, didn't you? Banned from teaching in the Sunday school, I was, and not allowed on any of the outings. And you, Gracie . . .' Mary leaned forward now, almost menacingly. 'I thought you was my best friend.'

Gracie looked ashamed. 'I was, Mary. But mi dad was as hard as yours. He forbade me to see you.' Now she leant forward and touched Mary's hand. 'I came round here one day though. Sneaked out, I did.'

'I don't remember that.'

'You'd gone,' Gracie said, and even after the intervening years there was still sadness in her tone. 'Run away, you had. I came to tell you that I was still your friend, no matter what. Me and Georgie and some of the other village young 'uns. But you'd run away without a word to any of us.' Now there was reproach in Gracie's voice.

'That's as maybe.' Mary sounded a little mollified, but still not wholly believing.

'My dad found out and I got a right thrashing for coming here, I can tell you,' Gracie went on, but now she was beaming. 'But here I am, large as life and twice as natural, to tell you what I came to tell you then. I'm still your friend. I always was and I always will be.'

Mary stared at her for a long time and then said, quietly, 'Eveleen, would you make us both a cup of tea, please love. Me and Gracie here have got a bit of catching up to do.'

Things might have continued in a fairly settled way for by the end of the first week a routine had been established. Jimmy was learning a trade in his uncle's workshops and the three women were already working well together.

But then came Sunday and with it the first confrontation between Mary and her brother.

'Eveleen,' Harry said at breakfast. 'You will go with Rebecca this morning. She teaches at the Sunday school. You can help her and, in time, you may be able to teach too.'

'Yes, Uncle,' Eveleen said. She liked children and knew she would enjoy helping her cousin.

Harry now included Mary and Jimmy too. 'You'll all be ready for this afternoon's service by two fifteen,' he decreed as he rose from the breakfast table. 'And you, young man,' he added, pointing a finger at Jimmy, 'don't think you can go out roaming the streets, making an exhibition of yourself. In this house we read the Good Book on a Sunday and Rebecca will play hymns on the organ for us later. Then there's Chapel again tonight at six.'

Eveleen saw Jimmy's horrified face and wanted to giggle, but knew she must not.

It was Mary who answered Harry. As she rose and

began to stack the breakfast dishes, she said, 'I'm well aware of the debt we owe you, Harry, and that because we are living in your house there are rules we must abide by. Jimmy will not disgrace you and both he and Eveleen will accompany you and Rebecca to the services in the chapel.' She faced him squarely. 'But I will not be attending any service in that chapel. And I think you know why.'

Eveleen heard Rebecca's little gasp of alarm and then it seemed as if everyone in the room was holding their breath.

The frown that seemed to be ever present on Harry's brow deepened and his voice was harsh as he said, 'You will attend each and every service, Mary. Everyone who lives in these four houses and in Chapel Row,' he waved his hand to encompass the neighbouring homes and even those in the rest of the street, 'indeed, all the people from the village who work in my workshops attend the services. Why should you be any different, might I ask?'

Mary's voice rose. 'You should know why. Or have you forgotten how that Christian congregation' – her tone bitter – 'treated me?'

'That was your own doing.'

'And are you still denouncing young people who "fornicate"?'

'Mary!' His admonishment was like a whiplash. Eveleen saw her mother flinch and knew that despite her valiant show of strength she would not defeat Harry. He ruled his small world and while Mary was a part of it, while they all were, they would obey him.

By two o'clock that afternoon Eveleen was proved right for when they all assembled in the living room Mary was dressed in her best black costume with its tight-fitting waist and leg o' mutton sleeves. She held a hymnbook in her hands, but her face looked as if she was about to be led to the scaffold.

'I'll go and help Gran,' Rebecca murmured and scurried out of the house.

Mary was startled out of her own problems enough to say, 'You don't drag poor Mother to Chapel surely, Harry?'

'It does her no harm,' he said pompously. 'The rest of the week she only moves from her bed to that chair and back again. It does her good to get out twice a week.'

'No doubt you consider it's good for her soul, too,' Mary said tartly before she could stop herself. She was rewarded by Harry's deepening frown.

As they trooped outside, Eveleen saw her grandmother, leaning heavily against Rebecca, coming along the path in front of the houses. Bridget winced with each step she took and their progress was so painfully slow that Eveleen hurried forward to take her other arm.

'There, Gran, lean on both of us. Is that easier?'

The old lady paused a moment, bringing them both to a standstill. She glanced from one to the other and smiled. 'My two granddaughters,' she murmured, pride in her tone. Then she looked towards Jimmy and her smile broadened. 'And that scallywag of a grandson.' Eveleen felt Bridget squeeze her arm. 'I'm glad to have you here, mi duck. All my grandchildren together. It's grand, isn't it, Rebecca?'

Rebecca smiled across at Eveleen and agreed. 'It is, Gran, it is.'

It took them ten minutes just to cross the narrow street to the chapel.

'You young 'uns shouldn't be bothering with the likes of me,' the old lady said. 'Mind you,' she added and gave

142

her cackling laugh, 'I'd be hard put to even get there without you.'

Mary was pacing up and down outside the door.

'You going to stay there all day?' Bridget asked her. Then her tone softened. 'Come on in with us, lass. They can't bite you.'

Mary did not pause in her pacing. 'Can't they?' she said bitterly. 'They had a good try once.'

Eveleen and Rebecca helped their grandmother inside and down the aisle to the front pew where Harry was already seated, his head bent forward in prayer. Beside him, kicking his heels against the wooden seat, Jimmy sat gazing around him, turning every so often to gape at newcomers.

As Bridget sat down heavily, Eveleen turned to her brother. 'Stop that this minute,' she hissed at him. Then she put the flat of her hand at the back of his head and, none too gently, pushed his head forward. 'Say a prayer. And make it a good 'un, 'cos I reckon you need it.'

She was about to sit down next to him so that she could keep him in check during the service when she realised that her mother had still not followed them in. Giving a click of exasperation, Eveleen hurried out to find her.

'Come on, Mam. It'll be starting soon.'

'I don't want to come in, Evie. You don't know what they're like.'

Perplexed and anxious, Eveleen spoke more sharply than she intended.'It'll mean trouble for all of us if you don't come in. Please, Mam,' she begged and took hold of her mother's arm. She was shocked to feel that Mary was shaking but she could not, dare not, give way. 'Come on,' she urged, more gently now. 'It'll be all right. Sit between me and Jimmy. You'll have too much to do to keep him in order to have time to worry about other folks.'

At that moment Gracie Turner came hurrying up the street, puffing and panting, afraid of being late. Summing up the situation swiftly, she linked her arm through Mary's. 'Come on, mi duck. You can sit with me, if you like.'

'Thanks, Gracie, but I'd better sit with my family.'

To Eveleen's relief Mary allowed Gracie to lead her inside and settle her in the family pew before taking her own place further back. But as Eveleen slipped in beside her, Mary clung to her arm as if she would never let it go.

'I want to go home, Evie. Take me home,' she whispered yet again.

Eveleen patted her hand, distraught that she could not respond to Mary's desperate plea, for she knew that her mother did not mean back to the house across the street, but back home to Lincolnshire.

Although their mother had never been religious, Walter had taken both his children to church regularly, but this service was like nothing Eveleen had ever attended before. Sitting in the front pew, they were directly beneath the preacher. He was a tall, heavily built man with white hair and a long, white beard. Thick curling eyebrows, white too, overshadowed deep-set eyes, and his face was set in stern lines. Not once did a smile even touch his mouth. He led the congregation through the service, through the prayers and the hymns, and while Eveleen did not know some of them, much of the form of the service was familiar.

But it was when it came to the sermon that the atmosphere changed completely. The preacher stood in the pulpit and harangued the congregation for their sinful ways. He shouted and stormed and could promise them only hell and damnation from a vengeful God unless they repented their sins this very moment and from this day forth led a blameless life.

At the first blast of his outrage, Eveleen had jumped physically. Her heart had thudded in trepidation and she had begun to understand her mother's fears. But as his diatribe continued with what seemed to the young girl mounting hysteria, Eveleen found her thoughts wandering, her mind shutting out his accusations.

This was not how she imagined the Lord. To her mind – and she recognized it might be a rather naïve and childish picture – God was a huge figure, about ten times the size of an ordinary man, who sat on a giant throne somewhere up in the clouds. He had a long, silky white beard and a wrinkled face that was wreathed in smiles. His eyes twinkled merrily at the mischief his creation caused. He would take his children on to his huge lap and pat their heads and pardon them their so-called sins when they sincerely begged his forgiveness. Even when faced with real wickedness, his eyes would be sorrowful rather than angry or vengeful.

On his right hand sat his son, resembling, Eveleen thought, the picture she had once seen of Jesus called "I am the Light of the World". He had a sweet, rather sad face. But then hadn't he suffered so terribly to save the whole world?

As the preacher shook his fist above the heads of his congregation and castigated them, Eveleen took her mother's trembling hand and put it through her own arm.

She patted it and, giving a disparaging nod of her head towards the preacher, whispered, 'It's all right, Mam. God understands, even if he doesn't.'

Whatever Mary had done in her life, she had already, to Eveleen's mind, been punished enough here on earth. With the confidence of youth, Eveleen had a firm trust and faith in a loving Father rather than a vengeful God. Her earthly father had been kind and loving and forgiving, so why should her Heavenly Father be any different?

'It's all right, Mam. Everything's going to be all right,' she murmured again, and was reassured to feel Mary's fingers squeeze her arm.

Twenty

'Gran, what happened to Mam at the chapel all those years ago?'

Later that day, Eveleen had entered her grandmother's house and sat down opposite the old woman. Wearied by the painful walk to the day's two services, Bridget leant back in her chair. She was lost in thought for a few moments, perhaps deciding how much to confide in her granddaughter, before she went on, 'When your mother got herself into trouble, we had a minister here at that time called Tranter.'

It was the name Eveleen had already heard but she said nothing and allowed her grandmother to continue.

'He was very – very . . .' Bridget sought for the right words. 'Hell-fire and brimstone.'

'I thought the one today was a bit like that.'

'Old Tranter was ten times worse than him – or better, according to your point of view. Years ago, it was the practice in our chapel to denounce wrongdoers before the congregation and Tranter believed in carrying on the old tradition. That's what he did to poor Mary. She was made to stand up in front of the whole congregation and confess her sins.'

'You mean – you mean, the minister shamed her in front of the whole village?'

'Oh aye,' Bridget said in a matter-of-fact way. 'Usually, the two concerned are brought before the chapel elders, but of course, they couldn't get hold of Brinsley Stokes. His family considered themselves a cut above the rest of us poor stockingers and they were church-goers anyway. I suppose they thought of themselves as gentry.'

'The man who was the father of Mam's baby was gentry?'

'Not what we'd think of as gentry. Middle class, maybe.' Bridget gave a cackling laugh as she added, 'It's what the *real* gentry would call "new money", earned from being in trade.' As she said the final word, she pulled the corners of her mouth down, imitating the condescending attitude of the upper classes towards a man who, by the dint of his own efforts, raised himself to a higher standard of living.

'How did my mother meet him?' It was important to Eveleen to fill in the gaps in the picture she was already building up.

The old woman sighed. 'His father was the bag hosier then. Brinsley was a nice young man, but that was the trouble, he was so young. They both were. But that didn't stop them falling in love and, of course, her father and Harry didn't approve. Neither did his parents when they found out.'

'And you, Gran? What about you?'

'Me? Oh, I just did as I was told.'

'I don't believe that for a minute.'

Bridget's bright eyes twinkled. 'Oh, lass, you're so like me, you know me already, don't you?' Her expression sobered. 'But be careful, love. Curb that wilful streak just a little, because it's still a man's world out there. You can kick against it now and again, and sometimes you can get your own way. But only for a while, because they'll win in the end. They always do.' She sighed. 'Aye, it's still a man's world all right.'

There was silence between them for a few moments before Eveleen prompted gently, 'So, what happened when everyone found out, apart from the scene in the chapel, I mean?'

'In a way, I could understand your mam running away, though I was so hurt and angry at her for not letting me know where she was and that she was all right. Oh yes, I'd've tanned her backside for her and no mistake if I could have got me hands on her.'

With the intervening years having lessened the anger, Eveleen now felt able to say with a saucy smile, 'Perhaps that's why she didn't keep in touch.'

Bridget laughed too and Eveleen thought, She *is* like me. Just like me. We even have the same sense of humour. Though they'd only known each other a few days, already a strong bond was growing between Eveleen and her grandmother.

Now Eveleen said soberly, 'But I have to agree with you, she should at least have let you know she was all right. It was cruel not to. Mind you, from the bits she has said, and even yet I can't quite piece it all together, I think the truth is that for some time after she ran away from here, she was anything but all right.'

Bridget sat up straight. 'Tell me.'

Eveleen spoke slowly, trying to tie all the threads of her mother's story together. 'I think she found work on the land and I suppose, being with child, it was very hard for her. She – she said her child was born in a field while she was working. In the cold and in a ditch, she said, and that's how it died.'

Bridget closed her eyes and sank back against the chair. Concerned that she had said too much, Eveleen leant forward and took her hand.

'Gran, I'm sorry. I shouldn't have told you.'

'Of course you should, child. I need to know. Even after all this time, I still need to be able to understand why.'

There was silence in the small room until Bridget asked, 'So when and how did she meet your father?'

'I think he was living alone at the time. His parents had died and he took her in. She was very ill and he looked after her, I think, but when she got better the wife of the man he worked for' – for a moment her own memories of the Dunsmore family threatened to overwhelm her, but she went on bravely – 'didn't approve of them living in the same house and not being married. She went to work at the big house for a while until' – an impish note came into her tone – 'Dad "took her on" and married her.'

Her grandmother did not respond to her humour. Instead she looked straight into Eveleen's eyes and said, 'Your father must have been an extraordinary man to do that.'

'He was,' Eveleen said simply. 'He was kind and gentle and – and *good*.' She met her grandmother's gaze steadily and said, 'He was what *I* would call a true Christian.'

Now Bridget did smile and said softly, 'Aye, I know what you mean, lass.'

After another pause, Bridget asked gently, 'If it doesn't hurt too much to talk about it, tell me about your life, about your father and what happened to him.'

So, sitting in the tranquillity of that first Sunday afternoon in Flawford, in the tiny parlour of a stockinger's cottage, Eveleen told her grandmother about her family's life in the farmhouse on the Dunsmores' estate.

'He was gathman—'

'A what?'

'He was responsible for all the livestock, even the herd

of milkers and the beasts kept for beef. Both Jimmy and I worked on the farm, me in the dairy mostly, but I'd have to help out wherever there was work to do. Sometimes, in the middle of the night, I'd have to help Dad deliver a calf. Oh I loved that,' Eveleen's eyes shone as she relived her former life. 'Snug and warm in the cowhouse, even on the darkest, coldest night with the wind whistling through the rafters. Just me and Dad helping a new life into the world. And then at harvest-time, all the workers on the estate had to help get the crops in. That was fun too when our dinners would be brought out to the fields and we'd sit in the shade under the trees . . .'

On and on she talked but not once did she mention Stephen Dunsmore. Her memories of him were locked firmly away. The happy times when she had truly believed he loved her were buried deep, so deep that they could not surface above the final hurt and insult he had inflicted upon her.

'You make it sound an idyllic life,' Bridget said.

Eveleen shrugged. 'It was hard work for all of us and we weren't well off. But we were never hungry or without boots on our feet.' Softly, she added, 'Mam misses it dreadfully. All she wants is to go back and I've promised her that, one day, I'll take her home. One day we'll go back to Lincolnshire where she was happy.'

'Aye, aye, I can understand that too,' Bridget said, a note of sadness in her tone. 'But you must realize, Eveleen, she will never be able to recapture her former happiness.'

'Why?' Eveleen asked defensively. 'Do you think I can't, or won't, keep my promise to her?'

Bridget leaned forward and said seriously, 'I think you'll do everything you possibly can to keep your promise, even to the extent of sacrificing your own happiness.

What I mean is that she can never know that same happiness, because *he* won't be there. Even you can't bring back the dead, lass, and her Walter won't be there, now will he?'

'No,' Eveleen whispered. 'But I have to try, Gran. I have to try. It's the only thing that will keep her going.'

Before she left her grandmother's cottage, Bridget asked, 'Has your mother taught you how to make bobbin lace then?'

Eveleen shook her head.

'Right then,' the old woman said firmly. 'Every Sunday afternoon after Chapel, you come here to see me and I'll teach you. I may not be able to see well enough to do it myself any more, but I can still teach you. I've already taught Rebecca and I'd like to think that both my granddaughters were carrying on the family tradition.' She wagged her forefinger playfully at Eveleen. 'But not a word to your uncle, mind. He's very strict about no work being done on the Sabbath and we wouldn't want to upset him, now would we?'

Although a smile twitched at the corner of her mouth, Eveleen managed to say seriously, 'Oh no, Gran, we wouldn't.'

Twenty-One

It was on a Sunday afternoon, a few weeks after their arrival in Flawford, that Eveleen was obliged to change her opinion of her uncle just a little. The impromptu cricket match had already shown her, very briefly, another side to the stern, dour man who forced his own rigid principles and beliefs on all his family and even on all those who worked with him.

She arrived outside her grandmother's cottage as usual and was about to enter, had even lifted her hand to push open the door that was already ajar, when she heard voices from inside. The shrill voice of her grandmother and her uncle's deep rumbling tones. She was about to move away again to return later but then the sound of her own name being spoken caught her attention and held her there. She knew it was wrong, knew she should have gone away, but the temptation to eavesdrop was too strong.

'I'm not one given to handing out praise,' Harry was saying.

'Don't we know it.'

He went on, ignoring Bridget's sarcasm: 'Eveleen has mastered the Griswold very well. Between the three of them, they've more than doubled what Rebecca could manage on her own. And she's a neat worker with her needle at seaming.'

'Earning their keep, are they?'

'Ah well now, I wouldn't go as far as that,' Harry said

cautiously. 'But Eveleen's a worker, I'll say that for her. She carries on long after the others of an evening. I've watched her. She examines her own work with a critical eye and tries to improve all the time.'

Bridget gave her cackling laugh. 'Well, if she's a worker, then she might even earn your approval, Harry Singleton. Eventually.' Harry gave a grunt and Bridget went on. 'What about the lad? How's he shaping up?'

Now Harry had not even the faintest praise for his nephew. 'He's less than useless. He'll find any excuse to leave his frame, and when he is sitting at it his work is not fit to sell.'

'Oh dear,' Bridget said, but Eveleen could still hear the sarcastic amusement in her grandmother's tone. Then, more seriously, Bridget urged, 'He's not the stuff the girl's made of, I grant you. They might be alike in looks, but that's where the likeness ends. They're totally different in character. But those youngsters've been through a lot just recently. Give the lad a bit of time, Harry.'

He gave another grunt of disapproval. 'I'll give him a bit longer. He's operating an old frame that's not needed for anything else at the moment, but he's heading for trouble, you mark my words. Eveleen tries her best to keep him in line, but she's not going to manage it for much longer.'

'It's a great pity,' Bridget mused, 'that Eveleen wasn't born the boy. She's strong and determined to do the best for her mother and brother. But whether she'll get any thanks for it is another matter. Strikes me . . .' The old lady was musing now and her voice dropped a little so that Eveleen could scarcely hear. 'Mary's soft with the lad, but too hard on the girl. Now, I wonder why?'

After a moment's pause, while Eveleen stood on her

toes ready to flee at the sound of her uncle preparing to leave, she heard him speak again. 'You're right, Mother. Eveleen's twice the character of the lad. She'd've made a fine framework knitter.'

'And,' Bridget put in slyly, 'you'd've had someone to carry on the family business then, wouldn't you?'

'Maybe. Aye, maybe so.' There was the scrape of a wooden chair on the brick floor and Eveleen moved away but not before she had heard her uncle's final words. 'And don't think I don't know about your Sunday afternoons teaching the lass your bobbin lace. But this time I'll turn a blind eye. At least it's keeping the Devil from finding work for her idle hands. She's better here with you than consorting with the village lads on a Sunday afternoon like her brother.'

Bridget's shrill laugh followed Eveleen as she scurried away down the path. 'Oho, you can turn a blind eye, Harry Singleton, when it suits you. When you can see a few more shillings being earned . . .'

As Eveleen hurried away towards the coal store on the pretext of collecting coal for her grandmother's fire, she could not help feeling the warm glow of her uncle's approval, even though she knew he would never say it to her face.

Perhaps, after all, things weren't going to be so bad for them here. If only, she thought, I can make Jimmy toe the line.

'Ugh, what's this? It's like eating a jellyfish.'

Jimmy prodded the thick white fleshy substance on his plate, while Eveleen stifled her laughter and kept her own eyes downcast. She knew what Jimmy meant. On their only trip to the seaside years earlier – a Sunday school outing from Bernby to the east coast – they had found a jellyfish on the beach and prodded it with a stick. Digging her fork into whatever it was on her plate, Eveleen thought, felt much the same.

'It's tripe and onions,' Rebecca said in a small voice. 'If you don't like it, Jimmy, I can get you something else.'

'You'll do no such thing, Rebecca. Sit down and eat your tea,' Harry boomed. 'Jimmy will eat what's given him or he'll go without.'

Jimmy pushed his plate away and muttered, 'Then I'll go without.'

'They're not used to it, Harry,' Mary put in tentatively, then turning to Jimmy, pleaded, 'Please, love, just try a little more.'

But Jimmy was already standing up. 'Sorry. I'm off out.' He glanced round the table and grinned. 'I'll go and see Jane.' Jane lived near the village green with her parents. Her father and brother were both framework knitters in Harry's workshops.

Jimmy pushed his chair under the table and moved to the door. Taking down his scarf from the peg behind the door he turned back and, as a parting shot, he added, 'Her mam makes a lovely stew.'

Eveleen risked a glance at her uncle's face. It was purple with rage. Instead of shouting after Jimmy, he seemed bereft of speech. Mary was nervous, her knife and fork trembling in her grasp. But it was the expression on Rebecca's face that shocked Eveleen the most.

Her dark eyes were huge in her pale face and she was staring at the closed door through which Jimmy had just left. She looked hurt and, yes, Eveleen thought, rejected.

Jimmy had done far more than insult the meal she had prepared. He had wounded the girl herself.

The rest of the meal continued in a stony silence, but Rebecca ate nothing.

The tension between uncle and nephew grew worse over the days that followed.

'You'll serve that up to him, Rebecca, each and every meal until he does eat it,' Harry boomed after Jimmy had left, his bushy eyebrows almost meeting above the bridge of his nose as he frowned. 'Do you hear me?'

Rebecca, pale and tearful, said, 'Yes, Father.'

Eveleen said nothing, but she knew her brother. There was going to be trouble.

The horrified look on Jimmy's face when the tripe and onions were placed before him the following morning at breakfast would have made Eveleen laugh if the atmosphere in the room had not been so fraught. Mary glanced from Jimmy to Harry and back again. With trembling fingers, she touched Jimmy's hand.

'Please eat it, love. You'll get used to the taste.'

Jimmy stood up, pushing back his chair in such a swift movement that it toppled backwards and crashed to the floor. 'I won't. It's horrible. I'd sooner starve.'

'Then as far as I'm concerned,' Harry boomed, 'you can.'

The two men glared at each other, while the women looked on helplessly.

Jimmy turned and left the house, slamming the door behind him. Mary began to wail. 'Eveleen, let's go home.'

Eveleen put down her spoon and got up from the

table. She left the house, but more quietly than her brother, and went in search of him.

He was leaning moodily against the pump and, as she neared him, he repeated his mother's plea, 'Let's get out of here, Evie. Let's go back home.'

Eveleen stood with her hands on her hips. 'Look, Jimmy,' she said firmly. 'It's high time you started acting like a man instead of a boy. Start taking a bit of responsibility, for Heaven's sake. You're the man of the family. Why do you leave it all to me?'

'Because you're so much better at it than me, Evie.'

'You mean I'm the bossy one.'

'No, no, I don't mean that. I'm being serious. You're the only one who can look after Mam. I can't.'

'But you're her blue-eyed boy. You can't do any wrong in her eyes. We both know what's going to happen now, don't we? With this tripe and onion nonsense.'

He glanced at her questioningly.

'You're going to stick it out and so's Uncle Harry. Neither of you is going to give way. That meal is going to be served up to you until there's green mould growing on it. And then what's going to happen?'

Jimmy grinned. 'I'll die of food poisoning and all the girls will weep at my funeral.'

'No. Mam is going to be caught in the middle and will be smuggling food to you. Rebecca, too, I shouldn't wonder.'

Jimmy's grin widened. 'She's all right, is Rebecca.' Then he appeared to be calculating. 'How long do you reckon it'll keep?'

Eveleen shrugged. 'A day maybe.'

'Right then. I'll stick it out today and I'll eat it tomorrow morning. I'll make my point and then I'll let the old bugger think he's won.'

'It's not quite the way I meant, but I suppose it'll do.'
'It'll have to. 'Cos it's all you're getting.'

The cricket season was over, but that did not stop the young men and boys employed in Harry's workshops from practising in the yard on fine evenings until the deepening dusk made seeing the ball quite impossible. Then, much to Eveleen's dismay, she would hear them clattering out of the yard, not to go home, but to the pub the Brown Cow, at the end of Chapel Row. If they could no longer play cricket, then they could talk about it, and where better than over a pint?

'You wouldn't think they'd have a pub at the end of the street where there's a chapel,' Eveleen said, ranting herself for once.

'It was probably there first,' Mary put in. 'Besides, there are two chapels further along the road on the opposite side. Don't you worry about Jimmy. He'll not go into a pub. And he'll be home by ten, just like he's always been.'

Eveleen wondered if her mother was really as blinkered about her son as she made out. But Mary was sitting placidly by the fire, her bobbin lace on her knee, her head bent over her work. Eveleen felt a lump in her throat. At any moment Mary might glance up and expect to see Walter sitting on the opposite side of the hearth. The tranquillity would be spoilt. But Mary did not look up. Eveleen wondered if her mother were deliberately inhabiting an imaginary world of her own, pretending that she was back home beside her own fireside with her husband. Anxious not to break the spell, if it gave her mother comfort, Eveleen tiptoed out of the house and across the road to the chapel where she had promised to help her cousin with the Wednesday night evening classes for the Sunday school children.

Later that night when they all went up the stairs to their rooms, Jimmy was still not home.

'Don't lock the door, Harry. He'll be home any minute,' Mary pleaded, but Harry, frowning and silent, made a great performance of turning the heavy key in the door. For once, Eveleen was in sympathy with her uncle. If Jimmy couldn't come home at a decent hour, she thought, then he can sleep in the pigsties.

It was half past one in the morning when she heard the gate into the yard bang and two drunken voices be raised in song and then collapse into silly giggling.

'Oh no,' she breathed and quietly slipped out of bed without disturbing Mary. She descended to Rebecca's room, opening the door as quietly as she could, but the click of the latch woke the girl.

'What is it? What's the matter?' Rebecca's fearful voice came out of the darkness.

'It's Jimmy. He's shouting and carrying on outside. If he wakes your dad—'

She didn't need to say more, for already Rebecca was throwing back the covers and getting out of bed. 'Oh dear. I'd better come down. I know where Father puts the key. I'll let him in.'

'You stay there. You'll only be in trouble.'

'I don't mind. Not – not if it's for Jimmy.'

There was silence between them as Eveleen strained through the darkness to see Rebecca's face. She would have said more, but at that moment there was such a banging and rattling on the door that both girls scuttled down the stairs as fast as they could.

'Quick, Rebecca, you find the key while I light a candle. He'll wake everyone in the row at this rate.'

Rebecca was shivering with cold and fright but laughing nervously at the same time. She could hardly get the key into the lock. 'Thank goodness Father's a heavy sleeper.'

'Even he won't sleep through this if it goes on,' Eveleen muttered. 'Hurry up, do.'

At last the key turned and Rebecca pulled open the door. Jimmy fell against her, almost knocking her over.

'Oh there you are, pretty Rebecca. See Andrew, Rebecca's come to let me in. Andrew?' He raised his voice, but, sensibly, Andrew had gone into his own house next door.

'Shush,' Eveleen hissed and grabbed hold of Jimmy by the scruff of his jacket. 'Come in and just keep the noise down.'

Jimmy swayed and put his finger to his lips, imitating Eveleen. 'Sh-shush. Quiet as little mi – hic – mice. Sh-shush.'

Between them, the two girls hauled Jimmy into Harry's chair.

'You go back to bed, Rebecca. I'll see to him.'

'No, no, you go. If your mother wakes up and finds neither of you there, she'll likely start a commotion that will wake Father.'

'That's true, but—'

'Go on,' Rebecca urged. 'I'll stay with him. No one will miss me and I'm always up first anyway.'

Eveleen glanced doubtfully at the frail girl and then at her brother, his head lolling to one side, a glazed look in his eyes and a stupid grin on his face. 'Well, if you're sure . . .'

'Of course I am. Go on, before you're missed.'

Reluctantly Eveleen saw the wisdom of the girl's suggestion and went back upstairs to bed. Though she slept fitfully, she did not hear Jimmy come to his bed under the eaves nor Rebecca return to her room.

When Eveleen came down the next morning, there was no sign of Jimmy. Rebecca was bustling between pantry, scullery and kitchen preparing breakfast.

'Where is he?' Eveleen asked. 'I'll knock their heads together, him and Andrew, when I catch up with them.'

Rebecca smiled, a pink tinge to her cheeks. 'He's all right. He – he slept it off on the hearthrug. He's outside having a wash under the pump.' Her smile widened. 'Waking himself up.'

Eveleen glanced out of the window and saw Jimmy with his head under the spout, while a green-faced Andrew Burns pumped the icy-cold water.

'Serves 'em both right,' she muttered and then turned to ask, 'What about you? Did you manage to get some sleep?'

Rebecca, the pink tinge in her face deepening, avoided meeting Eveleen's frank gaze. 'Me?' she said airily. 'Oh don't worry about me. I'm fine.'

Twenty-Two

Eveleen was chafing at what she thought of as idleness.

After a few weeks of living in Flawford, she had learnt to make socks on the Griswold machine in the house. She helped Rebecca with the seaming of the garments knitted in the workshops and, of course, shared all the household chores. And her grandmother had told her that already she had surpassed her own mother's skill in making bobbin lace.

'Mary never got her work as neat and even as that,' Bridget confided. 'But don't you let on.'

Daily now, Eveleen listened to their uncle ranting that Jimmy was hopeless and that he was taking up a knitting frame that could be put to better use. Jimmy had passed his seventeenth birthday and she, her eighteenth, yet her brother seemed to have gained nothing in the way of common sense or a willingness to apply himself.

'I'll run away to sea if you keep on at me, Evie,' he said morosely when she tried to reason with him.

'Look, Jimmy, we're lucky that Mam's family took us in. And even luckier that Uncle Harry is prepared to teach you a trade. And a good trade at that.'

'Huh. I don't see him making a fortune even for all the hours he works. And the other fellers who work here take home a pittance.'

'And you think you'll make your fortune at sea, do

163

you?' she answered sharply. 'What are you going to be? A pirate?'

Jimmy grinned. 'Now, there's an idea.'

She had to laugh in spite of her exasperation with him. 'Oh you!' She punched his shoulder playfully, then asked seriously, 'You wouldn't really run away and leave us, would you? We ought to stick together. At least until we can go back home.'

'And how do you think we're going to do that when we only make a few miserable pence a week between us?'

'You've got to try harder, Jimmy. Uncle's fast losing patience with you.'

'Well, if you think you can do any better on one of those frames, why don't you have a go. It's hard work, let me tell you—'

'Me?' Eveleen said and then again, suddenly thoughtful, she repeated, 'Me?' As Jimmy's derisory challenge took root, she murmured, 'Why not me?'

Now Jimmy was scoffing. 'He'd never let you. He won't have women working in there, I can tell you. Andrew told me.'

But Jimmy had not overheard the conversation between their uncle and grandmother. There was a determined glint in Eveleen's eyes as she said, 'We'll see about that.'

'Huh,' Jimmy said again, shoving his hands deep into his pockets and turning away, 'Pigs might fly.'

Over the following few days, Eveleen gave a lot of thought to the idea. She made several excuses to visit the workshops and lingered as long as she dared to watch the men at work. She was careful not to catch her uncle's eye, for he would certainly have gestured that she should be about her own work. No doubt he would have misconstrued her reasons for being there, thinking that she was flirting with the young lads. She kept her distance from Andrew Burns, for he never lost an opportunity to talk to her and would wink cheekily at her.

She was confident that she could learn how to operate a frame and the only thing that worried her was the physical strength that was obviously required. But she had worked on a farm, she reminded herself. She had lifted churns of milk and sacks of corn. She had stood on the top of a stack at threshing time and wielded forkful after forkful of straw. Her muscles flexed involuntarily at the memory.

Eveleen left the workshop and walked back down the brick path towards the cottages, returning to her own work. On Sunday, she decided, she would talk to her grandmother. Bridget and she had drawn even closer and she knew the old woman would be her ally.

If anyone could help her persuade Harry to give her a trial at one of the frames, then it was her grandmother.

'Gran,' Eveleen began the following Sunday, as she sat working the pillow lace under her Bridget's guidance. 'Do women ever operate the frames?'

The question obviously startled the old lady.

Eveleen paused in twisting the bobbins one over the other to form the spidery web of lace and repeated her question.

'I don't know about anywhere else, but they never have here.' Bridget's shrunken mouth widened into a smile. 'Your uncle would think it a distraction to the fellers to have a woman working alongside them.' She put her head on one side and eyed Eveleen thoughtfully.

As shrewd as ever she said bluntly, 'Are you thinking of taking Jimmy's place?'

Eveleen met her grandmother's gaze squarely. 'I'd like Uncle to teach me how to operate a frame.' Then she added deviously, 'Perhaps with me there, Jimmy would work harder. He'd not like to be outshone by his sister.'

Bridget laughed. 'You crafty little monkey.' Then, thinking aloud, she murmured, 'Well, your uncle doesn't like to have frames standing idle, and by what he said yesterday there'll be another from tomorrow morning. One of the older fellers was taken ill on Friday.' She shook her head and sighed. 'Poor old Alfie. He worked for your grandfather ever since he started this place.' The old lady's mind was wandering off into her own memories but far from being irritated, Eveleen was fascinated.

'When we first got married we came to live here in an old tumbledown cottage.' She pointed down to the ground. 'That stood where these houses are now. Your granddad started with just one frame at home and I worked the stocking-machine and made pillow lace. We worked from dawn to dusk and then some. He had this dream, you see, that he'd build workshops, run his own little factory. He bought this place because it had a good-sized garden to it and he could see the possibilities. Then he started to build the workshops, brick by brick with his own hands. It took years.'

She fell silent and gazed out of the window as if her old eyes, which could not see clearly around her now, could see perfectly back into the past.

'If Uncle would only teach me,' Eveleen said, trying to keep her growing excitement in check, 'there might be other people who would employ me.'

Bridget was dragged back to the present by Eveleen's remark.

'There might be,' she said guardedly, not sounding too hopeful. 'But I'm not sure any of them would employ a woman, let alone a young girl.'

Eveleen's smile broadened and her eyes twinkled as she said, 'We'll see.'

'No, no, it's impossible.' Harry shook his head. 'It's unheard of.'

'Why, Uncle Harry?' Eveleen said evenly, keeping her tone respectful and deferential.

'Well, because it is.' She could sense he was wavering. Whatever her uncle was, strict and uncompromising, he was also honest and truthful.

'But is there any good reason why I shouldn't learn, Uncle Harry? Other than that it isn't usual?'

Now he looked her up and down, appraising her.

'I worked on a farm, Uncle,' she reminded him gently. 'I'm used to hard work. Physical hard work. I'm not afraid of it. Oh, I'm not saying I could operate a frame at once. I can see how difficult it is—'

'So that's why you've been hanging around the work-shops is it? I thought you were eyeing young Burns.'

'You needn't be afraid of anything like that with me, Uncle Harry.'

The man put his head on one side and regarded her thoughtfully. 'You're a pretty young lass and one day—'

Eveleen shook her head firmly. 'No, Uncle. I'm not interested.' There was no need to tell him of the unhappy experience that had destroyed her trust in men. Instead, she used the weapon that she knew would be most effective with this forbidding man. 'I only want to work and work hard. You and Grandmother have been very kind to us, taking us in, especially after what happened

167

years ago. I know that. But we don't want to be beholden to you for ever. I have to get this family back on its feet.'

Harry nodded. 'Well, lass, you've got spirit, I'll give you that. Pity your brother isn't out of the same mould.' His expression lightened and Harry came as near to smiling as he ever would. 'You know your grandmother has been pleading your cause?'

Eveleen smiled up at him. 'I hoped she might. And she did say' – Eveleen's heart was in her mouth as she played her final card – 'that there's a frame not working now, because of Alfie.'

The frown was back and yet Eveleen could see the calculating look in his eyes. Anything – even this slip of a lass – was better than having a frame standing idle. 'Aye. It's his frame, mind you. I'd have to ask him. In fact, I'd have to ask the other fellers. Can't risk having a riot on my hands.'

Eveleen waited in a fever of excitement, pressing her lips together to stop more words tumbling out.

'Tell you what. After work at night, I'll give you a trial. If you shape up, lass, then we'll see. Can't promise more than that.'

'No, Uncle, you can't. But I won't let you down. I promise you.'

'You'd better not, lass.'

'Now, I'll show you first and then you can have a go. We'll only do one strip although this is a wide frame and would usually produce three strips at once.'

Harry hoisted himself on to the leather straps that formed the seat in front of the frame. First he pointed out all the different names of the parts: needles, jacks, sinkers, presser bar and treadles.

'You've got this metal frame and inside this you've got these plates. These are called the sinkers and they push the yarn around the needles to create loops. The needles are spring-bearded needles.'

He picked up a loose needle from a box of parts at the side of the machine and held it out towards Eveleen. 'The pointed end is bent into a hook which is closed by the presser bar.'

'Do the needles move in and out like the Griswold's move down and up?' she asked.

'No, no. On the Griswold they're latch needles but on this machine the needles don't move at all. Now, watch carefully, Eveleen. It's all a case of operating your feet and hands in a series of movements. At the base, look' – he pointed down to his feet – 'there are three pieces of wood called treadles. The two outer treadles are attached to that large wheel.'

Eveleen bent and peered through the workings to see a large, solid wooden wheel at the back of the frame. Harry went on explaining while Eveleen tried to take it all in, her quick mind racing to keep pace with his demonstration.

'And also attached to that wheel by these cords is the yarn carrier taking yarn from the bobbins at the top. Now, this treadle in the middle is attached to this bar called the presser bar and that's brought down to close the needles. So, Eveleen, my hands work these handles on either side of the machine with my thumbs on these two metal plates. My left foot is always on this sinking pedal and my right moves between the two treadles and the presser bar in the middle.'

Eveleen nodded, her eyes bright with excitement as Harry began to operate the machine. 'First, I bring the sinker bar forward . . .'

169

Fascinated, Eveleen watched the various parts of the machine begin to move under Harry's experienced hands and feet. There was a sudden noise as the yarn fled across the needles and the jack sinkers fell between the needles creating a loop across every two needles.

'You can't make a loop round every needle at once,' Harry explained. 'The yarn would snap. So, now we bring down a second series of sinkers by pressing on these thumb plates and these form a loop over every needle. See?'

'Yes, yes, I see,' Eveleen could hardly contain her eagerness and her fingers itched to try for herself. 'The first set of sinkers went up a bit,' she said.

Harry glanced over his shoulder. His beard hid his mouth but there was a smile in his eyes. 'That's right.' There was a hint of pleasure in his tone at her quick understanding. 'That's so that all the loops are equal. Now.' Harry pulled the carriage forwards and the new loops were pushed into the hooks. The carriage was lifted, the presser bar brought down to close the hooks and then the carriage was pulled forward again to bring the old loops over the closed hooks. A new row of knitting was formed.

'And then we start again,' Harry said as he carried on working several rows, but at a much slower rate than the knitters normally worked. 'The best knitters can work forty-two rows a minute,' he told her.

At last he stopped and swung his legs over the seat. 'Right, now you have a go.'

Her palms were clammy as she wriggled on to the seat.

'If you can't reach the pedals, we'll have to get you your own seat made.' He gave a short bark of laughter. 'That's if you shape up, lass.'

Licking her lips, Eveleen put her hands and feet where she had seen her uncle place his on the machine.

'Take it steady and I'll tell you what to do.'

She followed his instructions carefully and when the first row of loops fell to form a new row, she felt a thrill of achievement.

'And again,' Harry said, and repeated his instructions.

Again and again, row upon row, until cramp seized the back of her calves and her thumbs ached from pressing on the metal plates, but Eveleen kept on.

There were no words of praise from Harry, but there was no criticism either. And that, for Harry Singleton, was praise enough.

Gradually, he stopped repeating every single move, just giving a reminder now and again, until finally he fell silent and watched her steady, rhythmic flow of movements and the rows of neat, perfect knitting.

Eveleen went on until the yarn ran out on the bobbin. Then she turned to the man still standing at her side. He gave a brief nod and said, 'Tomorrow night I'll show you how to take off the finished strip and thread it all up from scratch. Leave it for tonight. No one will touch this machine tomorrow. Come along, now, Rebecca will have our supper ready.'

Eveleen swung herself off the seat. She staggered a little as she stood up and found her legs were trembling. Her neck and shoulders burned with pain and, as she stumbled after her uncle, she rubbed her aching thumbs and wrists.

But her physical discomfort was nothing to her for she was filled with exhilaration and hope.

Harry paused at the top of the stairs. 'You've got the hang of it now and all you need is practice. Come up

171

here every night and in a week I'll see how you're shaping. You can use that old yarn there.' He pointed to a basket of hanks lying in the corner. 'It's below standard, but it'll do for you to practise on.'

'Thanks, Uncle Harry,' Eveleen said, sounding a little breathless after the exertion it had taken to operate the heavy machine.

He nodded and, as he turned away and clumped down the stairs ahead of her, she heard him mutter again, 'Pity the lad's not like you.'

Twenty-Three

'What did they say, Uncle Harry?'

Eveleen had not been able to keep still but had paced up and down outside the row of cottages. It was a week since Eveleen had sat in front of the frame for the first time and her uncle was asking the workers now, this very minute, if they had any objection to his niece working alongside them. Eveleen felt as if her future – the whole future of her family – depended upon their answer. She pictured each of the men in turn, trying to guess whether they would be for her or against her. The younger ones, Andrew Burns among them, would be on her side. They would laugh and tease her, she knew, but she couldn't for one moment imagine them objecting. It was the older workers who worried her. They didn't like change. They didn't like going against tradition. A woman's place was in the home, not in the workplace. A young lass like Eveleen should be occupied within the home or sent into service. That was their thinking, she knew.

As she paced, she wrapped her arms around her, the pit of her stomach churning with nerves. She wished she dared to creep up the stairs and listen to what was happening, but she did not want to risk being caught eavesdropping.

As she reached the end house and turned to walk back again, she heard a sharp tap on the window and turned to see her grandmother beckoning her inside. She opened the door and stepped into the warm living room.

'For Heaven's sake, child, stop pacing up and down like a caged lion,' the old lady grumbled, easing herself back into her chair beside the fire. 'You're getting me all of a dither just watching you.'

'But, Gran, it's so important to me. I've tried so hard.'

'I know you have. Harry's been telling me.'

'He has?' Eveleen still could not sit down, but moved restlessly about the room.

'Oh aye. Singing your praises, he was.'

'He was? Really?'

'Yes, really. And that's rare. Harry's not one to hand out praise, not even when it's due, I can tell you.'

Eveleen bit her lip to stop herself blurting out what she had overheard previously. She sat down opposite Bridget and leaned forward. 'What did he say? Tell me.'

'Said you'd surprised him by the way you'd stuck at it. He knows how tough it is and he didn't think you'd even manage to operate the machine, but you're stronger than you look, he says. And you've got a will of iron.' Bridget laughed. 'He said it was a pity the boy isn't the same as you.'

Eveleen pulled a wry face but said nothing even though, silently, she was forced to agree. She didn't want to be disloyal to her brother but Jimmy was giving her increasing cause for concern. He'd taken to going out every spare moment, hanging about with the other village lads, especially Andrew Burns. Eveleen wasn't sure that Andrew was a very good influence on Jimmy. But then she sighed. She had no illusions about her brother at all and if she were to be absolutely honest, she had to admit that Jimmy was more than likely the bad influence on Andrew.

At that moment the door opened and Harry came in,

his huge frame filling the small room. Eveleen, her gaze on his face, rose slowly to her feet, her heart thudding painfully.

She could tell nothing from his expression. It was as stern and unreadable as ever.

'Well?' Bridget said sharply. 'Don't keep this poor lass in suspense any longer.'

Harry nodded. 'They've agreed to give you a try. Mind you, some of 'em weren't keen.'

Eveleen gave a cry of delight and flung herself against Harry, throwing her arms about him. 'Oh thank you, thank you, Uncle Harry.'

Harry pushed her away. 'Now, now, there's no need for such unseemly behaviour. If you're going to act like that . . .'

At once, Eveleen stood back. 'I'm sorry, Uncle. It was – it was just that I'm so relieved, so thrilled.'

He nodded and said gruffly, 'Well, all right, then. But remember, you must keep yourself to yourself in the workshops. I don't want any goings-on with those lads. Especially that Andrew Burns. He'll chase anything in skirts. Why, he's even dared to cast his eyes at Rebecca.'

Eveleen didn't know whether to laugh or cry. Poor Rebecca, she thought, not allowed even to speak to boys. Kept at home as a drudge, her only outing on Sundays to the chapel just across the road. Though she must respect her uncle's wishes, at least for the time being, there was no way Eveleen was going to allow herself to be treated in the same way.

She could guess who the objectors in the workshops had been without them being named and her mouth tightened with determination. I'll show them, she thought. I'll just show them. But she did not voice this, knowing that her uncle would not take kindly to such bravado. Instead, with pretended meekness, she said once more, 'I won't let you down, Uncle.'

'Well, lass, time will tell,' was all he said this time. Eveleen's heart sank. She could see in his eyes that he was still doubtful about her.

As he left the cottage and she made to follow him, Bridget hissed, 'You'll show 'em, lass. You'll show 'em.'

Heartened, she bent and kissed the old lady's cheek. 'Oh, go on with you,' Bridget flapped her away but not before Eveleen had seen the pink tinge of pleasure that suffused the wrinkled cheeks.

Andrew Burns was there to greet her early the following morning when Eveleen presented herself for her first day. Wearing her plainest, most shapeless dress and with her wayward hair tied firmly back beneath a headscarf, Eveleen considered she was hardly likely to inflame the senses of even the most flirtatious male in the workshops.

But there he was, waiting for her at the bottom of the steps, grinning widely. 'I'll look after you, Eveleen,' he said, bounding up the stairs ahead of her. 'Any trouble and you just let me know about it.'

'Thank you, Andrew, but—'

Before she could say any more, he stopped suddenly, turned and bent down towards her to whisper, 'I've made you your own seat. Come on, I'll show you. It's just for you and you take it with you wherever you go.'

Eveleen stared at him blankly. 'How do you mean?'

Patiently, he explained. 'You know the seats made with leather straps stretched across pieces of wood?'

She nodded.

'Well, everybody has their own, made to measure, if you like, and if he moves frames, he takes his seat with him so that it's just the right size and shape for 'im to be comfortable. You need to be comfortable, Eveleen, if you're going to sit all day long at a frame.'

Now she understood. She had only operated the machine for a few hours each evening when all the men had gone home. Even then, she had found her arms and legs aching when she stumbled down the stairs.

'Only,' Andrew was saying, 'yer've got to help me in return.'

Standing on the step below him, Eveleen gaped up at him. 'Me help you? How?'

'You can help me to get to see Rebecca wi'out her dad knowing.'

'Rebecca!'

'Shh.' He glanced fearfully up the stairs, but already the clatter of machinery was drowning their conversation from eavesdroppers. 'Her dad mustn't know. If he finds out, he'll sack me.' He grinned. 'Or worse.'

Eveleen shook her head, 'Oh, Andrew, I'm sorry. I'd love to help you, but I can't. My uncle's been very good to me – to all my family. And now he's giving me this chance, I can't do anything behind his back.'

The young man's face fell but then he shrugged philosophically. 'Oh well then. But you won't tell 'im, will you? You won't give us away?'

Eveleen shook her head. 'No, I won't do that. But I'd rather not know anything about it.'

'Fair enough.' He started back up the stairs, but then hesitated once more. 'There is something you could do for me though.'

'What?'

'Keep that brother of yours away from Rebecca. She's mine.' Then he turned and hurried up the rest of the stairs, leaving Eveleen staring after him in astonishment.

Jimmy interested in Rebecca? Oh no, surely not. He was only a boy.

No, he wasn't, Eveleen reminded herself. He was seventeen now and he'd been working since the age of twelve.

Already her little brother would think himself very much a man.

Eveleen's first day in the workshop did not go well.

She was nervous of the other men's reactions towards her and consequently overanxious. And now she had another worry on her mind. A worry put there that very morning by Andrew. She would have to watch Jimmy and Rebecca for herself. She could not allow a liaison between them. Her uncle would be appalled and she didn't think even her grandmother would condone it.

The work she produced that day was a mess with uneven stitches and broken threads that she would have to darn by hand.

Harry stood over her. 'You'll have to do better than that. And you've a needle broken there. It's missing a stitch.' He pointed to the ladder-like line of missed stitches. 'Didn't you notice?'

Mortified, Eveleen shook her head.

Harry gave a grunt and turned away, sounding every bit as if he now thought he'd made a grave mistake in giving her a trial.

Andrew was at her side. Close to her ear, he whispered, 'Don't worry. Stay behind tonight and I'll show you how to put a new needle in. We have to do minor repairs to the frames ourselves.' He jerked his thumb over his shoulder. 'He won't employ a framesmith unless it's something really serious.' He winked and grinned. 'That'd cost too much for that old skinflint.'

When she left the workshop that night every muscle in her body seemed to be aching. It was the longest period of time she had worked at the machine. As she stepped into the cottage, more trouble awaited her. Mary had lapsed into one of her moods of depression and was sitting by the fire, a shawl drawn around her shoulders, while Rebecca scurried between the kitchen and the parlour, hurriedly laying the table. It was a job that Mary normally did.

Eveleen sighed and closed her eyes, thinking to herself, This is all I need. Then she went to lay her hand on her mother's shoulder and shake it gently. 'Come on, Mam, it's suppertime.'

Mary shook her head. 'I don't want any. I'm not hungry.' She raised a tearful face, reached up and clung to Eveleen's hand. 'I want to go home, Eveleen. Take me home. I hate it here.'

'Mam, hush . . .' Eveleen began, but too late, Harry had heard his sister's words as he came in from the scullery after washing his hands.

'If that's how you feel, Mary, then you'd better leave. We've put ourselves out for you and that's how you repay us. The ingratitude, Mary. And don't forget . . .' He wagged his forefinger at her. 'Don't forget, we could be letting the room you and your children are occupying to proper rent-paying lodgers. And they'd be better workers than either your son,' and he added with pointed emphasis to remind Eveleen that she had not fared well that day, 'or your daughter.'

'She doesn't mean it, Uncle Harry,' Eveleen said

swiftly. 'We are grateful to you. You know we are. But she's missing Dad.'

'She's not the only one to lose someone. Don't you think I still miss my Rose every single day? But my faith carries me through.' He nodded towards Mary. 'You'd do better to pray to the good Lord for His help, Mary, than sitting there wringing your hands, wallowing in self-pity and being ungrateful to those who've taken you in.' Then he added with the bitterness that even now he could not quell, 'Even against their better judgement.'

Mary dropped her head into her hands and wailed aloud. 'Oh, you're cruel, Harry. Cruel and heartless. You were twenty years ago and haven't changed.'

'I am what I am, Mary, and I've no intention of changing.'

Eveleen looked at her uncle, torn between sticking up for her mother against his unforgiving attitude and trying to keep the peace between them to safeguard their future. Common sense prevailed. With a supreme effort to hold her temper in check, she said, 'I'm sorry, Uncle Harry.' Then turning to her mother she said, 'Come along, Mam. If you're sure you don't want anything to eat, let me take you to bed.'

She eased her mother up and helped her climb the narrow stairs, Mary moaning and complaining every step of the way. 'I want to go home, Eveleen,' was all she would say, over and over again.

An hour later, when Eveleen wearily descended the stairs to eat her cold supper, it was to find Jimmy and Rebecca in the scullery, whispering and giggling with their heads close together, while Harry snored in his chair by the fire in the parlour.

*

The following day, Eveleen determined to put all her other worries out of her mind and concentrate on her work. If she didn't make a good showing today, then her uncle would change his mind – and quickly – about allowing her to work for him. Her future was hanging by a very tenuous thread anyway. He had only agreed to train her because he didn't like to see a machine lying idle and, at present, he could find no one better to operate it. Should a man, or even an inexperienced boy, come along, Eveleen knew she would be replaced at once.

She had to be twice as good as any man to hold on to her place at the machine.

So, as she strode down the brick path to the workshops, she was annoyed to see Andrew Burns hanging about in the doorway, watching for her.

''Morning,' she said briefly and made to pass him to climb the stairs. Andrew caught hold of her arm.

'Tell 'im to stay away from her,' he hissed. 'I know they're cousins, but he's not acting like a cousin towards her.'

Their faces only inches apart, Eveleen stared at him. 'Whatever do you mean?' she asked, trying to sound as if she couldn't begin to guess, even though she had more than an inkling now about what was going on between her brother and Rebecca.

'They were out here in the yard last night. In the dark. And he was kissing her.'

Eveleen gasped. Now her surprise was genuine. Things had gone even further than she had thought. She glanced fearfully up the stairwell, hoping no one had overheard Andrew. 'I'll speak to him,' she muttered and pulled herself free.

'You'd better.' His threat followed her as she ran up the stairs. 'Else I will.'

At least there was one good thing about it, Eveleen thought as she slid on to the leather straps forming the seat in front of the frame. It's not me that Andrew Burns is interested in.

She was unprepared for the sudden shaft of jealousy that ran through her. It wasn't that she was attracted to Andrew Burns or that she wanted him to court her. It was just the thought that her life stretched before her, empty and lonely.

But that is the way it has to be, she told herself firmly. I'm never going to let another man hurt me the way Stephen Dunsmore did. Besides, I've a promise to keep, she reminded herself.

But the thought brought her no joy and the burden of the vow she had made settled even more heavily on her young shoulders.

Twenty-Four

'Jimmy, it's got to stop.'

Jimmy scowled and looked mutinous. 'What?'

'You know very well "what". Your carryings on with Rebecca, that's what,' Eveleen muttered as they walked down the path towards the cottages at the end of the day.

'Huh, chance'd be a fine thing. If the old man's not watching us like a hawk, then Burns is making sheep's eyes at her and looking daggers at me.' He laughed. 'Good job duelling is out of fashion. Reckon I'd be called out.'

Eveleen grasped her brother by the shoulder. She was as tall as he was and now, almost as strong. 'Just you listen to me. If you upset Uncle Harry, we'll be out on our ears.'

'So? Why should I care? I'll go to sea.'

'If you don't care about yourself, then spare a thought for poor Mam. And me.'

Their faces were close together in the gathering dusk. 'Please, Jimmy,' she pleaded.

'Look, Evie, I don't want to rock the boat any more than you do. At least,' he said mysteriously, 'not yet.'

'What do you mean – not yet?' Eveleen asked sharply.

Slyly he glanced at her and then looked away. 'I don't want to stay here for ever, any more than our mam does.'

Eveleen kept her voice low so that none of the workers passing by them on the path to go home would overhear.

'So why don't you work a bit harder? The sooner we get some money together, the sooner we can go home.'

'Do you think of Bernby as home too, then?'

'Of course I do. Whatever made you think I didn't?'

He scuffed the toe of his boot on the ground. 'I didn't think you'd want to go back there. Because of . . .' He cast her a sideways glance. 'Because of *him*.'

Eveleen felt her mouth tighten. 'He's nothing to me. Not any more.'

Jimmy arched his eyebrows as if he didn't believe her for a moment, but he said no more about it. Instead, he said, 'Besides, you seem to be getting well in with the old woman. I thought you was feathering your nest, like.'

Eveleen was appalled. 'Oh, Jimmy, how can you think that of me?'

'S'what I'd do. Given half a chance.'

Her grip on his shoulder tightened. 'Is that what you're doing with little Rebecca? Trying to wheedle your way into the family by the back door? Because that's not the best way to get into her father's good books.'

''Course not,' Jimmy said defensively. 'I – I really like her. Honest, Evie.' He grinned suddenly. ''Sides, I couldn't get into his Good Book unless I grew wings and polished me halo.'

'All right then,' Eveleen said, but for once she was not laughing with him. She was still not wholly convinced of the purity of his motives. 'Because I'll tell you something, Brother dear. Whatever your reasons for chasing after Rebecca are, genuine or otherwise, Uncle Harry's not going to like them one bit.'

Through the gloom she saw his grinning white teeth. 'Mebbe not. But that doesn't bother me. Just so long as Rebecca does.'

With that he twisted himself free and, stuffing his

hands into his pockets, walked towards the house, whistling jauntily.

'Oh, Jimmy,' Eveleen murmured. 'Just what trouble are you getting us all into now?'

Eveleen decided to tackle the problem from the other angle. She decided to speak to Rebecca. Her opportunity came when Harry asked her to give Rebecca a hand with the washing one morning instead of going to the workshop.

'There are several long johns and men's vests got oil on them. And Mr Buxton will be here for them at the end of the week.'

'Who's Mr Buxton?'

'He's the bag man or bag hosier.'

'What does the bag man do exactly?'

'He gets the orders for us. He supplies the yarn and then collects the finished garments and takes them back to the warehouse in the city. And he won't be happy if they're less than perfect. Here,' she pushed a bundle into Eveleen's arms. 'These all need washing. Then they need stretching and laying out to dry in the sun.'

'Where?'

There seemed little room here. Not like at home, she thought, where there had been the yard and the fields and . . . She closed her mind against her memories.

'On those boards there.' Rebecca pointed to four or five wooden boards leaning against the wall in the washhouse. 'Line them up as many as you can along the pathway. The rest can hang over the washing line.'

As they worked together, plunging the knitted garments into the warm water, squeezing them and then laying them on the boards, stretching them into the finished shape, Eveleen said, 'I've been wanting to talk to you.'

The girl glanced up swiftly and then bent her head over the tub as if she guessed what her cousin was about to say.

Eveleen came straight to the point. 'Look, Rebecca, you can tell me to mind my own business if you like, but be careful of our Jimmy. He's – he's . . .' She bit her lip. She didn't want to be disloyal to her own flesh and blood, yet she had to be truthful. She tried to phrase it casually. 'He's only young and all young fellers want a bit of fun before they settle down. Just don't take him too serious, will you?'

Rebecca kept her face hidden as she worked the dolly peg in the rinsing water, swirling the garments round and round. As the silence between them lengthened, Eveleen went on again, feeling almost as if she were plunging herself into hot water.

'And what about Andrew? Isn't there some sort of understanding between you two? Don't let Jimmy—'

She could not finish her sentence before the girl's head shot up and she almost shouted, 'No, there isn't anything between me and Andrew Burns. He likes to think there is. But there isn't and there never will be.' She thumped the dolly peg into the water, causing it to splash even over the high sides of the tub as she added, 'Not now.'

Not now, Eveleen thought with a sinking heart. That could only mean one thing: not now that Jimmy has come on to the scene. Eveleen plunged another garment beneath the soapy water, wishing that it was her brother's head she was dunking.

*

The weeks flew by for Eveleen in a haze of weariness. She worked long hours at the frame as well as still doing her share of household chores and even took a turn at the Griswold in the winter evenings when it was too cold to continue in the workshops.

'Do you know,' Jimmy grumbled, 'there's ice on the *inside* of them long windows and sitting next to them to work is worse than living in an igloo.'

'You'll have to work a bit harder.' Eveleen didn't dish out any sympathy. Nor did she tell him that her own fingers were often blue with cold and her feet felt like blocks of solid ice in the morning. By the time all the workers arrived and the machines were clattering busily, it didn't seem so bad to her.

'Only one fire to heat the whole room.' Jimmy was determined to find fault.

'It'd be colder still out at sea.'

But he was not to be cajoled out of his gloom. 'Well, I'd rather be out there than stuck in this place. And one day, I just might be.'

Eveleen laughed. She'd heard his threats so many times before, she no longer believed them.

Christmas came and Eveleen was surprised to find that the small community celebrated in style. On Christmas Eve Harry planted a Christmas tree in one of the vegetable patches in the yard and decorated it with lighted tapers and bright, shining trinkets fastened to the branches. There were presents for everyone; shawls and scarves, socks and ties. While, quite naturally, their revels were firmly rooted in the traditions of the chapel, nevertheless, they ate heartily on Christmas Day – goose, plum pudding and fruit cake. Mellowed by good food, everyone attended the service at the chapel, including, to Eveleen's surprise, Jimmy, sitting between her and Rebecca. Even Mary, greeted at the chapel door with open arms by a red-cheeked Gracie Turner, needed no persuading to attend.

The Christmas spirit seemed to last into the New Year, but then, towards the end of January, the whole nation was cast into mourning by the death of the queen.

'There's not many folk left alive who can remember us having a king,' Bridget remarked. 'Why even I wasn't born until a year after she came to the throne and I'm as old as Methuselah's mother!' She gave a cackle of laughter and earned herself a reproving glance from a solemn-faced Harry.

'We'll close the workshops on the day of her funeral as a mark of respect,' he said.

Bridget, sharp as ever, remarked, 'According to the paper it's not going to be 'til a week on Saturday.' She eyed him speculatively. 'So you won't be losing a full day's work anyway.'

But Harry, as ever, had the last word. 'There'll be a special service in the chapel,' he said. 'And everyone will attend. Including you, Mother.'

As he left the cottage, Bridget grumbled, 'Why do I always have to open my mouth and let it say what it likes.'

Eveleen stifled her laughter. It was what she often said of herself.

Winter gave way to spring at last and cricket bats were brought out from the back of cupboards and practice at the pump in the yard began in earnest. There was great rivalry between Andrew and Jimmy as to who would be picked to play for the village team that year. But it was on the Sunday school outing when the trouble Eveleen had feared really came to a head.

When the weather improved and may blossom dappled the hedgerows, Harry announced, 'There's to be a picnic for the Sunday school children a week on Saturday.' The men and the youngsters, he decreed, would go on bicycles, the ladies and very young children would ride in horse-drawn wagons with forms from the chapel to provide seating.

'We only go just outside the village to a meadow near the brook,' he told Eveleen.

Her heart missed a beat. 'I – I don't think we'll come, Uncle,' she began and, seeing his perpetual frown deepen, rushed on. 'It might upset Mam. Going into the country-side and especially beside the brook might remind her too much of home. There was a beck that ran behind our house. That – that was where I found my father.'

'I see.' Harry pondered for a long moment before saying, slowly, 'Mary can stay at home, then, with Mother. But you and that brother of yours will come.'

'Father will find you both a bicycle,' Rebecca said, her eyes sparkling with an unaccustomed excitement.

'A bicycle!' Eveleen was horrified. 'But I've never ridden one.'

Rebecca's eyes widened in surprise. 'Then it's high time you did. You've ten days to learn. You can borrow mine and I'll teach you.'

For the next few days for an hour after tea, when the men went off to the cricket field to play now that the evenings were lighter, Rebecca wheeled her bicycle out of the washhouse and into the street. While Eveleen stood watching, Rebecca mounted the cycle and rode solemnly up and down.

'Now, your turn.'

Eveleen eyed the contraption warily. 'I'll fall off,' she muttered.

'Of course you won't. Come on. Hitch yourself on to the saddle. I'll hold you.'

With Rebecca almost supporting her bodily at first, Eveleen took her first tentative lesson. After the first week she could ride up and down Ranters' Row with Rebecca running alongside and only holding on to the back of the saddle.

'You're still steering too much,' Rebecca panted. 'You're sort of – doing it too deliberately. Just pedal and move the front wheel only as much as you feel you need to keep your balance. It just becomes – well – a sort of instinct really, I suppose.'

Three days before the picnic, Rebecca said, 'You're getting too good for me.' She put her hand to her breast, pretending to be breathless. 'I can't keep up with you.' So saying, she let go of the saddle.

'Oh no,' Eveleen cried. 'Don't let go.'

For a moment the bicycle wobbled dangerously, but then suddenly she was riding completely unaided. As she rode to the end of the street, turned in a wide arc and rode back towards her, Rebecca clapped her hands. As Eveleen slowed the bicycle by putting her feet to the ground and came to a standstill near Rebecca, the girl said, 'And now all you need is an outfit.'

Eveleen stared at her.

'We can't have you going on the Sunday school outing dressed like a milkmaid.'

'Thanks,' Eveleen said tartly, sounding offended.

At once, Rebecca's eyes filled with contrition. 'I'm sorry. I didn't mean it . . .'

But Eveleen laughed aloud. 'I'm teasing you, Rebecca. I know my clothes are old-fashioned and countrified. But what can I do? I can't afford to buy any smart new clothes.'

Rebecca regarded her thoughtfully. 'You've got a long black skirt, haven't you?'

Eveleen nodded.

'Well then, all we need to do is to shorten it a little to just above your ankles. And I've got a pretty white lace blouse you can have. And Gran's got a piece of black silk. I'm sure she'd let us make you a tie and a band to match to go around your straw boater.'

'I haven't got a boater.'

'Ah, but I've got two.' Rebecca's eyes twinkled triumphantly. 'So you can have one.'

'But I can't—' Eveleen began.

'Yes, you can.' Rebecca contradicted her with far more asperity in her tone than Eveleen had ever witnessed from the shy girl. Linking her arm through Eveleen's, Rebecca went on, 'Please take it. I absolutely love having you here. You and Jimmy.' Her cheeks were faintly pink and then she added hurriedly, 'And Aunt Mary, too, of course.'

'Of course,' Eveleen said demurely. The two girls glanced at each other and burst out laughing.

The day of the outing began well enough. Picnic hampers and baskets of all shapes and sizes were loaded on to the wagons and then at nine o'clock everyone met on the village green.

'Are you sure you don't feel like coming, Gran?' Eveleen had asked Bridget.

'My Sunday school outing days are long gone.' She squinted up at Eveleen. 'Is your mother going?'

Eveleen shook her head. 'No. I – I haven't told her exactly where we're going so, please, don't tell her, will you?'

The old lady looked surprised. 'Why ever not? You're only going just outside the village, aren't you?'

Eveleen explained the reason for her concern. 'Luckily,' she went on, 'Mam doesn't want to come anyway. Says she'd rather stay here on her own and have a bit of peace and quiet. So she hasn't asked too many awkward questions.'

'She won't be on her own. I'm here. Tell her I expect her to come for her dinner.' Bridget frowned. 'And I won't take no for an answer.'

'All right, Gran.' Eveleen stooped and kissed Bridget's cheek. 'I'll tell her.'

As Eveleen rode her borrowed bicycle to the green, she saw that Rebecca was already there with Andrew on one side of her and Jimmy on the other. Bright spots of colour burned in the girl's cheeks. As Eveleen watched, Rebecca deliberately turned away from Andrew and began an animated conversation with Jimmy.

'Isn't it a lovely day? We're always lucky with the weather.'

Eveleen pursed her lips as she dismounted and wheeled her bicycle near to Andrew. She raised her voice and said pointedly, 'I didn't know you could ride a bicycle, Jimmy.'

''Course I can. I learnt on Ted's.'

Eveleen glared at him. Yet another skill that Jimmy had learned under Ted Morton's guidance. She wished everything that Ted had taught him could have been as useful.

Andrew confided in a whisper, 'And I was daft enough to lend 'im a bicycle an' all. Now he's going to be riding alongside Rebecca all day. I don't know which would be worse. Ridin' beside her but knowin' he's on her other side or not being able to be with her at all.'

'Oh dear, you have got it bad.' Eveleen tried to tease him out of his despondency, but the only reward for her pains was a baleful glare from the lovesick young man. 'Don't worry,' she tried to reassure him. 'When my uncle gets here, I expect Rebecca and I will have to ride alongside him.'

But when Harry arrived riding his own bicycle, sitting very upright so that his bowler hat did not fall off, he solemnly led off the procession from the green and did not appear to have noticed that his daughter was riding between two very attentive young admirers.

Twenty-Five

It was, as Rebecca had remarked, a beautiful day. The sun was high in a cloudless sky as the cyclists forged ahead, shouting and laughing with the horsedrawn wagons plodding along behind them. They passed through the village and came to the place where the brook, bordered by trees and bushes, meandered through the fields.

Already she could hear the shouts and squeals as the youngsters took off their boots and stockings and paddled in the cold water. When the wagons arrived with the rest of the party, the younger children ran about the meadow, shrieking and laughing, like caged wild birds suddenly set free. Eveleen smiled. She could remember herself and Jimmy on their one and only outing to the sea, running across the sand to the sea to dance like mad things at the water's edge, playing catch-us-if-you-can with the waves rolling on to the shore. Now she watched indulgently as the youngsters pranced about at the edge of the brook, daring each other to put a toe into the water.

She turned to see Andrew offering his hand to Rebecca to help prop her cycle against a tree while Jimmy fetched the wicker basket that she had packed for their picnic from one of the wagons. Andrew offered her his arm and, when Rebecca put her hand through it, Eveleen saw the look of triumph that the young man threw at his rival, who was struggling with the heavy basket.

If it had not been for her niggling worry about her brother and Rebecca and the trouble it might cause, Eveleen would have been amused by the antics of the two young men.

Andrew spread a rug on the grass for Rebecca to sit on, while Jimmy placed a cushion behind her. Andrew handed her the parasol he had been carrying for her. Jimmy opened the basket and offered her a cooling drink.

Eveleen had never seen her brother playing the courteous suitor and soon her concerns were pushed aside by the comedy being played out. She saw Rebecca glance around her, but her father was taking a walk along the banks of the brook, one of the local preachers at his side. They were deep in conversation, no doubt on chapel business, Eveleen thought, so engrossing, it seemed, that for once he had completely forgotten about his daughter.

Rebecca, seeing her father at a safe distance, lay back against the cushions. The two young men glared at each other and then sat down, one on either side of her. They lay down too.

Andrew snuggled his shoulder close to hers. Boldly Jimmy took hold of her hand. Rebecca closed her eyes and Andrew's eyelids began to droop.

Only Jimmy lay staring up at the bright sky above them.

Eveleen sighed and leant back against a tree, resting her head against its gnarled trunk. She felt comfortably, blissfully drowsy in the warm sun with only the sound in the distance of the children's laughter as they played among the trees and splashed in the brook. A light breeze rustled the leaves above her and bumble bees buzzed close by . . .

*

'There's a fight in the woods. Come and see.'

At the sound of a voice close by, Eveleen awoke with a start.

The young lad who had made the announcement was already running back towards the trees on the far side of the meadow. All the youngsters, the children and youths and girls, rose with one accord and began to run too.

Eveleen glanced round. The rug where she had last seen Rebecca and her two admirers was unoccupied. Feeling as if her heart was rising into her mouth, Eveleen scrambled up. Instinctively she knew that the fight would be between Jimmy and Andrew.

Eveleen began to run.

'Come on. Through here.' The lad leading the way was already crashing through the undergrowth, brushing aside branches in his excitement. 'This way.' He panted out an explanation to those nearest to him as he ran. 'Burns started it. He found Hardcastle in the woods with his girl. Kissing and carrying on, they were. There's going to be fireworks when her father finds out.' For the sake of those who had not already guessed, he added triumphantly, 'It's Rebecca Singleton.'

When they arrived at a small clearing and ranged themselves around its edges, the fight was still going on. Already, Jimmy's nose was bleeding and Andrew had a cut above his left eye. But neither seemed to feel, or even be aware of, their injuries. They stalked around each other like fighting cocks. A sudden flurry of punches was exchanged, bringing exclamations from the watchers.

'Go on, Andrew, smash his face in.'

'My money's on you, Jimmy. Go on.'

Several of the lads watching were already inching forwards, punching the air themselves as if they were already involved.

Jimmy stepped forward and landed a punch directly on Andrew's nose. He fell to the ground while Jimmy stood over him, victorious. The shouts around them grew louder but Andrew was already struggling to regain his feet. Jimmy stood back and allowed his opponent to get up, but the lad, though upright, was unsteady, swaying backwards and forwards. One more punch and . . .

Eveleen pushed her way through the crowd and ran towards them. 'Stop it. Stop it, this minute.'

She ran between them, turning towards Jimmy, trying to protect Andrew from any further punishment. With his blood up and intent on his adversary, Jimmy did not see her and the punch intended for Andrew's chin landed instead on Eveleen.

She fell, face downwards, and lay quite still.

At once their fight was forgotten as both youths bent over her prostrate form.

As if through a thick blanket of fog, Eveleen heard Jimmy shouting at her and felt him shaking her shoulder. 'You stupid thing, Evie. What did you do that for?'

Then everything seemed to go very dark.

Eveleen could not understand why her bed felt so hard and cold and why, as she slowly opened her eyes, she could see sunlight filtering through the trees and hear the rustling of leaves. Then she became aware of voices around her and of someone stroking her head. She opened her eyes, saw faces peering down at her and heard Rebecca say, 'Oh, Evie, please wake up. Please be all right.'

Then she heard another voice, louder and angrier.

'What's going on? Make way.'

Harry was standing over her, a towering giant of disapproval.

'They was fighting, mister.' A village lad, too young to be at work yet and therefore ignorant of Harry Singleton and his harsh rules, piped up. 'It was that Jimmy Hardcastle and Andrew Burns.' The boy's grin widened. 'They was fighting over your Rebecca, mister.'

'What?' Harry grabbed the informer, as if it was his fault. 'What's that you say? Fighting over my daughter? What do you mean? Speak up.'

The boy squirmed in his grasp. 'Le' go, I'll get my dad on to you.'

There were sniggers around them. The boy's father was a stockinger at the workshops and would not get involved in an argument with Harry Singleton if he valued his livelihood. Harry released the boy, pushing him away from him so that the youngster fell to the ground. The boy scrambled up and shoved his way through the crowd, realizing, too late, his mistake in opening his mouth. It would earn him a hiding from his father.

Harry reached down and hauled Eveleen to her feet. Already the side of her jaw was swelling. 'What's all this about, Eveleen? I demand to know.' He glanced at his daughter. 'Rebecca?'

'Nothing, Father. It was just Jimmy and Andrew being silly. They – they were just messing about and then it – sort of – got out of hand.' Her voice faltered and faded away and she hung her head to hide her face, now no longer flushed with excitement but fiery with shame and embarrassment.

Eveleen put her hand to her head. The earth still felt as if it were swimming around her. All she wanted was to lie down somewhere and go to sleep. She felt sick too.

Harry released her and she swayed, threatening to fall again, but Rebecca put her arm about Eveleen's waist to support her. 'Please,' the girl whispered, close to Eveleen's ear. 'Please don't tell him, Evie.'

Tell him what? Eveleen thought stupidly, her thoughts still reeling.

Then, as her senses began to return, she asked, 'Where – where are they?'

'Gone. They fled when they saw Father coming.'

Eveleen closed her eyes and shook her head a little, trying to clear it. 'Just as well,' she said tartly. 'But wait till I catch up with the pair of them, never mind your dad.'

'Whatever were you thinking of?'

When they arrived home, Eveleen grabbed her brother and hauled him into a corner of the yard, anger giving her strength.

'I'm sorry, Evie, I didn't mean for you to get hurt. You shouldn't have stepped between us like that.'

'I'm not bothered about that.' Eveleen brushed aside her own discomfort and the swelling bruise on her jaw. 'Are you stupid? Uncle Harry knows now, doesn't he?'

'It was him. Burns. He started it,' Jimmy muttered morosely.

'I don't care who started it. What I want to know is, what's going on between you and Rebecca? I've warned you before. You'll get us thrown out of here.'

'So what?'

'So what? You ask me "so what"? Are you stupid, Jimmy Hardcastle?'

'Oh leave off, Evie. You're getting as bad as him. Preaching. You'll be standing in that pulpit alongside the minister soon.' He pulled away from her. 'I'm going out.'

'You'll do no such thing.' She lunged at him, trying to

catch hold of him again, but he stepped smartly away. 'You'll come to Chapel tonight, Jimmy. At least that might—'

'Oh no, I won't. 'Bye, Sis. I'll be late home. I'm keeping out of his way till he's calmed down a bit.' Safely out of her reach now, he grinned cheekily and added, 'Say one for me.'

'It's more than one you'll be needing, Jimmy Hard-castle.' Eveleen shouted after him. 'I'd wear me knees out before I'd said enough to save you.' But he was gone, banging the gate behind him.

Shaking her head in exasperation, she opened the door into the cottage to be met by the full force of her uncle's wrath.

'I want him out of here.' He shook his fist in her face as if she were to blame for all the trouble. Eveleen faced him bravely, though her heart was thudding painfully. Out of the corner of her eye, she could see her mother sitting in the chair by the fire, her head in her hands. 'He's not to go near Rebecca again. As for Burns, well, I'll deal with him.'

Eveleen licked her lips. 'Uncle Harry,' she said, with far more calmness than she felt. 'I'm sure Jimmy and Rebecca are only friends. Just—'

'Oh aye. And do "just friends" lie on the ground, deep in a wood, kissing and—'

Eveleen felt the flush creep up her neck and face. 'Who told you that?'

'Rebecca, of course. I got it out of her. She's in her room. I've warned her, I'll take me belt to her if I catch her even speaking to either of them again.'

'It was wrong of them. But . . .' Before Eveleen realized what she was saying, her rash tongue was asking, 'But are you going to keep Rebecca locked away from young fellers all her life? She's seventeen. Surely . . . ?'

Harry's face was contorted with rage. 'You dare to question me, girl,' he thundered and began to raise his hand. For a moment Eveleen thought he was going to strike her, but then he seemed to be aware of what he had been about to do and, with a supreme effort, the big man controlled himself. Instead, he shook his fist close to her face. 'While you live under my roof, you'll do as I say. You hear me?'

'I hear you, Uncle,' Eveleen said, her quiet tones a deliberate contrast to his wrath.

'I want him out of this house,' Harry said again. 'I'll not sack him this time, but if he dares to try anything again, he's out. In fact, you're all out.' He glanced around at Mary, but she made no move, gave no sign that she had even heard his threats. 'Now.' Eveleen could see that he was making an effort to control his temper. 'I'm going to the chapel. I'll expect you to be there for the special service in half an hour. All of you.' He jerked his thumb upwards indicating his wayward daughter sent to her room in disgrace. 'And mind she comes, Eveleen. I'm counting on you.'

As the door slammed behind him Eveleen looked helplessly at her mother. It was gong to be a hard enough job to get Mary and, possibly, Rebecca too to the chapel in time for the service Harry evidently always insisted should be held after every Chapel outing. As for Jimmy, she had no chance.

Andrew Burns was already seated with his mother in their usual pew when Eveleen entered, pushing a reluctant

Mary in front of her. Rebecca, her head down, followed dutifully. She, more than any of them, knew what her father would be like if she dared to disobey him again. Eveleen glanced at Andrew and saw that his left eye was swollen and closed. It looked raw and painful and his mother kept darting anxious glances at him. But the young man stared sullenly ahead and did not even acknowledge the presence of the girl over whom he had been fighting. Eveleen hoped that perhaps he had learned his lesson and would leave Rebecca alone. Moments later she was on her knees praying fervently that this was so.

As for Jimmy, well, she would think of a way to deal with him.

Twenty-Six

'You're to go and lodge at Gran's,' Eveleen told Jimmy later that same night.

She had waited up for him and now, gone midnight, he was creeping into the darkened house expecting that everyone would be safely in bed.

'Heck, Evie, you made me jump. I thought it was him waiting for me with a big stick.'

'You can joke, Jimmy. You'll be laughing on the other side of your face soon if you don't watch out. He's given you a final warning. Any more trouble and you're out. We all are.'

Jimmy pulled a face at her and Eveleen felt the urge to slap him. But she kept her hands clenched and firmly by her sides. 'So,' she went on, trying to keep her voice low so that no one would hear. 'You can sleep here tonight, but tomorrow you move your things to her house.'

'There's no room,' Jimmy argued. 'She's got lodgers.'

'One of them's going to Mrs Burns. It's all arranged.'

'I see. Trying to put as much distance between us as he can, is he?'

'He'll put a lot more distance between you, if you don't watch it. And keep your voice down. We don't want him down here.'

'I'm not frightened of him,' Jimmy said boldly, but Eveleen, even in the dim lamplight, had seen the flicker of fear in his eyes.

'Of course you're not,' she tried to appease him. 'But you ought to respect him more, Jimmy. He is giving us a home at the moment and employment, don't forget.'

'I'm hardly likely to,' Jimmy muttered, glowering. 'Since you keep pushing it down me throat every five minutes. I'm off to bed.'

As he made to pass her towards the stairs, she caught hold of his arm. 'Jimmy, please, for my sake, and Mam's, please do what you're asked.'

'What I'm told, you mean.'

Their faces close together for a moment, the brother and sister looked into each other's eyes, seeing themselves mirrored in each other's face. At last Jimmy smiled. 'All right, Evie. I'll be a good boy.' But then he added ominously, 'For now, at any rate.'

Eveleen had been wrong about Andrew Burns. She had thought he would be frightened off by Harry's threats, but the following morning as she went down the path towards the workshops, he was waiting for her.

He grabbed her arm. 'Eveleen, I've got to see Rebecca. I've got to talk to her.'

'Andrew, don't. The poor girl's in enough trouble as it is.'

His eyes widened. 'Trouble? What sort of trouble? You don't mean she's – that he's . . .' His grip tightened on her arm. 'If she is, I'll kill 'im.'

'What are you talking about?'

'She's not in the family way, is she?'

Eveleen gasped and said swiftly, 'No, of course she isn't.'

Andrew looked into her face. 'She might well be, from

what I saw yesterday. Half undressed, the pair of them were.'

Eveleen stared at him in dismay and she began to tremble. 'You – you're not serious. You're making it up to make trouble for our Jimmy.'

Andrew's face twisted. 'I'd like to make trouble for 'im all right and no mistake. But no, I wouldn't make trouble for Rebecca. I love her, Eveleen. I have done for a long time. And until your blasted brother came on the scene, I thought I had a chance. I thought she liked me. And we were doing it all proper. Not behind her dad's back. But now, all because of Jimmy, 'er dad'll tar me with the same brush. I won't stand a chance either now.'

'Andrew, I'm sorry. Truly I am, if Jimmy's come between you. Look, I've got to get to my work now. And you'd better too. Let's talk later. Maybe we can help each other.'

Andrew's face lightened. 'You'll help me? I thought you'd be on Jimmy's side.'

'Not this time,' Eveleen said grimly. If what Andrew said was true about what he had seen the previous day in the woods, then even Rebecca had not admitted the whole truth to her father. 'This time,' she went on, 'he's really gone too far.'

Preoccupied with her family's problems, Eveleen had a bad day at her frame, but her uncle, no doubt just as worried, did not notice. Eveleen slipped out of work early that evening to make sure that Jimmy was gone from the house before their uncle arrived home.

'I'll go altogether,' Jimmy grumbled, hoisting a pillow-case of his few belongings on to his back. 'At least, I would if it wasn't for Rebecca.' He grinned archly. 'I've got a good reason to stay now.'

'Oh no, you haven't. Uncle Harry would never let her marry you.'

'Who said anything about marriage?' Jimmy said airily. 'I'm not the marrying kind.'

'And what if she gets pregnant?' Eveleen asked baldly.

'That's her problem.'

'Jimmy! How can you be so callous?'

She remembered he had said something very similar before and, unbidden, into her mind came the image of Stephen Dunsmore. His fair hair and handsome features. And those brilliant blue eyes that could shine with love and then, so suddenly and ruthlessly, turn cold.

'Typical,' Eveleen said bitterly. 'Just like a man.'

'Thanks for the compliment,' Jimmy said, as he slammed the door of the cottage and walked along the path in front of the row of houses towards their grandmother's home.

Eveleen breathed a sigh of relief and vowed to keep the two cousins apart. She turned and went into the scullery to find Rebecca peeling potatoes. She was sobbing, her tears falling into the water in the bowl. Her hands were shaking so much that Eveleen expected the knife to slip at any moment.

'Here, let me do that,' Eveleen said gently, taking the potato and the sharp knife out of the girl's hands.

Rebecca made no protest.

'Now, dry your tears and set the table,' Eveleen went on, briskly but not unkindly. 'Where's me mam?'

'Taken to her bed. She – she says all the trouble's upset her.'

'It would,' Eveleen said shortly and then rebuked herself for her impatience. No doubt this particular bit of family trouble was bringing back some very unhappy memories for Mary.

As the girl moved between kitchen and parlour, setting the table for supper, Eveleen pondered on the best way to help ease the situation. If only she could persuade Rebecca to focus her affections on Andrew Burns rather than Jimmy, then all might be well. She sighed. But even then, it sounded as if her uncle had no intention of letting his daughter walk out with any young man. As she dropped another potato in the saucepan of water, she wondered if the best way might be to talk to Harry himself first. Then she shook her head. No. That was not the way. She had tried already and he was so angry at the moment he would not listen to reason.

Perhaps her grandmother might help. Bridget had admitted that she regretted not standing up for her own daughter at the time of her troubles. Maybe, now, she would stand up to her son and persuade him to let Rebecca walk out with a young man.

A young man of whom Harry could approve.

'The table's ready,' Rebecca interrupted Eveleen's thoughts. 'I'll shell the peas.'

Eveleen nodded and took the heavy pan of potatoes through to the parlour to put on the hob to boil. Straightening up she went to the window overlooking the yard. There was still a light in the workshop window near where her uncle's frame stood.

Going back into the kitchen, she said carefully, 'Rebecca, Andrew was asking after you today. He wants to talk to you.'

The girl looked up. 'Well, I don't want to talk to him.'

'Why not?'

The girl shrugged. 'I don't like him.'

'He's very fond of you.'

Rebecca hung her head and said nothing, but Eveleen

was not about to let the matter rest. 'From what he said, I thought that you were friends.'

Rebecca's head came up quickly. 'What did he say?'

Eveleen decided that the time had come for complete honesty, if she was to prise Rebecca away from Jimmy. 'He said that he loves you and that before Jimmy came on the scene he thought he had a chance with you.' Eveleen bent towards her. 'Did he?'

'Maybe,' Rebecca was defensive now. 'But not any more. It's Jimmy I – I love now. And he loves me. I know he does.'

'Have you – have you . . . ?' Eveleen was at a loss as to how to ask the question delicately.

'That's none of your business,' Rebecca almost snapped, showing the most spirit that Eveleen had ever seen.

But her defensive answer told Eveleen what she most feared to hear.

'Gran, will you help me sort Jimmy and Rebecca out? We've got to put a stop to it. Right now.'

The old lady leant back in her chair and closed her eyes. 'Oh, Eveleen, I'm too old for all this trouble. Maybe if I was a few years younger—'

Before Eveleen could hold back the words they were out of her mouth. 'But you didn't do anything when you *were* younger, did you? You didn't stick up for my mother against her father. You let them make her life so awful that she ran away.' Instantly the words were said, Eveleen regretted them. 'Oh I'm sorry, Gran. I shouldn't have said that.'

Bridget sighed wearily and tears watered in her old

eyes. 'Tell the truth and shame the Devil, eh, Eveleen?' she murmured and smiled sadly. 'But you're right. I'm all talk and no do. That's me.' She lifted her head and looked straight into Eveleen's eyes. 'You're like me, but you've more spirit than I ever had. Mind you never lose it, love. Don't let anyone rule you, Eveleen. Not anyone. Not even if you fall in love. Don't fall so hard that you lose your own personality. You're someone in your own right, Eveleen. Never forget that.'

Softly Eveleen said, 'I won't, Gran. But what are we going to do about Jimmy and Rebecca?'

The old woman rested again. 'It'll sort itself out,' she said tiredly.

Eveleen watched as Bridget's eyes closed and she dozed. But would it? the girl asked herself and found no answer.

Over the following days, Eveleen watched the pair like a hawk. As far as she could see, Jimmy seemed to be obeying Harry's orders. He never came to their cottage. He didn't even linger to talk to Rebecca when he passed through the yard to work and she just happened to be going to and fro between the house and the washhouse, her arms full of laundry. If either of them looked about to disobey, Eveleen had to admit that it was Rebecca who looked the most likely.

Often she would find the girl standing at the parlour window overlooking the yard. She was watching for someone. That much was obvious. In the evenings when the young lads played cricket in the yard, Jimmy was no longer among them. Andrew always positioned himself behind the pump, playing wicket keeper so that he could be close to the window of the cottage. Eveleen saw him casting anxious, pleading glances towards it, but Rebecca would turn away, deliberately ignoring him.

'Rebecca,' Eveleen said at last, exasperated. 'Forget Jimmy. He's not worth it. Believe me.'

'I don't know why you're so against us.' Rebecca turned tearful eyes upon Eveleen. 'I'd have thought you'd have been happy for us. Don't you like me, Eveleen?'

'Oh, Rebecca. It's because I like you – I love you – that I'm so afraid for you. For both of you.' Eveleen ran her tongue over her lips before saying carefully, 'I know he's my brother, Rebecca, but even I have to admit that he's not – not reliable. And your father can see that. He'll never allow you to marry Jimmy, even if . . .' She faltered, unwilling to hurt the girl further by telling her of Jimmy's own views on marriage.

'My father will never allow me to marry anyone,' Rebecca said bitterly. 'He wants to keep me here an old maid. Just to look after him.'

'Oh no, surely not.'

'Oh yes, surely yes,' Rebecca mimicked bitterly. 'If I want to get married, the only way I'll ever be able to do it is to run away. Just like your mother did.'

'That was different. That was because she was in disgrace and – and she was . . .' Eveleen faltered, staring at Rebecca. She noticed now the girl's white face, the blue smudges beneath her eyes.

'So,' Rebecca whispered. 'Where's the difference?'

'Oh no,' Eveleen breathed, feeling as if she had been punched hard in the stomach. 'Oh, Rebecca, no!'

They stood for several moments just staring at each other, Eveleen with a look of horror on her face, while Rebecca was pale and silent and yet with a strange expression of relief. Eveleen guessed that the girl had carried her secret for some time and now, sharing it with someone, eased the fear, even if only a little.

But Eveleen felt as if she had been handed yet another burden to carry; a weight that threatened to crush them all.

She put out her arms and enfolded the girl to her. At the show of kindness, Rebecca's resolve crumbled and she wept against Eveleen's shoulder. Awkwardly Eveleen patted her back. 'There, there, don't cry. We'll sort it out.'

But Eveleen's brave words held far more confidence than she was feeling inside.

Now there was going to be real trouble.

Eveleen still fretted over Rebecca and fumed over Jimmy. How could he have been so thoughtless, so stupid? The only respite she got was when she was at her work. For a few hours she determined to put aside all thoughts of the impending cataclysm and to do her work well. Ruefully she admitted that she had every need to. Soon, she thought, they would be leaving here. When the news broke, as break it must, they would be out on the streets once more.

And where to this time? Back home? But to what? They were no better off now than when they had left Bernby. She sighed. Perhaps they should never have left. Perhaps they should have tried harder, she and Jimmy, to find work locally in or near Grantham and to rent a small cottage somewhere.

But we did try, she reminded herself. We tried very hard. At the time, coming to her mother's family had seemed the best solution, but she had not known exactly what they were coming to. She had pictured her mother's family as being like her own, with a kindly, understanding father at its head. Harry Singleton was no Walter Hardcastle. And that had been Eveleen's mistake.

'Here, I want a word with you.' One evening after work she grabbed hold of Jimmy's arm and, anger giving her strength, hauled him into the empty washhouse, slammed the door behind her and leant against it.

'What's got into you, Evie?' For a moment he looked angry. Then he grinned. 'Oh, I get it. You've arranged for Rebecca to meet me here, have you? I knew it. I knew you'd be on our side eventually.'

'Nothing of the sort,' Eveleen snapped.

His face fell. 'Well, in that case, I'm off. I've got a date in the village.'

'Oh aye,' Eveleen's voice hardened. She had suspected as much for she had heard Jimmy's whistling as he came back into the yard and towards Bridget's cottage late at night. He was either out with a group of youths in the village or seeing a girl. 'Oh aye,' she said again. 'Going to get another one pregnant an' all, are you?'

In the dim light, she could see that Jimmy's jaw dropped. It gave her a second's devious pleasure to see that he actually looked shocked.

She nodded and folded her arms, still leaning against the door. 'That's wiped the smile off your face, hasn't it?'

'You – you don't mean it.' He tried to laugh, but the sound was brittle. 'You're having me on.'

She bent towards him, her gaze holding his. 'Do you think I'd really joke about a thing like that? Rebecca's having your child and the poor girl's frightened out of her wits. So, Jimmy Hardcastle, what are you going to do about it?'

He stared at her and then his lip curled. 'Nothing.'

'Nothing? What do you mean, nothing?'

He stuffed his hands into his pockets and cocked his head on one side as he returned her gaze boldly now. 'How do I know it's mine?'

Eveleen lifted her right hand and slapped his face hard.

Twenty-Seven

Eveleen never told Rebecca the full conversation that had taken place between her and Jimmy in the wash-house, merely that Jimmy now knew about her condition.

'Oh, you shouldn't have told him,' Rebecca wailed.

'He's got to know. You can't keep it secret for ever, Rebecca.'

A look of sheer terror crossed the girl's face. 'Don't tell my father. Please, Eveleen.' She clung to Eveleen's hand in desperation.

'He'll have to know,' Eveleen said quietly. 'Sooner or later.'

'Then – then let it be later. As late as possible.' She cast about her, seeking escape. 'I'll go away. Yes, that's what I'll do. I'll have to. I can't stay here. Jimmy will take me, won't he?'

'I think,' Eveleen said slowly, 'that once the truth comes out, we'll all have to leave. Your father won't want us here any longer.'

'It's not your fault. Or your mother's.'

'Maybe not. But I doubt your father will see it that way.' She thought a moment and then added, 'Rebecca, maybe we're misjudging your father. Maybe he will stand by you. You're his only daughter. You're all he's got. Surely he won't turn his back on you.' She hesitated and there was doubt in her own voice as she added, 'Will he?'

'If you think there's the slightest chance of that, then you really don't know my father,' Rebecca said bitterly.

'Then I really think we should tell Gran.'

Rebecca shrugged her thin shoulders. 'She'll not do anything.'

To that Eveleen had no answer. She was very much afraid that Rebecca was right.

They were singing Eveleen's favourite hymn. Sitting close together in the pew, they looked like any other happy, close-knit family. But Eveleen could feel the tension in the air so tangibly she could almost reach out and grasp it. Jimmy was sitting at the far end of the pew, squashed against the wall, while Rebecca had been placed almost at the opposite end with her father sitting on her right-hand side near the aisle.

After the service, Eveleen planned to take Rebecca with her on her usual afternoon visit to their grandmother. But today there would be no lace-making done.

Today they had something to tell Bridget. And the good Lord alone knew what would happen after that. Eveleen closed her eyes and offered up a fervent prayer.

If ever she had needed to pray in her life, she needed to do so now.

'This is nice. Both my granddaughters paying me a visit.'

Unaware of the bombshell about to explode, Bridget welcomed them. 'Sit down, sit down. Don't make the place look untidy,' she joked.

They obeyed her, but both of the girls sat on the edge of their chairs, glancing at one other, each waiting for the other to begin.

Seeing how white and frail Rebecca looked – far from gaining weight because of her pregnancy, the girl looked to have lost it – Eveleen licked her dry lips and said, 'Gran, we need to talk to you. We've . . .' She glanced across at Rebecca, but the girl was now sitting with her eyes down-cast, her fingers laced tightly together in her lap. 'We've got a bit of a problem.' Even as she said the words she almost laughed hysterically at the understatement.

Bridget leant forward in her chair, looking from one to the other.

'There's no easy way to tell you this, Gran. Rebecca is expecting a baby.'

The old lady closed her eyes, groaned and flopped back in her chair. Eveleen half rose but then Bridget opened her eyes. Looking at Rebecca she said harshly, 'You little fool!'

'Gran—' Eveleen began.

'You keep out of this, miss. This is family business.'

'But we're family. We're—'

'Aye, you are. But I wish you weren't. If it hadn't been for you coming here, this would never have happened.'

Eveleen felt the colour drain from her face as she stared at the woman in front of her. The woman she had believed loved her, loved all her grandchildren. She had thought that Bridget would help them. But already the old woman's mood had turned against them. She was ready to side with the person who she knew would be the victor in any family quarrel. Her son, Harry.

And then Bridget said the words that Eveleen had expected to hear from her uncle, but never from her grandmother.

'You've brought trouble back to our door, Eveleen. Your mother's a bad lot and she's tainted this girl with her wickedness.' She leant back in her chair. 'You'd better pack your things. You'll be out of here before nightfall, I can guarantee you that. And you'll be taking her with you.'

'Oh Gran, I thought you'd help us. I thought you would understand. When we've talked you've sounded as if you regretted what happened twenty years ago. As if you wish you'd acted differently. Now's your chance to—'

The sharp eyes in the wrinkled face opened wide. Now there was a look of vindictiveness in them that Eveleen had never seen before. 'Don't you tell me what I can or can't do, girl. When Harry finds out about this, you'll be out on your ears. The lot of you. And there's nothing I can do to stop it.' Her head dropped and though she muttered the last few words, Eveleen heard them. 'Even if I wanted to.'

Shocked, Eveleen rose. Rebecca was now in tears. Sobs shook her thin shoulders and she sat hunched in her chair. As Eveleen looked down on her, she knew that from this moment on she had another being for whom she was responsible. Two, if it came to that. For there was the unborn child to consider too.

'You'd better get your things packed. We'll likely be homeless by tonight. We've told Gran so I don't expect it'll be long before Uncle Harry hears.'

'What did you want to go and do a daft thing like that for?'

Eveleen clicked her tongue against her teeth in exasperation. 'You're as naïve as Rebecca. She thought that as long as no one knew, the problem would go away. Well, it won't.'

'You're the one that's naïve, our Evie, if you thought

any of them here would help. Why didn't you let me find us somewhere else to go first before you went opening your big mouth?'

'Oh thanks. So it's my fault we're in this mess, is it? I rather think it's your fault, not mine.'

'Mebbe. Mebbe not.'

'Don't start that again.'

'How do you know it's not Andrew Burns' kid? He's always sniffing round her.'

'I do know,' Eveleen said shortly. 'And if you cared about Rebecca at all, you wouldn't even think such a thing of her.'

'If she let me, how do I know she didn't let others.'

Eveleen shuddered. Her brother had just confirmed what she had believed. He was no better, but probably no worse either, than most men. They wheedled and begged and promised the earth and then, afterwards, they believed the worst. Thank goodness, she thought yet again, she had held out against Stephen Dunsmore.

Sadness washed over her. Was there no man in the world who would really love and cherish her?

Twenty-Eight

Eveleen had been wrong about one thing. Bridget did not tell her son and so Eveleen had a few days' grace to think and to plan.

Nottingham, she decided. There would be work there. Now that both she and Jimmy could operate frames, she was sure that there would be work in the hosiery industry for them. Somehow she would have to take a day off from work to go to the city. But it was going to be difficult to explain her absence to her uncle.

The solution came from an unexpected quarter.

'She is, isn't she?'

The very next morning, Andrew was waiting for her as she went to work, barring her way up the staircase until she answered him.

Eveleen nodded, miserably.

'I could break 'is neck,' the lad muttered, and Eveleen believed that if her brother had been there at that moment, Andrew would have done just that. 'What are you going to do, 'cos he'll throw you out, once he knows.'

'I know,' Eveleen whispered hoarsely, aware that Andrew was now referring to her uncle. 'I want to get to Nottingham to see if I can find us work and a place to live, but,' she spread her hands helplessly, 'I don't know what excuse to make to Uncle Harry.'

Andrew looked thoughtful. 'Pity you haven't got some lace to take to the city.'

Eveleen gripped his arm. 'But I have. My grandmother's been teaching me pillow lace. I've got balls of it in my bedroom.' She didn't tell the young man that the work had been done every Sabbath afternoon.

'There's your answer then. Tell your uncle you're going to sell your lace in Nottingham.'

Eveleen blinked. 'Can I do that?'

He shrugged. 'There's something called the Lace Market there. I 'spect it's where folks sell their lace.'

Eveleen's face brightened. 'You've been?'

'No, but I've heard talk about it.'

'Do you think I might find work there?'

'Dunno, but if you don't there are big factories. They employ a lot of folks to work their machines. You could try them.'

'Where are they?'

'Dunno. You'd have to ask.'

Now that she had two possibilities, however vague, Eveleen said, 'Right then. I'll go. In fact,' she added with a calculating gleam in her eyes, 'I'll ask Uncle Harry if I can go with him on Saturday.'

Once a month on a Saturday, Harry went to Nottingham to sell the stockings and socks knitted on the Griswold and assorted garments that had been made in the workshops other than those the bag man disposed of.

'By heck!' For a brief moment the two young people forgot their trouble and smiled at each other. Andrew shook his head and glanced at her admiringly. 'You've got some nerve, I'll say that for you. Doing it right under his nose.'

Eveleen's smile faded and her mouth was grim. 'Serves

him right. He should be the sort of father poor Rebecca could turn to.' Tears prickled at the back of her eyes as she thought about her own father and how, if she had found herself in such trouble, she could have gone to him immediately. Oh, he would have been saddened, disappointed in her, but he would have stood by her and helped her.

Hadn't he done just that years ago with Mary when Harry Singleton had helped to turn out his own sister?

Harry grumbled and groused when Eveleen asked if she could go to the city with him the following Saturday. Usually, anxious to please and to earn a few extra pennies, Eveleen worked all day on Saturday, when the young lads and even her uncle occasionally took time off to play cricket matches.

'I know you're not very fast yet on the frame, but your work is very neat and saleable.' It was all that mattered to Harry Singleton.

'I thought I could learn how things are done. I know you go yourself once a month, just to make sure the bag man isn't cheating you . . .'

'Oh now, hold on a minute.' Harry held up his hand, palm towards her. 'That is man's business, Eveleen. I won't have you interfering in trading.'

'But I wanted to take my lace to sell at the Lace Market,' she said, facing him. Eveleen Hardcastle, her conscience smote her, you are becoming an adept little liar.

A look passed between them, she with a wide-eyed and innocent expression, he with the knowledge deep in his eyes of what exactly did go on in Bridget's cottage on a Sunday afternoon. 'It's not the kind of market you're thinking of. But I can sell that for you. I can get a better price than ever you would get. I know the right people.'

Eveleen thought quickly. She needed to take the lace to show prospective employers her skills. She could cut small pieces off each pattern she had made and hide them in her reticule. He would never know. She smiled at him. 'Thank you, Uncle, I'd be very grateful.' She cocked her head on one side and added, coyly, 'But I really would like to see the city.'

'Well, I suppose you can go. But don't start making a habit of wanting to go gallivanting off to the city, will you?'

'No, Uncle Harry. I won't.' She turned away before he could change his mind.

The omnibus from Flawford set them down in Broad Marsh. Eveleen looked about her. This was her first visit to a big city and she felt a tremor of excitement.

'Come along. Don't dawdle. We haven't got all day.'

Pretending obedience, Eveleen followed. Harry had said they would be returning home in the early afternoon, but Eveleen had ascertained when the very last omnibus left for Flawford. That was the one she would be catching, she promised herself.

Harry set off, his long legs striding out so that Eveleen had to take little running steps every so often to keep up with him. They turned to the left and walked a distance, then to the right and walked again. Eveleen found herself craning to look up at the grand buildings as she passed by. One street was lined with elegant houses.

'This is where a lot of the lace manufacturers and warehouse owners live,' Harry said. 'They make a better living than we do.' He sounded bitter, but Eveleen couldn't help thinking that the Singleton family had done quite well for themselves. Finally they turned to the left again and Harry said, 'This is Stoney Street.'

They walked a distance and came to stand in front of a magnificent building shaped like a huge E. It was four storeys high.

'This is the warehouse where I do my business.'

'Where do we go in?' Eveleen asked. 'Up those steps and through that arched doorway?'

'I do, yes. But you can't come with me.'

Eveleen's heart skipped a beat. Unwittingly her uncle was playing right into her hands. She had wondered how she was going to be able to slip away from him and now here he was giving her that very opportunity.

'Now, give me your lace. I'll show it to the buyer I deal with. But I can't make any promises, mind.' Eveleen handed her uncle the bag containing the rolls of pillow lace. It represented hours and hours of fine work, but all Harry said curtly, was, 'Now don't go wandering off.'

Absently, her gaze on the finely dressed men climbing the steps in long coats and bowler hats with stiff wide collars and ties, she nodded. Further along the street, she noticed men and women, dressed more like she was, hurrying in through a much lowlier entrance. They must work here, she thought.

As her uncle disappeared through the huge, ornate door, Eveleen walked towards the other entrance.

'Excuse me,' she stopped a woman about to hurry in through the door. 'Do you work here.'

'Er – yes, mi duck.'

'What do you do?'

The woman looked wary for a moment and she glanced Eveleen up and down. Then, appearing to like what she saw, she smiled and said, 'Well, I don't exactly work *here* but mi daughter does. She works on the third floor trimmin' and scallopin' lace. But sometimes I do work at home for 'em.'

'So they don't make anything here then?'

The woman shook her head. 'Not really. The lace is made in the factories and then brought here to the warehouses to be finished. And, like I say, they have a lot of homeworkers an' all.'

'Do – do you think they have any vacancies? I'm a quick learner and I don't mind what I do.' She fished in her reticule and brought out the small samples of her lace work that she had kept back from uncle. 'This is my work. Is it any good?'

'I don't reckon they've any jobs going at the moment, but you could ask.' Then the woman examined Eveleen's lace closely. 'That's very good.' Eveleen felt the woman's keen gaze on her. 'But you'd not make enough for a livin' just working at home, mi duck. The miserable beggars don't pay much, even for the finest work. You'd be better off trying to get work in a factory or a warehouse and doing this on the side at home to make a bit extra.' She gave a wry laugh. 'Aye, and you need to, I can tell you. Even the men's wages are a pittance. Anyway, don't get me going on that subject, else we'll be here all day. If you're lookin' for work,' she went on. 'The best way is to go to the factories.'

'Do you know where they are?'

'I should do. My old man works at one. Reckitt's on Canal Street. I do work at home for them an' all.'

'Do you? Do you really?' Eveleen's heart leapt hopefully. 'How do I get there?'

The woman rattled off directions, naming so many streets that Eveleen was mesmerized. Seeing her helpless look, the woman said, 'You don't know Nottingham, do you?'

Eveleen shook her head. 'No, this is my first visit. I got off the omnibus in Broad Marsh.'

'Ah well, that helps a bit. Canal Street isn't far from there. Go back and ask directions from there. It'll be easier for you.'

Eveleen smiled, instinctively liking the first person in the city she had met. 'Thank you,' she said as they parted. 'You've been very kind. I hope we meet again.'

The woman chuckled. 'Nottingham's a big place. But I wish you luck. And you never know, if you get a job at Reckitt's then you might meet up with my old man. Tarr-ra, mi duck.'

Twenty-Nine

Eveleen had a good sense of direction and found her way back to the corner turning into Broad Marsh without difficulty. Then she asked a man for directions again.

'Keep straight on this road and you'll come to a junction with Canal Street to the right and Leen Side to the left. Where are you looking for?'

'Reckitt's.'

'Oh aye, well, you can't miss it. It's got big green gates with the name painted in white lettering.'

'Thank you,' Eveleen said and set off once more. She was wishing now that she had had the sense to stop and buy something to eat and drink. She had seen a tiny shop selling teas, sweets and ice cream – a rare treat that would be – but she was so anxious to find work that she had ignored the messages from her rumbling stomach and her dry mouth. She walked on, pausing only to flatten herself against a wall as a fire engine, drawn by two black horses, their smooth coats shining in the sunshine, came rattling past her at full gallop. On the four-wheeled carriage sat eight firemen dressed in dark tunics with shiny brass buttons and helmets. The pedestrians in the narrow street parted quickly to let the vehicle through, but as soon as it had passed they continued going about their business.

Startled by the clanging bell and the thundering horses, Eveleen stared after the engine as it disappeared round a corner. She glanced about her. No one else appeared unduly concerned. For them, she thought, this must be an everyday occurrence. Recovering her composure, she walked on. She was coming now to a poorer part of the city. No longer were there grand houses, but tall, terraced houses with doors stepping straight out on to the cobbled street. Grubby-faced children played in the road while careworn mothers scrubbed the step outside their homes, trying to keep the city dirt at bay.

And yet, even here, Eveleen still felt that prickle of excitement. The place seethed with life. Here, Eveleen thought with fresh hope, her family could lose themselves, away from Harry and his strict regime.

She saw the green double wooden gates. One stood open, but the left one was still closed and bore the single name "Reckitt". Already she could hear the clatter of machinery. She glanced up and saw the now familiar sight of the long line of windows on the top storey.

'I can't escape him even here,' she murmured, thinking of her uncle's workshops.

Taking a deep breath, she stepped through the door and went towards the factory entrance.

'You need to see Mr Carpenter. He sets folk on. He's about somewhere.'

Eveleen was tired now and hardly looked her best for an interview for a job. She smoothed down her hair and adjusted the shawl about her shoulders. She lifted her head and straightened her back, trying to ignore her aching feet and weary limbs.

'What does he look like?'

The girl grinned. 'He's big and fat and ugly. And watch yourself, 'cos he's a devil for the girls. But he's not so bad. He's fair, I'll give him that. Look, wait here a minute, I'll see if I can find him for you.'

The girl's kindness brought tears of gratitude to Eveleen's eyes, but she blinked them away and smiled. 'Thanks.'

Eveleen stood in the cold and waited. Already the light was beginning to fade and lamps were being lit in the factory so that the workers could continue late into the evening. Unbidden, the picture of her uncle's round globe above his frame came into her mind. She sighed. If only Jimmy hadn't been such an idiot, they could have settled in very happily there. In time, Eveleen might have been able to buy her own frame and, with a lot of hard work, she could have made enough money to take them all back home.

Back to Lincolnshire where her mother wanted to be.

But Jimmy had ruined everything and now they were in a worse situation than before. There were times, Eveleen thought, when she could quite cheerfully wring her brother's scrawny neck.

'I've found him.' The girl was back and beckoning to her. 'This way.' She winked at Eveleen. 'I've told him there's a pretty girl wants to see him. He won't refuse to see you now. Come on.'

The girl led the way round a corner and along twisting, narrow passages. Arriving at a door leading into a tiny office, she gestured to Eveleen to go inside. 'Good luck,' then she smiled and whispered. 'And mind you stay this side of his desk.'

With a laugh she was gone, running along the passageway towards the stairs to the upper floors.

Eveleen stepped into the room. The bulk of the man sitting behind the desk seemed to fill the small office and she marvelled that he could even fit into the chair he was sitting on. As he looked up, his jowls wobbled and Eveleen had to stifle her laughter. The girl's saucy description of him had been most apt. His face was round and florid, his fat cheeks marked with tiny red veins. His bulbous nose fought for prominence over his thick, wet lips and he had dark folds of skin beneath his eyes. And yet, when she looked into those eyes, Eveleen could see the man inside the mound of flesh. There was humour and kindness and, yes, like the girl had said, a spark of devilment.

'Mr Carpenter?'

'That's me, young lady, and what can I do for you?' His bold glance appraised her and yet Eveleen did not find it offensive. She did not fear this man as she might have done a more handsome one. In a strange way, she felt sorry for him. He had feelings, just like everyone else, even though he presented a ridiculous figure.

'I'm looking for a job, Mr Carpenter.'

'Ah well, now.' Josh Carpenter leant back in the chair, which creaked in protest. Eveleen found herself holding her breath in case it should give way beneath him. 'Then we'd better have a nice little talk, hadn't we? Pull up that chair, mi duck. Sit down and tell me all about yourself.'

So Eveleen sat and found herself telling him about herself, *all* about herself. The words tumbled out and it seemed as if, once the floodgates were opened, she could not stop the deluge. She told him about her father's death and how she now felt responsible for her mother and younger brother. She told him about her uncle, his workshops and his devotion to the chapel. She even told him how Harry Singleton inflicted the rigid way of life he led himself upon all those around him.

'There's nothing wrong with that,' she said hastily. 'He's a good man and I'm sure his way of life is right, but—'

The big man finished for her. 'But it takes a lot of living up to, mi duck, doesn't it?'

Eveleen nodded.

'Aye, there's a few manufacturers and warehouse owners round here who worship at a particular church and expect all their workers to attend regularly too.'

Perhaps she had told him too much, perhaps she had sounded disloyal to her own family. He seemed so understanding, but he was still a man, Eveleen reminded herself sharply.

'And now,' he was asking. 'You feel it's time to move on? To get away?'

'There's more to it than that, I'm afraid.' She had come this far, she thought, he might as well know the full story.

'My uncle has a daughter. He keeps her very . . .' She strove to find the right words to be fair to her uncle. 'Well, she's all he has and—'

'Keeps her well and truly under his thumb, does he?'

Eveleen nodded, startled by this man's astuteness. There was a lot more to Mr Carpenter than being big, fat and ugly. She'd only just met him and yet there was something so comforting about him.

'My brother and Rebecca have become – have been . . .' She faltered, but again the big man let out a long, sympathetic 'Ahhhh.'

'Rebecca is expecting my brother's child. And when my uncle finds out—' There was no need to say more for Josh Carpenter nodded, understanding at once.

'You've taken a lot on for one so young.'

Eveleen sighed. 'We'll all have to leave. Rebecca too.

We'll have to look after her now. And the child, when it comes.'

'So the girl's father really won't stand by her?'

Eveleen shook her head vehemently, cutting in, 'No, he won't.'

Josh Carpenter rubbed his hand on his face and murmured, 'Well, now, let's see. You say you can make pillow lace?'

Eveleen bent down and picked up the bag she had dropped beside her chair. She pulled out the pieces of lace she had made and passed them to him.

Josh examined it keenly. 'This is well done. Very well done.'

'And I can work one of my uncle's knitting frames.'

Josh pulled a wry face. 'Sorry, mi duck, but we don't have women working the machines.'

Eveleen felt a swift stab of disappointment. It must have shown on her face, for Josh said quickly, 'But you say your brother can operate a machine? They're not knitting frames we have here of course. They're twist lace machines, but I'm sure your brother would soon pick it up.'

She nodded and bit her lip, stopping herself telling him that Jimmy was neither as good a worker as she was nor as reliable. She would just have to make sure that her brother changed his ways. Instead, she asked, 'But do you have any jobs for women in the factory?'

'Oh yes. This is a factory-cum-warehouse, see. So the goods that are made on the machines go straight to the warehouse building next door and we have different workshops and a lot of the workers there are women. So, young lady, when you get settled in Nottingham, bring your brother to see me and we'll see what we can do for both of you.' He held out his hand to her and Eveleen

231

stood up. She smiled at him and shook his hand. 'Thank you, Mr Carpenter. Thank you very much.'

As she walked out of the gates of the factory, Eveleen gave a little skip of sheer joy. Their luck was turning, she could feel it. The sky above the tall buildings was darkening now and she could feel a few spots of rain on her face. She would have to hurry to catch the last omnibus to Flawford. If she missed it, she faced a walk of five miles or more.

She had no time left now to seek lodgings for the family, but she had achieved a great deal that day and, though she felt tired and very hungry now, she was also elated. She had the promise of work for Jimmy and herself and she had seen the trading area known as the Lace Market. It was not quite the kind of market she had expected, with open stalls and traders standing behind them shouting their wares. It was a much more refined way of trading, but at least she now understood how it all worked, or at least she thought she did.

'We'll have to stay a night or two at a small hotel at first,' she murmured to herself. Not for long though, she vowed, for it would be expensive. Maybe a temperance hotel would be the answer. She smiled a little at the thought that her uncle would approve of her thinking, then pulled a wry expression as she remembered that he would have very little else to approve of. She still had to face his anger for disappearing and losing herself in the city, and missing the omnibus home.

The two solid green doors were now both closed, but Eveleen pulled one open, passed through and pulled it to behind her. She paused a moment to take one last glance back at the name painted in big letters on the doors. Now that they were both closed she could see the name of the factory and warehouse in full.

Reckitt and Stokes.

She felt a strange tremor run through her. Oh, it couldn't be. Could it? Stokes was the surname of the man who had been her mother's sweetheart. The man who had, so heartlessly, run away from his responsibilities and left poor Mary to face the shame and humiliation alone.

It couldn't be him. It was too much of a coincidence. And yet she remembered that her grandmother had said that Brinsley Stokes was in partnership in a factory in Nottingham now.

Eveleen, her mouth a tight line, stared at the name, almost as if it might come alive and materialize into the person himself.

'Well, whoever you are, Mr Stokes, I'll work for you,' she murmured. 'I'll work as hard as I know how. But perhaps you'd better keep out of my way or I might not be responsible for what I do.'

As she turned to hurry back to Broad Marsh, she realized that she would have to be very careful not to mention the name to her mother. And she would have to swear Jimmy to secrecy too.

Thirty

When Eveleen returned to Flawford, no mention was made of where she had been and why she was so late home. A far worse storm had broken and her mother had been the cause of it.

Mary, hearing Rebecca retching over the chamber pot in her bedroom, had remarked on it at breakfast.

'I only asked,' Mary wailed, spreading her hands in supplication to Eveleen as soon as she stepped into the cottage. 'Was she ill? Was it something she'd eaten? Then I laughed and said it sounded just like morning sickness. I was only joking, Eveleen, I never thought for one moment that she – of all people . . . But she turned as white as a sheet and burst into tears. Then, of course, Harry—'

'Don't tell me,' Eveleen said wearily. 'He got it out of her.'

Mary nodded.

'Where is he now?'

Mary plucked at her apron. 'He's – he's gone to the chapel.'

Eveleen's face was grim as she put down her bag, pulled her shawl about her shoulders and said firmly, 'I'll go and find him.'

'Do be careful, Eveleen, I've never seen him in such a temper. Not ever – not even . . .' Her voice faltered and she dabbed at her eyes with the corner of her apron. 'Not even twenty years ago.'

Eveleen walked across the road and opened the door leading into the chapel. Closing it quietly behind her she stood a moment watching her uncle kneeling alone on the cushioned step in front of the rostrum, his arms resting on the communion rail. His forehead was resting on his hands clasped tightly in prayer. Even from here she could hear his low murmuring. In front of him a vase of flowers rested on the small communion table and towering above him were the dark polished panels of the pulpit with steps on either side. Resting on the top rail of the pulpit was the lectern with the heavy Bible, still open at the page where the preacher had left it the previous Sunday.

As she watched her uncle, Eveleen felt a stab of pity for him. Rebecca was his only child, his beloved daughter. She was all he had left in the world and now, in his eyes, she was despoiled, shamed and full of sin.

Eveleen crept forward and sat down in the family pew to wait until Harry had finished. She pulled one of the embroidered hassocks forward and knelt, bowing her head in a prayer of her own. At once her vision of God came into her mind. He was stretching out his hand towards her and his face, though sad, was full of compassion. She prayed to him to give her strength, to give her the courage to do the right thing and the common sense to know what that was.

She heard a movement and opened her eyes to see her uncle easing himself stiffly to his feet. He turned to look at her. For a long time they stared at each other. The sadness had etched another ten years into his face in the space of a day, Eveleen thought, her heart going out to him. But there was no compassion in her uncle's face, no understanding or forgiveness.

She began, 'Uncle—' but he raised his hand to stop her.

'Don't say a word, Eveleen, because there's nothing you can say that can alter anything. Your mother has brought shame to my door again.'

'My mother is not to blame for this. It's Jimmy's fault and – and Rebecca's.'

He shook his head. 'Not Rebecca. She was a sweet, innocent flower who would never willingly have allowed him to – to—'

'Are you accusing Jimmy of – of . . .' The word was too ugly, too appalling for Eveleen to utter, especially in this holy place.

'He must have forced her. It must have been against her will.'

Eveleen stared. Then she realized that her uncle was twisting the truth to fit what he wanted to believe. He could not bear to think that his precious daughter could have committed such a sin and the only way around that was to accuse her lover of rape. This was worse than even she had feared. Jimmy was in danger. Harry Singleton could have him arrested. Her heart began to thud painfully. Perhaps he had done so already. Then she took hold of her wild thoughts. No, no, her mother would have told her at once if anything like that had happened. She would have been hysterical.

Trying to speak calmly, Eveleen said, 'We'll leave at once.'

'It would be for the best, Eveleen.'

She stood up and turned to leave but not before she had lingered a moment to say huskily, 'I'm sorry, Uncle Harry. Truly I am.'

For a moment, his head was bowed. When he raised it she saw tears in his eyes. 'Take Rebecca with you, Eveleen. I do not want to look on her face again.'

The lump that rose in Eveleen's throat threatened to

choke her. At that moment she did not know for whom she felt the sorrier, Harry Singleton or his daughter. He looked a lost, lonely and desolate man.

'It's late now but we'll be gone by Monday,' she promised him.

He seemed about to say more but then, looking away, he nodded. As she moved out of the family pew, he took her place and she left him sitting there, alone in the chapel. As far as she knew, that was where he stayed for the remainder of the night.

He could not bear to be under the same roof as the rest of his family.

Eveleen slept very little. She lay beside her mother in the attic room, staring into the darkness listening to every creak of the house settling itself for the night. Her mother, too, was restless, tossing and turning and muttering in her fitful sleep. Below them, Eveleen could hear Rebecca moving about her bedroom. No doubt she was collecting her bits and pieces together to leave. Every so often, she caught the muffled sound of the girl sobbing.

Throughout the following day, Harry did not return to the house and none of the family attended the Sunday services at the chapel.

Very early on the Monday morning, Eveleen knocked on the door of her grandmother's cottage. She opened the door and called softly. 'Jimmy, are you up?'

'You can come in,' Bridget called. Eveleen stepped into the room and was surprised to see her grandmother fully dressed and sitting in her chair by the fire. Then she realized that Bridget had probably not been to bed the previous night either.

'So, he's found out then,' Bridget said without preamble.

Eveleen sighed and sat down opposite her, feeling a pang of regret that this would be the last time she would be able to sit and talk to her grandmother. Despite her moods, Eveleen had become very fond of Bridget. She didn't even blame her – not any more – for not having the strength to stand up to her son and champion Rebecca. She was old now and frail. Though her spirit was still there, Bridget was not as resilient as she might once have been.

What Eveleen could not forgive her for was that she had not stood by her own daughter all those years before.

'He's like his father,' Bridget said suddenly. 'Unforgiving.' As if reading Eveleen's thoughts, she went on. 'I know you think I should have done more to help Mary, but you didn't know her father. John was a hard, God-fearing man. A good man, mind you, like Harry. No one can say he wasn't. But he was unforgiving of anyone's weaknesses. To his mind, Mary had committed almost the worst sin possible that a woman can commit. If I'd stood up for her against him, I'd've had to leave with her.' The old eyes were looking straight into Eveleen's now. 'I had to make a choice.'

Eveleen nodded but could find no words to say except the same as those she had said to her uncle. 'I'm sorry, Gran. So very sorry.'

'It's not your fault, love. I know that and so does Harry at the bottom of him, but he can't admit it. It's that no good brother of yours that's to blame. Him and Rebecca. She's not so innocent as Harry would have us believe. Oh, I know what he thinks, but I have told him I don't agree with him on that. She's weak and imagines herself in love with your Jimmy and she was daft enough to give way to his pestering.' She nodded wisely towards Eveleen. 'But you'll have to make him toe the line now, girl, and face up to his responsibilities, else he'll bring yet more trouble your way.'

Eveleen nodded. 'I know.'

'I'm sorry to see you go. I was proud to have all my grandchildren around me.' The old lady lapsed into silence and Eveleen knew that that pride had been cruelly snatched away.

She sprang to her feet. 'Jimmy,' she called out harshly. 'Get down here this minute. We're leaving.' She bent and kissed her grandmother's papery cheek. 'I'll miss you, Gran,' she said with a catch in her throat.

'Aye, and I'll miss you.' For a moment Bridget clutched at Eveleen's hand. 'What's to become of us, eh? What's to become of us all?'

For the first time, Eveleen spared a thought for the old lady. There would be no one left here to care for her now. No doubt Harry would employ some girl from the village to cook and clean and wash for him and his mother.

But it could never be the same for Bridget as having her own family around her. She had drawn strength from their youth and vigour and, despite the sharpness of her tongue, Eveleen truly believed she had rejoiced in her daughter's return.

They took the carrier's cart to Nottingham rather than the omnibus. Between them they carried their personal belongings. At the last moment, Eveleen had hurried to the workshop and snatched up the seat that Andrew had made for her.

'I don't know what you want to lug that thing about with you for,' Jimmy muttered morosely.

Eveleen said nothing. She was so angry with her

brother that she only spoke to him when it was absolutely necessary.

Their journey was a nightmare. Rebecca did nothing but sob and cling to Jimmy's arm and Mary complained bitterly. 'I don't want to go to the city, Eveleen. I want to go home. Back to Bernby. We were happy there. Take me home, Eveleen.'

The words seemed to echo round and round in Eveleen's mind. The promise she had made to her mother was going to be harder to achieve than ever.

Thirty-One

As they alighted from the cart, once again in Broad Marsh, Eveleen asked the driver, 'Do you know of any cheap hotels where we could stay? Only for a couple of nights,' she added hastily.

'Not that'd be suitable for ladies, mi duck.' The man pondered a moment and then added, 'You'd do better to go to one of the working girls' homes. There's one or two of them.' He glanced at Jimmy. 'Don't know if they'd take him, though. He might have to try the Young Men's Christian Association.'

'Not bloody likely,' Jimmy muttered and Eveleen gave him a sharp nudge.

'Wash your mouth out and shut up. You'll do as you're told for once.'

Jimmy glowered and, though he said no more, Eveleen noticed that he pulled his arm free of Rebecca's limpet hand causing the girl's sobs to grow louder.

The carrier cast a strange look at Jimmy but turned back to Eveleen. 'I reckon they have a house of refuge on Chaucer Street. He could try there, but it's a fair step. Right the other side of Market Place.'

Eveleen did not even know where Market Place was, but she was sure they could find it.

'Where is there a working girls' home? We'll try there first.'

'That's easier. There's one in Castle Gate. Go along

241

here to the end of Broad Marsh.' He pointed in the opposite direction to that which Eveleen had walked with her uncle. 'Turn right and then left and that's Castle Gate. I'm not sure where the house is exactly, but you can ask then.'

'Thanks,' Eveleen said. 'Thanks very much.'

The man glanced round at them and, seeming to catch something of the atmosphere of misery and desperation, he murmured, 'Good luck, mi duck.'

'Thanks,' Eveleen said again and added, under her breath, 'I'm going to need it.'

As Eveleen hitched up the baggage she was carrying and began to lead the way along the street, Jimmy said, 'I aren't staying in no Christian place. I've had enough of ranters to last me a lifetime.'

Eveleen dropped her belongings to the ground, whirled round on him and gripped his shoulders. She shook him hard, 'It's your fault we're in this mess. You'd do better to try to help—'

'It's not Jimmy's fault,' Mary said rousing from her apathy. 'Don't blame him. I won't have you blaming him.' Her glance went to Rebecca and then came back to rest on Eveleen. 'It's your fault, Eveleen, bringing us here in the first place.' And, unspoken, other words lay between them. *And it was you who caused your father's death.*

Mary linked her arm through Jimmy's. 'Never mind her. You'll look after me, Jimmy, won't you?'

'I don't know where to go.' Jimmy glanced resentfully at Eveleen. 'We'll have to do what she says.'

Eveleen picked up her bundles, tucking the seat under her arm. 'It's only for a night or two until I find us a house to rent or something. I'll ask at the factory. Mr Carpenter might help.'

242

'Who's he?' Jimmy asked as they began to walk again, this time with his mother hanging on to his arm.

'The man who's going to give you a job, that's who. And you'd better be nice and polite to him. No making fun of him. You hear me?'

'Why? What's the matter with him? Got two heads, has he?'

'No.' Eveleen tried to explain. 'He's a rather – rather large gentleman, and – and – he's not exactly handsome. But you just remember, our livelihood might well depend on that man.'

'You mean he's a big, fat, ugly bugger,' Jimmy said and then dodged smartly out of the way as Eveleen dropped one of her bags again and her hand came up to swipe good-naturedly at him. 'He'll be just right for you, our Evie, 'cos you can't seem to keep the good-looking ones, can you? If you'd raised your skirts for Master Stephen, then maybe we'd all be living in clover by now.'

Laughing unkindly, he marched ahead along the street, dragging Mary with him and leaving Eveleen to help Rebecca.

They found the Home for Working Girls and the woman in charge was happy to take the three women but shook her head at Jimmy.

'We can't take men in here.'

'Oh please,' Eveleen cajoled. 'It's only for a couple of nights. Just until I can find us a place to rent.' Eveleen swallowed hard before she offered, 'I'll pay you a little extra.'

The woman eyed Jimmy dubiously, even though he was trying to adopt the most innocent expression he could muster. But then her eyes began to gleam at the thought of some extra money in her pocket. 'He'll have to behave himself else I could lose mi job.'

'He will,' Eveleen said firmly.

'All right then, just so long as it is only for a couple of nights or so.'

The following morning as they stood together side by side in front of Mr Carpenter, Eveleen could feel Jimmy shaking with suppressed mirth. Unseen by the man on the other side of the desk, she put out her foot and trod heavily on Jimmy's, and she held it there until he put his hand behind her back and pinched her arm. They glanced at each other, each of them testing the other out. Then Jimmy grinned in capitulation and turned towards Mr Carpenter.

'Good morning, sir. I think my sister has told you we're both looking for work. I'm a good worker, sir, and I'll give you no trouble.'

The shrewd man eyed him suspiciously. Eveleen bit her lip, wondering if Mr Carpenter was going to let slip all that she had told him about her family. But all he said was, 'Aye well, lad, we'll see, won't we? Now, you go down this passage here. Turn left at the bottom and you'll see a little office on your left just before the door into the machine shop. Ask for Bob Porter. Tell him I've taken you on as an apprentice on a Levers machine.' Josh's round face broke into a smile. 'Tell Bob to put you with Luke Manning. He'll keep you in line.'

Politely Jimmy touched his forelock and said, 'Thank you, sir.' Then he stepped out of the tiny room and out of sight of the big man, he winked at his sister, jerked his thumb towards Mr Carpenter and mimed lifting his skirt, had he been wearing one.

Eveleen almost took a step towards him, but Jimmy laughed, winked again and, thrusting his hands into his pockets, set off down the passageway, whistling merrily.

She turned back to meet Mr Carpenter's eyes and before she could stop herself, she said, 'I don't know what he's got to be so cheerful about. It's all his fault we're in this mess.'

The man nodded sympathetically. 'I can see he's got a bit of the devil in him. But he's not the only one. We've a lot of apprentices here, lass, and I have to keep me eye on 'em all.' He tapped the side of his huge nose. 'Don't you worry, love. He's just one more I'll be watching.'

Her smile was genuine as she said with relief, 'Thank you, Mr Carpenter.'

'Now, mi duck. Let's see what we can find for you to do, eh?'

'Thank you, sir. There's just one more thing. Do you know of anywhere where we could take lodgings? There's four of us.'

'Soon to be five, eh?'

Eveleen nodded.

He rubbed a handkerchief across his forehead wiping away beads of sweat. 'Now I'll have to think about that. Where are you staying at the moment?'

When Eveleen told him, he pulled a face. 'That'll be costing you.' He smiled, his jowls wobbling, 'And the rules'll be a bit rigid, I bet.'

Eveleen smiled. 'We're used to worse than that, Mr Carpenter.'

'Can't promise anything, mind, but I'll see what I can do. I'll ask around the factory.'

Eveleen thanked him again and then waited while he heaved himself up from the chair and lumbered his way around the desk and out into the passage. 'But for now, we'd better set you to work, lass.'

He led her to the adjacent building. They climbed five flights of stairs with Josh pausing on every landing to regain his breath. 'I don't – come up here – very often,' he puffed and smiled. 'You can see why.'

Eveleen smiled kindly at him but could not think of a suitable response. When they reached the top floor Josh led her into a large, airy room with large windows on all sides. The noise greeted them as they opened the door, but this time it was not the clatter of machinery but the chattering of the forty women at work in the room. They were all seated, except for one woman who appeared to Eveleen to be some kind of supervisor.

The sound of their voices died away as they became aware that Josh Carpenter had entered the room. One or two glanced up, stared for a moment at Eveleen and then bent their heads again over their work. The woman and young girls were all neatly dressed in high-necked blouses and long dark skirts and everyone seemed to have their hair smoothly coiled or plaited into the nape of their neck. In stark contrast Eveleen felt suddenly wild and unkempt and her dress and shawl shabby.

'This is the inspection and mending room,' Josh explained. Each worker had a bale of lace fabric spread over their knees and spilling on to the floor and Eveleen could see that they were examining the material carefully and mending any faults.

Josh raised his voice. 'Miss Brownlow, could you spare me a moment please?'

The supervisor left the table where she had been inspecting a length of dress lace and came towards them.

'This is Miss Eveleen Hardcastle. She has shown me some of the pillow lace she has made and it is very fine.'

He glanced at Eveleen and smiled, 'Very fine work indeed.' He turned back to Miss Brownlow. 'So I am sure she would be suitable for the work here.'

It was a statement not a request and the woman, thin-faced and with a hooked nose that dominated her features, could only purse her small mouth and nod in reluctant acquiescence.

Josh turned to Eveleen. 'Miss Brownlow will look after you and I'll not forget what you asked me. I'll see what I can find out. Come and see me after work.'

As the door closed behind him, Eveleen felt the curious eyes of all the women in the room upon her. She heard the soft laughter that rippled through the room like a breeze. Close by she heard a young girl murmur, 'Another one for Josh's harem, eh?' And Eveleen felt an embarrassed flush creep up her face.

Thirty-Two

'Miss Binkley,' the sour-faced supervisor called forward one of the young women. 'Look after her and show her what to do.' Miss Brownlow's scathing glance raked Eveleen from head to foot. 'I don't expect she'll be much use, but we'll have to take her if he's taken a fancy to her.' She gave a loud sniff. 'And perhaps a little responsibility will do you no harm.' With her back ramrod-stiff, the woman went back to her table. Unseen, the girl pulled a face. Miss Binkley, about the same age as Eveleen, was fair-haired with blue, mischievous eyes, a small nose and a laughing mouth. She touched Eveleen's arm in a friendly gesture and whispered. 'Don't worry, she's only jealous. I don't reckon she's ever had a man in her life, not even one like old Carpenter. Come on,' she led the way carefully through the mounds of delicate fabric on the floor. 'My name's Helen, by the way. Sit near me and I'll show you what to do.'

One or two of the other women sitting nearest to Helen looked up and smiled, but soon, resuming their chatter as they worked, they had forgotten all about the new girl.

At the end of that first working day, Eveleen found her way back to Josh Carpenter's office.

'I'm sorry, but I've been so busy this afternoon. One

of the machines went wrong.' He pulled a face and Eveleen held her breath, praying that it had nothing to do with Jimmy. But as Josh continued, she let out her breath in relief. 'I haven't had the time to ask around. But I'll see what I can do tomorrow.'

She smiled her thanks and went outside. Jimmy was already halfway along the street with two or three other youths of his own age. Eveleen had the uncomfortable feeling that her dear brother would not arrive back at their lodgings until much later that night and then probably he would be rolling drunk and likely get them thrown out.

For once, however, Eveleen held her impetuous tongue in check. If she called out to him, belittled him in front of his newfound friends, Jimmy would then do it deliberately.

Eveleen sighed. Either way, she couldn't prevent the inevitable.

'Please, just one more day.' Eveleen was obliged to plead with the woman running the home the following morning, after Jimmy had woken half the house – maybe even half the street – sitting on the steps outside in the early hours and singing at the top of his voice. Eveleen had scuttled down and dragged him in but not before the warden, or whatever she was called, had heard him too.

'I am sorry,' she added.

The woman mellowed enough to say, 'It's not your fault, Miss Hardcastle. I can see that. But I stretched the rules to let him stay here at all and see what he does?'

'I know,' Eveleen said helplessly. 'And we'll move out as soon as I find somewhere, I promise.'

'All right then, but if he comes back in that state tonight, I won't have him in the house. He'll have to sleep in the street.'

Eveleen nodded and went upstairs to drag her leaden-headed brother from his bed. 'Come on, you,' she said roughly. 'You've cost us our place here. I'm not going to let you lose your job an' all.'

Nearing the lunch break, a man came into the inspection room. He stood in the doorway and looked about him. He spoke to one of the women nearest the door and she gestured towards Eveleen.

Helen nudged Eveleen. 'Looks like you've got yourself an admirer already.'

'That's Fred Martin,' Sarah, who sat near Helen and now Eveleen too, remarked. 'He's married to Win and they've got six kids. Their eldest daughter works at the Adams' place on Stoney Street.'

Helen pulled a face at Eveleen and grinned. 'He can still come looking, though, can't he?'

'Not if Win catches him, he can't,' someone else close by said.

That was the thing about factory life, Eveleen was swiftly learning. Whatever was said to the person sitting next to you was overheard and usually taken up by half a dozen others.

The laughter rippled around them as the man stepped carefully among the workers towards Eveleen.

'Hello,' he said, nodding at her in greeting. 'My missis has sent me. Said to watch out if any new girls turned up here and I was to be sure to ask you if you was getting on all right.'

Eveleen dropped her work, stood up and held out her

hand, smiling as she did so. 'Oh you must be the husband of the kind lady I met in Stoney Street when I came the other day looking for work. It was her suggested I came to Reckitt's. She said you worked here.'

The man's smile broadened. 'That's my Win. She collects lame ducks. No offence, love.'

'None taken,' Eveleen said at once. 'I was certainly a lame duck that day by the time I'd finished tramping the streets.' The man laughed and those listening around them joined in.

'So,' he went on. 'Are you all right, 'cos I'll have to report back now I've found you.'

'Yes, thanks. I'm fine. And it's thanks to your wife I am.'

'Good,' he nodded, raised his hand and made to turn away. 'I'll tell her that. She'll be pleased to have helped you, love.'

'There is just one thing,' Eveleen said hastily. 'You don't happen to know of anywhere to rent do you?'

'Just for you?'

Eveleen shook her head. 'No. There's four of us.' Eveleen bit her lip. She had been about to say more but there were too many listeners for her to want to confide more. All around them the women had fallen silent and were listening intently.

Fred wrinkled his forehead and said, 'I don't know of anywhere but I'll ask the wife. She might. I'll let you know tomorrow.'

'Thanks. I'd be ever so grateful.'

As he left, she sat down again and resumed her work. The buzz of conversation rose again and soon Eveleen and her problems were forgotten. Only Helen said, 'I'll ask around too for you.'

Eveleen opened her mouth to express her thanks when

she noticed that once again the workers had fallen silent. Then a whisper rippled through the room like a breeze.

'It's him. It's Mr Stokes himself. By the door, look. He's just come in.'

'I hope that handsome son of his is with him.'

'Shut up, Lucy. You're too old for him. The lad's not even twenty.'

'Mebbe he'd like an older woman. I'd like the chance to teach him a thing or two.'

Eveleen looked up to see that two men had entered the room. The first was a man in his mid-forties. Tall and slim with dark hair that was greying at the temples, he had clear-cut features, a long straight nose and a firm jaw. The second man was much younger and, quite obviously, the son of the older man, for he resembled him in looks and build. The first man looked about him, his expression stern, but the young one smiled and nodded to the women nearby.

'Oh, isn't he the most handsome man you've ever seen in your life?' Helen sighed ecstatically.

Eveleen stared at the young man until, as if feeling her eyes upon him, he turned to look at her. Boldly she held his gaze for a long moment, then dutifully she bent her head over her work again.

'No, he isn't, actually. But then I have no liking at all for handsome men,' Eveleen said, unable to keep the bitterness from her tone as Stephen's fair, chiselled features were suddenly in her mind's eye. 'I'd sooner have an ugly one who was kind and reliable.'

'In that case,' Lucy piped up. 'Look no further. Old man Carpenter's going free.' The ripple of laughter around her made the older man look across towards where Eveleen was sitting and frown.

Eveleen concentrated on her work and took no more

part in the whispered conversation among the other women. She didn't want to incur the wrath of one of the owners of the factory on only her second day there.

Not until the two men had gone did she say, 'Who did you say they were?'

'That's your employer, Eveleen. That was Mr Brinsley Stokes and his son, Richard.'

So, she had been right. The older of the two men had been her mother's lover more than twenty years earlier. And now it was too late. She had the promise of work for both her and Jimmy. Work she dare not give up just because one of the owners had once treated her mother so shamefully.

Eveleen frowned over her work and, for a moment, her fingers trembled as she thought of the shock it would give her mother if she ever found out.

She would have to make sure that never happened.

'You're quiet,' Helen said. The muted buzz of conversation had begun again once Mr Stokes and his son were out of earshot.

Eveleen looked up and forced herself to smile. 'Sorry.'

Helen leaned closer. 'You're taken with him, aren't you? Master Richard.'

'Of course not,' Eveleen snapped. 'I've told you, I'm not interested in handsome men. You can't trust them any further than you can throw them.'

Instead of taking offence at her sharpness, Helen said quietly, 'You've been hurt, haven't you? Someone's hurt you very badly.'

At the kindness in her new friend's voice, Eveleen felt a lump in her throat and tears prickle behind her eyelids. She bent her head and tried to hide them, but Helen touched her arm. 'I'm sorry. I didn't mean to upset you. Forget him, whoever he is. He's not worth it.'

Eveleen gave a watery smile and looked up. 'You're right there. He wasn't.'

'But they're not all like that, you know,' Helen said gently. 'Don't tar 'em all with the same brush, just 'cos one's been a right bastard.'

Eveleen said nothing. She couldn't expect Helen to understand.

She had fallen in love with Stephen Dunsmore. She had given him her heart completely and he had crushed it. She was never, she vowed, going to give herself to any man like that again. She was not going to give anyone the chance to hurt her again.

The meeting – although it could hardly be called that – with Brinsley Stokes and his son had disturbed her. She couldn't confide in Helen, nice though the girl seemed, and by lunchtime she was in such a state of agitation that she went in search of Jimmy.

She slipped into the machine room, even though she knew she should not be there. She walked down the aisles of machines until she came to where her brother was working. She stood watching him, taking in his every movement.

Luke Manning, the skilled twisthand deputed to train Jimmy, shouted orders above the clatter of the machinery. He was a thin man in his late forties or early fifties, with thinning grey hair and a slight stoop to his shoulders. His face was pale and gaunt, but his mouth was pursed in a cheery whistle, even though his tune could not be heard above the racket. Catching sight of Eveleen, he winked at her, pointed to Jimmy and then raised his eyes to the ceiling and shook his head in mock despair.

Then she saw Luke gesture with his hands, explaining yet again an operation that even Eveleen had just witnessed him showing her brother. A few minutes later,

Luke pointed to her and signed that Jimmy could take a short break to speak to her.

Shouting above the noise she said, 'Can't you try a bit harder? I saw him having to show you the same thing twice and I've only been here a minute or two.'

'Reckon you could do better, do you?' Jimmy snapped.

'I could make a darn sight better job of it than you're doing.' She moved closer and dropped her voice, although above the clanking machinery all around them it was doubtful they would be overheard anyway. 'Look, Jimmy. You need this job. Try and make a go of it.'

Jimmy glared at her resentfully. 'Don't boss me about, Evie, else you'll be sorry. I've enough of 'em round here shouting orders at me all day long. And the feller who takes over from us' – the twisthands, as the machine operators were called, worked in shifts so that the machines were kept running for twenty hours out of every day – 'he's been tittle-tattling to the foreman already. I'm sick of it, I tell you. For two pins, I'd be off to sea.'

Eveleen's patience snapped. 'This is only your second day.' She stopped and sighed. She didn't want to fall out with her brother. 'Look, I'm sorry. At least give it a go, eh?'

'Well,' he said slowly and then grinned at her. 'Just for you then.'

They smiled at each other, then Eveleen said, 'I didn't come here to find fault with your work'

'There's plenty doing that already,' Jimmy grimaced but his good humour had been restored. 'What did you come here for then?' He grinned cheekily at her. 'Just wanted to walk past all the fellers, eh? Let 'em all see what a fine figure of a woman you are.'

Eveleen laughed at his absurdity. Nothing had been

further from her mind. Then her expression sobered. 'I shouldn't really be here anyway, but I had to see you. I have to talk to someone.'

'What's up?'

'Do you realize who we're working for?'

He blinked. 'What d'you mean? I'm working for Luke Manning and over him is this bugger of a foreman called Porter. And above him, it's Carpenter—'

'Watch your language, Jimmy.'

Jimmy laughed. 'Oh, I aren't working for Holy Joe now, Evie. There's worse language than that flying round here, I can tell you. I reckon that's why they keep the "ladies" from coming in here.'

'Is that what they used to call Uncle Harry behind his back? Holy Joe?'

'Oh aye. And worse.'

Eveleen still had such mixed feelings about her uncle. Part of her admired him for the way he tried to live his life and yet . . . She pulled herself back to the problem of the moment. 'Never mind about that now. No, I mean do you know who the boss is? The man whose name is painted on the factory gates. Stokes. It's Brinsley Stokes.'

Jimmy still looked puzzled. 'So? What about it?'

'That's the man who caused our mam all that trouble. Years ago.'

Jimmy stared at her. 'You're not serious?'

Eveleen nodded. 'I am. Gran told me his name. And how many other Brinsley Stokes do you think there are round here?''

'What on earth did you want to get us a job here for then? I'm likely to kill him if I get near him.'

Eveleen spread her hands. 'I thought it was a coincidence. That it couldn't be him. It wasn't until I heard his first name this morning – Brinsley – that I knew for definite. It's such an unusual name, it's got to be him.' She leant closer, speaking urgently, 'Look, just don't tell Mam, that's all. She needn't know.'

Jimmy opened his mouth but before he could speak, a loud voice spoke close behind Eveleen making her jump. 'What the bleedin' hell are you doing in here, girl? Get yourself out of here. Right now.'

Eveleen turned to find herself facing the irate face of a stocky, balding man.

'Sorry, Mr Porter,' Jimmy was saying at once. 'It's me sister. Spot of family bother. Off you go, Evie. I'll see you later.'

'And don't let me catch you in here ever again. Women aren't allowed in here.' He looked her up and down with a leering glance. 'Takes their minds off their work, see.'

'Sorry, Mr Porter,' she mumbled and hurried away, her face burning, as, behind her, she could hear catcalls and whistles from the men working the machinery.

It was certainly a very different place to her uncle's workshops.

Thirty-Three

Jimmy finished his shift at six in the evening, the same time that Eveleen left the warehouse.

'I should be working 'til seven,' she told him, 'but I told Miss Brownlow I was feeling unwell. She let me go but I don't reckon she believed me. 'Eight until seven are my hours and until twelve on a Saturday.' She smiled. 'Bit different to life on a farm, eh? When we had to work the clock round at lambing time or when one of the beasts was calving.'

'Give me that any day, though, even if we did have to work the clock round. These shifts are getting to me, Evie. I don't know if I'm coming or going.'

'You'll get used to it,' was all she said. 'You'll have to.'

They fell into step together.

'So,' he began, continuing their earlier conversation that had been interrupted. 'You're not going to tell her?'

'What'd be the point? It'd only upset her. He's hardly going to come riding up on a white charger and carry her off into the sunset to live happily ever after. Life's not like that,' Eveleen said, her thoughts drifting back once more to Bernby and the fair-haired, blue-eyed man who had promised her heaven.

Jimmy grinned. 'She might want to see him. Get to know him again. You never know, they might—'

'He's married,' Eveleen said impatiently, surprised by

258

Jimmy's romantic nonsense. 'His son was with him when they came into the inspection room today.'

'Oh well, I don't care what you do. I shan't tell her.' He cast Eveleen a sly look. 'There's a lot I don't tell me mam.'

'Now why doesn't that surprise me,' Eveleen said, but Jimmy's grin only widened. Then he went on. 'They came into our place an' all this afternoon. Handsome chap, ain't he, the son? Just your type, Evie. That'd be a turn-up, wouldn't it, if you married the son.'

'Don't talk daft.' Eveleen was angry now. 'His sort don't interest me.'

'They did once,' Jimmy said, watching her closely.

'Well, they don't any more,' she snapped back and marched up the steps and into the home. I've far more pressing things on my mind, she thought. Getting us out of this place, for one.

The following morning when she arrived at work, the first thing Eveleen did was to ask Helen if she had heard of anywhere for them to rent.

The girl shook her head. 'Sorry, Eveleen, I haven't.'

Eveleen managed to smile and say, 'Thanks for trying.'

'I'll keep asking,' the girl promised.

About halfway through the morning, Fred appeared again at the doorway of the workroom to be greeted by calls and saucy remarks from the women. Eveleen could not stop herself from smiling. They're almost as bad as the men, she thought.

But Fred was only grinning good-naturedly and making his way towards her. 'You're in luck, lass. The missis has heard of a house in our yard, would you believe? If you like to come home with me after work, she'll take you to see it. She's going to get a key from the owner today.'

Eveleen leapt to her feet and threw her arms around him. 'That's wonderful. Oh thank you, thank you.'

She became aware of the laughter around her and she stepped back, embarrassed by her own behaviour.

'Miss Hardcastle!' came Miss Brownlow's voice. 'I think you forget yourself.'

'I'm sorry,' she said at once to Fred. 'But you don't know what this means to me.'

The man nodded kindly, quite unperturbed by her impetuosity. 'That's all right, love.' He laughed. 'I enjoyed it, but don't tell the missis.' He winked at her and said, 'See you outside the gate at knocking-off time, eh?' Fred worked in the warehouse carrying the heavy bales of cloth up and down the stairs to the different levels for sorting, dying, scalloping and trimming as well as to the very top for final inspection. He was lithe and muscular, no doubt from all the exercise he got each day.

She nodded, 'Thanks, Fred. I'll be there.'

'Hello, mi duck. It's nice to see you again.'

'Oh Mrs Martin, I'm so pleased to see *you* again. I wanted to thank you for all you've done to help me. You were so kind that day and you're still helping me now.'

The woman flapped her hand in embarrassment. 'Do call me Win and think nothing of it. Glad to help.' She turned to her husband. 'Your supper's in the oven, Fred, I'll just take this lass down to look at the house, though whether we'll see much in the dark, I don't know.'

'Take some candles,' Fred suggested. 'Or better still, I'll light a lamp for you.'

While they waited, Win said, 'I don't even know your name.'

Eveleen told her and then went on to explain why she needed a house so desperately.

'There are four of us, me mam, me brother and our cousin.' She bit her lip and said no more about Rebecca. Time enough for Win to find out about that later.

'Well, it won't be much of a place, love. This whole area's called Narrow Marsh and this is Foundry Yard. It's overcrowded and you have to share privies, but if you keep your own place clean, it's not so bad. Me and Fred have lived here ever since we got married and I wouldn't move if you gave me a palace. Folks is friendly round here and we all help each other.'

Eveleen smiled. Win Martin was certainly friendly and if all her neighbours were the same, then Eveleen could put up with harsh conditions.

'Ah, here's Fred with the lamp. Let's go and have a look.'

Only minutes later, they were walking into one of the back-to-back houses.

'There'll be three floors,' Win explained as they stepped into the room on the ground floor. 'There's the range . . .'

It was smaller than the one back home in Bernby, but Eveleen said nothing. She looked down at the cold, damp brick floor and thought, The sooner we get a fire going in here the better.

The furnishings were sparse: a table and three wooden chairs. They had left more than this behind in the farmhouse.

'There's a cupboard under the stairs for food and that.' Win opened it to show the empty shelves.

'It's all been left very clean,' Eveleen remarked, feeling she should say something as Win led the way up to the next floor.

'There's only one bedroom,' she said flinging open the door, 'but it's a good size.'

'I thought you said three floors.'

'Oh aye, of course, you could maybe use the room above here as another room for your brother.'

They climbed the ladder to the attic room under the eaves. It had the long window down one side.

'These houses are often occupied by stockingers,' Win said. 'And this is where they'd work. I use our top room for drawing lace. The younger girls help me too with the jennying.'

'Tell me, what is jennying?'

'The twist machines make the dress lace in breadths, each one separated by a draw thread.'

Eveleen nodded.

'When it comes off the machine all in one piece, it goes to you in the inspection and mending room. There are various other processes – bleaching, dyeing, dressing an' all that – and then it's sent out to homeworkers who separate all the breadths by "drawing". They wind the lengths of lace on to cards and that's what's called jennying.'

'So now I know,' Eveleen laughed and turned her attention back to their new home.

Jimmy could sleep to one side of this room, she was thinking, and leave space for her mother and Rebecca to work up here in the day.

'There's a tap in the yard we all share. It's all right until it gets cold in the winter and freezes up.' Win pulled a wry face. 'The privies are at the end of the yard and they're all right until it gets too hot in the summer and they pong to high heaven.'

She cast her eyes to the ceiling, but she was laughing.

'It's great, Win. Thank you so much.'

'It's in good order,' Win said, holding the lamp high. 'There's no damp patches on the ceilings or walls. When we moved into our place, you should have seen what Fred had to do to make it weatherproof.'

'It wonderful, really,' Eveleen said, clasping her hands. 'And it's so near to work too. Only just round the corner. How can I ever thank you?'

The woman looked at her and said gently, 'The look on your face is thanks enough, mi duck. Leave everything to me. I'll see the rent man tomorrow and get you a rent book sorted out. Now, come back home with me and have a bite to eat before you set off back to that home. You've a fair walk back and it's starting to rain.'

By the time she arrived back at the home, Eveleen was soaked to the skin, but she didn't care. She and Jimmy had work and now she had found them a house with friendly neighbours.

The relief was enormous and the move, which they were able to do the following Sunday, was far less traumatic that either of their two previous, hasty departures.

Of course all her worries and responsibilities were not going to disappear overnight, but at least now her family were housed, fed and clothed. There was just enough money coming in from both her and Jimmy to keep them. There would be none to spare for luxuries, but at least they had enough for the moment.

'And you can both earn a little extra here at home

lace-making,' she said to her mother and to Rebecca once they were settled into their new home. 'Or drawing and jennying.'

Rebecca said hesitantly, 'Eveleen, I'm sorry, but I'm not very good at pillow lace.'

'What? Didn't Gran teach you?'

Rebecca shook her head. 'Yes, but I've never done much. Father always wanted me to work the stocking-machine at home. He – he said there was more money to be made.' She hung her head. 'I'm sorry.'

Eveleen sighed and murmured, 'It's not your fault.'

This was a double blow. If her mother was refusing to help and Rebecca was not able, how were they ever going to earn that little bit extra that they needed so desperately?

'Mam, will you at least teach Rebecca pillow lace?'

Mary shook her head. 'Oh, I can't think about that just now. Leave me alone, Eveleen.'

Eveleen turned away. There was no getting through to her mother when she was in this mood. She'd leave it a few days and then see.

But Mary's mood did not dispel. She seemed permanently sunk in depression and despair and all she would say again and again was a pitiful, 'I want to go home, Eveleen.'

Thirty-Four

'I just hope this isn't tripe and onions again.' Jimmy pulled a face as he sat down at the table and looked down with suspicion at the plate Rebecca placed before him.

'No – no, Jimmy. I know you don't like it. I wouldn't do that.' She smiled uncertainly, her eyes never leaving his face.

Watching, Eveleen sighed inwardly. Rebecca's adoration of her rogue of a brother was plainly written on her face.

Jimmy stabbed at the food experimentally. 'What is it?'

'Pig's fry. We call it "Poor Man's Goose". Silly name really.' She tried to laugh light-heartedly, but the sound was forced. 'There's nothing of a goose in it. It's pig's liver, heart and kidney.'

'It's like Mam makes,' Eveleen said.

Jimmy brightened visibly. 'Is it?' He twisted round to look at Mary huddled in her chair by the fire. 'Did you make it Mam?'

Mary shook her head. 'I'm too ill, Jimmy. I have a dreadful headache. It's the smell of this place and having to share the privy with all these awful people.' She gave a dramatic shudder. 'I can't stand it.'

Eveleen was tempted to defend their neighbours. She liked the inhabitants of the yard; they were friendly and had welcomed the Hardcastle family into their midst. But she bit back the words while Jimmy pulled an unsympathetic face, rolled his eyes, and turned away. He took a mouthful, chewing it round and round, considering.

'Not bad,' he said. 'Not bad at all.' He cast a sideways glance at Mary before adding, 'Not as good as yours, of course, Mam, but not bad.'

Rebecca was pink with pleasure and emboldened to ask, 'After supper, shall we go out for a little walk, Jimmy?'

Jimmy stared at her as if she had taken leave of her senses. 'A walk? Where to, for Heaven's sake?'

'Well,' the girl stammered, her colour deepening but now through embarrassment. 'I – I'd just like to get some fresh air, that's all. I don't mind where we go.' The remainder – 'as long as I'm with you' – went unsaid.

'Fresh air,' Jimmy scoffed. 'Here? You must be mad. All you'll get is a lungful of smoke or the smell from the sewers.'

'The air at home was fresh and sweet and clean and . . .' Mary dissolved into tears. 'You see, Eveleen, Jimmy misses it as much as I do. Don't you, Jimmy?'

Eveleen could not let this pass. 'I seem to remember when we were living in the country, all he could do was talk about going to sea.'

'And I still might,' Jimmy said and, as Mary's sobs grew louder, silent tears ran down Rebecca's face.

The brother and sister glared at each other, but all Jimmy said was, 'What's for pudding?'

'I don't think Jimmy loves me any more, Eveleen.'

'Oh Rebecca, I'm sure that's not true. He's so young.

You both are. Only just seventeen. You were both very foolish, you know.'

'But I thought he loved me.' The girl's eyes filled with easy tears. 'He said he loved me and wanted us to get married.'

'That's what they all say.' Eveleen could not stop the bitter remark.

Her eyes brimming, Rebecca said, 'Did he just want to marry me because of my inheritance? That's what Father said.'

'Did he indeed?' Eveleen murmured, her mind calculating swiftly. Her uncle was sitting on a little gold mine. Perhaps if Jimmy and Rebecca had not been so hasty, all that might one day have become theirs. Why hadn't she thought about that before? She wondered what consideration Jimmy had given to it.

Rebecca was speaking again, 'Father said that if anyone ever did want to marry me, it'd only be to get their hands on his business.'

'What a cruel thing to say.'

'It looks like he was right, though, doesn't it?'

Eveleen took the girl's hands. They were cold. She chafed them, trying to warm the girl physically and raise her spirits. 'Look, I know my brother's not perfect. He's thoughtless and irresponsible but he's not cruel and calculating.' Hoping she sounded convincing, for she knew it was not quite true, Eveleen added, 'Besides, he's not clever enough to have thought all that out.'

She could see that Rebecca was still not reassured, so she went on, 'And he would hardly have got you into this state if that had been his reasoning. It wasn't quite the best way to worm his way into your dad's good books, was it?'

Rebecca smiled tremulously and shook her head. 'It was what he always said though, if anyone showed an interest in me. Any young man, I mean. He said it about Andrew.'

'Well, that's plain daft,' Eveleen said at once. 'Andrew truly loves you. Even I could see that and I'm certainly not the best judge when it comes to men.'

Rebecca's eyes were wide. 'Why?'

'Oh never mind just now. Maybe I'll tell you one day. But not now. I can't talk about it now.'

Rebecca nodded. She didn't understand, yet she sensed that it was a painful subject for Eveleen.

'Now then,' Eveleen said briskly, changing the subject. 'I've got a surprise for you. Since I can't persuade my mother to teach you to make lace I've been keeping my eyes and ears open. I asked Josh Carpenter if he knew of any way I could get hold of a Griswold. Like the one you had at home?'

Rebecca nodded.

'And guess what?' Eveleen went on triumphantly. 'He's found me an old one lying in one of the outbuildings at the factory.'

She smiled as she remembered the pleasure on the big man's face when he had presented her with the rusting machine. 'Needs a bit of cleaning up, but if you smile nicely at Fred Martin, I bet he'd do it up for you. Good with machinery, is Fred.'

Eveleen had been ecstatic in her thanks and had even reached up and planted a kiss on the man's fat cheek. He put his arm around her waist and squeezed her against his belly.

'You're a nice lass,' he said gruffly. 'Not like most of the girls here. They only know how to poke fun at a feller.'

Eveleen had felt a moment's fear. Had her rash gesture of gratitude given him the wrong idea? But in the next moment he had released her, patted her shoulder and said kindly, 'Run along, mi duck, before I forget myself.'

Now she told Rebecca, 'Fred's cleaning it up. He said it'll take him a week or so. All the needles are rusty.'

Rebecca looked the happiest she had looked for weeks. 'That's wonderful. Now I'll be able to earn some money to help out. You've been so good to me, Eveleen. I do so want to help.'

Good to her, Eveleen thought. We've been anything but good to her. It's all our fault that she's in this predicament and she's saying we've been good to her. But Eveleen kept her thoughts to herself and hugged her cousin.

Alone, Eveleen began to think more rationally about what Rebecca had told her. Rebecca was Harry's only daughter, his only child and consequently his only heir.

Maybe . . . Eveleen's eyes narrowed thoughtfully, calculating objectively. If Jimmy could be persuaded to do the decent thing and marry Rebecca, then maybe one day, Uncle Harry would relent. Jimmy would be set for life and she could take their mother back home to Lincolnshire.

For once, Eveleen vowed, her rebellious young brother must be made to toe the line.

'Jimmy, I want a word with you.'

Eveleen grasped his shoulder with a strength that was surprising for a girl. But her days on the farm were still not forgotten and, with walking to and from work each day and housework when she got home each evening, she was as physically fit as she had ever been. Instead of being defeated by the sheer hard work of it all, Eveleen seemed to thrive on it.

'Now what?' he said, trying to shake her off, but Eveleen kept tight hold of him.

'Walk home with me tonight and I'll tell you. It's the only time we get to talk alone. You never seem to want to stay at home in the evenings now.'

'What, with that miserable pair? Mam just sits in her chair all day long and Rebecca keeps bursting into tears. She won't even let me near her any more. Y'know, for a bit of you-know-what.'

'Wash your mouth out, you,' Eveleen said angrily. 'Don't talk about your future wife like that.'

'My what?'

If it hadn't been such a serious matter, Eveleen would have laughed out loud at the look of horror on his face. Instead she forced herself to say primly, 'Well, I hope you're going to do the decent thing by her. Surely you're not going to let the baby be born a – a . . .'

'If you think I'm going to tie mesen to that miserable cow, you can think again.'

'Jimmy, please. Don't talk about her like that. You've caused her misery.'

He twisted himself free of her grasp. 'Leggo. I've got to get back to work.'

Eveleen released him, but she realized that her devious brother had said the one thing that would make her let him go.

Her eyes narrowing, her gaze followed him as he walked into the factory.

This time, there was no swaggering walk and cheerful whistle.

She was waiting for him outside the gates when she knew his shift ended. It had meant her leaving her work an hour early but it was the only time she could snatch a few moments alone with him to try to talk some sense into him. She had pretended to be suffering stomach cramps to persuade the supervisor to allow her to leave.

'I meant what I said, Jimmy. It's your child she's having. You know very well it is. I don't want you trying to wriggle out of it by putting the blame on someone else. Rebecca's a good girl and if you hadn't filled her head with your lies just to get your way, she wouldn't be in that condition. And you know it, don't you?'

'Do I?' Jimmy was determined to be defiant to the last.

'Yes, you do,' Eveleen flared.

They walked in silence until he said, 'We're too young to be tied up, Eveleen.'

'You should have thought about that before. She's well and truly tied up now, isn't she?'

'She should have said no.'

'Oh yes, here we go. The old, old story. It's all the girl's fault. Jimmy, you took advantage of a young lass who's hardly been allowed out the door except to go across the road to the chapel. For all I know she might not have been told the facts of life properly. Maybe she didn't even know what you were up to.' She glanced sideways at him. 'Did she?'

'*I* don't know,' he muttered. 'It's not my problem.'

'Of course it's your problem. It's your bairn she's having.'

Again there was silence until he said suddenly and triumphantly, 'We can't get married. We're both under age. Even if I was willing – and I'm not – her father would never give his consent.'

'I intend to go to see him and ask him.'

Jimmy stopped walking and stared at her, causing her to pause too. 'Go back there? To him? You wouldn't?'

'Of course I would. I'm going on Sunday.'

For a moment the young man looked frightened. Then his face cleared. 'You can't. I bet there's no carrier's cart on a Sunday.'

'Yes, there is. I've checked.' Quietly, but with her tone full of steely determination, Eveleen added, 'And even if there wasn't, it's only about six miles. I'd walk.'

Thirty-Five

'You've got a nerve, girl, I'll say that for you. Showing your face here again.'

'I had to come, Gran. I have to speak to Uncle Harry.'

'I don't expect he'll want to speak to you.' Bridget looked up sharply, suddenly anxious. 'Is something wrong? Is it Rebecca?'

'No, no. She's fine. At least, as fine as she can be. She's very unhappy.'

'She's brought it all on herself,' the old woman said stiffly. 'I haven't got a scrap of sympathy for her.'

'So I see,' Eveleen said grimly.

Bridget glared at her and then looked away. 'What do you want to see her father about?'

'I need his permission for them to get married.'

'He won't give it.'

'Why ever not? Why won't he help us to make the best out of the situation? What's done, is done. At least we can make sure that his grandchild – and your great-grandchild – is born in wedlock.'

'Go and ask him yourself. He's in the chapel. Spends half his time there now. He'll tell you.'

'I will,' Eveleen said determinedly and marched out of the cottage and along the brick path, but before she reached the gate, she heard someone calling her name.

'Eveleen. Eveleen. Wait.'

She turned to see Andrew Burns coming towards her.

'How is she? Is she all right?' he was asking before he even reached her.

'She's fine.'

The look of relief on his face left Eveleen in no doubt, if indeed there had ever been any in her mind, of this young man's feelings for Rebecca.

'I thought something must have happened with you coming back here.'

Eveleen shook her head, reluctant to tell Andrew the reason for her visit. It could only bring him more pain. But Andrew was far more astute than she had given him credit for.

'You've come to see about them being married, haven't you? You've come to get his permission?'

There was nothing Eveleen could do but nod assent.

'Well, if he does marry her, he'd better treat her right. Else he'll have me to deal with. And I'll make a proper job of it next time. I'll mind you're not there to break us up.'

'Andrew, I'm so sorry.' She was reaching out to touch him, but he turned away. Sadly she watched him go.

A few minutes later she pushed open the door of the chapel, her heart thudding with nervousness. Her uncle was standing high up in the pulpit at the lectern reading silently from the huge Bible that always lay there.

She walked down the aisle knowing he must have heard her come in, yet he did not look up. She stood right beneath him near the communion rail and even when she spoke his name softly he did not look at her.

'Uncle Harry, please hear what I've come to say.'

He closed the old leatherbound book with loving care and, at last, he met her gaze.

Eveleen licked her dry lips. 'Uncle, please will you give

your permission for them to be married. So that – so that the child can be born in wedlock.'

She could see that he was struggling with his conscience. His inner turmoil showed plainly on his face. Then he stepped down from the pulpit and came to her. He took hold of her shoulder and pushed her into the family pew.

'We'll pray together, Eveleen. We'll ask for guidance.'

Willingly Eveleen knelt beside him, put her hands together in prayer and closed her eyes.

Half an hour later when her knees were sore and her legs cramped, her back aching and her hands cold, she was still in the same position. She opened her eyes and stole a look at the man beside her. He was still muttering quietly in prayer as he had done throughout the time they had both been kneeling there. Eveleen eased her aching limbs and shifted her position but her uncle droned on. Then she began to heave herself up to sit on the seat, but his hand shot out, pressing her firmly on the shoulder to keep her kneeling position.

Another ten minutes passed before he allowed her to rise and sit back on the pew. Stiffly he did the same and they sat in silence while she tried to rub life back into her limbs.

She felt his gaze on her and turned to look into his eyes. The sadness she saw there turned her heart over with pity for him.

'Have you an answer?' he asked her quietly.

She nodded. 'Whatever they've done wrong – and I know it was wrong, Uncle – it's not the unborn child's fault. Why should it be born without a proper name? Why should it have to go through life with the stigma of being called a . . .' She hesitated over the word. She had no wish to blaspheme in the chapel. '. . . dreadful name,' she finished instead. Softly, she added, 'Can't you forgive them, Uncle, because He will?'

He looked away from her then, his gaze roaming around the chapel and coming to rest once again on the Bible. Slowly, he nodded. 'Very well, Eveleen. I will agree to their marriage, but I – I can't bring myself to attend the ceremony.'

For a moment his stern face threatened to crumple, but he rubbed his hand across his eyes and with a supreme effort controlled his emotion. 'It's every father's wish to walk his daughter down the aisle on her wedding day. But now I have no wish to do so. I cannot bring myself to see her ever again.'

There was no more she could say or do to persuade him and while she had got what she came for – his written permission for his young daughter to marry – the victory was a hollow one.

She decided to walk back to Nottingham rather than wait for the last omnibus late in the evening. By the time she reached the yard where they now lived it was dark.

She pushed open the door thankful to be home and looking forward to a cup of tea and warming her toes by the range. She was met by the sound of Mary's wailing. When she heard the door, Mary rose from her chair by the fire and rushed towards Eveleen, her arms flailing.

She hit out at her, striking her on the shoulder and then about the head, 'He's gone. You've driven him away. He's left us. Jimmy's run away to sea. My Jimmy. My baby. He's gone.' More blows rained about her head and shoulders before Eveleen was able to catch hold of her mother's wrists and hold them firmly.

'Calm down,' she shouted above Mary's hysterical

shrieking. She pushed her into a chair and held her there until her cries subsided into hiccuping sobs. Eveleen glanced round to see Rebecca cowering in a corner, her arms folded over her stomach as if to protect her unborn child.

'Did she go for you, an' all?'

The girl nodded.

'Has she hurt you?'

'Not – not really.'

Beneath her grasp, she felt her mother go limp and Eveleen loosened her hold. Once she was sure that the onslaught was not going to begin again she let go completely and stood up. 'Now then. Will one of you tell me what's been going on?'

Rebecca only huddled further into the corner, sobbing quietly. Eveleen looked down at her mother. 'Well?'

'After you'd gone this morning, he was in a right temper. Shouting and carrying on. "Eveleen'll get that old bugger to agree to it," he said. "Everything always has to be her way. She always gets what she wants. And she will this time."'

Eveleen gasped and felt the colour drain from her face. How could Jimmy say such things about her? All she'd ever tried to do was take care of the family after their beloved father had died. Her knees gave way as the spirit drained out of her. Though she continued to stare at Mary as she ranted on, Eveleen sank into the chair opposite.

'"She's done it now," he said. "I'm really going to do it this time. I'm off to sea." And with that, he packed his things and went.'

Mary raised resentful eyes to Eveleen. 'If you hadn't pushed him to marry the girl, he'd have stayed with us. It's all your fault, Eveleen. All of it.'

Guilt pressed heavily upon Eveleen. Her mother was right. All their troubles had started back home in Lincolnshire when she, Eveleen, had believed the sweet words of a handsome young man.

Thirty-Six

Though her body ached with weariness, Eveleen slept little that night. Her mind was in turmoil. Her first thought, after the initial shock had worn off, had been to go in search of her brother. He could hardly join up on a Sunday, but she knew it was pointless. He could be anywhere by now in the vast city of Nottingham, and early the following morning he would no doubt be on his way to London or to a seaport to sign on.

She felt a stab of envy that he had broken free and then, despite his callous act, admiration for his daring. But there would be no such escape for her and he had left her with even greater problems than before.

Now she had to earn enough money to keep all of them.

The following morning Mr Porter stormed into the women's workroom.

'Where is he? Where is that idle blighter? You, girl, where's that blasted brother of yours?'

For some reason, Eveleen's instinct told her to hold back the truth, at least for a day or two. Knowing Jimmy, he could well be home by nightfall.

'Isn't he here?' she looked up with wide, innocent eyes. 'I'm so sorry, Mr Porter. I'll wring his neck when I catch up with him.'

The man grunted and seemed a little mollified by her willingness to condemn her brother. 'Well, see you do, lass. Meantime, get him back to that machine. He's not much use at his job yet, but Luke is a good teacher and if anyone can lick him into shape, Luke can.' Then he wagged his finger at her. 'And you can tell him, if he doesn't buck his ideas up and work harder, he'll be out on his ear anyway. I don't mind telling you, if I could find a youngster who was a quicker learner than him, he'd be out. Luke says he has to keep showing him what to do every morning. He can't seem to remember anything from one day to the next.' Perceptively, the man added, 'Or he doesn't want to.' Bob Porter turned away, grumbling and muttering to himself.

Eveleen stared after him as a daring and devious plan began to form in her mind. Her heart began to thud with excitement. Could she pull it off? If she was found out, she'd be sacked at once. But it was worth a try. They could hardly be worse off than they were at this moment. Her wages were a pittance – the family could not survive on those alone.

But if she could earn Jimmy's wage, then . . .

Eveleen bent her head over her work, trying to still her trembling fingers, trying to do her own work properly, at least for the rest of the day.

For tomorrow she would take her brother's place in the machine shop. They hadn't been here long enough for people to get to know him that well. And yet Jimmy had worked alongside Luke Manning for a few days. Would he guess? Could she really pull off such a daring deception?

Eveleen pressed her lips together determinedly. She had to.

There was only one thing she was going to regret. Tonight she must cut off all her glorious hair.

'Oh Jimmy, Jimmy. You've come back.' Mary rose from her chair and held out her arms to the figure that stood in the doorway. It didn't seem to register with her that the person had come from upstairs and not in from the yard. 'I knew you wouldn't desert us. Didn't I tell you, Eveleen?' She looked around her and then raised her voice. 'Eveleen? Where are you? Come here. Jimmy's come home.'

Rebecca came running from the scullery, her face alight with joy.

From her position by the door, it broke Eveleen's heart to have to say quietly, 'No, he hasn't, Mam. It's me.'

Mary turned startled eyes back to stare at her and Rebecca's mouth dropped open. Then tears of disappointment welled in her eyes.

'I'm sorry,' Eveleen said swiftly.

Mary, too, dissolved into tears, holding the corner of her apron to her mouth. 'How could you be so cruel, Eveleen? To dress up and pretend to be him. How could you do it?'

'It's not a game, Mam. I mean to take his place at the factory.'

Surprise caused Mary's tears to cease. 'You're not serious. You'll never get away with it.'

'I deceived you, didn't I? His own mother.'

'The light's poor in here,' Mary persisted. 'Besides, you don't know how to do his work.'

Eveleen moved forward and sat down. Mary sank into her chair and Rebecca, drying her tears as she became intrigued by Eveleen's bold plan, sat down too.

'I've watched him work, only the once I grant you, but when Mr Porter came looking for him yesterday, he said that Jimmy was not much of a worker anyway and Luke Manning – that's the twisthand who's training Jimmy – had to keep showing him what to do. I saw it with me own eyes an' all. Now, if I can only get him to do that for another day or two, I can soon pick it up.'

'Oh, Miss Clever,' Mary said sarcastically. 'You think you can do a man's job better than Jimmy, do you?'

'Jimmy could have done it if he'd really wanted to.' Eveleen sighed. 'But let's face it, Mam. All he's ever wanted was to go to sea. Maybe now he's going to be happy.'

'He was happy on the farm,' Mary insisted defensively. 'He was happy back home.'

'No, he wasn't, Mam. If you're honest, you know he wasn't.'

'What will happen if you're found out?' Rebecca asked softly.

'I'll be sacked on the spot. I know that, but it's a risk worth taking.'

'But if you're fired, we – we'll have nothing.'

'There are other factories. Other places to work. I'd soon get work again.' She pulled a face. 'Even if I have to go back to women's work.'

'What about Fred and Win? She's always popping in here. What are we going to tell them?'

Eveleen had been concerned only about the people at work: Mr Carpenter, who had been so kind to her and Helen, who was fast becoming a firm friend. And then, of course, there was Luke Manning. He was her greatest fear. Even Bob Porter was another threat, but the man she really had to convince was Jimmy's teacher at the lace machine.

Now she stared at her mother in horror. She had completely forgotten about Win and her husband.

She thought quickly. 'We could say that I've had to go back to Uncle Harry's to look after Gran. That she's not well.'

'Wouldn't it be me who would go back?' Rebecca asked in a small voice. 'I would want to if it was true.'

Eveleen bit her lip. She did not know how to answer the girl without sounding heartless. Rebecca saved her the need for she answered her own question sorrowfully. 'But they wouldn't want me there, would they? You're right, Eveleen. If anyone had to go back, it would be you.'

The following morning, Eveleen dressed in clothes that, fortunately for her, Jimmy had left behind. Striped shirt, braces and trousers and a black waistcoat and jacket. She stood looking at herself in the mirror. She did indeed look just like her brother except that her features were softer and there was no downy growth on her chin. She frowned at her reflection. She hadn't stopped to think about that. But then, Jimmy hadn't started shaving yet, so perhaps no one would notice. At least her hair, cut short now, curled just as Jimmy's had done, and beneath the shapeless man's clothing all sign of her womanly shape was well hidden.

She slipped out of the house into the darkness of early morning to arrive at the factory for Jimmy's early-morning shift. Four o'clock in the morning until nine and then again from one o'clock until six in the evening, with another worker taking the hours in between and afterwards until midnight. At least, she thought, I can get some work done at home between nine and one.

As Eveleen walked up to the gate, her heart was pounding and her mouth was dry with nervousness. Any moment she expected a raucous voice to shout, 'Hello, Eveleen. What are you doing dressed up in your brother's clothes?'

But as they all hurried, hunched with the cold, into their work, the other men did not even glance at her.

Feeling as if her heart was rising into her mouth, Eveleen took a deep breath and walked in through the factory gates.

Thirty-Seven

'Again? You're asking me to show you again?'

Eveleen nodded. 'Just once more, Mr Manning. I'm sure I'll get the hang of it soon.' She tried the sort of joke she was sure Jimmy would have used. The sort of quip he always made to get himself out of trouble. 'It's a lot different to milking cows.'

'Well, we'll try for a bit longer but you know, it doesn't rest with me. And Bob Porter's got his eye on you. If you don't buck your ideas up, lad, you're going to be out on your ear. And where were you yesterday? Bob doesn't like anyone taking the odd day off here and there.'

Eveleen had her answer ready. It would make her sound more laddish. She hung her head as if in shame. 'I had a drop too much to drink the night before.' It had been a Sunday night, so she added, 'One of the lads had a party at his house. It won't happen again, though, I promise.'

Luke pulled a wry face. 'It had better not. I'll say no more this time, but watch it. And don't you ever turn up the worse for wear after a night out, lad, else you'll be sacked on the spot. That's one thing Porter's a stickler on. And rightly so.' Luke nodded. 'Oh yes, rightly so. You've got to have your wits about you operating these machines.'

Now Eveleen could answer him far more truthfully

than ever her brother would have been able to do. 'I won't, Mr Manning.'

'Right then, lad. Let's show you all this once more.'

As she watched Luke, Eveleen felt a growing excitement. She could do this. She knew she could. Until this moment, she had worried that she might not be able to carry out all the tasks of an apprentice twisthand. The machines were heavy to operate. But Eveleen was strong and now she knew she could do it.

Luke stood back. 'Now then, let's see you have a go.'

As she stepped forward and laid her hands on the levers, Eveleen felt a thrill run through her such as she had never felt in her life before. At her fingertips she had a new skill, a skill that could earn her good money.

A few minutes later, Luke said, 'Well, you're shaping up better this morning. Mind you keep it up.'

Eveleen did not turn round, did not even answer him. Her whole concentration was on this wonderful machine; she was fascinated to see how the threads twisted into a pattern as delicate as a spider's web.

As she walked out of the factory gates again that night, Eveleen wanted to skip with joy. She had loved every minute of the day and the final cherry on the cake had come only a few moments ago when Luke had said, 'You've done much better today. Why you couldn't work like that before beats me.' And he had gone away shaking his head at the callowness of youth.

Eveleen had hidden her smile. The following morning and every morning after that, she knew she would not need to ask for his help any more. Already she knew exactly what was expected of her. Except perhaps when new work was given to them, but then he would expect Jimmy to have asked to be shown how to do it too.

As she walked along, she pushed her hands into the pockets of the trousers that had once been Jimmy's and tried to adopt his swaggering walk. She even tried to whistle, but that was going to need more practice.

'Jimmy!' She heard the familiar voice calling behind her and stopped. It had been bound to happen. There she was, she thought, congratulating herself that she'd pulled it off. She had been jubilant, but her celebrations had been premature. Now she was going to be found out. This was one of the people she had most feared meeting.

With a sigh of resignation she turned to see Josh Carpenter hurrying towards her as fast as he was able. His size made him walk with a rolling gait like a sailor on board a ship. Wheezing with the effort, he reached her and panted, 'Jimmy. Glad I've caught you. Where's your sister today? Not ill, is she?'

Eveleen felt a stab of guilt for her deceit when she saw the genuine concern in the man's eyes. Just in time she remembered not to lick her dry lips. It was not a habit of Jimmy's. She dropped her voice a tone lower and tried to speak in the offhand way that he would have done.

'Aw sorry, I was supposed to come and tell you. I forgot.' It was so alien to her nature to act as if she were unfeeling but it was the way Jimmy would have behaved. 'She's had to go back to Flawford. The old woman's ill.'

Josh's face fell. 'I'm sorry to hear that. But she will be coming back? I'll keep her job open for her. Tell her that. Tell her I'll keep her job open for her.'

A lump rose in Eveleen's throat at the man's kindness. But his eagerness was pathetic and she knew that Jimmy would have sneered at Josh Carpenter at this moment.

Eveleen could not bring herself to do that. The new Jimmy would have to retain some of the real Jimmy's character traits, but by degrees Eveleen would act more like herself. Now, she said, 'I'll tell her, Mr Carpenter. But I think it might be a while before she's back.'

The way was cleared now for whatever might happen. If Jimmy stayed away, their grandmother could remain in her make-believe sickbed. If he came back, then Eveleen too could be said to have returned home.

As Mr Carpenter looked even more dejected, Eveleen turned away, unable to bear the look on the big, kind man's face.

'I really liked your sister,' she heard him murmur as she moved away. Eveleen swallowed. Jimmy would have laughed out loud, jeered at the man, even if it had jeopardized his job.

That was one thing that Eveleen would never do. As she walked out of the gates and turned for home, she smiled to herself. They say leopards never change their spots, she thought. Well, Jimmy Hardcastle, you certainly are doing now.

When she arrived home it was to find Fred Martin standing proudly in front of the Griswold stocking-machine sitting on the table. The once rusty piece of machinery now positively gleamed.

Eveleen opened her mouth and began to say, 'Oh Fred,' in the tone of voice that the delighted Eveleen would have used. Just in time she caught herself.

'You've made a good job of that, Fred.' Jimmy was cheeky enough to have dispensed with the polite 'Mr Martin' by now.

'Rebecca's just been telling me that your sister has had to return to Flawford. I'm sorry to hear that.'

Eveleen and Rebecca exchanged a glance. In her chair by the fire Mary glowered, but to Eveleen's relief she said nothing.

With a forced brightness, Rebecca said, 'But it's me who's going to be using this, Mr Martin. I don't know how to thank you. It means I can work at home and help out a bit now that we've lost one of the wages.'

Eveleen let out her breath. Rebecca was prepared to play along with her scheme and she suspected that Mary would too, especially if it meant that she could continue to sit idly by the fire all day long.

Well, that was going to have to change too, Eveleen promised herself as she gave a brief nod towards Fred Martin, turned and headed for the stairs, leaving Rebecca to express the effusive thanks that once Eveleen would have done.

After a hurried supper, which Rebecca was anxious to have cleared away, the girl sat down at the table with the restored machine in front of her.

'Mr Martin's even brought me some yarn to get me started. Isn't he kind?'

'A lot of people have been very kind to us since we arrived in Nottingham,' Eveleen murmured and Rebecca looked up.

'Kinder than we were to you when you came to us, eh?'

'Oh I didn't mean that,' Eveleen said at once.

Rebecca sighed. 'But it's true, Evie. I know it is and I'm ashamed that I didn't do more to make you welcome.'

Eveleen sat down at the table opposite her and looked

at Rebecca. The girl had been sunk in misery since Jimmy's departure and Eveleen had despaired that she was ever going to raise her or Mary from their depression. But now, watching Rebecca as she ran her hands knowledgeably over the machine and threaded up the yarn in readiness to begin work, even at this late hour in the day, Eveleen could see that her young cousin now had a new purpose. The Griswold had restored her pride. It was something she could do and do well and she could contribute to the family's income.

'Don't tire yourself, though, will you?' Eveleen said gently to her, but forbore to add, You must think of the baby. At this moment she did not want to spoil the girl's pleasure by reminding her of her problems. She was only too happy to see a tentative smile returning to Rebecca's wan face.

Eveleen stood up and moved to the hearth to stand over her mother. It was time Mary Hardcastle started to pull herself together too.

'Now, Mam,' Eveleen began, firmly, but not unkindly. 'Rebecca's going to be busy earning a bit extra for us, so you're going to have to look after the house. And it's high time.' She reached up to the shelf at the side of the fireplace and brought down Mary's workbox holding all the bobbins for making pillow lace. She opened it and carefully lifted everything out. She moved one of the wooden chairs usually placed at the table in front of her and rested the pillow on its seat. Then she began to sort out the bobbins to try to pick up the threads of the piece of lace that her mother had started just before the tragedy of Walter's death had happened. She had worked on it spasmodically during their time at Flawford, but since their arrival in Nottingham it had lain untouched in her workbox.

She heard a gurgling sound and both she and Rebecca looked swiftly at Mary. Startled, they saw that she was leaning back in her chair, tears running down her face. But to their amazement, her tears were of laughter.

'Oh,' Mary gasped, holding her midriff as if the laughter actually hurt her. 'You don't know how funny you look sitting there, dressed as Jimmy but doing a woman's work. If he could see you now. If Jimmy could see you now.'

Eveleen and Rebecca glanced at each other and then back at Mary. And then they, too, began to laugh until their sides ached.

Thirty-Eight

After that evening when their laughter had broken the tension, everyone seemed in better spirits. Rebecca was the happiest she had been since the awful moment she had realized she was pregnant and even Mary roused herself enough to attempt a little lace-making during the day. She and Rebecca shared most of the household chores in the morning and then sat down to their stocking-making and lace-making in the afternoons.

If there was no supper on the table when Eveleen arrived home after a long day's work, she forbore to complain. She was only thankful that the atmosphere was a great deal pleasanter in the house and also that they were making productive use of their time. For the first time since her father's death, Eveleen had caught a brief glimpse of the woman her mother used to be when she had been loved and cherished by the gentle Walter Hardcastle. It gave her a glimmer of hope.

'I don't know how long you're going to be able to keep up the pretence,' Mary said. 'I'm surprised no one's twigged on to you yet.'

Eveleen had been playing the part of her brother for more than a week, and while there had been one or two moments when she thought her deception might be discovered, she had still carried it off. The hardest part was not letting her façade slip, not even for a moment, and always remembering to act as Jimmy would have done.

Already she had become a willing apprentice to Luke and had earned praise from him. 'Well, you've turned out better than I expected, lad. See what you can do when you put your mind to it?'

Eveleen had hidden her smile.

Now, she answered her mother. 'I don't think Jimmy'd been there long enough for anyone to really get to know him.'

'If you get caught, you'll be out.'

'Yes, Mam. I know that, but for the moment, it's a risk worth taking.'

'But you can't be a boy for ever, Eveleen,' Rebecca said softly. 'I mean you might meet someone nice and want to get married.' Her voice trailed away. Her future hopes and dreams were in tatters, but it didn't stop the young girl having romantic notions for someone else.

'That's the least of my worries,' Eveleen said with feeling.

Josh Carpenter rarely came to the machine room. Although he was in overall charge of the factory and answerable only to Mr Stokes, the day-to-day running of the machine shop was Mr Porter's domain. Eveleen had thought herself safe from having to speak to Josh and the only times when she feared she might encounter him were when she arrived and left each day.

So it was a surprise one morning to glance up and see him standing near by. She gave him a brief nod – as Jimmy would have done – and concentrated on her work, but her fingers were trembling. Had she been discovered? Had Josh realized just who she really was?

Josh watched her working for a few moments, then leaned towards her and shouted above the clatter. 'I don't want to stop you working, but come to my office when you knock off, will you?'

Eveleen nodded. Her heart sank and she sighed inwardly. Only just over a week in the job and she had been found out. She doubted she would be even allowed to go back to her job in the workroom with the other women. No one in the management or workforce would take kindly to her deception.

Later that day, as she stepped nervously into his office and stood facing him, she remembered to keep up the act. She stood facing him with her hands in her pockets, a resentful expression on her face. It was how Jimmy would have acted at being delayed from escaping from the place.

'Have you heard from your sister? Is she all right? When is she coming back?' Josh, far from being the imposing figure Eveleen had once thought him, now looked rather vulnerable.

'She's fine,' Eveleen said truthfully, but then the lies had to start and did not come so easily to her lips. 'But Gran's still ill. We don't know when she's coming back.'

Disappointment etched lines into the florid face. 'Oh.' He gave a great sigh that seemed to come from deep inside his huge frame. 'Do you go to see her on a Sunday?'

Jimmy would certainly not have made any such effort, so Eveleen shrugged and said evasively, 'I might.'

'If you do, give her my regards. Her job's still here for her.'

'Righto,' Eveleen said and left the office whistling through her teeth. She had been practising on the way home each night and now had Jimmy's whistle almost perfect. But once outside the factory gates, she ceased her merry tune. She didn't feel in the least merry tonight, even though she was relieved that the reason Josh had wanted to see her had not been what she had feared.

She had mixed feelings about Josh's obvious interest in her as Eveleen. She wasn't sure whether she was completely comfortable about it. Surely a man of his age – he was old enough to be her father – could not be interested in her romantically? Surely he couldn't imagine . . . In a world where his position isolated him anyway and where his size made him a figure of fun for cruel, unthinking people, she had been nice to him, polite to him. Like a flower thirsting for water, he had soaked up her kindness.

I could write to him, she thought. I could write and thank him for getting us the Griswold and for his kind messages. Then 'Jimmy' could bring it into him next Monday morning as if he had seen me on the Sunday.

She felt so sorry for the man. Surely that couldn't do any harm. Besides, Eveleen wasn't even here, at least, not that he knew.

So, after chapel on the Sunday evening, Eveleen sat down to compose her letter. It had been at Rebecca's surprising insistence that they still attended Chapel.

'It's so much a part of my life,' she had said simply. 'I have to go. I *need* to go.' So Eveleen had gone along with her and had found some solace for herself in the services conducted by a young preacher who was far less fiery than the minister in Ranters' Row.

Now, as she sat down to write, Eveleen thought, At least I don't have to pretend for a few moments. At least I am writing this as myself.

Dear Mr Carpenter, she wrote. *Jimmy tells me that you have been asking most kindly after me, for which I thank you.* She hesitated to write anything about her

Gran. Suddenly, she felt overcome with a strong sense of superstition. What if by acting out her grandmother's illness, she made it become a reality? Was she tempting Fate? Then Eveleen shook herself and put such fanciful notions out of her head. *I can't say when I'll be back so if you have to let my job go, I shall understand.* As the days passed, Eveleen was increasingly sure that Jimmy would not come home. And she wanted to try to be as fair as she could to Mr Carpenter. She was deceiving him enough already, her guilty conscience reminded her.

I also want to thank you so much, she went on, *for getting us the stocking-machine. I hear that Mr Martin has finished repairing it and Rebecca is thrilled. She is making stockings faster than we can find people to buy them. With many thanks, yours sincerely, Eveleen Hardcastle.*

She read the letter through three times before she was satisfied that she had not made any glaring mistakes.

She folded the paper into four and wrote on the outside *Mr Carpenter – Personal* and then laid it on the table for 'Jimmy' to deliver the following morning.

Thirty-Nine

It was not Josh Carpenter who caused Eveleen any awkward moments the following day, but Richard Stokes.

Brinsley Stokes and his son, making their daily rounds through the factory, passed close to where Eveleen was working. Glancing up she saw them approaching and, fascinated to see the man who had once been her mother's lover close to, she stared at Mr Stokes senior. He did not appear to notice her scrutiny, but the son paused by her machine, a slight frown of puzzlement creasing his forehead. So intent had been her concentration upon the father that when Richard spoke to her she jumped.

'You're new here, aren't you? How long have you been here?'

'Couple of weeks, mister,' she said in the offhand way her brother would have answered.

The young man was still frowning. Close to, he was even handsomer than she had thought him the day she had seen him in the women's workroom. His hair was like jet, smooth and shining. His skin was dark, his jawline was strong and clearly defined. His thick black eyebrows were a gentle arch, but it was his dark brown eyes, so like her own, that caught and held her attention. He smiled at her now and the tanned skin around his eyes wrinkled endearingly with laughter lines.

'You seem familiar,' he murmured. 'Have I seen you before?'

Eveleen's heart was in her mouth. He knew her. He recognized her from the workroom and now she was about to be unmasked.

She manufactured a shrug. 'Dunno,' she muttered. 'You might have.' Then, a little belligerently, she added, 'I've been stood here for the past two weeks at this machine and you come every day.'

'Mm,' he said, seeming to accept her reasoning, but his thoughtful gaze was still upon her. 'Possibly.' His frown deepened. 'But there's something about you. You look . . .' Then he appeared to shake himself and laughed. 'I must be imagining it. For a moment, I thought . . .' He laughed again and added, 'Oh well, never mind what I thought.'

As he moved away, Eveleen's heart was hammering so loudly inside her chest she thought that he must hear it even above the noise of the machinery around them. She could easily guess what had been in his mind. He thought that the young lad standing at the lace-making machine was remarkably like a girl he had seen in the women's workroom.

Well, I am, Eveleen reminded herself. I mean, I am even if it really was Jimmy standing here. But somehow she had the uncomfortable feeling that Richard Stokes had seen something more than just the likeness that had always been between the brother and sister. He had looked so deeply into her eyes that the depths of her soul had trembled.

He was very good-looking. *Nice* looking, she thought, not just handsome. He's got kind eyes – warm brown eyes, not cold blue ones. Then she reminded herself sharply that she had better concentrate on her work. She didn't want to slip back into Jimmy's ways and lose Luke's respect. It had been hard enough to earn after

Jimmy's careless start. One more mistake and she could be out of a job.

Besides, she reminded herself fiercely, she wanted nothing to do with handsome young men. But the girl inside the boy's outward appearance was startled by the sudden stab of disappointment she felt that Richard Stokes could no longer see her as a woman.

He came again the following day and the day after that. And always he paused beside her workplace, allowing his father to move ahead out of earshot while he spoke to her.

On the third day, he was smiling broadly as he approached her.

'Now I know why I thought you seemed familiar,' he said at once. 'Mr Carpenter has just been telling me about your sister in the workroom. I saw her in there a week or two back.' He winked conspiratorially and leaned closer. 'Such a pretty girl. Marvellous hair.'

Eveleen tried to adopt the expression that she knew would have been on Jimmy's face. A slightly sneering, disbelieving look. Never in a million years would Jimmy have acknowledged that his sister was remotely nice-looking, never mind pretty!

Eveleen shrugged and said gruffly, 'She's all right, I suppose. Got a temper on her, though.'

'Mm.' Richard was looking keenly at her. Even now Eveleen had the uncomfortable feeling that somehow he was disbelieving the evidence in front of his eyes. 'Well, perhaps she has reason,' he said in softer tones, so that, above the noise, Eveleen did not hear his words. Working in the machine shop, however, she was fast becoming adept at lip-reading and so guessed what he had said. In reply, she gave the nonchalant laugh of her brother.

Richard was leaning closer again. 'When you see her, give her my best wishes and tell her I hope your grandmother will soon be well enough for her to return to us.' He nodded, stepped back and then moved away, walking down the aisle between the rows of machines with an easy grace.

Despite her vow to have nothing to do with handsome young men and the impulsive and dramatic change in her persona, Eveleen began to look forward to Richard's visits to the factory each day. He would smile and nod to her though he would not always stop to speak. Often Eveleen was too busy to pause in her work, but she was always very aware of his nearness.

Against her will, she began to watch the doorway for his arrival, and more than once was reprimanded by Luke for inattention.

'You're slipping back into your bad ways,' he grumbled. 'I'll have to tell Bob Porter about you if you don't buck your ideas up. I've my own job to think about, y'know.'

'I'm sorry,' Eveleen said, uncharacteristically as Jimmy. Luke cast a sideways glance at her and Eveleen could have kicked herself, not only for her inattention at her work but for allowing herself to think about Richard Stokes.

For the remainder of that week she refused to glance at him when he paused at the end of the long machine.

But always, even without looking up, she was acutely conscious of his presence.

*

A week later it was Richard who caused her to make her most disastrous mistake yet – even by Jimmy's standards. It was ironic that she had been so intent upon her work that she had not seen him enter the machine shop and was unaware of him until she felt him touch her shoulder.

She jumped physically and, to her chagrin, gave a girlish gasp. But Richard was smiling and mouthing the words, 'How's your sister? Any news?'

Eveleen shook her head and Richard shrugged, raised his hand in acknowledgement and moved away.

Her gaze followed him.

Suddenly she felt a clout across the back of her head that sent her reeling and she fell to her knees in the aisle between the rows of machines.

Luke was standing over her, his face purple with rage and roaring at the top of his voice above the noise.

'Look what you've done.'

Eveleen scrambled up. To her horror a thread had broken and she had failed to notice it. Now a flaw was running the length of the fabric.

'That's it, I've had enough of you. I'm telling Bob Porter to fire you. I thought you'd mended your ways, but the first few days you were here I had my doubts about you. Seems I was right all along.'

Eveleen felt her face grow crimson as Luke's tirade continued. There was nothing she could do to prevent the girlish blush.

'You've had enough chances now,' the man went on waving his fist in her face. 'You're out.'

'Hold on a minute,' a voice spoke behind them and they both turned to see Josh Carpenter standing there, a letter in his hand. 'What's going on?'

'It's this young lad. He's useless.'

'But you told me only last Friday that he was shaping

up much better.' Josh glanced worriedly from one to the other. 'My office when your shift ends – both of you.'

He turned away, still carrying the letter, which, Eveleen was sure, had been another addressed to her.

She turned to Luke unable to stop tears glimmering in her eyes. 'I'll put it right, I promise.'

'Pigs might fly,' he grunted. 'Well, I'm not letting my work go to the inspection room like that. They'll likely try to get my pay docked.'

'I'll mend it. I—'

Luke shot her a strange glance. 'That's women's work. Know someone who'll do it for you, do you?'

Eveleen bit her lip but did not answer. Even if she risked revealing her identity she intended to repair the long mend, as they called the flaw.

When the length of lace came off the machine, Eveleen bundled it up and, at the end of her shift, carried it with her as she and Luke Manning walked side by side to Josh Carpenter's office.

'So, what's all the trouble?' Josh was frowning, his face even redder than usual as he mopped at his brow with a large, greyish handkerchief.

'No trouble, sir,' Luke said smoothly. 'Not now.'

'Well, what was the trouble then? Come on, I want to know. I saw you clout this young lad. You're not the sort to do that, Luke, without good reason. I know that.'

Although she kept her voice gruff and resentful, Eveleen could no longer stay totally in Jimmy's character. She liked Luke and it had been her foolishness that had caused the problem.

Damn and blast all handsome young men, she thought, including Richard Stokes.

'It was my fault, Mr Carpenter. A thread broke and I

didn't notice it.' She indicated the fabric she was carrying. 'But I'll get it mended.'

For a moment, Josh's jowls sagged sorrowfully. 'If your sister were here, lad, she'd mend it.' He glanced up at Luke. 'Lovely worker, she is.'

'Aye, well, we all mek mistakes. And if he can get it mended . . .' Luke, his anger gone, was now prepared to champion his young apprentice.

Josh leant back in his chair and linked his podgy fingers across his belly. 'So you're prepared to give him another chance.' Josh's tone seemed to Eveleen to be more of a statement than a question. Luke must have noticed it too, for he said deferentially, 'If you think I should, sir.'

Josh looked sternly at Eveleen. 'As long as you'll be more careful in future and keep your mind on your work, lad.'

'Yes, sir,' Eveleen whispered. 'Thank you, sir.'

Josh leant forward again. 'That'll be all, Luke, thank you.'

As Eveleen turned to leave too, Josh said, 'A moment, lad, if you please.'

When Luke had left the office, Josh handed the letter across his desk. 'Take this to your sister when you see her again, will you?'

Eveleen merely nodded as she took the envelope. She could not, at this moment, trust herself to speak. So guilty did she feel that she was on the verge of breaking down and confessing her deception.

As she escaped into the passage outside, she found Luke was waiting for her. 'Looks like you've got a champion, boy.' His tone was friendly again, his earlier anger forgotten, but as he put his hand on Eveleen's shoulder and walked alongside her out of the factory, he said, 'Or is it your sister that old bugger's interested in, eh?' When Eveleen did not reply – she did not know what to say – Luke dropped his hand and added, 'Well, just you tell that lass of yours to mind herself with him. See you tomorrow, bright and early.'

Eveleen nodded. 'Thanks, Mr Manning.'

Again, just briefly, there was a strange look in his eyes as he said, with a veiled warning, 'And no more chatting when we have – er – visitors round the factory, eh?'

Eveleen's heart skipped a beat. It was obvious that Richard's attentions had not gone unnoticed. At once Eveleen said, 'Mr Richard was asking me about me sister an' all.' Feigning resentment, she added, 'Can't think why.'

Now Luke laughed and there was a look of relief in his eyes. 'From what I've heard, your sister's a very pretty girl. Can't say I've seen her but it sounds as if I've missed something if even Mr Richard's asking after her welfare. She must be summat special.'

They had reached the gates and Luke turned in the opposite direction to the way Eveleen went.

Still chuckling, Luke shouted, 'Tarr-ra,' leaving Eveleen standing very still, staring after him.

His remarks had left her with a warm glow and, despite her resolve, the image of Richard Stokes's handsome face was in her mind's eye.

Forty

There was little privacy in the house in Foundry Yard so Eveleen waited until her mother and Rebecca had gone upstairs before she pulled the letter from her pocket and opened it.

Dear Eveleen, Josh had written in forward sloping script. *I am sorry that your grandmother's illness keeps you from us. We miss your lovely smile.* Eveleen drew in a sharp breath. The word '*We*' had obviously been altered from '*I* ' and all that the single letter implied.

'Oh no,' she groaned aloud to the dying embers in the grate and the soft lamplight. 'Don't say they're right and he really has got a thing for me?'

She sighed. Was there no man who would be a true friend? Young or old, handsome or ugly? Were they all just after the one thing? Perhaps she was being naïve. Perhaps there was no such thing as a true friendship between the sexes.

She read on. *Don't worry about your job. There'll always be room for a good worker like you in our workroom. Your brother is shaping up very nicely now, Luke tells me. Maybe with you being away, a bit of responsibility is good for him. Although I hope that part of it doesn't last for too long. I am so glad the Griswold is proving useful. I might be able to help with the selling of the socks. Tell your brother to bring some to show me and I'll see what I can do. Take care of yourself and hurry back. With kind regards, Josh.*

The letter was innocent enough, she supposed, but then she gave an involuntary shudder. If it had fallen into the wrong hands, there was enough in the words to hint at something more. What factory manager, Eveleen asked herself candidly, writes to a lowly girl worker from the inspection room?

They don't, was her honest answer.

She sat there until the embers had grown cold. By the time she rose from the chair and went up the stairs she had decided that she would not reply to Josh's letter, but then she caught sight of the pile of socks that Rebecca had made waiting for a buyer. Eveleen bit her lip. Just one more letter to thank him, she promised herself, and, as Jimmy, she would take some samples for Josh to see. After that, no more letters. As Jimmy, she might have to fend off his enquiries about Eveleen, but surely when she did not reply to any future correspondence from him and did not return to work, Josh would eventually forget about her.

As she slid quietly into the bed she shared with her mother, Eveleen could not prevent a stab of disappointment as she realized the full extent of the charade she had undertaken.

Never again could she talk to a man, any man, as a pretty, lively young girl.

The pattern went on much the same for the next two weeks. Even though Josh answered her second letter immediately, this time Eveleen did not write back. She was managing to concentrate on her work, although she was intensely aware of his nearness whenever Richard

Stokes was standing in the aisle close by her. And almost daily Josh would waylay her on her way into or out of the factory.

'I've found an outlet for your cousin's socks and stockings. Bring 'em all in tomorrow.'

'Right,' Eveleen said. 'Ta.'

And then, as he always did, Josh asked, 'How is your sister? Any news?'

Towards the end of the second week, as the shift ended, Josh handed her another letter as she was leaving.

'Take this to your sister. You'll be seeing her on Sunday?'

'I dunno,' she answered gruffly and shrugged.

'Then tell me the address and I'll post it,' Josh said, his fingers closing again on the letter as if to retrieve it from her grasp.

'No,' Eveleen said swiftly, suddenly afraid. If letters started arriving in Ranters' Row addressed to her from a strange man, her uncle's view that she and all her family were destined for hell and damnation would be justified in his eyes.

'I'll take it to her,' she said brusquely, snatching it back from his reaching fingers. She pushed it into the depths of her pocket, crumpling the offending letter carelessly.

Why, oh why, she asked silently, did he have to go on writing to her? It's your own fault, a small voice inside her head answered. You shouldn't have encouraged him. You should never have replied to his letter in the first place. You should have killed this before it even started.

Several men passing by had witnessed Josh handing the letter to her but Eveleen walked out boldly with the rest of the workers. To try to avoid them, to linger behind until they'd all left, would look even more suspicious. So, pushing her hands into her pockets, she walked jauntily out of the gates and set off for home.

They were waiting for her round the corner at the end of the street. A gang of lads and one or two of the older men from the machine shop.

'Here he comes. Carpenter's little darling.'

'We knew the old bugger liked the lasses, didn't know he had a liking for lads,' one of the older men leered, pretending to give a shudder as if the mere thought offended him. 'What's he put in the letter, eh? Asking you to meet him down a dark alley, is he?'

Eveleen glanced at him out of the corner of her eyes. 'The letter is for me sister . . .' She couldn't stop herself hesitating pointedly before she added with heavy sarcasm, 'sir.'

'Oh aye, I'll believe you. Thousands wouldn't.' His eyes narrowed as he added, 'But who do you like, boy? Carpenter or young Stokes?' He prodded his finger at her. 'I saw you eyeing the boss's son. Well, you're barking up the wrong tree there, son. He'll be earmarked for some society girl, you can bet your last 'apenny on that.'

Forgetting for a moment just who she was supposed to be, Eveleen felt the tears prickle at the back of her eyelids. She bit hard down on her lower lip. Her deception was bringing more ridicule to Josh. Was that the way to repay the man's kindness?

They encircled Eveleen, calling her filthy names and punching her so that she was pushed from one side of the circle to the other, then to and fro until she fell to the ground on her hands and knees.

She was sick with fear, terrified of what they meant to do to her. But she was trapped. They were all around her. There was no escape and no friendly face. They stood over her, leering down at her, jeering at her.

One of the young men straddled her back, as if to ride her like a horse. Holding her, he pushed his hand into her pocket and pulled out the letter. 'Let's see old Carpenter's love letter.'

Still, sitting astride her, his weight crushing her, he ripped open the letter and held it aloft.

'*Dear Eveleen.*'

All around there were whistles and ribald remarks. 'Oho, is that your name, ducky, when you're not at work?'

'No, it is his sister's name,' another spoke up, for the first time with a word in her defence.

'I bet there ain't no sister,' the young man still sitting on her back sneered.

'No, no, there is. She used to work in the warehouse.'

But the lad on Eveleen's back was not listening. '*Dear Eveleen,*' he went on. '*I was disappointed not to hear from you again.*' There were loud jeers around her and, straining not to give way beneath the lad's weight, Eveleen caught the sob that rose in her throat. '*Please write back and let me know how you are faring. Your friend, Josh.*'

'Oho, *your friend.*' He caught hold of Eveleen's short hair and jerked her head upwards. He stood up and hauled her to her feet. 'Well, let's have a look at just what it is that old Carpenter likes.'

'I tell you, it's not him, it's his sister Carpenter's after.' But the lone voice of protest was shouted down.

They crowded closer with willing, eager hands to grab her and wrench off her jacket.

Eveleen began to scream but they only laughed.

'He screams like a girl,' someone said, still unaware that he spoke the truth.

They pulled the braces from her shoulders and while

one man holding her lifted her off her feet, others yanked at her trousers. Eveleen kicked out and caught one of them in the face with her boot. He cried out and stepped back, holding his cheek. Then, swearing at her, he lunged at her and tore off her shirt.

'Come on, let's finish the job. Let's make him walk home naked through the streets. That'll teach him.'

Though she struggled she was powerless against their number. They ripped off the man's vest and long johns she was wearing and then there was a sudden silence. They stood back and the man holding her set her on the ground.

'My God. He's – she's a girl.'

Eveleen stood, her head bowed, tears coursing down her face, trying to cover herself with her arms. Then a sudden spurt of anger made her lift her head to face them all. She dropped her arms and, shamelessly, stood naked before them.

'Aye, come on, take a good look, 'cos that's all you're going to get.'

They were shuffling uneasily now. One or two picked up the items of clothing and handed them back to her, sheepish and embarrassed. They were trying not to look at her and yet, being healthy, lusty men, they could not stop themselves looking upon the young, firm and shapely body of the girl.

Eveleen, her anger driving out her embarrassment, pulled on her clothes. 'There, seen enough, have you?'

They parted the circle and allowed her to walk out of it, but then one of the younger men said, 'Hey, wait a minute. Do you mean to say you've been posing as a lad to get work in our machine shop?'

Eveleen turned to face him. Now her secret was out, there was nothing more to lose. The following morning even Josh Carpenter would not stand up for her. Not this time.

She held up her head proudly. 'Yes. My brother, Jimmy, did start work on that machine but then ran away to sea. I was working with the women, but the pay's rubbish. So I took his place. I needed the money.'

'We've all got families to support,' someone muttered. 'You're taking a man's place. A man who needs a job.'

'I needed the job.' She glared round at them. 'I've my mother and the girl my dear brother's left pregnant to support.'

There was grumbling among them until one of the older men spoke up. 'We don't mean to be hard on you, love. In a way, I admire you for what you've done. Those machines aren't easy to operate and from what Luke was saying, you're coming on a treat now even though you weren't much good to start with.' He glanced round at the others and grinned suddenly. 'That explains it. She must be a better worker than ever her brother was.' Then his face sobered. 'But it's not fair on the rest of us. If we let you carry on, there's no telling where it'll lead.'

'Aye, we'll have women taking over. Taking all our jobs.'

The first man, who seemed to have appointed himself as spokesman, spread his hands apologetically. 'So you see, we can't let you stay, even if we wanted to.'

A lump in her throat, Eveleen nodded. 'I know,' she said huskily and turned away before they should see the tears in her eyes.

'We'll put in a good word for you, love,' one of the older men shouted after her. 'See if Carpenter will give you your old job back.'

'Or mebbe you could work as a winder,' someone else suggested.

'We'll ask Carpenter not to sack you, love.'

Not trusting herself to speak, Eveleen glanced back over her shoulder and raised her hand in acknowledgement.

Not until she arrived home did she allow the tears to fall.

Forty-One

'I told you it wouldn't work. I said you'd get caught.'

Mary was triumphant that her pessimism had been proved right.

Rebecca put her arm about Eveleen's shoulders. 'Don't cry, Evie. You'll get work somewhere else. There's plenty of other factories round here. Or you can work at home with us.'

Eveleen did not answer. She didn't want to hurt the girl's feelings by saying that while their money was very useful, even necessary, the bit that homeworkers brought in, even three of them, would not be enough to support the household. And very soon Rebecca would have a baby to care for and even less time to work.

'If you hadn't driven my Jimmy away,' Mary said resentfully. 'None of this would have happened. In fact, if you—'

Eveleen's patience gave way and she snapped, 'Yes, yes, I know. It's all my fault. Everything that's happened is my fault.'

Mary wagged her finger at her, seeming for a brief moment more like the mother Eveleen remembered. 'Don't you back answer me, miss.'

'I'm sorry, Mam,' Eveleen said, as the fight drained out of her. She took a deep breath and tried to concentrate on their current problem. 'Maybe if I can get a job like I had before in the women's workshop and then work at home at night too, it wouldn't be far short of the pay I was getting at the machine.'

'You can't work the clock round, Evie,' Rebecca said gently. 'You'll make yourself ill. Why don't you go and see that nice man you mentioned. What's his name?'

'Mr Carpenter.'

'Yes. Him. Maybe he will help you.'

Eveleen shook her head. 'Not this time,' she said sadly and then, thinking aloud, added, 'It's a pity, though. I really don't want to leave Reckitt and Stokes. They're one of the best places to work around here.'

'What name did you say?' Mary's voice was shrill.

In an unguarded moment, Eveleen had let slip the name she had meant to keep from her mother.

'What name did you say?' Mary repeated. She was not going to let the matter drop.

'Reckitt's,' Eveleen murmured, desperately trying to divert her mother's attention.

'No, no. You said another name.'

Reluctantly Eveleen said, 'Stokes. The firm's called Reckitt and Stokes.'

She was quite unprepared for the light that shone in her mother's eyes. Eyes that had been doleful, almost lifeless, for so long. 'It's him, isn't it? It's Brinsley Stokes.'

Eveleen nodded.

Mary reached out and touched her daughter's hand. 'Have you seen him? How does he look? Tell me, Eveleen. Please.'

'He looks fine. He – he . . .' She hesitated to cause her mother further pain, yet it was better that she knew the truth. 'He visits the factory most days and he – he brings his son with him. Richard Stokes.'

'His son? He has a son?'

Eveleen nodded.

Mary sat a moment, digesting this new information. 'Of course,' she murmured, lost in her own thoughts. 'He's moved on. Got married. I should have expected that.' She sighed, accepting the fact, coming to terms with it though the knowledge brought her no pleasure. She rallied again and asked, 'You say he looked well?'

'Yes. He's very handsome. He's still got dark hair but it's grey here.' Eveleen touched her own hair just above her temples. 'It makes him look distinguished.'

A smile played around Mary's mouth and her eyes had a faraway expression. 'Oh yes, he always looked very distinguished. Tall and slim. Is he still slim? He's not run to fat, has he?' Her tone was scathing as if the very idea appalled her.

Eveleen hid her amusement and shook her head. 'No, and his son is very like him. The same looks, build, everything.'

By looking at the son, she could see the man that her mother had fallen in love with so desperately all those years ago. Now she could understand. To believe oneself loved by such a man would have been heady wine indeed.

'Mm.' Once again Mary was lost in her own thoughts, years away from the kitchen in the little back-to-back house. But to Eveleen's surprise her mother did not seem distressed. In fact the conversation seemed to have brought comfort to her.

Eveleen shook her head. Her mother was a mystery to her. She doubted she would ever understand Mary's strange mood swings if she lived to be a hundred.

'I should like to see him again,' Mary murmured. 'Just once more.'

*

The following morning Eveleen dressed in her own clothes and tied a scarf over her cropped hair. She was fearful of the interview ahead, but it had to be done. She had to face Josh Carpenter.

'How could you do it, Eveleen?' he said the moment she stepped into his office. 'How could you deceive me so?' He was red with anger and hurt pride. 'You've made a laughing stock of me.' Bitterly, had added, 'Or I should say, more of a laughing stock, because I'm that already.'

His anger was dying even now and all that was left was the hurt and sorrow. 'I really thought you liked me. Oh, I don't mean any romantic nonsense. I'm not that blind or stupid. I'm a big fat bugger and old enough to be your father. But I thought you liked me as a person. I thought you could see beyond this mound of blubber to the person underneath.'

Now that any lingering doubts were swept away by his admission of the nature of his interest in her, Eveleen was able to say genuinely, 'But I do like you, Mr Carpenter. And I'm truly sorry I deceived you. But when Jimmy went off, I was desperate. I couldn't keep the family on what I could earn in the workroom.'

'Why didn't you come and talk to me? I could have helped you.'

'Could you?' There was a challenge in her tone. 'Could you really? Could you have paid me more than you paid the other women? Could you really have employed me anywhere in this factory on better pay? As a woman?'

Josh stared at her for a moment and then dropped his gaze. 'No. You're right. I couldn't.'

'No,' Eveleen said softly, 'you couldn't. So – I had no choice.'

'But you must have realized you'd be found out eventually.'

'I had to do something.'

'Eveleen, was it all lies?'

She frowned. 'I don't understand what you mean.'

'Was it all part of the cunning plan?' The bitterness and anger were back in his tone. 'Did you write to me just to make it more plausible that Eveleen was away from home?'

Her surprise at his suggestion was so genuine that he could not fail to see it.

'I wanted to thank you for giving us the stocking-machine. Really I did. I was so very grateful. I still am. And then, when you replied, well, I didn't know what to do. Part of me wanted to keep on writing to you, but I . . .' It was her turn to be embarrassed to admit that she had feared his interest in her was more than that of a friend. She leaned towards him. 'I meant every word of what I said in those letters.'

'Right then,' he said and hastily cleared his throat. 'Well, we'll forget all about it, shall we? Only thing is,' he looked at her and smiled, 'I can't let you go back into the machine shop.'

Eveleen managed to smile. 'I didn't for one moment think you could.'

He heaved himself up from behind his desk. 'I'll take you back to the workroom. Set you to work in there again.'

'You're – you're not going to fire me?'

Josh smiled. 'You deserve it, you little minx, but no, I don't want to do that. I can understand why you did it. Besides, you're a good worker.' He winked at her. 'And I'm not in the habit of cutting off my nose to spite my face. There's just one thing though. They'll all know in there what you've been up to. You might get a bit of trouble.'

'I can stand that,' Eveleen said, determined that she would. If Josh Carpenter was on her side, she didn't care about anyone else.

He took her to the workroom and informed the woman in charge in a loud voice so that most of the other women could hear too that Eveleen Hardcastle had returned home from looking after her grandmother.

The thin woman pursed her mouth in disapproval and glared at Eveleen, but she dared to say no more than, 'Yes, Mr Carpenter.'

As she took her former place, Helen looked up. 'You've got a nerve,' she hissed. 'Expect us to welcome you back here with open arms after what you've done, do you? Well, we're not going to speak to you. Not any of us.'

Eveleen looked around her. It seemed as if everyone was looking at her. Then, one by one, they averted their eyes and carried on with their work.

There was total silence throughout the workroom.

'I've got me old job back,' Eveleen told Mary and Rebecca when she returned home that evening.

'We've been thinking about you all day,' Rebecca said, placing a hot meat and potato pie in front of her. 'We didn't know whether you were still working there or were tramping the streets looking for other work.'

Eveleen pulled a face as she sat down and picked up her knife and fork. After all the tribulations of the day, she was ravenous now. 'I would be, if the other women had their way. None of them are speaking to me.'

Rebecca gasped. 'Not even Helen? I thought she was your friend.'

Eveleen shook her head and said sadly, 'Not now, she isn't.'

It was hard to brave the hostility every day. The silence continued for three days until the women began to talk among themselves, a little at first, and before long the buzz of the workroom was back to normal. But still they excluded Eveleen.

The supervisor, never particularly friendly with anyone, now seemed to pick purposely on Eveleen. She found fault with her work and gave her the most difficult tasks to do. But the worst to bear was the averted eyes, being passed on the stairs with heads turned away. It was as if she wasn't there, as if she didn't exist.

Eveleen kept her head down and worked steadily. She didn't even look up when Brinsley Stokes and his son made their daily rounds.

It was Richard Stokes who unwittingly made matters even worse. As soon as he saw her, he wove his way between the workers and came to stand in front of her. 'I'm pleased to see you back.' His deep voice was soft and gentle and there seemed, even to Eveleen's cynical heart, to be genuine concern in his tone.

She glanced up at him briefly and murmured huskily, 'Thank you, sir.'

She swallowed painfully. He didn't know about her deception, she thought. He's acting as if he thinks I've just returned from caring for my sick grandmother. She could feel the tension around her. The disapproval of the other women seemed to come at her with the physical force of waves pounding the seashore. She bent her head over her work wishing he would go away and leave her alone.

He was bending over her now, speaking softly to her. 'I must leave you to your work, but I'll see you again.' As he moved away, she breathed a sigh of relief but once he had left the room, the taunts began.

'Oho, what's she got that the rest of us haven't, eh?'

'Lifting your skirts for him an' all, are you?'

'Dropping her trousers, more like.'

Eveleen said nothing, but her fingers trembled. She had experienced the cruelty of men, but she had never thought that women could be so spiteful.

Eveleen put up with the situation for two weeks but then, even she had had enough. One evening as their working day ended, she rose to her feet and addressed the whole room.

'I want to apologize to you all for what I did. It was nothing personal against you. A lot of you' – her glance took in Helen and one or two others sitting closest to her – 'were very kind to me when I first came here and I was very grateful.'

'You've got a funny way of showing it,' someone muttered.

'I'm not going to stand here and give you a sob story to try to win your sympathy—'

'You'll have a job,' someone else said scathingly.

Eveleen carried on. 'But I did have my reasons for what I did. And they were good reasons.'

'Aye, you wanted more money. Don't we all? You didn't stop to think of that, did you?'

Eveleen licked her lips. 'It's true, I did want more money, but not just for myself.'

Beside her, Helen slowly rose to her feet. 'She won't tell you herself, but I will.'

'No, Helen, please—' Eveleen began, but Helen held up her hand to silence her. 'They ought to know. Then they can make up their minds whether they're going to carry on treating you this way – or not.' Without even waiting for Eveleen's agreement, Helen climbed on to her chair. Now she had the undivided attention of everyone in the room. It was time to go home, but no one made a move to leave. Someone opened the door and stepped into the room, but no one looked around. No one took any notice. Even the supervisor was listening.

'A few months ago Eveleen was living on a farm in Lincolnshire. Then her father died suddenly. He was found face down in a ditch.' There was a ripple among the listeners. 'It was Eveleen who found him.' The ripple grew louder and now there was a tentative feeling of sympathy. 'They lived in a tied farmhouse and so the family were turned out of their home. They came to Flawford, to Eveleen's uncle. Jimmy, Eveleen's brother' – Helen smiled a little now – 'was a bit of a lad. He got friendly with their cousin – their *girl* cousin . . .'

Already some of the listeners were ahead of her. 'That's right,' Helen nodded. 'He got her pregnant. Her father turned them out and so they came to this district bringing their cousin with them. So now there's four people to support.' Helen ticked them off one by one on her fingers. 'Eveleen, her mother, Jimmy and Rebecca, the cousin. And there's a baby on the way. Eveleen got both her and Jimmy a job here. She worked here with us and Jimmy was in the machine shop.'

Now there was puzzlement among some of the listeners. Someone shouted from the back, 'So how come she ended up dressing up as her brother and working in there?'

'I don't know,' Helen said, looking down now at

321

Eveleen. 'That's the story as far as I know it. Will you tell us the rest yourself, Eveleen?'

'I don't want your pity,' Eveleen said, tight-lipped.

'Don't worry. You won't get it,' someone snapped. 'Just get on with it and tell us. I've got a home to go to, even if the rest of you haven't.'

'All right.' Eveleen was reluctant to tell her family's secrets to these women who had treated her so harshly, yet she knew this would be her only chance to explain. She ran her tongue over her dry lips and went on. 'I tried to persuade Jimmy to marry Rebecca. I even went back to Flawford to get my uncle's permission. She's under age. They both are. But – but then he ran away. He's gone to sea and we haven't heard a word from him since.'

The women stood quietly absorbing this information. She didn't need to say any more. They could work the rest out for themselves. With her brother's wage – the only man's wage – gone, there would not be enough to support three women and a baby.

Now they could understand, but whether they could sympathize and forgive was another matter. They shuffled their feet and murmured to each other, moving now towards the door. They would sleep on it and only by morning would they decide.

As the room emptied, Eveleen glanced at Helen as she climbed down from the chair. 'I don't know whether to smack you or hug you,' she said.

The girl grinned. 'As far as I'm concerned we'll carry on as we did before all this happened. All right?'

Eveleen nodded and said a heartfelt, 'Thanks.'

'See you tomorrow,' Helen said and moved towards the door.

Only as her gaze followed Helen across the room did

Eveleen become aware of the person who had entered the room earlier.

Richard Stokes, leaning against the wall near the door, with his arms folded and looking directly at her, must have heard every word.

Forty-Two

'Well, well, well.'

He pushed himself off the wall and came towards her, his gaze never leaving her face. He stood in front of her and looked down at her. A small, amused smile played at the corners of his mouth and then widened so that his eyes sparkled and the laughter lines deepened. 'I can't tell you,' he said very softly so that she had to strain to hear the words, 'how glad I am to discover that you are – and have been all along – Eveleen.'

'I am sorry for the trouble I've caused. Mr Josh has given me another chance and I promise it won't happen again.' She spoke stiffly, already on her guard against this handsome man standing so close to her and looking at her so intently.

Richard Stokes shrugged. 'I wouldn't mind if it did. Just,' he added impishly, 'so long as I know that underneath those dreadful boy's clothes you really are Eveleen.' His gaze was roaming over her now. 'The only thing that's a real shame,' he murmured, 'is that you've cut off that glorious hair.'

Eveleen stiffened. Why did he have to start to get personal, almost flirtatious? Why couldn't a young man just be friendly without . . . ? Eveleen sighed inwardly but her guard against his flattery went a little higher.

'I must go,' she said, just short of sounding curt.

She side-stepped to go around him towards the door,

but he put out his hand to touch her arm. He did not take hold of her but his gesture was meant to delay her. He was still looking at her earnestly, his dark brown eyes now filled with concern. 'It's a sad story. If there's anything I can do . . .'

'I don't want your pity,' she snapped and he withdrew his hand swiftly, as if the touch of her burned him.

He gave a stiff, almost mocking, bow. 'I'm sorry. I did not mean to offend you, Miss Hardcastle.'

'I just want the chance to work hard and earn a living. If you really want to help, you could think about the pitiful wages you pay your women workers.'

With that she turned away and marched out of the room leaving him staring after her.

Her anger carried her out of the factory gates and halfway home before she sighed and groaned aloud. 'Now you've really done it. You won't even have a job to go to by the morning.'

Like her mother had always warned her, sometimes she was far too outspoken for her own good.

But the following morning she was not summoned to Josh's office and she took her place in the workroom as usual. Only this morning there was a subtle difference in the atmosphere. Helen greeted her cheerfully.

'I don't know about anybody else,' the girl said in a loud voice so that most of the other women could hear her. 'But I've decided to forgive and forget. What you did was wrong, Eveleen, but I reckon you had good reasons.'

No one else said a word, but throughout that day and the days that followed, there was a noticeable shift in the general attitude towards Eveleen. Some of the other women followed Helen's example and gradually began to include Eveleen in their conversations once more. Only a few continued to ignore her completely and refuse to speak to her. She didn't let this bother her but what did sadden her was that Josh Carpenter now seemed very careful in his treatment of her. She had little reason to go to his office so there were no chances for private conversations. Though he would nod to her when they happened to meet accidentally, there was wariness in his eyes.

Eveleen sighed inwardly. She hadn't meant to hurt the big man who had shown her such kindness. Despite the jibes from others, she had never really felt threatened by his interest in her.

But if Josh's interest in her was waning, there was one whose attentions were becoming more noticeable.

It wasn't long before Helen remarked, 'Mr Richard's coming to the workroom a lot more these days. I reckon he's sweet on you, Eveleen.'

Eveleen shuddered. Uncannily, the girl had used the very same phrase that Jimmy had used about Master Stephen Dunsmore.

The very words that had started all the trouble.

Life continued in much the same manner for the following weeks and months. Eveleen brought home her pay from the factory while Rebecca worked hard, often late into the night, at the stocking-machine. Mary helped in fits and starts. Some days she would be reasonably cheerful and would willingly contribute to what she regarded as their 'going home' fund. On other days she would be sunk in depression once more and would sit by the fire all day, lost in self-pity and sobbing because there was no word from Jimmy.

'I don't even know if he's alive or dead,' she wailed. 'Oh my baby boy.' Then she would say harshly to

Eveleen, 'It's all your fault. If you hadn't caused your poor father so much worry in the first place. And now you've driven Jimmy away. Now I've lost two sons.' On and on the tirade would continue and always ending with the same wailing plea, 'Take me home, Eveleen.'

'Get to bed, Rebecca,' Eveleen said gently late one night when the girl looked pale and wan in the lamplight. 'You look worn out and, besides, you can hardly reach the machine now for the bump.'

She was trying to make light of the situation but she was becoming increasingly concerned about Rebecca's welfare. While the girl never complained, there were dark shadows under her eyes and her cheeks were hollowed. Although her pregnancy was obviously far advanced, the rest of her body looked thin.

Rebecca heaved herself up. 'I will if you don't mind. I've got the most dreadful backache—'

'What?' Mary spoke suddenly from her chair by the fire, making both girls start. They turned to look at her. 'Backache, you say?'

'Yes, I've had it all day.'

'Hardly surprising,' Eveleen remarked. 'You're having to sit at such an unnatural position now to reach the machine.'

'It's not that,' Mary snapped. 'It's the baby. Lots of women start their labour with back pains. I did.' For a moment both girls stared at her. 'Get her upstairs, Eveleen. I'll go for Win.'

The most animated they had seen her for weeks, Mary was already reaching for her shawl hanging on a hook behind the door. 'Go on. Don't stand there all night. Get the girl upstairs else she'll be giving birth here on the hearthrug.'

Eveleen was to look back on the hours that followed as a nightmare. Win arrived only minutes after Mary's first pronouncement that Rebecca must be in labour and followed the two girls upstairs to the back bedroom.

'Plenty of hot water, Eveleen, and towels.'

Eveleen hurried downstairs at once to carry out Win's instructions, leaving the older woman to say comfortingly to the frightened young girl, 'You'll be fine, love. It's going to hurt a bit, but just think in a few hours you'll have a lovely baby in your arms.'

'I don't want it . . .' were the last words Eveleen heard Rebecca say as she left the bedroom. 'I want my father. Please – I want Father.'

As she hurried down the stairs, Eveleen made herself another impossible promise. I'll get him for you, Rebecca. I'll bring him here if it's the last thing I do.

Forty-Three

By five o'clock in the morning, Win said, 'You'll have to get a doctor, Eveleen. The poor girl's exhausted. She's so tiny. I – I can't cope with it.'

'Is there something wrong?'

Win looked helpless. 'I don't know. I'm fine at births if everything's straightforward, but . . .' She said no more but the unspoken words frightened Eveleen.

Eveleen pushed aside the thought that they could not afford the expense of a doctor and said, 'Where's the nearest?'

'Go and knock my Fred up. Tell him I said we need a doctor. He'll know then that it's urgent. He'll get one.'

It was two hours before a doctor arrived at the house. The moment he entered the bedroom, he took one look at the girl on the bed and opened his bag.

'You'd better go downstairs,' he said to Eveleen. 'Mrs Martin can assist me.' The middle-aged man with kindly, well-worn features, smiled briefly at Win. It was a face that had seen all of life's tragedies. 'We're old team-mates, aren't we? As soon as I get a message from Mrs Martin, I know I'm really needed.'

When he drew out huge forceps, Eveleen hurried away feeling sick and closing her ears to the girl's screams. She was glad of the excuse to escape, yet she would have braved it out and stayed if the doctor had needed her.

'Will she be all right?' was Mary's first, anxious question as Eveleen sat down in front of the fire beside her mother. She was shivering, but from anxiety, not the cold.

'Oh I hope so. I do hope so.' Eveleen's fervent whisper was like a prayer.

As if sensing the girl's feelings, Mary held out her hands. 'Come, kneel with me on the rug,' she said gently. 'Let's pray together.'

Eveleen gave her mother a startled glance, but then she sank to her knees. It was strange, she was thinking. While her mother flatly refused now to attend services, there must still be a deep-rooted faith in her. A faith that had been planted in her childhood and, though it might have withered, refused to die completely.

Eveleen closed her eyes and put her hands together and pictured the huge figure dressed in white sitting on his throne in the sky. His face, in her imagination, was etched with deep lines of sadness and his eyes were fathomless depths of compassion. She pictured him reaching out with a huge hand, the hand that held the world in its palm. She imagined she felt him touching her head. So vivid was the scene that she fancied she could feel his power flowing into her and seemed to hear him say, in deep comforting tones, 'Be strong, child. Be brave and strong. I am here to guide you.'

But however hard she willed herself to hear the words, the voice in her head gave her no promise that everything would be all right.

Later Eveleen made hot drinks as she and Mary sat together straining to hear sounds from upstairs.

'It's gone awfully quiet,' Eveleen said worriedly.

'At least she's not lying in a stinking ditch with only an old gypsy woman to hold her hand,' Mary murmured.

'Oh, Mam.' Eveleen reached out and took her mother's hand.

Mary said no more. Now was not the time to be dwelling on that time and its tragic outcome. 'Just so long as they both come through it this time,' she whispered.

The baby girl came into the world at eight o'clock in the morning but in the same moment the mother's life ebbed away.

When they had first heard the child's cries, Eveleen and Mary had leapt up from their chairs and clutched each other in excitement. 'It's over. Oh thank God.' But when the doctor came down the stairs, his face was grave. At once, they guessed the worst.

'I'm so very sorry.' He stood before them, weary and dishevelled. 'There was nothing I could do.' The concern, the disappointment at his failure was written in the man's eyes and in every line of his face. He glanced from Mary to Eveleen and back again. 'She – she was asking for her father. Is he not here?' He glanced around him as if looking for the man.

Not knowing the circumstances the doctor had perhaps presumed that Rebecca was Mary's daughter and Eveleen her sister.

Stunned by the news, Eveleen could only shake her head, while Mary let out a wail and covered her face with her apron. She rocked to and fro in the chair.

'The baby's strong and appears quite healthy, though I'll call back to examine her properly later today.'

'A girl,' Eveleen murmured. 'She's had a baby girl?'

The doctor nodded. 'Have you a name for her?'

Eveleen realized that they had never even discussed a

name for Rebecca's baby. She glanced down at her mother but Mary was lost in her own misery. The years fell away and she was mourning that other loss too.

Eveleen's mind was in turmoil. She couldn't think properly and yet the doctor was waiting for an answer. He seemed to want the child to have an identity before he left the house.

'Bridget,' Eveleen murmured, thinking of the old woman in the cottage – only a few miles away but separated by a deep chasm of bitterness. 'After her great-grandmother.'

The doctor nodded, satisfied. 'And the surname,' he asked gently, aware that not only was the young girl's father missing, but there had been no sign, no mention even, of the baby's father.

Eveleen had to say, 'I don't know.' Then she was obliged to say, haltingly, 'The child is my brother's, but – but they weren't married. Rebecca is . . .' Tears blinded her for a moment as she was forced to say hoarsely, '. . . was our cousin.'

'In such circumstances,' the doctor's voice was infinitely kind, 'the child takes the mother's surname. 'Unless the father is here.'

'He isn't,' Eveleen said shortly, unable to hide the resentment in her tone.

The doctor nodded understandingly but probed no further. 'In that case then, I'm afraid that the father's name cannot appear on the birth certificate.'

Eveleen flinched. The child would be registered as illegitimate and the stigma would follow her all her life.

'Shall you put her into an orphanage?' The doctor's tone was gentle but his question appalled Eveleen. Her head snapped up and she looked directly into the man's eyes. 'Oh no,' she said, determinedly. 'Never. I'll look after her. She's my responsibility now.'

Eveleen stood beside the bed and looked down at Rebecca's still and silent form. Her face was pale, but two bright spots of colour still burned in her cheeks. Eveleen picked up the girl's limp hand and held it to her cheek. It was still warm and Eveleen, though she knew it was hopeless, for a moment fancied that Rebecca was only asleep.

'Poor darling,' she whispered. She closed her eyes and held Rebecca's hand to her lips. Against the slim fingers, she promised, 'I'll look after your little one. I promise.'

Another promise made. Another burden to carry. And yet, she thought as she whispered 'goodbye' to her cousin, what else can I do?

She left the bedroom, closing the door softly behind her and stood a moment at the top of the stairs to wipe away the tears that filled her eyes. Then she took a deep breath, squared her shoulders and went downstairs.

Entering the kitchen, she found Win sitting in Mary's chair, feeding the baby.

'Where's my mother? She could be doing that.'

Win's eyes softened as she looked down at the tiny mite in her arms. 'I don't mind.' Then she cast her eyes to the ceiling. 'Your mam's gone upstairs. To the top floor, I reckon. She says she's going to sleep in the room your Jimmy had.'

Eveleen nodded but her heart sank. She had a feeling that her mother was slipping into one of her moods.

'Win, could you look after the baby for a day? I'll have to go to Flawford to see my uncle. He has to know.

Besides . . .' She bit her lip. 'I don't know what he wants to do about the funeral.' It was already late to be setting off to travel to Flawford, but Eveleen could delay no longer.

'Of course I can, mi duck. But what about your mother? Doesn't she want to look after her?'

Eveleen shook her head and her mouth tightened. 'I suspect my mother has taken to her bed for a while.' She glanced at Win, unwilling to confide all her family secrets, yet the woman had been so kind. So she told part of the truth but not all of it. 'Years ago she lost a baby and this has brought it all back.'

Win nodded sympathetically. 'I'll look after them both, love. And I'll see to poor Rebecca too.' The woman sighed and said sadly, 'I help 'em into the world and I help 'em go out of it.'

Touched by her thoughtfulness, Eveleen hugged her.

'There, there,' Win murmured, patting Eveleen's back, trying to give her some crumbs of comfort. 'Off you go. You go and do what you have to. You haven't got an easy job either, love.'

Eveleen was lucky. A carter gave her a lift part of the way and soon she was turning into the narrow street in Flawford. Her heart was beating fast as she stepped into the yard. The noise of machinery came from the workshops. That was where he would be.

As she walked towards the door leading up to the stairs to where her uncle sat at his frame, Andrew Burns was coming down.

He stopped on the bottom step and stood looking down at her. His face was in shadow, but she could feel the tension in him. 'What is it? What's happened?'

Eveleen opened her mouth to say that she must speak to her uncle first, but no sound would come. Sorrow choked her and tears filled her eyes and spilled down her cheeks.

He stepped down and came to her, holding out his arms. Sobbing, Eveleen clung to him, burying her face against his shoulder. 'Did she lose the baby?' he asked gently.

Against him Eveleen, still unable to speak, shook her head.

She felt his whole body tremble as he breathed against her ear. 'Oh no. Dear Father in Heaven, no!'

Eveleen raised her tear-stained face and drew herself gently out of his arms. 'Will you – will you go and fetch my uncle down, please?'

The young man nodded as if now he too were unable to speak. He turned and dragged himself back up the stairs.

Eveleen leant against the whitewashed wall and closed her eyes. When she opened them again, her uncle was standing at the turn in the stairs looking down on her. He came slowly down to her, his gaze fastened on her face as if he was trying to read there what the dreadful news was before she even spoke.

As she stood before him, Eveleen thought these were the hardest words she had ever had to say in her life, harder even than breaking the news to her mother about her father's death. Then there had been other people with her. Jimmy had been there and their neighbours.

Now, Eveleen faced her forbidding uncle alone.

'Uncle Harry. I'm so sorry. Rebecca, she – she's gone.'

Harry frowned and asked harshly, 'Gone? What do you mean gone? Run away?'

'No, no.' She was handling this very badly. Giving him

false hope when there was none. Then the words came out in a rush. 'No, she had the baby. A girl, but – but she had such a bad time. There was nothing the doctor could do. She – she died, Uncle Harry. This morning. Rebecca died this morning.'

The man's big frame was immobile and his expression did not alter, except perhaps that the frown deepened. He was motionless for several minutes before he said steadily, 'Thank you for telling me, Eveleen.'

Then, to Eveleen's amazement, he turned and began to climb back up the stairs to his work.

She caught hold of his arm. 'Uncle Harry. What am I to do? What do you want me to do?'

'Me?' His voice was hard, as unforgiving as ever, and his words chilled her. 'Why should it be anything to do with me?'

'She's your daughter. I thought—'

'Then you thought wrong.'

He pulled free of her grasp and clumped up the stairs. Eveleen stared after him unable to believe what she had heard. Then she blurted out, 'She was calling for you. The last words I heard her say were, "I want my father".'

He paused. He stood still for a long moment but he did not look round. Then slowly he continued his way up the stairs.

Forty-Four

Eveleen stumbled her way to her grandmother's cottage, opened the door and went in without waiting for an invitation.

Bridget was sitting in her usual chair before the fire. She glanced up at the sound and, unlike her son, read the dreadful news in Eveleen's face before she spoke. 'So one of 'em's gone then? Which? Or is it both?'

Eveleen sank down into the chair opposite and stared at her grandmother. 'He – he doesn't seem to care,' she said, still in shock at her uncle's response.

The old woman's face worked before she said, 'He cares, but he can't show it. He hides behind this unforgiving front. But underneath . . .'

Eveleen, regaining some of her senses though her uncle's attitude had left her reeling, said, 'You could have fooled me.'

'So,' Bridget was looking at her granddaughter. 'Tell me what's happened.'

Eveleen related the dreadful events of the past day and night, ending with, 'The baby's strong and healthy. We're going to baptize her Bridget.'

The old lady smiled wistfully. 'Another little Bridie,' she murmured. She lapsed once more into a perfect Irish brogue. 'Ah me dada would have been that proud, so he would.'

'Is that what they called you, Gran?'

Bridget nodded. 'Me dada always called me Bridie.' She smiled gently as she remembered but her eyes were sad and watered as she gazed into the flickering flames in the grate. 'Michael O'Hallaran,' she murmured, slipping into the Irish brogue once more, the speech of her childhood. 'The foinest Irishman that ever drew breath, so he was.' There was silence between them before she murmured, 'We should never have left Ireland.'

'Why did you?' Eveleen prompted gently, though she knew something of the story already.

Bridget sighed deeply. 'The potato failure in 'forty-five. Not one year, but four years in a row. A lot of families left then. Some went to America. We came to England. I was about nine. To London first and then, because my father got work as a hosier, we moved to this area. Later, of course, I married Alfred and I've been here ever since.'

'Your husband must have been a very clever man to have built all this from nothing.' Eveleen waved her hand briefly to encompass the cottages, the yard and the workshops.

'I don't know about "clever". He worked hard, I know that. All the hours God sent, as they say.'

There was another long silence before Eveleen, rolling the name around in her mind, then spoke it aloud. 'Bridie. I like it. That's what we'll call Rebecca's little one. Bridie.'

As she was leaving, with still nothing resolved about Rebecca's funeral, Eveleen found Andrew waiting for her by the gate.

'Did she suffer?' he asked bluntly.

Eveleen could not meet his eyes and her hesitation told him the answer. He groaned and said bitterly, 'Tell that brother of yours if I ever set eyes on him again I'll kill him.'

Eveleen pulled her shawl closely around her shoulders. 'You'll have to stand in line then, because if I ever catch up with him, I'll kill him an' all.'

'What do you mean?'

Of course, she reminded herself. Andrew didn't know. None of them here knew about Jimmy. The last time she had visited Flawford, it had been to ask for her uncle's permission for them to be married.

Gently she said, 'He ran away. The day I was here last time, when I got back, he'd gone.'

'You – you mean, he never married her?'

Eveleen shook her head.

Andrew punched his fist into the palm of his hand. 'I wish I'd known. I wish you'd told me, Eveleen. I'd have married her, if she'd've had me. I'd have given her baby my name.'

Eveleen reached out and touched his arm. The lump that seemed to have been constantly in her throat since the previous day grew. This man's love for the dead girl overwhelmed her. After her own disastrous romance, she had never thought that such an unselfish love existed in any young man.

But before her stood a young man who would have done anything for the girl he loved.

'I'm sorry, Andrew,' she said.

They stood together in silence until he said, 'What's – what's going to happen to her? Are you bringing her back here?'

Eveleen shrugged helplessly and told him of her uncle's attitude. 'I don't understand him. He won't even tell me what he wants me to do.'

'Bring her back here,' Andrew said firmly. 'Have a service in the chapel for her' – he nodded across the road – 'and have her buried in the cemetery. I'll look after her grave.'

'Are you sure? Won't my uncle . . . ?'

'Never mind about him. Do it, Eveleen. It's what Rebecca would have wanted.'

Eveleen nodded. 'She was calling for him. For her father. Her last words were of him.'

'Did she – did she ever ask about me?' The young man's decisiveness deserted him.

'Of course,' Eveleen answered quickly. Too quickly. 'When I got back last time, she wanted to know how you were.'

Andrew smiled sadly. 'Good try, Eveleen. But you don't fool me. But thanks for the lie.'

He turned away before she should see the tears that brimmed in his eyes begin to fall.

'What on earth are you spending all our savings on her funeral for?' Aroused from her lethargy, Mary now screamed at Eveleen. 'We'll never get home at this rate if you go squandering every penny we've earned.'

'Just remember who it was who earned us that little bit extra that we could put away,' Eveleen shot back. Mother and daughter glared at each other, then Mary's glance fell away.

'It should be Harry paying for it all, not us,' she muttered.

'I'd agree with you there, Mam, but since Uncle Harry wants nothing more to do with his daughter, not even her funeral, I don't have much choice.'

340

'Why are you taking her all the way back to Flawford? You don't need to do that.'

'Maybe not.' Eveleen was trying very hard to hold on to her patience. 'But Andrew says it's what Rebecca would have wanted. It's the least we can do.'

Mary shot another resentful glance at her daughter, but said no more. It was not the least they could do and they both knew it. But in their hearts both women knew it was what should be done.

'Oh have it your way then,' Mary muttered, and climbed the stairs to the top-floor room where she slammed the door as if she meant never to open it again.

Two black horses, groomed to shine in the pale sunlight, pulled the enclosed box-like hearse in which the coffin rested. High on the driving seat a man in a black coat and silk top hat held the reins and the long whip in black gloved hands. The sad little funeral party set off from the back street in the city and into the country, Eveleen driving the pony and trap she had hired behind the hearse.

'I 'spect we'll be the only ones there,' Mary grumbled. 'That lot' – she referred with scathing bitterness to the villagers of Flawford – 'won't come to a sinner's funeral.'

Mary had taken a lot of persuading to come, but Eveleen had managed it. Now she sat in the trap clutching Rebecca's tiny baby, who was warmly wrapped in a lace shawl that Win had given them.

'Andrew will be there.' Of that, Eveleen was confident. 'And what about Gran? Won't she come?'

Mary sniffed. 'Shouldn't think so. Not if Harry's not going. She wouldn't dare. She's all talk and no do, is your grandmother.'

'She might surprise you,' Eveleen said, but even she was not hopeful.

As the ponderous procession reached the village, Eveleen said, 'The place seems deserted. There's nobody about.'

'They're all staying indoors out the way so they don't have to take their hats off or bow to the coffin.' Mary's bitterness went deep, very deep, Eveleen realized sadly.

But as they turned into Ranters' Row, Eveleen gasped. The narrow street was full of people, so crowded in fact that the driver had to halt the vehicle to allow the throng to part to let them through.

Several of the women wore black bonnets and shawls and all of the men wore something black as a mark of respect. Whatever they could unearth among their own belongings, or beg or borrow from neighbours, Eveleen suspected. One or two, perhaps unable to find anything else, wore black armbands on their sleeves.

As the horses' hooves clattered on the cobbles the gathering fell silent.

'Nosy beggars,' Mary muttered as Eveleen helped her down from the trap. 'Coming to gawp and revel in some poor girl's downfall.'

Eveleen glanced about her. There didn't seem to be much revelry. One or two women held handkerchiefs to their faces and all the men had removed their hats and caps and stood, solemn-faced, with their eyes lowered. To the forefront, stood Gracie Turner, tears running down her cheeks.

As they stepped through the door of the chapel, even Mary's eyes widened in surprise. Not another villager could squeeze inside. Only the Singletons' family pew had been left empty for the chief mourners. As Eveleen, carrying the child now, and her mother moved down the aisle they could see that only one person was sitting there already. Bridget.

Men, women and even children were squashed into every pew and those who could not find a seat lined the aisle so that the bearers, Andrew among them, had difficulty in carrying the coffin to the rostrum. The door was left open so that the people who were still in the street could hear the service. It seemed that out of the whole village there was only one person missing.

Harry Singleton was not present at his daughter's funeral.

Eveleen was quite unprepared for the warmth, the sympathy and the compassion that enfolded the family. The minister was a young man whom Eveleen had not heard preach before. She was struck at once by his humanity, by the caring and forgiving attitude that was so evident in the way he conducted the funeral. As the service continued she was overwhelmed by his solicitude, and when it came to his address and he spoke with such love and concern for the dead girl that Eveleen broke down and sobbed, burying her face in the shawl wrapped around the motherless baby in her arms.

The service over, the four young men hoisted the coffin on to their shoulders and walked slowly out of the chapel and down the street. They made no move to slide the coffin back into the hearse. They would carry their sad burden on their shoulders all the way to the cemetery. With one accord the whole of the congregation fell into step behind them. As they passed by the windows of the cottages that looked out on to the street, Eveleen glanced up, straining to see beyond the glass and into the scullery of her uncle's home.

Standing well back from the window, hoping not to be seen in the shadows but caught by Eveleen's sharp eyes, Harry was watching.

Later, back in Eveleen's grandmother's house, Andrew tenderly took the baby from her arms. Holding her, he looked down into the tiny face, searching, Eveleen was sure, for a likeness to the girl he had loved so much.

'She's a pretty little thing,' he said and even managed a tremulous smile. 'I thought she'd be all red and wrinkly, being so little.'

Eveleen shook her head. 'No, she was even pretty when she was born. She's been good this morning, thank goodness, but you should hear her when she's hungry and starts to yell. She's a real little fighter.'

'Good job,' Andrew said soberly. 'She's going to need to be.'

'And there's something else she's going to need too.' Eveleen's tone was a mixture of sadness at the mother's death and bitterness at the father's desertion.

Andrew looked at her, a question in his eyes.

'We're going to have her baptized. I'm going to see the minister before we leave today. And I feel . . .' Eveleen ran her tongue over her lips. 'I think she ought to have godparents. Andrew, would you be her godfather?'

Despite the sadness of the day, Andrew's smile lit up his face. 'I'd be honoured, Eveleen. Thank you.' They seemed to Eveleen to be only the dregs of comfort yet as he looked down at the sleeping infant in his arms Andrew said again, 'Oh thank you,' as if she had given him the moon.

Forty-Five

Eveleen had not been to work since Rebecca's death. On the morning following the funeral, there was a knock at the door of their home.

'Who can that be at this hour?' she grumbled, picking up the baby who was whining. Any moment now Bridie would open her mouth wide and start to yell lustily.

Carrying the infant in her left arm, Eveleen opened the door to find herself staring into Josh Carpenter's face.

'Oh!'

Eveleen had been so preoccupied for the past few days that she had not given a thought to letting her workplace know what had happened.

'Please, come in, Mr Carpenter.' She led him into the kitchen. 'Do sit down,' she invited. 'You'll excuse me if I get on with her feed. She'll start to raise the roof any minute now.'

Josh eased his large frame into the chair at the side of the range and watched, fascinated, as Eveleen deftly juggled with the feeding bottle and tube. In a few moments the infant was sucking noisily.

Sitting opposite him, Eveleen said, 'I am so sorry. I never thought to send word. Fred Martin would have told you for me if I'd thought to ask him.'

His gaze still upon the child, Josh nodded. 'He did come to tell me that he thought you would be off work for a few days. But he was very evasive. Wouldn't tell me exactly what was the matter.' He glanced up briefly at Eveleen but then his gaze went back to the child. 'I thought you were ill, Eveleen. Of course, I should have guessed, but you never told me when the baby was expected.' He dragged his gaze away from the infant and glanced at Eveleen. 'How is the mother?' He gestured towards the child as if to say, Shouldn't she be doing that?

Eveleen was touched by his concern. He had taken the trouble to leave work and walk all the way to her home. She sighed, and when she had finished telling him the sad events of the past few days, Josh shook his head in sympathy. 'I wish I'd known what was happening, Eveleen. Maybe there is something I could have done to help.'

Eveleen hesitated and then took the plunge. 'There is something I would like your advice about.'

Josh spread his hands. 'Anything.'

She looked down at the baby. 'I just want to do everything right by her. I want to know that I'm doing everything legally. That I can be her – what do they call it – her guardian?'

'You want to adopt her?'

'I suppose so. You see, my brother is her father but his name can't be on her birth certificate because they weren't married. She's had to be registered in her mother's name. Singleton.'

'Leave it with me. I'll find out about it for you.' He frowned. 'There is just one thing. I think you're too young to adopt her yourself. It would have to be an older person. Your mother, for instance.'

Eveleen nodded.

'What's her name? Just so I've got all the facts.'

'Mary Hardcastle, now, but she was a Singleton before

she was married. Rebecca's father and my mother are brother and sister.'

Josh nodded and heaved himself up out of the chair. 'Leave it with me,' he said again. He stood a moment uncertainly, looking as if he wanted to ask something else but did not know quite how to phrase it delicately.

'I'm – er – afraid they will have stopped your pay at the factory for the time you've had off.'

'Oh yes, I understand that.' She smiled up at him. 'Just so long as I haven't lost my job altogether.'

'No, no,' he reassured her swiftly. 'Mr Richard said I was to be sure to keep it for you.'

'Mr Richard?' Eveleen was so startled she let the feeding tube slip and Bridie yelled in protest. When Eveleen had popped the teat back into the little mouth and there was a contented silence once more, Josh said, 'Oh yes. That's why I'm here this morning. Mr Richard sent me.'

'Oh,' was all a very surprised Eveleen could say.

Later that day, while the baby was sleeping, Eveleen climbed the stairs to the top floor where her mother was still sleeping in the makeshift bed that Jimmy had used.

Apart from the day of the funeral, Mary had not got out of her bed since the day after Rebecca had died.

'Why don't you come back down to our room? Win washed all the sheets yesterday. Everything . . .' Eveleen felt the familiar lump in her throat swell. It seemed to have been constantly in her throat for the past few days. She swallowed it determinedly. 'Everything's clean and . . .' She hesitated to say bluntly that all trace of the poor girl, who had given birth to her child there and then died, had been washed away.

'I'm all right here.' Her head buried beneath the covers, Mary's voice was muffled. 'Leave me alone.'

Eveleen let out an exasperated sigh and tried a different tack. 'Mam, I need to go back to work as soon as possible. You'll have to look after the baby.'

Mary burrowed even further beneath the covers so that Eveleen could hardly hear the smothered, 'I can't.'

For half an hour Eveleen begged, pleaded and finally got angry, shouting so loudly at her mother that even down two flights of stairs the baby began to wail. All to no avail. Mary flatly refused to get out of her bed.

'I don't know what to do to get her up,' Eveleen said helplessly to Win, who had arrived by the time she came back downstairs.

Picking up the baby, Win said, 'You might try setting fire to the bed.'

'Eh?' For a moment Eveleen stared at her and then she began to laugh. After the sorrow of the last week, it was good to have an excuse to laugh. Eveleen held her side and spluttered. 'Oh don't, Win. It hurts.'

The older woman chuckled. 'You go to the shops, Eveleen. I'll stay with this little treasure.'

'Would you?' Eveleen said gratefully. 'I do need a few things.' She pulled a face. 'Though how I'm to pay for them, goodness knows.'

'I can lend you—' the kindly woman began, but Eveleen held up her hand. 'Thanks, Win, but I'll manage.' She frowned and murmured, 'If only I could get back to work next week.'

She saw Win glance at her, a thoughtful expression on her face.

*

Two hours later when Eveleen stepped back through the door with her shopping, she stopped in surprise. Mary was sitting in her chair by the fire, fully dressed with her hair neatly pinned into a bun, and she was nursing the baby.

Win stood behind her chair and, unseen by Mary, winked at Eveleen above her head. 'We've got it all arranged between us. You can go back to work on Monday morning, mi duck. I'm going to bring my lace across here and between us, we'll look after the house, the baby and each other.'

Eveleen stared at her in disbelief, glanced at her mother and then looked back at Win. Later as she put her shopping away, she whispered, 'I don't know how you did it, Win, but you're a miracle worker.'

Win grimaced. 'I thought I'd gone a bit far at one point. I told her a few home truths and I don't think she liked it.' The older woman glanced shrewdly at Eveleen. 'Seems your brother was her favourite. That right?'

Eveleen nodded.

Win gave an unladylike snort. 'I thought as much. Well, I told her in no uncertain terms that you was worth ten of 'im and she was a very lucky woman that you hadn't washed yer 'ands of her a long time ago 'cos it's what she deserved.'

Eveleen gasped, startled by Win's frankness. Yet it seemed to have worked. 'I can't tell you how grateful I am,' she said.

The older woman chuckled. 'Tell you the truth, it gets very lonely some days working at home when the young 'uns are at school. I'll be glad of the company. Besides,' she added, a little sheepishly, 'I love little babies. I just can't stay away from 'em.'

'Well, thanks anyway. I do need to get back.' Eveleen held up her purse and shook it, adding, 'I've exactly one farthing left to me name.'

She didn't say any more to their neighbour but privately Eveleen thought, Hardly a sum of money that's going to get us back home to Lincolnshire.

Forty-Six

When Eveleen returned to work the following week, Helen was eager for news. 'She's had it then? Well, come on. What did she get and are they both all right? And when can I come and see the babby?'

Soberly Eveleen said, 'I thought you might have heard, with me being away from work so long.'

Now that she really looked at her, Helen saw Eveleen's sorrow. 'What's happened? Nobody's said anything.'

'She had a baby girl. She's a lovely little thing, but Rebecca died.'

'Oh no!' Helen whispered. 'I'm so sorry.'

There was a murmur of sympathy around her from the women sitting nearby. In that moment, the last vestige of resentment against Eveleen, at least among those working closest to her, died away.

'What's going to happen to the baby?'

'We're taking care of her. My mother, me . . .' She couldn't miss out the wonderful Win. 'And Win, who's been a very kind neighbour to us.'

At the look on Helen's face and her earnest, 'Oh, Eveleen, I am sorry. Me an' my big mouth.'

But Eveleen found it a relief to be able to talk to someone about the baby and now the women with whom she worked were friendly again, she chattered about the child, what she looked like and what they intended to call her.

The supervisor was standing over her. 'They want you in the office,' she said, sharply. 'I don't know who runs this place. You've been away over a week and now they're calling you out. If I had my way . . .' The woman turned away muttering and grumbling beneath her breath.

'Take no notice of the old sourpuss,' Helen whispered. 'But just you watch yourself with old man Carpenter. I reckon he's got his eye on you.'

For once the remark didn't bother Eveleen. She just grinned and said, 'Better to be an old man's darling than a young man's slave, eh?'

Helen pretended to wince as if being Josh Carpenter's darling was the worst fate she could imagine. Eveleen chuckled as she left the workroom to make her way to Josh's office. Halfway along the corridor, she was surprised to see Josh lumbering towards her.

'Eveleen, I wanted to catch you before you get to the office to explain.' He mopped his brow with his handkerchief and, breathless from hurrying, said, 'You know you asked me to find out for you about you caring for the child?'

Eveleen nodded.

'I didn't quite know how to set about it so I thought Mr Richard would be the best person to ask.' He paused a moment but when Eveleen remained silent, waiting for him to go on, he continued. 'I thought he'd know about the law, you see, or he'd certainly know someone who did. He's got friends among solicitors and people like that.'

Get on with it, Josh, Eveleen wanted to say, but steeled herself to stay silent and wait patiently.

'I gave him all the details, but he says he'd like to talk

about it to you himself. They're waiting in my office for you now.'

As she hurried away all Eveleen was thinking, her heart in her mouth, was, I hope he's not going to say I can't keep her. Oh dear Lord, please don't let him say that, she prayed to the huge figure in white sitting up there in Heaven. In her anxiety, it hadn't registered in her mind that Josh had said 'they are waiting for you', so when she reached the office, she was surprised to see not only Mr Richard sitting there, but also his father, Mr Brinsley Stokes.

The two men half rose from their seats as she stepped through the door. How polite they are, she thought, irrationally at such a moment, to get up out of their chairs for the likes of me.

'Sit down, my dear,' Mr Brinsley said. His voice was deep and his eyes were filled with concern. 'Mr Carpenter has told us something of the recent tragic events in your life.'

This was the first time Eveleen had been really close to the man who had been her mother's sweetheart and lover. This was the man who had caused her mother so much pain, who had deserted her when she had needed him the most. And, although he couldn't possibly know it, his show of kindness towards Mary's daughter now felt like a further act of betrayal to the girl.

He was more than twenty years too late.

'I'm sorry you've been troubled, sir. I thought Mr Carpenter might be able to help me. That's all. I didn't intend him to worry you with my problems.' Her hostile glance included Richard. 'Either of you.'

Father and son glanced at each other and then Mr Brinsley cleared his throat and leant towards her, resting his arms on the desk. 'But we would both like to help you, my dear. Please believe me. Now, I've asked my solicitor to find out what all the legalities are so that you can keep the child and bring her up as your own.'

'I can't afford fancy solicitor's fees.' Eveleen knew she was being unfair. The man sitting before her couldn't know who she was or even begin to guess at the reason for her rudeness.

'Don't concern yourself about the cost,' he said gently. 'We'll see to all that.'

Eveleen's chin defiantly went a little higher and there was no hint of the gratitude that should have been there in her tone. 'Thank you, sir, but I'll manage.' As long as it doesn't cost more than a farthing, she thought dryly.

Her antagonism was fuelled by Richard saying, 'I told you she'd be prickly, Father.'

Eveleen glanced at him and felt her mouth tighten. If you only knew, she thought. I could wipe that smile off your face in five seconds flat.

Brinsley cleared his throat. He shuffled some papers on Josh's desk unnecessarily and was obviously ill at ease. 'There's something I would like to ask you, my dear. I hope you don't mind?'

Eveleen knew she was in no position to refuse, so she sat there, her face like a thundercloud, while he struggled to find the right words. 'Er – the names Mr Carpenter gave us. Well, I just wanted to ask you. Er . . .' Still he did not seem able to phrase the question.

With blinding clarity, Eveleen suddenly realized what he was trying to say, but she kept silent. She took pleasure in seeing the man struggle.

'Your mother, Mary?' His dark eyes were looking directly into Eveleen's. 'Was her name really Mary Single-ton before she married?'

Eveleen nodded, watching him closely. 'Yes,' she said with deliberate emphasis on every word. 'She used to live in Flawford in Singleton's Yard in what they call Ranters' Row.'

She was quite unprepared for the effect her words had. There was such a look of longing and of loss deep in Brinsley Stokes's eyes. The colour drained from his face, leaving it ashen. His hands, still lying on the desk, trembled and he seemed, suddenly, to find difficulty in breathing.

'Father? Father, are you all right?' Richard was bending over him, his hand already on the older man's shoulder.

Brinsley waved one hand and said huskily, 'Yes, yes, I'm fine.'

He pulled in a painful deep breath and looked straight into Eveleen's wide-eyed gaze. Now it was Eveleen's turn to pull in a sharp breath. She was shocked to see unshed tears brimming in the man's eyes.

Brinsley closed his eyes and sighed. 'It must be,' he murmured more to himself than to anyone else. 'It can't be a coincidence. It must be her.'

'Oh it is, Mr Stokes.' She could not stop the words spilling out of her mouth, could not hide the years of resentment against him. 'It is the girl you deserted and left pregnant more than twenty years ago.' Bitterly, thinking of Jimmy, she added, 'It seems as if history repeats itself in our family.'

Richard's hand was still resting on his father's shoulder and she saw it tighten, but at this moment she dare not meet the younger man's eyes. She kept her hostile gaze directed solely at Brinsley Stokes.

He was staring back at her, his colourless lips slightly parted in a gasp. 'Deserted? And – pregnant? Mary was – pregnant?' His face worked, threatened to crumple as he whispered, 'You say she was expecting a child? *My* child?' Even Eveleen, determined to detest this man, to make him suffer as much as it was in her power to do so, could not fail to hear the incredulity in his tone.

All the anger and the hurt against him, and now Jimmy too, seemed to boil up inside her. 'Don't try to tell me you didn't know.' Remembering the more recent denial by her brother, she added, 'Don't you dare to say it wasn't yours.'

He was shaking his head in bewilderment. 'I didn't know about the child. I swear I didn't. But no,' he added hoarsely. 'I'm not going to deny that it's mine.'

'Oh!' That, more than anything, surprised her.

He leant on the desk and buried his face in his hands and groaned aloud.

'Father,' Richard was anxious now. He turned angry eyes towards Eveleen. 'I think you'd better leave.'

Brinsley looked up. 'No, no. I'm fine.' He patted his son's hand that still rested on his shoulder. 'Really.' Then, suddenly brighter and with renewed spirit, Brinsley began to flash questions at Eveleen. 'How is she? Is she well? And the child? Was that – is that you?'

Eveleen shook her head. 'No, she had a baby boy.' Still needing to twist the knife that she had already plunged in deep, she said, 'She gave birth to him in a ditch with only a gypsy woman to hold her hand.' Her voice flat, she added, 'The child died and my mother nearly died too.'

He was shaking his head again. 'And I never knew.' He was gazing at Eveleen as if trying to find a likeness in her features to his lost love. 'I must see her. Do you think she will see me?' The yearning in his tone was evident and against her will Eveleen found her resolve to hate him begin to crumble.

He sounded sincere. If she let herself, she could almost believe that what he said was true. That he had not known about her mother's pregnancy. But even yet she was not prepared to forgive. 'I was told you went away. That you left her.'

'I – did. My parents arranged for me to go away to London to learn other aspects of our trade. But I explained all that to Mary in a letter. I wrote to her time and again . . .' His voice faded away as realization came to them all. 'She never got the letters, did she?'

'I don't know,' Eveleen said truthfully, 'but it sounds very unlikely.'

'But what happened? Why – why did she – have to give birth in such dreadful circumstances? I don't understand.'

'Her family treated her very harshly and she ran away from home. She found work on the land, but after she lost the baby she was very ill. Then she met my father. He—' Her voice broke now in the telling. 'He was a wonderful man, who loved her dearly. She was happy with him, I think, through the years.' She stopped and there was an unspoken 'but' lying between them.

Brinsley cleared his throat and tried to speak, though she could see that he was deeply affected. 'Do you think,' he asked again, 'she would see me?'

'I don't know,' was all Eveleen could answer him. 'But I'll ask her.'

Forty-Seven

'No, no,' Mary's voice began to rise hysterically. 'No, I don't want to meet him. I – I can't.'

Eveleen stood looking down at her. Despite the protest, she thought that there was a tiny part of her mother that still longed to see Brinsley Stokes again. She had been too quick to refuse, too vehement.

'You said the other day that you wanted to see him.'

'*See* him, yes, but not to meet him. Not to have to talk to him.'

'He says, Mam, that he knew nothing about you being pregnant.'

Mary's head snapped up. 'He's lying then.' There was a pause and Eveleen saw the doubt creep into her mother's eyes. 'Isn't he?'

Eveleen sat down. 'I'm loath to admit it, but he – he seemed genuinely shocked when I told him. But you know me, Mam,' she added, 'I can't trust a man further than I can throw him.' She smiled, trying to lighten the tension with a little humour. 'And most of 'em I can't even pick up!'

A small smile flickered on Mary's mouth but it did not reach her eyes, clouded with doubt.

Eveleen leant back in the chair and gave herself a few moments' respite. The baby was quiet and she and Mary had had their supper. A few minutes' respite before she began her evening work at the stocking-machine wouldn't hurt. 'Maybe I'm wrong, Mam. Maybe there are some men you can trust.'

'You could trust your dad,' Mary murmured, gazing into the glowing coals in the range.

Eveleen closed her eyes and thought about her father. She could see his face so clearly she almost believed that if she opened her eyes he would be standing there in the room with them. He was smiling that slow smile and his eyes were twinkling with mischief, just like they had when she was being particularly stubborn.

Then the vision of him faded and a picture of Stephen Dunsmore's face thrust its way into her mind's eye. Fair hair and blue eyes that had once been bright with passion and desire had turned, overnight it seemed, so cold. The mouth that had kissed her so tenderly and whispered such promises had, in the end, uttered only lies. When his father had handed him the reins of running the estate, the power had gone to the young man's head and she was no longer 'suitable'.

Then that final insult when he had ridden by on the day of their departure. He had deliberately ignored her. She could never forgive him for that.

She dragged her thoughts resolutely away from Stephen and stood up. 'This isn't getting the work done.'

But Mary was still daydreaming. 'What does he look like now?' The wistful note in her tone made Eveleen pause and force herself to say quite truthfully, 'He's – he's a very handsome man.'

'He always was.' The longing that she had heard in Brinsley Stokes's voice was echoed now in her mother's.

'I wonder,' Mary murmured, 'if he really didn't know.'

Eveleen sighed inwardly and sat down again. This was not the time to be worrying about work. Tonight her mother's need was greater than Eveleen earning a few more coppers, precious though those pennies might be.

'I made myself believe he'd deserted me,' Mary went on. 'I clung to that thought.'

It was an odd thing to cling to, Eveleen thought. It would have seemed more natural to hold on to the belief that he had not known. Her mother's next words explained it. 'The anger kept me going, you see,' she said simply. 'If I could blame him more than I blamed myself, then I could survive.' She shook her head. 'Only my poor little baby didn't.'

It was all tangled up with her harsh upbringing, Eveleen thought. Mary had needed someone to blame. She had not been able to forgive herself for bringing supposed shame on her family nor for the death of her child. Blaming Brinsley for what she had believed had been his desertion of her had given her a focus and had eased her own conscience.

Softly Eveleen asked, 'Mam, what do you really want? Do you want to see him?'

'I . . .' Mary began. Slowly she nodded and whispered, 'But I'm so afraid.'

For a few days they let the matter rest, but Brinsley Stokes was impatient. Once more Eveleen was called to Josh Carpenter's office, much to her supervisor's annoyance, to find Brinsley pacing up and down the tiny space in front of the desk.

'Sit down, sit down,' he said his tone testy with impatience. 'Have you told her? What did she say? Will she see me?'

Eveleen remained standing and faced him squarely.

'She's like me,' she said, her tone betraying nothing. 'She doesn't quite know what to believe.'

The man continued his pacing and ran his hand distractedly through his neatly combed hair, leaving it ruffled and sticking up in all directions.

Relenting, though only a little, Eveleen said, 'Give her a little more time. Part of her wants to see you, yet she's so afraid.'

'Afraid? Of me?' The idea appalled and saddened him. 'But we loved each other. Oh I know we've married other people since and it reassures me to think that she knew happiness with your father.' He shrugged his broad shoulders. 'I've been happy with my wife. She's a lovely woman, a good woman, but . . .' He hesitated and for a moment seemed uncertain. Eveleen caught a glimpse of the young man he had once been. A little shy perhaps and diffident. So obedient to his parents that he had never questioned, had never dreamed that they would deceive him. As she stared at him struggling to find the right words, Eveleen felt some of the ice around her heart beginning to melt.

Huskily he said, 'You never quite forget your first love, Eveleen.'

'Don't you?' the ice hardened once again. 'Oh I think you can if you make yourself.'

She was close to him now, looking into his dark eyes that were so like his son's and those eyes were looking straight into hers, plumbing the depths of her soul. He shook his head slightly. 'It makes me very sad, my dear, to see such bitterness in one so young. Tell me, is it on your mother's behalf or on your own that you bear such a grudge against men? Or is it against just one man in particular?'

With a bluntness that was bordering on rudeness, Eveleen said, 'That's none of your business.' Belatedly she added a more polite, 'sir.'

But Brinsley only smiled, though his smile was sad and did not reach his eyes. 'If you ever want to talk about it,' he said quietly, 'I'm a good listener.'

'Are you? Are you really?' Eveleen burst out, all the worry and tension and bitterness flooding out of her. Before she could stop her rash tongue, she had said, 'Then it's a great pity you weren't listening twenty years ago.'

She turned and ran from the office, tears of frustration and rage blinding her. Just who did he think he was, trying to worm his way back into her mother's life after all this time?

Oh, he had a nerve. And so did his son. No doubt, she thought bitterly, he'll be just the same.

Forty-Eight

A week later Josh was waiting for her near the workers' entrance of the warehouse as Eveleen finished her shift.

He mopped his brow. 'I couldn't face the stairs, mi duck, but could I have a word?'

Eveleen smiled and said, 'Of course, Mr Carpenter.' She was aware of the whispering and tittering among the other women leaving work. With impetuous mischief, Eveleen's eyes glinted wickedly as she said to Josh, 'Come on, let's give the old biddies something to talk about.'

Boldly she stepped forward and linked her arm through his.

'Eh?' For one startled moment Josh's face was a picture, but then, realizing what she was about, he chuckled and said, 'You little minx.'

'Well,' she said as they walked side by side laughing softly. 'It'll give 'em summat to gossip about for a week. It'll make their day.'

'And mine,' Josh said gallantly, clearly enjoying the fun.

When they reached his office, he gave her hand a little pat and ushered her into the chair on the visitor's side of the desk. Then he took his own behind it, easing himself into it with a sigh of relief. 'I just wanted to tell you that Mr Richard asked me to let you know that all the legalities seem to be proceeding satisfactorily about your adoption of the little one.' He pulled a comical face and added. 'I rather think those are the solicitor's words, not Master Richard's and certainly not mine.' He laughed and his jowls wobbled.

Eveleen smiled, relieved at his words. But then she was surprised by a sudden shaft of disappointment that Richard had not sought her out to tell her the news himself. In fact, now she thought about it, neither Richard nor his father had visited the inspection room recently.

Not since the day she had run from this very office after her rash remark to Brinsley.

Haltingly, she asked now, 'Did – did Mr Richard say anything else?'

Josh wrinkled his brow thoughtfully. 'No, I don't think so.' He looked at her keenly. 'Was there something else?'

'No – no,' Eveleen said hurriedly, unwilling to confide further. The secrets of more than twenty years ago were not hers to divulge. She stood up. 'I'd better get home. Thank you for telling me.'

'Eveleen . . .' Now it was Josh who seemed a little uncertain. 'I was wondering – I mean – would you mind if I came to see the little one?'

Eveleen stared at him for a moment, but seeing genuine concern on his face, she nodded. There was something more. Deep in those kind eyes there was a haunting sadness. 'Of course you can.'

The Sunday of Bridie's christening dawned bright and clear.

'It's going to be a lovely day,' Win said as she came into the house almost before it was light. 'Fred's organized his mate to bring his pony and trap for us at eight o'clock. What time's the service?'

'After the usual service in the chapel this afternoon.'

Win tried, unsuccessfully, to hide her smile. 'How's Mr Carpenter getting there? You have asked him, I suppose?'

Josh Carpenter was now a frequent visitor to Foundry Yard. The first time he had settled himself in a chair beside the range and held out his arms to take the baby, Eveleen had stared at him open-mouthed. But she had placed Bridie in the crook of his arm and then stood back to watch him. The tiny child nestled against his soft body and gazed up into his face as if drinking in the man's features.

Josh smiled down at her. 'She's not frightened of my ugly mug, is she?'

Eveleen said nothing but watched Josh's gentleness with the tiny mite.

As he looked down at the infant in his arms, Josh said slowly, 'You might not believe it, but I was married once.' He paused and then added sadly, 'My wife died having our first child. A boy. He died too.'

Eveleen glanced at her mother who was staring, wide-eyed, at Josh, her fingers trembling against her mouth. Eveleen turned away and went into the scullery, leaving them together. If her mother wanted to confide in the big man, then that was her business.

Mary never said what had passed between them and Eveleen did not ask, but after that day, Josh came to the house once or twice a week, always bringing a little gift for the baby and sometimes a posy of flowers for Mary.

'He's making his own way there,' Eveleen said now in answer to Win's question.'

Win glanced about her and whispered. 'Is your mam all right? Is she going to go?'

Eveleen held up two crossed fingers. 'So far, yes. But you never know with my mam. This morning she might have changed her mind yet again.'

'Do you think the rest of your family will attend?'

'That's what's worrying her, I think. Part of her wants them to be there, the other part is dreading it.'

Win nodded, though she could not quite understand all that went on in this family. All she knew was that this spirited young lass, now busily feeding and dressing a tiny baby that was not even her own, had a lot on her plate.

Fred and his mate arrived promptly and everyone, including Mary, climbed up into the trap. They set off at a spanking pace in good time to travel the few miles to Flawford, a basket holding the baby's feeding paraphernalia at their feet.

'You'll need to go somewhere to feed and change her before the service, won't you?' Win said softly to Eveleen and glanced anxiously at Mary, hoping that above the noise of the wheels, she would not hear. 'Is there anyone's house you can go to?'

'When we went to the funeral, we went to my grandmother's. But today' – Eveleen looked up smiling – 'I think the godfather will oblige. He lives in one of the other cottages.'

'So,' Win said slowly, 'you're going close to your uncle's home? Right next door to Bridie's grandfather?'

Eveleen nodded 'And her great-grandmother's house.'

Win shook her head. 'I don't understand it. How anyone can hold it against a tiny mite like this, I don't know.'

With great feeling, Eveleen said, 'You don't know my Uncle Harry.'

'Maybe, after today,' Win said, determination in her tone, 'I will.'

Andrew must have been watching out for them for only seconds after the trap had drawn up outside the gates, and before they had had a chance to climb down, he was pulling open the gate and holding out his arms to take Bridie.

Eveleen saw the smile on Win's face and knew that even before he had been properly introduced, Bridie's prospective godfather had endeared himself to her.

'Come along in. Everything's ready.' He led the way to his cottage, which was between Harry's at one end and Bridget Singleton's at the other.

'Oh, Andrew!' Eveleen exclaimed as she stepped into his front parlour. Before her spread on the table in the centre of the small, cramped room were plates and plates piled high with food: sandwiches, scones and buns, dark brown squares of ginger parkin, and lacemaker's cake cut into slices and spread thickly with butter. 'You shouldn't have gone to all this trouble.'

Andrew, still carrying the baby, only grinned. 'Not every day do I get an excuse to have a party.'

'It's a grand spread, young man,' Win said and moved forward to greet him. 'I'm Win, one of Bridie's godmothers. Eveleen's the other, of course. I'm pleased to meet you.'

Andrew nodded, but keeping tight hold of the baby, did not put out his hand to take Win's. He smiled and echoed, 'Pleased to meet you. Make yourselves at home. Mrs Hardcastle, come and sit near the fire.'

The room was full of chatter and bustle as the party

all squeezed in to Andrew's front room. Now that he had welcomed everyone, Andrew sat down and gently eased open the folds of the shawl. 'Oh, but she's bonny,' he said. 'She's altered even since I last saw her.'

'They alter every day when they're little,' Win said, leaning forward to join in the admiration. 'You'll have to come over and see us as often as you can.'

'I will,' Andrew said promptly. 'I'll come on Sunday afternoons.' He glanced up at Eveleen and added, 'If that's all right with you.'

'Of course it is,' she said quietly, marvelling again at his devotion. He would come all that way every week, walking the six miles or so if necessary, just so that he could see Rebecca's baby.

There was a knock at the door and Eveleen, being the nearest, opened it.

'Mr Carpenter. You made it then? Do come in.'

The big man squeezed himself into the already crowded room. He mopped his forehead and said, 'Reckon I'll just stand by the door, Eveleen. And please, do call me Josh when we're not at work.'

Eveleen smiled and introduced him to Andrew, the only person in the room whom Josh had not met before.

Josh nodded and then craned to see the baby. 'How's the little one? Been all right on the journey, has she?'

'Good as gold,' Win said.

'Eveleen,' Andrew said. 'Do you want to make everyone a cup of tea? Everything's ready in the scullery and the kettle's boiling there on the hob. And please, everyone, help yourselves to something to eat.'

Eveleen smiled. Obviously Andrew had no intention of letting go of the baby. She pulled off her gloves and went through to the scullery.

While the adults drank tea, Eveleen prepared Bridie's bottle.

'I'll give it to her,' Andrew said. 'Just show me what to do.'

The women in the room exchanged a glance that said silently, what a wonderful husband for Rebecca and father this young man would have made. If only she had lived, there would have been some happiness for her if she had been prepared to take it.

Josh eased himself down on to a spindly-legged chair next to Mary and began a conversation. 'How are you, Mrs Hardcastle? Lovely day for a ride out into the country, isn't it?'

Eveleen, hearing his words, held her breath for a moment. That was not the best topic of conversation he could have chosen. Even though he had seen her often over the past few weeks, he probably still did not know of Mary's hankering to return to the open fields and the huge skies of Lincolnshire.

But, strangely, Mary was smiling at him. 'Oh, Mr Carpenter—'

'Josh,' he prompted gently.

Her smile widened. 'Josh, then. I wish you could see the place where we used to live. It's beautiful. My husband was head cowman for the Dunsmores and we lived in a tied farmhouse on the estate. That's why we had to leave when he died, you see.'

Josh nodded, understandingly.

'But we shall go back one day. Eveleen's promised to take me home again as soon as she can.'

Though his attention was on the child, Andrew had heard the conversation and looked up at once. 'You're leaving? You're going back to Bernby?' The disappointment was written plainly on his face and even Josh looked crestfallen too.

Eveleen pulled a comical face, trying to make light of it. 'It'll be a while yet on the wages I get.'

'Eveleen, you promised,' Mary's voice rose a little.

'Yes, Mam,' Eveleen said quietly, trying to calm her at once. 'And I'll keep that promise. One day we will go home, but it won't be for a little while yet.'

Now she was torn among those in the room. Her mother, to whom she had made a solemn vow, and the new people in their lives, who so obviously cared about them now: Andrew, Win and Fred, and even Josh Carpenter. Their feelings mattered too.

Into the silence, Eveleen said briskly, 'Time I was getting madam here ready for her big moment. Now, Andrew, unless you want to learn how to change her nappy . . .'

Andrew laughed and handed Bridie over. 'I think I'll give that a miss, if you don't mind.'

The laughter that followed lightened the tension and even Mary was smiling once more.

Just before it was time to leave for the service, Eveleen slipped out of the house and knocked on the door of her grandmother's cottage.

'Come in, come in,' came her imperious voice and Eveleen knew before she even stepped into the room what kind of welcome awaited her.

'So you've brought her bastard back to be christened, have you?'

'It's not the bairn's fault, is it, Gran?' said Eveleen quietly.

The old woman merely grunted and said, 'Well, I hope you're not expecting us to come.'

'I didn't expect Uncle Harry to, no. But I thought you might. You came to Rebecca's funeral.'

'Aye, and much good it did me. He wouldn't speak to me for a fortnight afterwards.'

'Then that's his problem.'

Bridget squinted up at her. 'Very forthright for a slip of a girl, aren't you?'

Eveleen smiled. 'Yes, I'm like you. Haven't you always said what you thought?'

'And a lot of good that's done me an' all. I'm still doing what other folks tell me to do. First, my parents, then my husband. Now I have to obey my son.'

'Why?' Eveleen countered. 'Why do you have to obey him?'

For a moment the old lady floundered. 'Because he – because he's the man. The head of the family.'

Craftily Eveleen said, 'I would have said you were the head. You're the oldest. What do they call it?' She sought in her mind for the right word. 'The matriarch of the family.' With a note of gentle pleading, she added, 'Won't you come, Gran? Please. She's your great-granddaughter.'

The old woman's face worked as she fought the inward battle, but years of obedience still remained strong. She shook her head. 'No, I can't. I'm sorry.'

From the tone of her voice, Eveleen believed her, but she returned to Andrew's cottage disappointed.

A little later as they trooped out of the house and across the road to the chapel, Eveleen glanced back to see her grandmother standing at her kitchen window, her face almost pressed to the glass. This time, however, there was no sign of her uncle skulking in the shadows watching his granddaughter being taken to her baptism.

Forty-Nine

Eveleen was amused to see that as they went to and from the chapel, Josh offered his arm to Mary, sat by her when they returned to Andrew's cottage and fetched and carried food from the table for her.

In the tiny kitchen, Win nudged Eveleen. 'I reckon your mam's found herself an admirer.'

Eveleen chuckled. 'Well, his excuse at first was that he came to see the baby, but now I wonder.' For once she was feeling relaxed, almost happy. The service had gone well, apart from the moment when the minister doused the baby with water and Bridie set up a squealing that echoed out of the chapel and into the street. Everyone had laughed and assured a flustered Eveleen that it was a good sign.

'Driving out the Devil, she is.'

Now, back at the house and surrounded by such loving, caring people, Eveleen was able, if only for a few brief hours, to lay aside her worries and enjoy the moment.

If only this day could last for ever, she found herself wishing.

'Why won't you let my father see your mother?'

The feeling of contentment had been all too brief. The following day, Eveleen found Richard waiting for her during her dinner break.

'I have asked her, and the idea upsets her.'

Richard's gentle eyes flashed with an unusual fire. 'I have my doubts that you've even told her.'

'I am not in the habit of lying,' Eveleen said loftily.

Richard's left eyebrow arched. 'Really?' he drawled. 'And you don't call impersonating your brother and deceiving us all a form of lying?'

Eveleen felt the colour suffuse her face. 'That was different. I was desperate.'

He leaned closer. 'And my father's desperate to see her again. He wants to help. He can't bear to think he caused her such misery and yet he never even knew about it.'

Now it was Eveleen's turn to doubt. 'Really?' she echoed. 'Do you honestly expect me to believe that he knew absolutely nothing about it at the time? Or did he "conveniently" not know? Surely, he must have known he might have left her pregnant?'

Richard was really angry now. 'I tell you he knew nothing. He was only nineteen, for God's sake. At that age, you still believe everything your parents tell you. You believe they know what's best.'

'Oh yes, they knew what was best for him all right. But they didn't care what happened to a slut of a girl who was daft enough to believe the sweet nothings of a young feller out for a bit of fun.'

Appalled, Richard stared at her. 'You believe that? You really believe that she meant so little to him?'

'You're all the same. You so-called gentry.' Her verbal attack was scathing. 'You'll take your fun wherever you can get it, but you'll always marry your own class.'

Now the conversation was more about the two of them than about his father and her mother.

'And you think my interest in you is just as – shallow?'

'What interest?' she snapped.

He blinked and, for a moment, was disconcerted. 'Well, I don't visit the workroom to see the other women, I can assure you, or to check up on the supervisor. Miss Brownlow does a good job.'

'You haven't been near the workroom for over two weeks.'

There was a hint of sarcasm in his tone as he said, 'So you noticed?' Eveleen felt her cheeks glow pink, but even she could not tell whether it was from embarrassment or anger. His tone was gentler as he went on. 'I've only kept away because of this business between your mother and my father. Don't you know how difficult it's been for me to stay away? How hard it's been not to see you?'

Eveleen echoed the words that her own mother had once used to her. 'What could the likes of you possibly want with the likes of me?'

He shook his head wonderingly, but his gaze never left her face. 'Eveleen Hardcastle, don't you know I'm falling in love with you? That all I want is your happiness? That I'd do anything to help you, to look after you. Yes, you and all your family. Even that reprobate of a brother of yours, wherever he is. If I could find him, I'd do my damnedest to bring him back to face his responsibilities.'

His declaration, so unexpected, shook her, but her indignant anger was so high now that she did not stop to think what she was saying. 'If you thought so much about me, you'd pay me more so I can keep my promise to my mother.'

'Promise? What promise?'

'To take her back home. Back to Bernby. That's the only place where she's ever going to be happy again. She doesn't want to be here, not with all the reminders of the past. And she doesn't like the city life. She wants to go home.'

As she turned and flung herself away from him, Richard stared after her thoughtfully.

'He's been. He's been here to see me.'

By the time Eveleen arrived home late that evening, Mary was hysterical and Bridie was shrieking. Hurrying to the makeshift cradle – the bottom drawer from a chest of drawers – she lifted the child out. The baby was soaking and red with anger.

Eveleen turned on her mother. 'Have you fed her?'

'I tell you Brinsley Stokes has been here.' Mary was wringing her hands agitatedly. 'This afternoon. How could you, Eveleen? I told you I was afraid to see him.'

Eveleen was enraged by the arrogance of the Stokes family. 'How dare he?' she muttered. For some reason she could not have explained herself her anger was directed not at the father but at the son.

As she busied herself preparing a bottle for the screaming child, Eveleen said, 'It's not my fault, Mam.'

'Of course it's your fault. It's all your fault. If you hadn't been carrying on with young Dunsmore, your father would still be alive. And if you hadn't brought us here, none of this' – she flung out her hand towards the innocent child – 'would have happened either. And I've lost my Jimmy too. My baby boy. Oh you've got a lot to answer for, Eveleen Hardcastle. I wouldn't like to be in your shoes on Judgement Day.'

Harassed and worried, Eveleen snapped, 'And I wouldn't be in your shoes in the next few minutes if you don't let me get this poor child fed and changed. Sit down, Mam, and for goodness' sake, just shut up!'

Mary sat down suddenly, so shocked she could only gasp, 'Eveleen!' As she recovered a little, she began to wail. 'You've no respect for your mother. You don't care how I've suffered. How I'm still suffering. And seeing him today brought it all back. I can't bear to stay here any longer. Eveleen,' her plea was pitiful as she said, yet again, 'take me home. Please take me home.'

Eveleen never knew what made her wake up in the middle of the night with a start. There was no sound from the cradle nor could she hear her mother's snoring from the room directly above her. Eveleen turned on her side as sleep threatened to claim her once more. Then her eyes flew open again. Suddenly she realized what had disturbed her peaceful sleep.

The house was too quiet. There was no sound of the baby's snuffling breathing or from Mary as she turned and murmured in her sleep or snored loudly, as she did when she lay on her back with her mouth wide open.

In one swift movement Eveleen had thrown back the bedclothes and put her feet to the floor. The cradle was empty, the blankets that wrapped the child gone too.

On bare feet, Eveleen rushed upstairs to the top floor. Her mother's bed was neatly made, looking as if it had not even been slept in that night.

Frantic now, Eveleen hurried down the two flights of stairs to the kitchen. The grate was cold, the room silent and empty.

Her mother and the child were nowhere in the house.

She went to the door and looked around the dark, wet yard. Rain was falling steadily and the night was black with not a glimmer of light from the moon or the stars.

'They'll be soaked through,' she muttered. 'Oh, Mam, how could you?'

Of course, she knew where they had gone. Seeing

Brinsley Stokes again had brought back all her unhappy memories. His visit must have disturbed Mary's mind so much that she had set off in the night to go home, taking the child with her. In her confused state, Rebecca's baby had become that other baby that she had lost. But Mary wasn't going to lose this one. No one was going to take this baby away from her.

'Poor Mam,' Eveleen murmured to herself as she dressed hurriedly, pulling on her warmest clothes. She was beside herself with anxiety, but she was no longer angry with her mother. The poor woman needed help and pity, not censure.

Once more, Eveleen felt the weight of guilt. She had been impatient and sharp with Mary's wailing last night when she should have been more understanding. She should have listened to her mother and comforted her and reassured her that everything would be all right. Promised her yet again that, one day, they would go back home.

But Mary had not been able to wait for that. She had set off in the dark, in the cold and the wet, with the child in her arms, to walk back home to Bernby.

Fifty

Eveleen's banging on Win's door threatened to wake the whole yard.

· A sash window above her was pushed up and Fred stuck his head out. 'Who is it?' he asked quite calmly, and then, at his next words, Eveleen understood why someone knocking on his door in the middle of the night was not an unusual occurrence for him. 'Want the missis, do you? Which is it?' he asked in a matter-of-fact manner. 'Birth or a death?'

'Fred, it's me. It's Eveleen.'

'Eveleen?' Now there was surprise in his tone. His head disappeared at once and she heard muffled voices. Only a minute later she heard the door being unlocked and opened.

'Whatever's wrong, mi duck?' said Fred, barefooted, his thin legs like sticks beneath his nightshirt. 'Is it the babby?'

'Sort of.' Breathless from running, Eveleen put her hand to her chest and leant against the wall. 'It's me mam. She's gone.'

'Eh?' the man was startled. 'What d'you mean? Died?'

'No, no,' Eveleen said swiftly, and pushed the dreadful thought aside that in this weather that eventuality was a strong possibility. And the child. Poor little Bridie out in the cold, crying with hunger.

'She's gone out and taken the baby with her. I – I think she's trying to walk home.'

'Right,' Fred said, and seemed to be thinking quickly. 'Right. Come inside, lass, and sit down while me and Win get dressed. Then I'll knock Joe up. He'll lend us his pony and trap again.'

'In the middle of the night?'

''Course he will. He's a good sort is Joe.'

The next half an hour was a flurry of activity. As they waited for Fred to return, Win asked, 'What brought this on, d'you reckon?'

'She – she's always wanted to go back home. Back to Bernby.'

'Oh I know that,' Win nodded. 'But why now? What happened to set her off in the middle of the night?'

Eveleen bit her lip. If these good people were going to help her they deserved to know the truth. The whole truth.

'It was Brinsley Stokes.'

Win's eyes widened. 'Mr Stokes? How on earth—'

Haltingly at first and then in a rush, Eveleen told Win her mother's pathetic story from the beginning right until the moment when Brinsley had found out who Mary Hardcastle really was.

'I never thought for a moment when I asked Mr Carpenter to help over my adopting Bridie that it would lead to all this. Mr Stokes came to the house yesterday to see her. When I got home she was hysterical. The baby was screaming at the top of her voice. Mam hadn't fed or changed her.'

'Oh, mi duck, I am sorry. I should have been there, but our Elsie was poorly and—'

'It's not your fault,' Eveleen said swiftly. 'If it's anybody's, it's mine. I shouldn't have snapped at her last night. I should have understood and . . .' Tears spilled down her cheeks and she covered her face with her hands. 'She's right. It is all my fault.'

'Of course, it isn't,' Win tried to reassure her, but her words brought no comfort to the wretched girl.

Fred returned with the disappointing news that Joe's pony and trap was already out on hire for the next three days. 'It's out of town an' all,' Fred reported dolefully. 'No way of getting it back quickly.'

'Who else has got a trap? Think, Fred,' Win said.

'I am, love. I am doing.'

Suddenly Eveleen sprang to her feet. Her tears dried as sudden hope spread through her. 'Josh – I mean, Mr Carpenter. He had a pony and trap the day he came out to the christening. He must have got that from somewhere.'

Fred's yes lit up. 'That's right, lass.'

'Do you know where he lives?'

Fred nodded. 'Round the corner from the factory.'

Eveleen clutched his arm. 'Oh please go and wake him up, Fred. He won't mind. I know he won't. I'll come with you.'

They hurried through the wet streets while Win stayed behind to pack food and drink into a basket and gather together warm blankets. 'Poor things'll be frozen when you find them,' she said as they left.

Eveleen bit back the words, If we find them.

It seemed an age before Josh lumbered down the stairs to answer their urgent knocking.

'What's up?' he asked before he had seen who was standing there. 'Factory on fire, is it?'

'Worse than that, Mr Carpenter,' Fred said. 'Eveleen's mother's gone off in the night.'

'Mary? Whatever for?'

'She's taken the baby with her.' Eveleen's voice rose frantically. 'Please, Josh, we need a pony and trap. Where did you get that one you came to the christening in?'

'Eh? Oh,' Josh, woken from a deep sleep, was having a hard time taking it all in quickly. 'It's Mr Stokes's. Mr Richard lent me it.'

'Oh no,' Eveleen breathed and sagged against the doorframe in disappointment. 'That's it then. There's nothing more we can do. At least till morning.'

Now Josh was fully awake and worried. 'Of course we mustn't wait until morning. If she's gone out in this lot' – he nodded at the weather – 'and with the baby. Oh poor little thing.' Then he pulled his mind back to the emergency. 'Mr Richard won't mind. He'll organize it. Even in the middle of the night. 'Specially when he knows who it is who's asking.'

The veiled reference to Richard's interest in her was not lost on Eveleen even in this moment. Grimly she said, 'It's all his fault that it's happened.'

'Why?' As Josh asked the question he was gesturing them inside and leading the way into his kitchen.

'Mr Brinsley visited my mother yesterday and I think his visit upset her so much that – that she's gone out of her mind a little.'

Josh stopped and turned to look at her. 'Mr Brinsley? Whatever would he go and see your mother for?'

So, Eveleen thought, whatever my mother had told Josh on his frequent visits to their house, she had not confided everything. She sighed. 'It's a long story, Josh. She knew Mr Brinsley years ago.'

The big man blinked and he and Fred exchanged a glance. Although Win now knew the whole story, there had been no time to enlighten Fred. 'Oh,' Josh said and then, with a kind of understanding, 'oh, I see.'

She knew he didn't. Not really. How could he? But perhaps he guessed at least a little of the truth.

Looking worried, Fred ran his hands through his hair and Josh mopped at his brow.

'We can't leave things till morning, lass,' Josh said. 'Something's got to be done. Leave it to me.'

'But—' Eveleen began to protest, but he was already lumbering towards the stairs.

'Just let me get dressed,' he said.

Fred laid a hand on her arm. 'Leave it, lass. Don't argue. He's the man to help you. Just accept it and be grateful.'

Eveleen bit her lip but said no more. She didn't mind Josh Carpenter helping, but she certainly did not want the Stokes involved. At this moment, she did not know which 'he' Fred meant.

It was only minutes before they heard Josh's heavy tread on the stairs again yet the wait had seemed like hours. Josh was wheezing as he came through the door, but he was smiling. 'Good job for us that Mr Brinsley likes to live in town. If he was the sort of man who wanted a fancy house on the outskirts of town, we'd be the rest of the night getting to his place. Now, Fred, you go and get the pony and trap from the stable at the factory and bring it up to the house.'

'Didn't we ought to ask first?' Fred asked.

Josh dismissed the necessity with a wave of his hand. 'He'll say yes, of course he will. But me and Eveleen will go to the house and tell him, just in case . . .' He did not complete the sentence but added authoritatively, 'Let's get going. The sooner we get that pony and trap the sooner we can get after them.'

While Fred hurried away towards the factory, Eveleen fell into step alongside Josh. He was in charge now and, for once, Eveleen was prepared to leave it to him.

She did not want to ask favours of the Stokes family, but she had no alternative.

Fifty-One

'How far do you think they could have got?'

They were driving through the streets. Richard, sitting on one side with Fred and Eveleen squashed on the seat beside him, held the reins, while Josh sat on the opposite side. The trap was scarcely big enough to hold the four of them, but the pony, despite the weight, was managing a good pace.

'I don't know,' Eveleen muttered. She was resentful because Richard had insisted on coming with them. 'I don't know what time she left. Her bed looked as if it hadn't been slept in. If she left soon after I went to bed, they could have been gone five hours.'

'Mm.' Richard seemed to be calculating. 'I would estimate that she would walk at about two miles an hour. It wouldn't be much quicker than that if she was carrying the child.'

'Wouldn't she stop to rest?' Josh put in, sounding as if he didn't think he would be able to walk one mile in an hour.

'Probably,' Richard said. 'Would she know the way, Eveleen?'

'I don't know. When we left home, we went to Flawford and from there, we came here.'

'Might she go back there? To Flawford?'

'No,' Eveleen snapped. 'Not in a million years.'

The three men were silent but not one of them could have failed to notice the bitterness in her tone.

More calmly Eveleen added, 'She'll be trying to get home. Back to Bernby. That's where she thinks of as home.'

'We'll take the main road out of the city towards Grantham, so let's just pray that that's what your mother has done.'

Silently, Eveleen began to pray to the kindly, white-robed figure in Heaven.

It seemed to the anxious girl as if the streets of houses were neverending but at last the buildings thinned out and they were passing through countryside.

'Now,' Richard said, 'keep a sharp look-out for any sort of place where she might have taken shelter. This rain's getting worse.'

It was driving against them now, stinging their faces, but the pony was trotting on valiantly at Richard's gentle words of encouragement.

'She'd shelter in a barn,' Eveleen said and couldn't resist adding, 'It's what she did last time.'

No one answered her, but squinted through the rain and the darkness, straining to catch sight of the woman and child.

Ahead of them the sky began to lighten and with the dawn the rain began to ease a little. Richard drew the trap to a halt.

'We must have come ten miles or more. She can't have got this far, surely?'

Josh looked anxiously about him. 'You wouldn't have thought so.'

'Do you think she might have got a lift with a carrier or on a cart of some sort?' Fred put in.

'That's a good point,' Richard said. 'What do you think, Eveleen?'

She shrugged. 'I doubt it. She doesn't like asking strangers for help.'

Richard turned away and muttered something beneath his breath but Eveleen, sitting furthest away from him, did not catch the words. Fred and Josh must have heard for she saw them exchange a look. Then Richard turned. 'So what do you all suggest we do now? Press on?'

'Yes,' Eveleen said firmly. 'But watch out for farm-houses and barns now. Bridie will be hungry . . .' There was a catch in her voice and tears welled in her eyes. Her anger and resentment against Richard Stokes died. She felt cold and wet and there was a knot of anxiety in the pit of her stomach. She covered her face with her hands and turned her head away so that they should not see her tears.

She felt Fred's arm around her shoulders. 'Hold up, lass. Hold up. We'll find them.'

Eveleen felt the trap jolt as she took a deep breath, lifted her head and said, with far more confidence than she was feeling inside, 'Of course we will. We've got to.'

They were passing the gateway into a farmyard, the house and outbuildings dark shapes against the grey sky.

'Stop a minute,' Eveleen said suddenly, and as Richard brought the vehicle to a standstill Eveleen forced her stiff limbs to climb down.

'What is it?' Josh asked, anxiety and hope in equal measure in his voice. 'Have you seen something?'

'No, but it's milking time.' If the moment had not been so serious she would have laughed at the puzzled looks the three men exchanged. She couldn't resist the temptation to say, 'Farm workers rise early. They're up and about and at work while factory workers are only thinking about it.' She gestured towards the farm. 'There'll have been someone about the yard for an hour or more. They might have seen something.'

The three men looked towards the farm and now, as they listened, they could all hear the sounds of life coming from the cowhouse.

'D'you want me to come with you?' Fred asked uncertainly. 'I will, but I don't like cows much.'

'I'll go,' Josh said and pushed himself up, rocking the trap as he climbed down. 'I've always fancied living in the country and working on the land.'

Eveleen glanced at him in surprise. 'Have you really?'

'Oh aye,' he went on as they walked towards the five-barred gate into the yard. 'When I was a little lad I came on holiday to a farm. Best holiday I ever had.' Then, despite the gravity of their mission, he laughed. 'Mind you, it was the *only* holiday I ever had.'

They reached the cowhouse and Eveleen opened the door to be met by the familiar smells of her childhood, the warm, comforting smell of the beasts and the straw that littered the floor. For a moment she stood breathing in the heady atmosphere and swayed momentarily as poignant memories of her father flooded through her.

No wonder, she thought, that her mother was so desperate to come back home. It was the only place Mary had known true love and security.

A man was walking towards them. 'What do you want? You're unsettling my beasts.' His tone was wary and held a note of warning as the cow nearest to the door where Eveleen and Josh were standing moved restlessly. It turned its head and looked at them with wide, nervous eyes.

Margaret Dickinson

Without thinking what she was doing Eveleen out of a long, inbred habit moved towards the cow and began to rub its hindquarters and croon softly in her throat. The farmer began to smile. 'Oh, so you know about cows, lass, do you? After a job, are you?'

She smiled at him, but the worry did not leave her eyes. 'Yes, mister, I do know about cows, but it's not a job I'm after at the moment. We want to ask you if you've seen anyone this morning. A woman carrying a baby.'

The man shook his head. 'No, can't say I have.' He looked at them and must have read the anxiety on their faces, for he murmured, 'Not the sort of morning to be out walking. And with a babby.'

Disappointed, but hardly surprised, Eveleen sighed heavily. She gave the cow's rump a final pat and turned towards the door. 'Thanks, anyway.'

'Wait a bit. Have you come far?'

'From Nottingham,' Josh said.

The farmer smiled. 'Then I reckon you could do with a bite. My missis'll be getting my breakfast. You're welcome to come in.'

'Well,' Josh looked towards Eveleen, guessing that she'd rather press on.

'We did bring a basket of food with us.'

'Aye, but it'll not be bacon, eggs and fried bread, will it?'

Eveleen could almost see Josh salivating and suddenly, despite the anxiety, she felt hungry too. 'That's very kind of you,' she said, trying to keep the surprise out of her voice. 'Are you sure your wife won't mind? There's two more waiting in the trap in the lane.'

The man threw back his head and roared with laughter. 'There's nowt my missis likes better than having a

388

houseful of folks to cook for. Bring 'em in. Bring 'em in and I'll go and tell her we've got visitors for breakfast.'

It was just what the four of them needed, though Eveleen fretted at the delay and felt guilty as she tucked into the food.

'You'll feel all the better. Dan, go and feed that pony, an' all. Poor animal looks that bedraggled and miserable. Now, Mr Carpenter, more fried bread?' The farmer's wife, who was almost as round as Josh and with a red face, beamed at him. She liked a man who enjoyed his food. 'Another sausage?'

Fed and warmed, though not quite dry, they took their leave of the kindly farmer and his wife. 'We'll keep a look-out,' the farmer promised. 'And if we see them we'll take them in and look after them.'

Eveleen smiled her thanks, knowing, for once, that their promise was genuine.

Richard shook the farmer's hand. 'If you do see them,' he said, 'send word to the Reckitt and Stokes factory in Nottingham.'

'Right you are, sir.' The farmer touched his cap respectfully, recognizing the voice of authority when he heard it.

Fifty-Two

They drove on for miles until Eveleen said hopelessly, 'She can't possibly have walked this far. We must have missed her.'

'Unless she got a ride on a cart with someone,' Fred reminded her.

'But we're almost at Bernby. We're almost home.'

She felt the three men glance at her, but her gaze was straight ahead now, searching for familiar buildings.

Was it really only just over a year ago that she had travelled this road taking her away? It seemed an age away, another life.

'Take the next turn to the right, Mr Richard, please.' A little later Eveleen murmured, 'And now left.'

Richard nodded and guided the pony and trap down the rough cart track that led to the farmhouse where the Hardcastle family had once lived. Without pausing to consider whether it was what she wanted, he drew into the yard and halted. Then he turned to her. His tone was gentle as he said, 'Is this where you used to live?'

Unable to speak, Eveleen could only nod. She was looking at the house, drinking in the sight of it, reliving the memories, good and bad.

Richard said softly, 'It doesn't look inhabited.'

Startled, Eveleen looked closer. She had been seeing the house as she had always known it, had almost expected her mother to step out of the back door in her white apron, calling, 'Walter, Walter, your supper's ready.'

Now she saw that although the same curtains still hung at the windows, the glass was dull and dirty. The door was shut and no hens scratched about the yard grumbling to each other. No sounds came from the cowhouse.

There was a deserted feeling about the whole place.

White-hot anger flooded through Eveleen. 'Nobody's living here. They drove us out and yet nobody's even living here.'

'There's one thing though, mi duck,' Josh said. 'Your mam might well be here. That is, if she could get in.'

Eveleen clambered down from the trap and with a sudden spurt of renewed hope ran to the back door. She bent and scrabbled under a loose brick near the wall. Triumphantly she stood up and turned back towards them holding a key in her hands. 'It's still here. They haven't moved it.'

The men were climbing down now to join her and Richard was the first to reach her. Then the hope in her face died. 'She can't be in the house, can she, if the key is still under the brick?'

'No, probably not,' Richard said gently, 'but we'd better take a look anyway now we're here. It is the most likely place she would come. Could she have found another way in?'

Eveleen shook her head. 'I don't think so.' But she turned the key in the lock, stiff now with disuse, pushed open the door and stepped inside. She wrinkled her nose. The house was damp and unlived in. The furniture they had been obliged to leave was still there. Eveleen glanced around her. The pots and pans they had used every day, now dull with dust and lack of care, still lined the dresser.

Walter's wooden rocking chair still stood in its place near the hearth. Even the scraps of paper they had burnt just before leaving were still in the cold grate.

'I can't believe it. It – it's just as we left it.' Tears prickled her eyes at the injustice of it. 'No one's even lived here since we left.'

Richard touched her arm. 'Do you want me to look upstairs?'

Eveleen shook herself out of her reverie. 'No, no, I'll go.'

Only moments later she returned downstairs to say sadly, 'No, she's not here.'

'We've looked in the parlour,' Richard said. 'But now I think we should search all the outbuildings, thoroughly.'

As they moved outside it was raining again and the pony stood looking woeful and, despite the kindly farmer's attentions, still hungry. Eveleen, reared to think of the welfare of the animals even before herself, said at once, 'I'll see to the pony. If they've not even bothered to clear the house out, then maybe there's feedstuff still here.'

There was and soon she had fed and watered the animal and had drawn him into the shelter of the barn while the men searched the cowhouse, the large barn and its hayloft and even the henhouse.

'I'm so sorry, Eveleen,' Richard said, and there was no doubting his sincerity. 'I really thought, like Josh, when we saw the place empty, that she might be here.'

They were standing just inside the house, sheltering from the rain but with the door open, while they decided what to do next. The sound of hoofbeats in the distance came nearer and slowed near the gate.

Eveleen, recognizing the rider, drew in a startled breath and felt the three men with her glance at her. But she was staring at the rider as he trotted into the yard and dismounted.

He was as handsome as ever. He hadn't changed in the months since she had seen him, of course. But she had. Oh how she had changed. The scales had tipped and her love had now become hatred. Her face coloured as she stepped towards him.

'So.' His languid voice now held no appeal for her. 'We've become squatters now, have we?'

'Don't worry,' Eveleen said tightly. 'We're going. I wouldn't want to live in a house owned by you if you paid me.'

He threw back his head and laughed. 'There's no fear of that. I can get what I want without having to pay for it.'

His glance took in the three men with her and his left eyebrow rose in the way she remembered so well. Yet now there was a cruel, sardonic slant to it. Perhaps it had always been there, Eveleen thought, but she had been too blind to see it. Stephen's gaze had come to rest upon Richard and now there was a sarcastic twist to his smile.

'I see you still aim high, Eveleen.' He gave a brief nod and said directly to Richard, 'I hope she gives you as much pleasure as she once gave me.'

Eveleen's face went red with rage. His words implied far more than had ever passed between them. He meant to humiliate her in their eyes, especially in Richard's.

'How dare you?' Before she had stopped to think what she was doing, she had flown at him, clawing at his face. She was crying with rage. 'How dare you say such a thing when it isn't true?'

He caught hold of her wrists and held her easily.

'I hate you!' she spat at him. 'Hate you.'

He was laughing in her face. 'No you don't. You still love me. You only held out because you thought I'd marry you.' His lips curled again. 'You really had the temerity to think that I'd marry the likes of you. The daughter of our gathman.'

She kicked out at him and caught him on the shin, noticing with satisfaction his wince of pain. He released her and she would have flown at him again if Richard's strong arms had not come around her waist from behind and held her firm, while Fred stepped between them.

'I don't know who you are, young feller, but I think you'd better leave.'

'Had I really?' Stephen's voice drawled, but his blue eyes glittered dangerously. 'You're the ones who had better leave. You're trespassing. On *my* property.'

'We're going.' Now Josh moved forwards and brushed passed Stephen, deliberately using his bulk to knock the young man off his balance.

Richard, still keeping tight hold of her, whispered, 'Come, Eveleen. Your mother's not here. We ought to press on anyway and we're serving no purpose here.'

Suddenly her defiance deserted her and her spirit drained out of her. The worry over her mother and poor little Bridie, the return to her former home to find it empty and just as they had left it and to realize there had been no good reason for them to be turned out, then to come face to face with the man she had thought she loved – it was all too much. She hung her head in shame and defeat and began to sob.

Gently Richard turned her in his arms towards him. She buried her face against his chest and he held her tightly against him.

'We're going,' he said above her head to Stephen. His voice was controlled, but Eveleen could feel the barely suppressed anger in him. 'But you haven't heard the last of this.'

'Oh, I think we have. This is my land and you have no right to be here.' Stephen's lip curled again as he added scathingly, 'Whoever you are.'

As he helped Eveleen climb into the trap which Fred had brought out from the barn, Richard said, 'You drive, Fred.' And he sat beside Eveleen and held her close as they drove away.

Fifty-Three

They had not gone far before Richard signalled to Fred to halt.

'Now,' he said to Eveleen, offering her a white, neatly folded handkerchief, 'dry those tears and let's try to think what we should do next.'

Eveleen drew in a shuddering breath, raised her head and took the handkerchief. She blew her nose and felt better though she knew the humiliation would stay with her for ever.

Richard, however, was sensibly concentrating on the task in hand and she must do the same. The longer her mother and Bridie were out in this terrible weather, the more danger they were in.

'Is there anywhere else in Bernby where your mother might go?' Richard asked.

'I – I suppose she might go to Bill and Dorothy's.'

'Where's that?'

'If we go a little further on down this road it's on the right. But it's still on *his* land.'

'Never mind about him. I haven't time to deal with him today,' Richard muttered, 'else I would.'

Eveleen noticed that the other men exchanged a glance, but nothing more was said apart from Richard deciding, 'Right, we'll go and find Bill and Dorothy.'

As they rocked their way down the muddy cart track towards Bill Morton's cottage, Eveleen saw their old friend emerge from the lean-to at the side of the house. As soon as they were close enough for him to recognize her, he hurried forward, reaching up his arms towards her, his face one big grin. 'Eveleen, lass. By, but it's good to see you. How are you?' His voice faltered as, closer now, he could see her distress. 'Oh, lass, whatever's wrong?'

As they all climbed down from the cart Richard swiftly explained, his manner towards Bill at once entirely different from his attitude towards Stephen a few moments ago.

'Eveleen's mother is missing. She left home last night and we thought she might have come back home.'

'It's all she's ever wanted,' Eveleen hiccuped miserably as Bill hugged her. 'I promised that one day I would bring her back, but . . .'

'I know, love, and I know you did. But it all takes time. Poor Mary. She never was the most patient of women, was she? Now,' he said briskly. 'Come inside. All of you and have a hot drink and a bite to eat. You look starved to death, lass.'

As he ushered his unexpected guests inside the tiny cottage, he was calling to his wife, 'Dorothy, Dorothy, look who's here. Get that kettle singing, lass. We've guests for dinner.'

When Dorothy appeared she gave a squeal of delight and hugged Eveleen. At once she was making everyone welcome and fussing round them.

'What a good job I've made a huge pan of stew this morning. I must have known.'

'We don't want to impose—' Richard began, but his protestations were waved aside.

While they ate, Eveleen found herself bombarded with questions from Dorothy and Bill. The whole, sad story of their life since leaving Bernby was told and Dorothy reached out and touched Eveleen's hand. 'You poor lass. What a time you've had. And all that on top of finding your poor father dead in the beck.' She glanced around at the strangers who had come into her home, but who she could see at once were trying to help the girl. 'Life can be very cruel at times, can't it?' she remarked.

Back among people who had known her family well, Eveleen felt able to say, 'Mam always blamed me for Dad's death. She – she said my wilful ways had brought on his heart attack.'

'That's nonsense,' Bill said at once. 'You must never think that, love. Your dad must have had a weak heart. It ran in his family. His father died in just the same way.' He glanced around, telling the three other men whom he presumed would not know. 'Found in a field, he was, just like poor Walter. Besides,' he went on, looking directly at Eveleen, 'I remember your dad having funny turns now and then. When we were haymaking or harvesting. He often had to stop for a rest.' He shook his head. 'That wasn't normal. Not for a feller of his age.'

Eveleen felt some of the guilt she carried for that event slide away, but now there was an even more pressing need for self-reproach.

'I seem to bring trouble on everyone,' she whispered. 'On poor Rebecca, on my uncle and grandmother . . .'

'That was Jimmy's doing, lass, not yours. You can't be held responsible for what he did. He always was a little rascal even as a young lad. It doesn't surprise me one bit.'

'But I am responsible for my mother being so unhappy that she walked out in the middle of the night.'

To this, no one around the table could think of a comforting answer.

*

'We'll organize a search all around this neighbourhood,' Bill said a little later when the decision had been made that Eveleen and the three men should try a different route back towards Nottingham.

'I'm sure that kindly farmer we met will keep a watch out for her,' Richard said. 'So we needn't retrace ground we've already covered.'

Once more, arrangements were made for messages to be sent should there be any news.

Bill and Dorothy hugged Eveleen and told her not to worry. Then they shook hands with the three men and received their thanks with nods and smiles. Although the smiles were genuine, they were tempered by the anxiety that everyone was feeling.

Just where were Mary and the tiny baby?

Fred took the reins this time without being asked and Richard sat close to Eveleen. She leant against him, allowing herself to give in, just this once, she told herself, and enjoy the feel of his arm around her shoulders, the strength of him and the confidence and common sense he exuded. It was a relief to hand over, even if only for a short time, the heavy burden she had carried for so long.

She was weary, worn out with the responsibility that had been thrust on her young shoulders. She closed her eyes and her head drooped. As the trap rocked, Eveleen slept against his shoulder.

She woke with a start as the trap halted. 'Mam?' she began, for she had been dreaming about her mother and the child.

'I'm sorry,' Richard said at once. 'We're almost back at Nottingham and we've seen no sign of her. We've asked along the way, but nothing.'

Anguished, Eveleen said, 'What do we do now? Call the police?'

'Unless she's been found, that will already have been done by now. I left word with my father.'

Eveleen felt a flicker of anger and opened her mouth to protest. She didn't want Brinsley Stokes involved. If anyone was to blame for this, then it was him. He was to blame for all the unhappiness in her mother's life.

But the retort died on her lips. At this moment, she should take any help she could get – wherever it came from. She looked about her. They were indeed nearing the city, but she recognized that they were even nearer the village of Flawford.

'We're not far from my uncle's,' she said glancing at Richard. 'I don't think for a minute that she would go there, but—'

He took the words from her. 'You think we ought to make sure?'

She nodded and, as Fred turned the trap in the right direction, Eveleen instinctively drew closer to Richard.

Fifty-Four

'Gone? Gone where?' Andrew's face was white with fear. 'And taken Bridie? My little Bridie? Oh, Eveleen, how could you let that happen?'

Eveleen's shoulders sagged. Although she had not held out much hope that they would be in Flawford – she believed it was the last place her mother would come – she was still disappointed. And once more she was shouldering the blame.

Gently, because he could see the young man's distress was genuine, Richard said, 'It wasn't Eveleen's fault. Mary left in the night while Eveleen was asleep.'

Andrew glanced at her and then looked away. 'I'm sorry,' he muttered. 'Of course it's not your fault. I'm sorry, Eveleen.'

Eveleen nodded, but could not speak. Bridie was all Andrew had left of his beloved Rebecca. He was beside himself with anxiety. Now he was firing questions at them. Where had they searched? Had they called in the police? What were they going to do next and how could he help?

Richard answered him calmly, adding, 'We should go now but we'll let you know.'

'Can I come with you?'

'Of course you can. But what about your work?'

'Sod that!' Andrew said. He jerked his thumb over his

shoulder towards the workshops. 'He can go hang, for all I care. There's other jobs.'

Eveleen glanced up at Richard. As an employer, it was not the sort of reaction he would like, but she could see the sympathy for Andrew's sentiments written in his features.

'Come along then,' Richard said briskly.

As they came out into the street and he saw Fred and the cumbersome figure of Josh already sitting in the trap, Andrew faltered. 'Oh, I'm sorry, I didn't realize there were more of you.' He thought quickly and then added, 'Look, I'll borrow my mate's pony and trap. I'll follow you. I know the way.'

Richard nodded. 'Right, because I don't think we should wait for you.'

'No, no,' Andrew urged. 'You go.' He gave Eveleen a quick hug and said, 'I'll be right behind you. I'll come straight to your house.'

Eveleen nodded and climbed back into the trap. It was only as they moved away that she realized she hadn't even asked after her grandmother and her uncle.

Although the police had been informed earlier in the day, Mary and the child had not been found nor had word come to the factory from those looking out for them in the countryside.

'You'd better both go home and change into dry clothes,' Richard said to Josh and Fred, but the two men glanced at each other. It was Josh who answered their employer but Fred nodded in agreement. 'We'd sooner stay here, Mr Richard, thank you. There might be news. And if there is, this is where it'll come.'

When Richard finally took Eveleen home, a pony and trap were standing outside the door. Eveleen felt a brief surge of hope and then she saw Andrew pacing up and down the yard. Behind him, Win was hurrying towards them.

'Any news?' she called out as Richard drew the trap to a halt and Andrew held out his hand to help Eveleen climb down.

Eveleen shook her head sadly and led the way into the house. She ran from room to room, leaving them to follow her inside.

'Mam? Mam?' But the house was still and silent.

She returned downstairs and sank into the chair at the side of the range. Win busied herself reviving the fire and setting the kettle to boil.

'Now what do we do?' Andrew, fresher than the others, who had been looking all day and half the previous night, was eager to carry on the search.

'First,' Richard said firmly, 'Eveleen must rest. She's exhausted.' She felt them looking at her and knew her face was white, her eyes dark-rimmed with fatigue and worry. 'And I'm going home for something to eat, a wash, a change of clothes and then, if there's still no news, we'll begin again.'

'It'll be dark by then,' Andrew persisted. 'We won't find them in the dark.'

'Well, we—' Richard began but whatever he had been going to say was left unsaid. Someone was thumping urgently on the door and shouting.

'Eveleen? Eveleen, they've found her.'

A rush of adrenaline brought Eveleen to her feet and running to the door. She flung it wide to see Fred standing there, leaning against the wall, his hand to his chest.

'I ran – all the way – from the factory,' Fred panted in staccato bursts. 'Word's just come – from that farmer. He's found her.'

'Who? Bill?'

'No. That other one. Joe Elgin. That was his name, wasn't it? The one that gave us breakfast. She was walking past his farm.'

'Are they all right? Is Bridie all right?' Andrew, having followed Eveleen to the door, asked urgently. Richard and Win were close behind him, craning to hear the news.

'I must go to them,' Eveleen said. 'I've got to see for myself. The baby could have taken a chill. Anything.'

Without waiting for an answer, Andrew was already climbing into the pony and trap he had brought. 'Come on, Eveleen.'

Richard moved forward. 'Eveleen, you ought to rest.'

'No, no,' she argued. 'I'm fine now. Honestly.' Before anyone could stop her, she had climbed in beside Andrew.

'Can't you just have something to eat?' Win called. 'And you ought to change out of those wet clothes.'

'Eveleen, wait—' Fred was reaching out towards them, trying to delay them, but Andrew flicked the reins.

'I'm fine,' Eveleen insisted and, as they moved off, she called out, 'Thank you. Thank you for everything.'

Turning the corner of the yard, they passed Josh, puffing and panting, on his way in. It took a moment for him to recognize them and then he began to wave his arms. Eveleen could see his lips moving, but above the rattling wheels she could not make out his words. He was shouting something and gesticulating that they should stop, but Andrew only drove the pony faster.

Eveleen smiled and waved and nodded, hoping that

Josh would understand that they had already heard the good news.

As the trap was headed out of the city, Eveleen linked her arm through Andrew's and hugged it to her. 'Oh thank goodness they're safe.'

Already she had forgotten her weariness and the wet clothes that clung to her and made her shiver from time to time. All she could think of was holding Bridie in her arms. She couldn't reach her fast enough.

'I just hope the babby's all right,' Andrew said. Eveleen smiled to herself. Andrew's only thought was for the child. And then, guiltily, she realized that Bridie had been uppermost in her own thoughts too.

The journey seemed interminable but at last Eveleen was directing Andrew through the gates and into the Elgins' farmyard. It seemed an age since she had been there and yet it had only been that morning.

The farmer was coming towards them. 'She's in the house with the missis,' he said at once, without any greeting. 'But we can't get any sense out of her.'

'She'll be upset,' Eveleen murmured as the farmer led the way to the house. 'Is the baby all right?'

Joe Elgin stopped and put his hand on her arm. 'I'm sorry, lass, but she had no baby with her.'

It was as if someone had knocked the breath from her. Eveleen's whole body began to shake.

'Oh dear God, no!' Andrew ran his hand through his hair and his eyes were dark with fear.

Eveleen grasped the jamb of the open door for a moment's support. Maybe that was what Fred, and then Josh, had been trying to tell them. She dragged in a deep, steadying breath and then forced her legs to move into the kitchen.

Mary was sitting in front of the range wrapped in a blanket. Mrs Elgin was bending over her, coaxing her to drink a steaming cup of tea.

'Mam, oh Mam!' Eveleen put her arm around her mother's shoulders and hugged her. 'Thank goodness you're safe.'

Andrew, following her in, asked harshly, 'Where's the baby? Where is my Bridie?'

Eveleen knelt on the hearthrug and took her mother's hands into her own. 'Mam,' she began, trying desperately to keep her voice calm as she looked into Mary's vacant eyes. She knew from bitter experience that anger would only drive her mother deeper into the trance-like state she was in, or worse still, it might induce one of her bouts of near-hysteria. 'Mam, where is Bridie?'

The vacant eyes focused on Eveleen's face and yet the girl felt a shudder run through her. It was as if Mary did not even recognize her own daughter. 'In a ditch,' the poor woman murmured. 'Born in a ditch. In the dark and the cold.'

Eveleen gripped her mother's hands tighter. 'Mam, that was a long time ago. Bridie's fine. She – she—' The lump in her throat threatened to choke her. Oh let her still be fine. Let her be safe, she prayed silently. 'Bridie is Rebecca's little girl. Mam, where is she? Where have you left her?'

Mary's eyes were vacant again, seeing only into the past.

Joe Elgin filled the doorway. 'I've got a search party out.'

Eveleen stood up slowly. It was no use. Mary was so

sunk into her own little world that they would get nothing from her. But Andrew was not going to give up so easily. He bent over Mary, grasped her shoulders and shook her so hard that her head snapped backwards and forwards. 'Where is she, you stupid, stupid woman? What have you done to my Bridie?'

'No, Andrew, no,' Eveleen cried, pulling at him, but it took the burly farmer to step forward and drag the distraught young man away.

'That'll do no good, lad,' he said firmly, but with a gruff kindness in his tone. 'Can't you see, she's in a bad way herself.' He glanced at his wife. 'I've sent word for the doctor. She needs help.'

Mrs Elgin nodded in agreement and fussed over Mary who began to wail. 'Jimmy. I want Jimmy. Eveleen, take me home to Jimmy.'

Eveleen glanced quickly around at the others and then looked down at her mother. She was still not thinking quite rationally, but at least she seemed to be coming back into the present.

Again Eveleen knelt in front of her and though her own instincts were exactly the same as Andrew's – she too felt the urge to shake the truth out of Mary – she managed to say calmly, 'I'll take you home, Mam, I promise you. But first, tell us where Bridie is.'

The wailing subsided to a quieter sob.

'Bridie?' Mary shook her head. 'Poor motherless little mite. Cast out, just like me. How can Harry turn his back on his own grandchild, Eveleen? How can he do it?'

Gently Eveleen said, 'Is that where you took her? Back to Uncle Harry?'

'She didn't—' Andrew began but was hushed by both Joe Elgin and his wife.

Mary was shaking her head and now there was spirit in her action. 'No, no. I wouldn't take her there. Not back to *him*,' she said bitterly.

'So, where were you going?'

'Back home,' Mary said simply. 'Back to Bernby where she'd be safe.'

'Is that where she is? Back at Pear Tree Farm?' Could they have missed finding the child earlier that day? Eveleen agonized. Had Bridie been there all the time and they'd not seen her or heard her cries?

Mary was shaking her head. 'No. No, she got so heavy to carry and it was raining. She was hungry too. Crying and crying. She wouldn't stop.' She covered her face with her hands and rocked to and fro.

Cold terror seeped into Eveleen's being. What had her mother done? Had the child's crying driven her over the edge? Oh, what had she done? Eveleen swallowed the fear but now even she could not keep the tremble from her voice. 'Where is she, Mam? What have you done with her?'

'If you've hurt her—' Andrew began and struggled to break free of Joe's grasp, but the farmer still held him firmly.

'Now, now, lad. Hold on. She'll tell us in a minute.'

'I left her in a barn,' Mary began and added quickly, 'She's all right. She's warm and cosy in the hay loft. I went to find some milk for her and I thought I'd be quicker if I went on my own . . .' The faraway look was back on her face. 'I started to walk, but I couldn't find a farm and – and I got so tired.' Her voice trailed away. 'I can't remember any more.'

Joe took up the story. 'She did look sort of lost when we found her and she didn't speak to us at all until you got here, but she let us bring her in here and look after her.'

'Where's the barn? Where have you left her?' Andrew demanded.

'It can't be far away. We'll find her,' Joe said with more determination than either Eveleen or Andrew could feel.

Eveleen was the first to reach the door. She flung it wide and rushed out into the yard, straight into Richard's arms.

Fifty-Five

The local police and all the men from the neighbouring farms joined in the search and, after four hours, the child was found in an isolated barn in the corner of a field.

'I heard her crying,' the searcher placed the child tenderly into Eveleen's arms. 'She's hungry, poor little thing. But she was cosy and warm.'

Andrew hovered close by, peering over Eveleen's shoulders, itching to hold Bridie himself. 'Is she all right? Has she hurt her?'

'Of course she hasn't hurt her,' Eveleen snapped, but even she was thankful to feel the baby wriggling in her arms.

Richard put his arm around Eveleen's shoulders and gently led her to the trap. 'Let's get her back to the Elgins' farm.'

When they arrived back, the doctor was with Mary. He examined Bridie too and pronounced her fit and well, but ravenous. Drawing Eveleen to one side he said, 'I'm concerned about your mother. Physically she's taken no harm, but I'm not happy about her state of mind. I've arranged with Mrs Elgin for her to stay here and I'll call each day. Good food, fresh air and plenty of rest should work wonders, but I want to be sure.'

Eveleen bit her lip but nodded agreement. She would worry about how to pay the doctor's bills later.

'And you, young lady,' he said with pretended severity, 'should take the same prescription.'

Eveleen felt as if her legs would give way any moment, but she managed to say, 'I'll be fine, Doctor, thank you.'

It was not Bridie, or even Mary, who took a chill and developed pneumonia, but Eveleen.

After a few days' rest and being cosseted by the farmer's wife, whose name they learned was Sarah, Mary and the child were fine, as the doctor had predicted.

'I just wanted to go home,' Mary said tearfully, when Eveleen sat beside the bed in the big room at the rambling farmhouse and took her mother's hand.

'It's all right, Mam,' she said gently. 'You're both safe now. That's all that matters.'

'Yes, but I shouldn't have taken the bairn with me. I – I might have lost her, like – like . . .' Her voice petered away and Eveleen knew she was thinking of that other tiny baby so long ago.

'It's over now,' Eveleen patted her hand. 'We'll say no more about it.' But as her mother drifted into sleep, Eveleen began to worry again.

I must get her back to the country. Somehow I must or else this could happen again.

When she could see that her mother was sleeping peacefully, Eveleen slipped out of the room and went downstairs. As she entered the warm kitchen, she felt suddenly dizzy. She clutched at a chair for support, but there were wavy lines in front of her eyes. The room began to swim around her and then she felt herself falling.

She awoke to find herself lying in a huge bed. The room and the bed were warm, for beside her in the bed were four heated bricks wrapped in scraps of blanket, and a cracking fire burned in the grate, the flames leaping and casting dancing shadows on the walls and ceiling. Yet Eveleen was shivering with chills that felt as if someone was pouring cold water down her back.

A shadow rose out of a deep armchair near the window and came towards the bed.

'Eveleen?' a deep voice said and a cool hand rested on her forehead.

'Andrew?' she said and heard the name spoken in a croak. Was that really her voice?

'No,' the voice came again. 'It's Richard.'

'I'm so sorry . . .' she began, but it was difficult to speak. She felt as if she were breathing through cotton wool. 'I didn't – thank you properly.'

'Don't try to talk. You must rest. But first, if you can sit up a little, you must drink this. The doctor said—'

'Oh,' she gasped. 'A doctor. I can't—'

'Now listen,' his tone was still gentle, but firm now. 'You're not to worry about a thing. Your mother and the child are fine. They haven't taken any harm for their adventure. But you must take care and get yourself well again.'

'Where am I?'

'At the Elgins' farm. You remember, the kind farmer who gave us breakfast that day and who later found your mother?'

'Mm.' Talking made her breathless and there was a pain in her chest when she tried to breathe deeply. 'But I can't lie – here,' she said in staccato gasps. 'I must—'

'You *can* lie here, Eveleen. And there is nothing you have to do except rest and get well again. Everything is taken care of.'

Her mind was playing funny tricks on her. Why was Richard Stokes, her employer, sitting on the bed beside her and holding her hand? Now he was slipping his arm beneath her shoulders and easing her up and holding a cup of warm liquid to her mouth.

She began to cough and the pain in her chest was worse. She shivered again, yet her head felt as if it was burning.

'Don't lift my feet up,' she murmured. 'It feels funny.'

'I'm not touching your feet,' the voice said, but it sounded faint now. Eveleen closed her eyes. 'I must get up,' she murmured, but her limbs felt like lead. 'I must go to work.'

Her mind was playing funny tricks with her. She seemed to hear her father's voice calling her from a distance. 'Eveleen. Eveleen.'

There was a bright light and she tried to run towards it. 'I'm coming, Dad. Wait for me. I'm coming . . .'

But the light disappeared as suddenly as it had come and she was tossing and turning in the bed again. She felt something cool bathing her forehead and a voice that said soothingly, 'Try to sleep, my love. I'm here and I'm not going to go away. Don't worry about a thing.'

The voice lulled her. She felt secure and cared for. It was a wonderful feeling, she thought, as she drifted away, to have someone looking after *her* for a change.

Her sleep was fitful and disturbed by dreams. She felt as if someone was lifting her up in strong arms and then there was a woman's voice and capable hands were taking off her nightdress and pulling on a warm, dry one.

'She's wringing wet, poor lass,' the woman's voice said. 'We ought to get the doctor to take another look at her.'

'No, no,' Eveleen tried to say. 'I can't afford a doctor.'

Then there were other voices in the rooms. A man's voice and he was pressing something round and cold against her chest and bending over her as if listening intently. She tried to speak but her throat was dry and her lips cracked and sore. And her head ached dreadfully. The man had moved away from the bed and was talking softly to someone else in the room.

Eveleen tried to speak, but all she could hear was this strange mumbling, a jumble of words that made no sense. Her mind was drifting, not thinking clearly.

In the end she gave up trying. She closed her eyes and slept.

The next time she woke up, she felt better. She didn't feel as if her whole body was burning and yet shivery at the same time. At least she was not having nightmares any more. Strange, muddled dreams where she was running and running but her legs would not seem to move because she was dragging a heavy weight behind her. But now her head did not hurt so much and her thoughts were clearer.

She pulled herself up in the bed and saw that although sunlight streamed in through the window, a fire still burned brightly in the grate. At her movement, Richard rose from the chair by the window and came to stand beside the bed.

She tried to smile at him. 'Whatever are you doing here?'

There were dark lines of tiredness beneath his eyes and a day's growth of stubble shadowed his face.

'Looking after you.' He smiled and some of his anxiety lifted. 'Mind you,' his smile broadened. 'I don't seem to be making a very good job of it. You look awful.'

'Thanks,' Eveleen said and heard for herself that her voice was stronger. 'I feel it.'

The bed creaked as he sat down beside her. To her surprise he reached over and laid his hand on her forehead.

'Thank God,' he murmured more to himself than to her. 'The fever's broken.'

'I'm still hot.'

'Yes, but you're sweating it out now. Not burning up. That's a good sign.'

'Is it?' she managed to say with a tremulous smile. 'I'll believe you.'

'I wish you would,' he murmured, and she had the feeling that he was not just referring to the state of her health.

'Are they all right? My mother and Bridie.'

He sat quietly, watching her for a few moments before he said softly, 'They're fine.'

'How long have I been here?'

'Five days.'

'Five days!'

If her weakened body had let her she would have leapt up there and then in horror. As it was, she tried to pull herself up but found she was as weak as a new-born kitten.

She groaned as she fell back against the soft pillows. Before she had thought to whom she was speaking, for her mind was still a little slow to work properly, she said, 'Oh, I'll lose me job.'

She heard his soft chuckle. 'I don't think so. But if you do, I'll have something to say to the boss.'

She realized then and could laugh at herself. 'I'm sorry. I'm not thinking straight.'

She felt him pat her hand and then he got up. 'Now that you're on the mend, I must get back home.'

She looked up at him, standing so tall over her. 'You mean – you've been here all the time?'

He nodded but then, before she could say more, he said briskly, 'But now I must go. I'll come and see you again and if' – he wagged his finger at her now with mock severity – 'I hear any bad reports that you are not behaving yourself, I'll bring a big stick.'

Before she could say any more he had left the room and she heard his footsteps running lightly down the stairs.

And I still haven't thanked him, she thought.

Fifty-Six

Eveleen slept for a while and awoke to find Sarah Elgin bending over her.

'You're feeling better.' It was as much a statement as a question.

Eveleen nodded but immediately wanted to know, 'Mam and Bridie?'

'They're fine and thriving. Your mother's churning butter in the dairy and singing at the top of her voice.'

'Churning?' Eveleen began and then, amazed, added, 'And singing?'

'Yes, singing. And little Bridie's outside in the sunshine. I got my Joe to fetch the old perambulator down from the loft in the barn. We've cleaned it up and even painted it. And she loves it. Just lies there gurgling and crowing all day long.'

'I seem to have missed an awful lot,' Eveleen murmured and glanced towards the window, longing to be outside in the sunshine herself.

'You'll soon be back downstairs with us now you're on the mend. You'll feel weak for a day or two, but once you start eating properly, my good food and this lovely weather will help you. I can't believe the change in the weather after all that awful rain we had.' She crossed to the window and pushed up the sash. Warm air flowed into the room and Eveleen breathed in deeply, revelling in its fresh country air smell.

Then she was overcome by a fit of coughing, but Sarah only laughed. 'Cough it up, lass,' she teased, thankful to see the girl was so much better. 'It might be a gold watch.'

Sarah had thought for a day or two that they were going to lose her. Privately the farmer's wife believed that it was only the young man's own determination and constant care that had pulled the girl through. Richard refused to let her go and his will power had somehow reached her even through the depths of her fever.

'Now, let me help you out of that bed and into a chair. I'll give you a blanket bath and then change the sheets. You'll feel much better.'

'A what?'

'A blanket bath. You've been having them every day for the last five days. Didn't you know?'

Eveleen shook her head. 'I don't seem to know much at all about the last five days.'

She soon found out what a blanket bath was and when the woman had washed her with warm water as she lay on the bed, Eveleen did indeed feel refreshed.

'Now, let's have you out of bed and I'll change the sheets,' Sarah said.

As she sat up, swung her legs to the floor and tried to stand, Eveleen was appalled at how weak and wobbly she was. She groaned aloud. 'Oh, it's going to take me weeks to get back to work.'

'Don't you be worritting about that, love.'

'But we can't impose on your goodness any longer,' Eveleen began.

'I'm loving having you all here. And your mother's making herself useful. She's a big help. And as for the baby, well, you can leave her here with me for good if you want.' Then seeing Eveleen's expression, she added hastily, 'Only teasing, love. Of course you couldn't bear to part with her. She's a little darling.'

'But you must have had so much work looking after me.'

Sarah shrugged her plump shoulders. 'Not really. That young feller did most of it.'

Startled, Eveleen stared at her. 'He didn't give me the blanket baths, did he?'

Sarah chuckled at the idea. 'Oh no. I wouldn't let him do that.'

While Sarah stripped the rumpled sheets and spread crisp, clean ones on the bed, Eveleen asked, 'Where's Andrew?'

'He had to go back home, but he said he'd be back at the weekend.' She wrinkled her forehead and added, 'That's tomorrow. He'll be so pleased to see you looking better.' Sarah chattered on. 'And Josh is coming on Sunday.'

'Josh? Really?'

'Oh yes,' Sarah looked up and winked at Eveleen. 'He's been here a time or two. Mind you, I think he's coming to see your mother as much as anyone. I reckon he's sweet on her.'

Time took a sudden tilt and for a moment Eveleen's senses reeled. She was back in the kitchen at home – at the farm – and once again she could hear Jimmy's voice saying, 'I reckon Master Stephen is sweet on our Eveleen.'

'Jimmy.'

'What, love? What did you say?'

Not until Sarah asked the question did Eveleen realize that she had spoken his name aloud. 'Nothing,' she said, as her gaze went out across the flat fields. 'I was only thinking aloud.'

As Sarah bustled about the bedroom, Eveleen sat lost

in her own thoughts. For the first time for many months, she had a chance to sit and think.

Where was her brother and why had they never heard from him? He might have sent word, even if only to their mother. He knew how much Mary had always doted on him. Surely he could have spared a thought for her? Eveleen prepared herself for the shaft of impatience that usually accompanied thoughts of her rascal of a brother. But nothing came, and thinking about him she even found an amused smile twitching involuntarily at her mouth as she remembered their childhood. The scrapes he got into and how he had expected his older sister to cover for him, never to tell tales of him to their mother. It was Eveleen who always had to take the blame. He always had such a winning smile for Mary. He could wind his mother round his little finger and she would believe any story he told her.

Oh, Jimmy, Eveleen sighed inwardly, but now the words were not spoken aloud. Why did you have to do it? Why did you have to stir up trouble for me and then bring such tragedy on poor Rebecca?

And still I'm left carrying all the blame.

Andrew arrived the following day and was invited to stay the night, and on the Sunday Josh arrived, driving Mr Richard's pony and trap.

Eveleen was still not strong enough to leave her bedroom, but each day she sat out of bed for longer periods of time.

Josh lowered himself into a chair near her as she sat beside a window, flung open to let in the warm day.

'How can I ever thank you, Josh?' she began but he waved her gratitude aside.

'I'm just so glad to see you getting well again and that we found your mother and the babby safe.' He was thoughtful for a moment before he remarked, 'She's a different woman out here, isn't she?'

Eveleen nodded and her gaze went to the scene outside the window. She heard all the usual farmyard noises she had known for most of her life. The clatter of buckets. The lowing of cattle. The grumbling and scratching of hens about the yard. The occasional squeal of a pig. The sound of horses' hooves and the rattle of cartwheels.

It was home, especially for her mother. It was the only place Mary had ever known real happiness.

Eveleen gave a deep sigh. 'I've got to get her back here. Somehow I've got to find a place for us to live back home.'

Her gaze was intent upon the idyllic country scene below her, so that she did not see the gleam in Josh Carpenter's eyes.

The following Sunday, Josh was late arriving at the farm.

'I wonder why he hasn't come,' Mary said, her glance going to the farmyard gate for the fiftieth time that morning.

'Mary, how many more layers are you going to take off that potato. You've peeled the same one three times now,' Sarah said, laughing.

'Oh!' Startled, Mary dropped the potato into the bowl, the earthy water splashing her white apron.

'Come on, Mam, you go and sit outside with Bridie and watch the lane.' Gently Eveleen took the knife from her mother's fingers. 'I'll do these.'

'Are you sure, love? Are you sure you're strong enough?'

Eveleen felt tears prickle her eyes. It was the first time in an age that her mother had voiced real concern for her. She put her arms around Mary's slim waist and hugged her.

To her surprise, she felt her mother's arms creep around her and hug her in return.

As they drew apart they smiled at each other, a little embarrassed, and Eveleen's voice was unsteady as she said, 'I'm fine, Mam, honest. Off you go.'

'Well, I don't think he's going to come now,' Mary said as they all sat down around the dinner table. Her voice was flat with disappointment. 'He wouldn't be late for one of Sarah's Sunday dinners, I know.'

'Maybe he's just got delayed,' Sarah said comfortingly as she placed a joint of beef in front of her husband for him to carve. Then she moved between the range and the table placing tureens of steaming vegetables before them. 'Help yourselves.'

There was silence around the table except for the clatter of cutlery and crockery. When they were all served and began to eat, Mary picked at the food on her plate. 'I'm sure he isn't coming.' She put a piece of meat into her mouth and chewed it round and round, but all the time her gaze was on the yard beyond the window.

It was as Sarah stood up to clear away the plates that they all heard the sound of wheels.

Mary sprang up with more energy than Eveleen had seen in her for a long time. Sarah beamed, 'There you are, you see.'

But Mary was gone, flying out through the back door.

Joe Elgin and his wife exchanged a glance and then Sarah winked at Eveleen. 'I told you, didn't I?' But now the girl was sure that her words held more meaning than that she had been right about Josh's late arrival.

They squeezed in through the door, with Mary clinging to his arm. 'Why are you late? We thought you weren't coming.'

'I've kept a plate warm for you, Josh. Come and sit down,' Sarah called.

Josh beamed all round and eased himself into a chair at the table while Joe carved slices of beef and Sarah piled his plate with vegetables. Mary pulled her chair close to him and, as he began to eat, picked up her knife and fork and finished her own meal too.

Eveleen and Sarah glanced at each other in amusement. She's right, Eveleen thought, there is something going on between Mam and Josh. The thought pleased her. She liked Josh, and if he brought a sparkle to her mother's eyes again, Eveleen would be the very last person to complain.

They all waited until Josh and Mary had finished their first course and then Sarah served the pudding. When at last Josh pushed away his empty plate and leaned back in his chair with a satisfied sigh, he glanced around and said, 'I've got some wonderful news for you. Mary – Eveleen – you're going home.'

Eveleen, though she was feeling stronger with each day, could not stop the stab of disappointment. But she had known the day would come and knew, too, that she and her family could no longer impose upon the Elgins' goodness.

'Sarah says I can stop the night so that I can take you in the morning.' He went on, rubbing his hands together.

'Tomorrow,' Eveleen murmured. 'So soon?'

'Yes.' Josh could not keep the gleeful note from his voice. 'Yes, by tomorrow, we'll have you all back home.'

Fifty-Seven

'Now, are you sure you're going to be all right,' Sarah said, wrapping warm blankets around Eveleen as she sat in the trap early the following morning.

'We'll be fine.' Eveleen tried to reassure herself as well as Sarah, but she could not help thinking of the cold, unwelcoming house that awaited them in Foundry Yard.

'Now, Mary, you sit beside me,' Josh was saying and added to Sarah, 'You can put the cradle on the floor, between our feet.'

Sarah had found a wicker cradle in the loft too and had lined it and made little blankets for it. Now she was looking as if she didn't want to part with either the cradle or the child lying in it.

Eveleen reached out her arms. 'Please, come and see us whenever you can. You know our address in the city. We'd love to see you.'

Sarah looked up and smiled, but it was at Josh that she directed her glance. 'Yes,' she said softly. 'Oh yes, I'll come and see you all right.'

There was a flurry of goodbyes and then they were moving off. As they turned out of the gate, Eveleen said, 'You're going the wrong way, Josh.'

'No, no, I'm not. I thought your mother might like a little ride in the country before we go home. All right, Mary?'

Eveleen watched as her mother slipped her arm

through the big man's and said with a coy smile, 'Whatever you say, Josh.'

They were going in the wrong direction all together. They were heading towards Bernby and even further away from Nottingham.

Eveleen bit her lip and glanced at her mother. She was anxious that if her mother saw their former home empty and deserted and falling into disrepair it would upset her.

It had upset her, Eveleen thought, never mind her mother whose emotions were very unstable. But Mary seemed to be enjoying the drive and when they neared familiar landmarks, she cried out excitedly, 'There's Bernby church on top of the hill. Poor Walter's buried there you know. We ought to take flowers there before we leave, didn't we, Eveleen?'

'Yes, Mam,' Eveleen agreed reluctantly and glanced at her worriedly. She would love to visit her father's resting place, but to take Mary might bring all the memories, good and bad, flooding back. But Mary was still smiling and looking about her. Then before Eveleen could protest, Mary was pleading, 'Oh, do take us to the farmhouse where we used to live. I'd love to see it, just one more time. Please, Josh.'

Josh's eyes positively twinkled. 'If you're sure you'd like to see it, Mary?'

'I would. Oh, I would,' she breathed and then directed him happily, not realizing that Josh already knew the way.

Eveleen pulled the blanket closely around her and hunched her shoulders miserably. She didn't want to cause an argument, but she was sure that seeing their old home would swiftly dispel Mary's new-found happiness. It might even topple her over the edge into a bout of confused depression once more. At the Elgins' farm and under Sarah's placid care, Mary had been like her old self. Now, Eveleen was sure, all that was going to disappear in an instant.

As they pulled into the yard, Eveleen saw at once the change in the place since their last, brief, visit.

Hens wandered about the yard and from the pigsties came the sounds of noisy occupants. In the field close by, half a dozen cows grazed contentedly. She looked at the house. Windows were flung wide and curtains – still the ones they had left but now freshly laundered – blew in the breeze. The back door stood open to the warm, sunny day.

'Josh, we mustn't stay,' Eveleen said at once. 'Someone's moved in. Someone's living here now.'

'That's right,' Josh said as he looped the reins and stood up to alight, his weight wobbling the trap dangerously. He stepped down and held out his hand to Mary.

'Come on, Mary. I'm sure they won't mind us taking a look. You too, Eveleen.'

'I'll stay with Bridie,' Eveleen said at once, not wanting to see some other woman in her mother's kitchen, another man sitting in her father's chair. She was surprised and worried too that her mother could even contemplate the idea.

'No, no, you must come,' Josh insisted. 'Here, push the cradle to me. I'll carry her.'

So the three of them, with Josh carrying the wicker cradle, walked towards the back door. As they neared it a figure appeared in the doorway.

'Dorothy!' Mary cried in delight and rushed forward with her arms outstretched to embrace her friend. 'This is wonderful. Oh I'm so glad it's you and Bill living here.'

Dorothy returned the hug, but above Mary's head, her

glance went to Josh. Eveleen saw him wink. Then he put his finger to his lips and gave a little shake of his head.

'Come in, come in,' Dorothy said. 'Bill's here too.'

'Shouldn't he be at work?' Mary teased. 'He'll be getting the sack.'

'No, he's got the morning off to be here to see you.'

Mary glanced at her and frowned slightly. 'You knew we were coming?'

Again, Eveleen saw Dorothy glance helplessly at Josh, almost as if she realized she had said too much.

They've planned it, Eveleen thought. They planned it that we should call round this way. She didn't know whether to be grateful or angry.

'In you go, Mary,' Josh said blandly, ushering her into her former home.

Mary stood in the kitchen and slowly turned round, drinking in the sight. 'Oh, Dorothy, you've got everything just the way we left it. I could almost think . . .' Her voice broke a little and there were tears in her eyes, yet she was still smiling as she went towards the man sitting in Walter's chair by the bright fire in the range. 'Bill. How lovely to see you again.'

'Mary, love.' He rose from the chair and kissed her cheek. 'It's good to have you back.'

Mary sank down into the chair that had once been hers and looked about her again. Dorothy bustled between the kitchen and the scullery carrying a tray with cups from Mary's best china tea service on it.

Seeing it, Mary pointed. 'Do you know, that's the only thing I really minded leaving behind. It was a wedding present.' She laughed wryly. 'The only one we got.'

'Well, here it is, all ready for you,' Dorothy said and began to pour the tea. As she handed round the cups,

Dorothy asked, 'Is the little one all right, Eveleen? Does she need a feed?'

Eveleen nodded. 'She will soon. If you wouldn't mind, I should like to give her a bottle before we leave.'

Dorothy smiled and nodded, but dropped her gaze.

Bill had not sat down again in the chair by the fire and now he gestured towards it with a broad grin on his face. 'Here, Josh, you'd better get used to sitting in it.'

Josh laughed and went towards the chair. With great ceremony he lowered himself into it. 'Bit of a tight squeeze,' he said.

Bill chuckled again and said, 'We'll soon work that off you.'

Eveleen exchanged a mystified glance with her mother and then they both looked at Josh. He cleared his throat and looked embarrassed. 'I suppose I had better explain.'

Quietly Bill and Dorothy stood to one side, though they did not leave the room.

'You see,' Josh began, 'I've bought this place and a little bit of the land around it too. I've always wanted to live in the country.'

Mary stared at him. 'You're going to come and live here?'

Josh nodded. 'And I was rather hoping you might come and live here too. As my – my housekeeper.' He reached across and took her hands in his. 'Mary, please say you will?'

Tears were running down her face, but now they were tears of happiness. 'Oh, Josh, of course I will, but what about . . .' She glanced at Eveleen and then at the cradle.

'I mean, all of you. Eveleen and the baby too, of course. You're a family.'

'You want all of us to come and live with you?' Eveleen asked.

Josh nodded. 'I'd like nothing better.'

Eveleen wasn't sure about all this. It had been thrown upon them so suddenly. She needed time to digest the idea. She glanced at her mother, but there was no mistaking the joy and happiness on Mary's face.

She was back home where she had always wanted to be. Mary Hardcastle was back where she really belonged.

Tears sprang into Eveleen's eyes and she turned away and walked from the room and out into the yard. She went as far as the gate and leant on it, looking out across the well-known view.

She couldn't tear her mother away from this, not again. Couldn't take her back to the terraced house in Nottingham. She had to agree to Josh's proposal for Mary's sake.

But Eveleen was troubled. There was something about this whole thing that didn't quite ring true. She felt as if she had been manipulated, as if the decision had been made for her and that she had been put in the position of not being able to refuse.

Fifty-Eight

'I don't know how you managed it all and so quickly,' Mary marvelled for the umpteenth time during their first week. 'And however did you get the Dunsmores to sell it to you?'

Josh smiled. 'They were persuaded. Everyone has their price,' he added with an unusual smugness.

Eveleen glanced at him across the dinner table. That was exactly what was troubling her. At first she had not been able to understand what it was about the whole story that mystified her. Josh wanting to live in the countryside, seeing the place where Mary and Eveleen used to live, falling in love with it and buying the house and a parcel of land from the Dunsmores all in under a fortnight just did not seem plausible.

'There are still some legal documents to be drawn up and signed and all that' – Josh waved his hand – 'but because the place was still empty, they could hardly refuse to let us move in.'

Eveleen looked down at her plate. It was not quite what she would have believed of the Dunsmores, especially not of Stephen. She could sooner believe that he would have tried to block the sale completely, if he had known who was moving back into the cottage.

She licked her lips. 'Did – did the Dunsmores know exactly who was going to be living here? I mean, did they know we were moving back?'

Josh appeared to be trying to remember. Vaguely, he said, 'I'm not really sure if it was ever mentioned. But that's none of their business.' He smiled broadly. 'They don't own it any more, do they? Or at least, they soon won't, once the papers have been signed and sealed.'

'You mean, the sale's not yet complete? They could still change their minds?'

'Of course they won't.' Josh winked at her. 'Like I said, everyone's got his price. It seems as if that young feller we met has been spending money a bit too freely. Gambling, I shouldn't wonder. Anyway, it was lucky for us – for me – that he was only too pleased to sell off a bit of the estate to get some quick cash.'

So, Eveleen thought, yet another flaw in the character of the man she had once thought she loved. But the knowledge brought her no satisfaction, only a feeling of foolishness, remembering how besotted and blind to his faults she had been.

Eveleen glanced at her mother, who was serenely ladling out the hot vegetable soup she had made that morning. The smile never seemed to leave her face now. Mary was happy and contented. She was back home and she had a kind man to fuss over once more and to care for her. With a start of surprise, Eveleen realized that her mother had not mentioned Jimmy once during the past few days. Perhaps even Mary had now accepted the fact that he was doing what he wanted to do and would not come back to them.

It was still thoughtless of him to leave them without even a word, however, to disappear so completely. But that was her brother, Eveleen thought. Selfish to the last. But even she wished that they could just know that he was all right. She believed he owed them that much.

Eveleen sighed and tried to dispel her anxieties. But there was one thought that would not leave her.

Just how had a man like Josh Carpenter managed to find the money to buy a smallholding?

A week later, after he had disappeared for a day back to Nottingham, Josh returned to tell them both gleefully, 'It's all signed, sealed and delivered. This place is really ours now.'

Eveleen glanced at him and said quietly, 'Yours, Josh.'

'No, no,' he insisted. 'I've had your names put on the deeds as well. It belongs to all of us.'

Eveleen's eyes narrowed as she regarded him shrewdly. 'In that case, isn't there something that we have to sign?'

For a moment Josh looked startled. 'Oh no, I don't think so. I've signed. Er – um – sort of proxy, or whatever they call it.'

He seemed to be avoiding meeting her direct gaze now. Eveleen glanced at her mother's ecstatic face and decided to say no more – for the present.

Later, in the yard, she cornered Josh.

'Now, Josh Carpenter, I want the truth and I want it now.'

'What do you mean, Eveleen?'

'Josh, don't take me for a fool. With the greatest respect, there's no way someone like you could save enough money to buy a place like this. Oh I know you had a good job at the factory, but you'd never earn enough there if you worked till you were a hundred.'

'I – I've never had anyone to spend my money on, Eveleen. I – I've saved.'

'So why spend it all on giving comparative strangers their old home back?'

Now she could see that she was hurting him, but she drove on relentlessly. She had to know the truth, and she was sure that the story that Josh Carpenter had bought the property, land and animals was not the truth.

'You're not strangers, Eveleen. Please don't say that. I'm very fond of you both, and little Bridie, too. I wanted to see your mother happy again.' His eyes had a haunted look for an instant, then he said hesitantly, 'Don't laugh at me, Eveleen, but I was rather hoping that one day your mother might consent to become my wife.'

Eveleen felt ashamed. The sincerity in the man's statement was apparent. She could see it in his eyes. But she saw also that he had craftily turned her attention away from the financial side to the more personal and emotional side, of which there could be no doubt in her mind.

She sighed and shook her head. 'I'm not laughing. I'm sure you'd make her very happy.'

'I know she'd make me the happiest man alive,' he said, smiling now, some of the loneliness chased from his eyes.

Softly Eveleen said, 'But you're still not telling me the truth about how you bought this place, are you? I know *why* now and I believe you. But I don't believe that you've bought it.'

Josh fidgeted and shifted uncomfortably. He ran his hand over his forehead and Eveleen could see that there were beads of sweat standing on his brow.

'All right, all right, I'll tell you the truth. But you've to promise me one thing first. That you won't do anything about it. You won't cause trouble. And especially that you'll never, ever, tell your mother.'

Slowly, she nodded, but the truth was becoming clear to her, even as Josh began to explain.

I was right. It's not Josh who's bought our home for us at all. It's him. He's behind all this.

She heard the words coming out of Josh's mouth, but now she could scarcely take it in. Her mind was reeling, the world spinning around her. She felt dizzy and sick.

How could she live with this, knowing that he, of all people, owned the house they lived in?

Fifty-Nine

'You're being very selfish.'

Richard Stokes was now sitting behind the desk that had once been Josh Carpenter's.

Eveleen, her eyes blazing and her mouth tight, leant across the wide expanse and shook her fist in his face. 'Don't you dare to tell me what I am. Aren't I giving up my whole life to taking care of my mother and Rebecca's child? I made a promise to her and I meant to keep it. I'll be the one to take her back to Bernby, not you.'

'Of course you would have kept your promise and taken her back home,' he said smoothly, but he added pointedly, 'one day.'

'Oh you know how to dig the knife in, don't you? Well, if you and your condescending father paid better wages, I might have managed it a bit quicker.'

He rose and came round the desk to stand close to her. In so doing, he placed himself between Eveleen and the door so that she could not flounce off before he had said what he intended to say.

'I didn't want you to know about any of this and I'll give Josh Carpenter a piece of my mind when I see him.' The twinkle in his eyes belied the threat. 'But since you know part of it, you'd better know the rest.'

'The rest? What do you mean, the rest?'

'Won't you sit down?'

'I'd rather stand, thank you.'

'Very well.'

There was tension between them and a spark that had nothing to do with Eveleen's anger, yet she held on to that indignation. That was why her pulse was racing and her legs felt weak. It had nothing to do with the fact that he was standing so close to her she could have reached out and touched his face, traced the line of his strong jaw, smoothed back the unruly lock of black hair that fell on to his forehead, drowned in those dark eyes . . .

'We did it for your mother as much as for you. More so, really.'

'We?'

'My father and I.'

Eveleen was stunned to silence.

'My father feels very guilty about what happened years ago.'

Eveleen found her voice. 'So he should,' she muttered.

'Even though,' Richard went on firmly, ignoring her remark, 'he knew nothing about your mother's pregnancy and the tragedy that followed at the time. Now he wants to try to make amends as much as he can.'

'And what would your mother say to all that?' Eveleen asked sarcastically. 'If she knew.'

'She does know. My mother is a wonderful lady and very understanding.' His words were like a rebuke to Eveleen. 'My father told her everything. About how much he had loved your mother, had wanted to marry her, but because they were so young he had bided his time, hoping that when he reached his majority, he could go his own way.'

'But he went away. He left her,' Eveleen argued, still unwilling to believe that Brinsley Stokes had been entirely ignorant and therefore also completely innocent.

'He was only nineteen and thought it politic to obey

his family's wishes until he was twenty-one. But when he came back home, your mother had disappeared. He searched for her, but never found her. He waited for more than a year, hoping she would come back, but then he came to the conclusion that she had gone away – just like her family said she had – because she no longer loved him.'

Eveleen was struggling with her conscience. For so long she had believed that Brinsley had deliberately and callously deserted her mother when she had needed him the most, and yet . . .

'You don't believe me, do you?'

'I . . . I want to. Really I do, but . . .'

With great understanding, he said softly, 'But you've lived all your life with your version of the story and you cannot change.'

She shook her head. 'Not that long, I knew nothing about it at all until we went to Flawford. My father must have known.' Vividly she recalled his evasive answers to her probing questions. 'But we – Jimmy and me – we didn't.'

'It's hardly the sort of thing a mother would like to tell her children, is it?'

Eveleen met his gaze. For a young man, not much older than she was, he was very kind and understanding. Or was it only a façade? Would this kind, generous face dissolve into twisted disdain if he didn't get his own way?

'Don't you trust me?' he asked gently.

She jumped at how accurately he had gauged her thoughts. Trust? How could she trust any man after what had happened to her? She had trusted Stephen Dunsmore. She had even trusted her own brother and so had poor, naïve Rebecca and look where that had got her.

'I know you've been hurt,' he was saying and his tone

hardened as he added, 'and I think I've now met the man who hurt you so, but haven't there been others in your life who haven't hurt you? People who have loved you and cared for you and about you? What about your father and those nice people at Bernby? Bill and Dorothy. Their affection for you was plain to see.'

It was as if a door opened in her mind. His gentle prompting caused her to think about the other men she had known in her young life.

Her father. But that was different. Of course her father had loved and cared for her and had never let her down. But Rebecca's father hadn't, a little voice reminded her. When Rebecca had needed him the most, he had turned his face from her.

And then the others queued up in her mind's eye, demanding to be remembered.

Bill Morton, who had stood by the Hardcastle family, perhaps even jeopardizing his own job by doing so. Then Andrew Burns. How could she ever doubt his selfless devotion to Rebecca and, now, to Bridie? And Josh. Josh Carpenter, whom everyone ridiculed, had a heart of gold. He wasn't a lecherous figure of fun. He was wonderfully kind and caring. And a very lonely man.

And yet he had readily been party to deception. He had deceived her into thinking he had brought about their good fortune.

Richard was watching her. Perhaps he was even reading on her face the signs of her inner struggle. He moved closer.

'Won't you forgive us? You must see that if we had told you the truth, you would never have agreed to it.'

That was true, Eveleen was forced to admit.

'What about Josh?' she burst out. 'Was that all a lie too?'

Richard frowned, obviously puzzled. 'I don't under-stand.'

'Once he's got my mother installed in the country, is he going to leave her?'

The puzzled expression was replaced by one of under-standing and then of gentle sadness. 'One day, I'll make the man who's hurt you so much pay for what he's done.' Richard's mouth tightened. 'Believe me, I'll make him pay. But as for Josh,' he shook his head. 'No, he's not going to abandon your mother. He's a happy man. A very happy man. You'll see. Over the next few weeks and months, he'll have shed several pounds and be as fit as a fiddle.' He moved closer and said softly, 'Oh Eveleen. Won't you believe us? Won't you trust me? Won't you at least give me a chance to prove how very much I love you?'

She looked into the depths of his brown eyes and she could see nothing but love and concern for her.

He took her hand and raised it to his lips. Gently, almost with a reverence, he kissed each one of her fingers. Then she felt his sigh as he looked up and met her gaze. She could not doubt the look in his eyes. Desire was there, yes. She recognized that. She had seen it before in another's eyes, but in Richard's deep eyes there was something more. So much more.

He gave a little shake of his head, a sad, almost defeated gesture. 'You're still in love with him, aren't you, Eveleen?'

'No, no,' she cried vehemently. 'I hate him. Hate him.'

Richard closed his eyes and sighed so deeply now that it seemed to come from the depths of his soul.

'Oh my love. My dearest love. Love and hate are blood brothers. Only indifference is truly the opposite of love.' He opened his eyes and, reaching out, tenderly touched her cheek. 'You can never truly love again until you can look at him and feel nothing. Absolutely nothing.'

She opened her mouth to protest but gently he laid his forefinger against her lips. 'But when that day comes, I'll be here waiting for you, Eveleen. I'll wait for you for ever, if I have to.'

Sixty

Eveleen was restless but did not know why.

She was back home in the country. The cows in the field nearest the house belonged to them now and were providing enough milk for the family with plenty to spare. She made butter and cheese and sold it in Grantham market. Another field was to be ploughed up and set with vegetables which would also be sold at market. With eggs from the chickens and a recent litter of pigs, Pear Tree Farm was becoming a thriving smallholding.

Josh looked to her to lead the way, but he worked alongside her in the fields, in the cowhouse, in the barn – anywhere where there was work to be done. The outdoor life had tanned Josh's skin to a healthy bronze and the happiness was written on his face.

As for Mary, she was back to her old self, happier, if that were possible, than she had ever been. She cosseted and fussed over the new man in her life and there was no denying that she was besotted with the baby. Mary had even, much to Eveleen's silent amusement, mellowed towards her. Gone were the sharp retorts and remarks that had always been the tone of the early relationship between mother and daughter.

There was only one cloud in her mother's sunny sky, as far as Eveleen knew. Still no word had come from Jimmy.

Everything should have been perfect in Eveleen's life,

so why did she feel restless? It was as if there was something missing. Why did she so often find her mind empty of rational thought and her dreamy gaze on the westward horizon?

She was happy here. Win and Fred had visited and Andrew came often, though she knew his main purpose was to see Bridie. She was back home, Eveleen told herself, where she had longed to be.

And yet . . .

'I don't know what's the matter with me,' Eveleen confided in Dorothy one day when she had pushed the perambulator down the track to Furze Farm to sit in the warm kitchen over a cup of tea.

'I s'pect you're missing the bright city lights.'

Eveleen laughed. 'I didn't get the chance to see any "bright lights",' she said. Then her smile faded. 'But do you know, I do miss it. The noise and the bustle.'

'And the people?' Dorothy prompted gently.

'Well, maybe one or two,' Eveleen said carefully.

There was silence between them, the only sound in the kitchen the settling of the fire in the range and the kettle singing on the hob, until Dorothy, changing the subject, said, 'I don't expect you've heard.' She was beaming. 'Our Ted and Alice Parks have got engaged.'

'Oh, that's wonderful news,' Eveleen said sincerely.

'Alice is so happy. Planning her trousseau and collecting bits and pieces for her bottom drawer.' Dorothy cleared her throat and glanced at Eveleen. 'They're getting married next month.'

Eveleen spoke without thinking, unable to keep the surprise out of her voice. 'Next month?'

Dorothy nodded. 'Yes, it's a bit sudden, but then

Alice's dad is holding a shotgun to our Ted's head.' To Eveleen's surprise Dorothy was laughing as she added, 'If you know what I mean.'

Eveleen's eyes widened and then she said tartly, 'Well, I hope Ted doesn't run off like our Jimmy.'

'He won't,' Dorothy said firmly. 'He's really looking forward to being a dad, even though they are both a bit young.'

'He's changed then,' Eveleen murmured.

'Why do you say that?'

'Oh nothing,' Eveleen said evasively. She could hardly tell Dorothy of the advice that Ted had once handed out to Jimmy. Obviously he was no longer following his own counsel.

'You – you don't seem to mind,' Eveleen said hesitantly.

'There's not a lot me and Bill could say. Our Ted was born only six months after we were wed. And he was a full-term baby.'

'Oh,' was all Eveleen could say but the comical look of confusion on her face made Dorothy burst out laughing.

There was someone coming down the track that led to Pear Tree Farm: a slim young woman, holding up her skirt to pick her way daintily around the puddles. Eveleen, emerging from the cowhouse, a bucket of milk in each hand, paused to watch her. The girl reached the gate, lifted her head and looked about her.

A wide smile spread across Eveleen's face and she almost dropped the buckets to the ground in her haste to reach her visitor. Her arms flung wide, she ran towards the gate calling out a greeting.

'Helen! Oh, Helen.'

'Eveleen!'

Their shrieks of joy, their laughter and the tumult of questions they fired at each other brought Josh and Mary out of the house. Linking her arm through her friend's, Eveleen drew her towards the house. 'Mam, Josh, look who's here.'

Josh came forward, smiling and holding out his callous-hardened hand. As Helen's eyes widened and her mouth dropped open, Josh chuckled, 'Yes, mi duck, it's really me.'

As she put her small hand into his, the girl said candidly, 'You look marvellous. So – so . . .'

'Much thinner,' Josh beamed and they all laughed.

'Come in, come in, love,' Mary said. 'We haven't met before, have we? But I've heard a lot about you.'

'This is my mam,' Eveleen made the introductions. 'And the little madam who's making all the noise is Bridie.'

They went into the house and Mary picked up the baby. 'You're hungry, my little precious, aren't you? There, there,' she crooned.

'You sit down, love. I'll make her feed,' Josh said, heading for the scullery.

Eveleen could not hide her laughter at the astonished look on Helen's face. 'Well,' the girl whispered, anxious not to cause offence. 'Who'd have thought it?'

Close to her ear, Eveleen murmured, 'Who indeed?'

For a moment the two girls watched the happy, domestic scene, then Eveleen said, 'I'll show you round.' She pretended to grimace as she said laughingly, 'We won't get our dinner until mi lady there has got hers. I'll take the milk into the dairy and then we'll go for a walk.' She hesitated and then added, 'Unless you're tired.'

Josh came back into the room as Helen answered, 'No, no, I'd love to see everything. I don't get into the country-side very often.'

'Dinner in half an hour then. If your mam hasn't finished feeding Bridie, I'll get it ready.'

The two girls exchanged another glance and hid their smiles.

'Oh, I nearly forgot.' Helen fished in the bag she carried and pulled out a dog-eared postcard. 'I've some-thing for you. Win said this came to the house you had in Foundry Yard.'

Eveleen took the card in her hand and turned it over. She drew in a breath sharply, making a little startled sound of surprise so that Mary and Josh looked up.

Eveleen raised her gaze to meet her mother's eyes. 'Oh, Mam, it's from Jimmy.'

'Jimmy!'

Eveleen nodded.

In Mary's arms the baby squirmed and protested. She could see the bottle but it wasn't coming to her mouth quickly enough.

'There, there, my pet,' Mary soothed and in a moment Bridie was sucking noisily. Then, quite calmly, Mary said, 'Well, read it out then.'

'It doesn't say much,' Eveleen looked down at the untidy scrawl. Schoolwork and her brother had never really been good companions. 'Just "*Dear Mam and Evie, I am well. Hope you are. I'm seeing the world. Love, Jimmy*".'

'Not a word of apology, I suppose?' Mary asked.

Eveleen shook her head and smiled. 'I can't ever remember Jimmy saying he was sorry for anything. Can you?'

'No,' Mary said tartly. 'But it wouldn't have hurt

him. Just once. He owes you that much, Evie, at the very least.'

For a long moment mother and daughter stared at each other. Then to Eveleen's surprise, tears filled Mary's eyes and ran down her cheeks. 'Oh, Evie, I'm so sorry. So very sorry. I don't know how you've put up with me.'

Eveleen hurried to her side and put her arms about her mother. Quietly Josh took the baby from Mary, who now clung to Evie and sobbed against her shoulder. 'I've treated you so badly, even when your poor father was alive.'

Stroking her hair, Eveleen soothed, 'It's all over, Mam. All forgotten.'

Mary pulled back a little and smiled through her tears. She patted Eveleen's shoulder. 'You're a good lass, Evie. And I do love you – very much.'

Now it was Eveleen's turn to feel the tears spilling down her face. Then suddenly they were laughing and crying and hugging each other, until at last Mary said, 'Go on, love. You go for a walk with Helen.' Her smile widened and her words included Josh and the baby. 'We're fine here.'

As Eveleen propped the card on the dresser, she murmured, 'I am glad we've heard from him. At least we know he's well.'

Again she and her mother exchanged a look. Eveleen knew that the arrival of news from Jimmy had completed Mary's contented world.

'It's like something out of a picture book.' Helen was ecstatic in her praise. 'Blue sky, green fields, even a stream and trees. Oh I've never seen so many trees.'

They were walking alongside the beck towards the

bridge, where they sat on the parapet and watched the water bubbling over the pebbles.

'Just look at the colours in that water,' Helen marvelled. 'Brown against the rocks but there's blue and green. Even purple.'

Fascinated, she sat watching the rushing water.

'You make it sound idyllic,' Eveleen teased. 'It's not so lovely in winter, when there's snow and ice and—'

Helen clapped her hands, 'Oh, I bet it is. Everywhere covered in white. How pretty it must look.'

'Pretty pictures, maybe, but not when you have to milk the cows with fingers you can't feel and trudge through two foot of snow to feed the pigs and—'

'Stop, stop. You'll have me crying in a minute.' They laughed, leaning against each other.

'Oh it's good to see you.' For Eveleen the sight of her friend had brought the touch of the city again: the pavements seething with life, the lighted shops, the bustle and the noise. She felt a sudden surge of excitement. 'Tell me,' she demanded eagerly, 'what's been happening?'

'Well,' Helen began slowly, with a coy glance. 'All the women in the workrooms have had a rise in their wages and we've been promised a little extra at Christmas. Oh, he's so good to us. Any suggestions we want to make for improving our working conditions, he said, we're to go straight to him.'

Eveleen swallowed and her voice was husky as she asked, 'Who? Who is this "he" who's doing such wonderful things?'

Before Helen spoke, Eveleen already knew the answer.

'Why, Mr Richard, of course. He's taken on the management of the warehouse now, while his father manages the factory side of things. But even he's making improvements, they say.'

So, Eveleen thought, another young man who had been given power over other people's lives. And yet, from what Helen was telling her . . .

There was the sound of hoofbeats in the lane coming closer and, intrigued, Helen twisted round to watch the horseman approach.

Eveleen kept her gaze fixed steadfastly on the beck, her back turned towards the lane. The rider reined in and Eveleen heard him speak.

'Good afternoon, ladies. I trust I find you well.'

She heard Helen's soft chuckle at her side and almost laughed aloud as in a very haughty tone Helen said, 'You do indeed, sir.'

'And you, Miss Hardcastle?'

She felt Helen's sharp elbow in her ribs and her whispered, 'Evie?'

Slowly Eveleen turned round and looked up into the face of the man on horseback. With a grand gesture she inclined her head and said quietly, 'I am very well, sir. Thank you.'

Stephen Dunsmore raised his hat and bowed his head towards them. He smiled his most charming smile and said, 'I bid you good-day, ladies.' Replacing his hat, he urged his horse forward. They watched him canter along the lane and turn in at the gates of Fairfield House.

'What a pompous, stuck-up little prig!' Helen said.

Eveleen gasped and stared at her friend until Helen laughed and said, 'Oh I know I've only just met him, but I'm pretty good at summing folks up. 'Specially fellers. I wouldn't want anything to do with him if he was the last man on earth.' Her merry laughter echoed across the fields as she spluttered, 'Mind you, whenever I say that me mam always says, "Don't worry, you'd be killed in the rush".'

Eveleen, her gaze still on the empty lane where Stephen had disappeared, said tentatively, 'How – how can you tell?'

'Tell what? What he's like, you mean?'

'Mm.'

'He's got cold eyes and a weak chin. I bet he can be a right charmer when he wants to be, but turn nasty if he didn't get his own way.'

Suddenly Eveleen was laughing and crying all at the same time. She put her arms around Helen and hugged her close. 'Oh, Helen, you're wonderful. I do love you so.'

'What did I say?' asked the mystified girl in astonishment.

But Eveleen couldn't tell her that when she had looked up into Stephen Dunsmore's face she had felt neither love nor hatred. No swift beating of the heart or trembling at the knees. No wanting to rush into his embrace or feeling the urge to scratch her nails down his petulant face.

At last she had been able to look at Stephen Dunsmore and feel absolutely nothing.

'So, when are you going back to Nottingham for good?' Mary, sitting contentedly by the fire with her pillow lace on her lap, her fingers deftly twisting and weaving the threads, asked her daughter.

'Trying to get rid of me, are you?' Eveleen smiled fondly at her mother and winked at Josh sitting in Walter's chair reading the newspaper. It didn't hurt her to see him in her father's place. He was a good, kind man – just as Walter had been – and she felt sure that her father would approve of Josh.

'Of course we are,' Mary said, laughing. 'What do I

449

want with a nineteen-year-old daughter around when I'm about to become a blushing bride myself?'

Eveleen gasped and looked from one to the other and back again. Then she leapt to her feet and flung her arms wide, trying to embrace them both at once.

'Oh when? Have you fixed a date?'

'We thought next Easter.'

The conversation turned to their plans; plans, Eveleen noticed with a pang, which did not seem to include her.

Her own thoughts drifted. She thought about the city that she had grown to love and the friendly people there. Win and Fred and Helen in particular, but there were others too. She loved Lincolnshire, the place of her birth, she always would, but she had seen something else now. She had witnessed another kind of life and it had twisted its way into her heart.

Her mother was home where she belonged and she had a good man to care for her once more. What did it matter how that had been achieved? That it had been accomplished was what mattered.

'Of course if you do decide to go back, we . . .' Mary hesitated and looked towards Josh who took up her words, 'We want you to leave Bridie with us, love.'

In that instant Eveleen felt the burden slip from her shoulders. She was free. Free to live her own life.

And, now, she was free to love again.

'Yes,' Eveleen murmured and began to smile. 'You're right, Mam. My life is back in Nottingham.'

'Right, that's settled then,' Josh said and added, mildly, 'Give my regards to Mr Richard when you see him.'

From behind his newspaper, he winked across the hearth at his bride-to-be.

The Clippie Girls
Margaret Dickinson

Sisters in love. A family at war. A city in peril.

Rose and Myrtle Sylvester look up to their older sister, Peggy. She is the sensible, reliable one in the household of women headed by their grandmother, Grace Booth, and their mother, Mary Sylvester. When war is declared in 1939 they must face the hardships together and huge changes in their lives are inevitable. For Rose, there is the chance to fulfil her dream of becoming a clippie on Sheffield's trams like Peggy. But for Myrtle, the studious, clever one in the family, war may shatter her ambitions.

When the tram on which Peggy is a conductress is caught in a bomb blast, she bravely helps to rescue her passengers. One of them is a young soldier, Terry Price, and he and Peggy begin courting. They meet every time he can get leave, but eventually Terry is posted abroad and she hears nothing from him. Worse still, Peggy must break the devastating news to her family that she is pregnant.

The shock waves that ripple through the family will affect each and every one of them and life will never be the same again.

Fairfield Hall
Margaret Dickinson

A matter of honour. A sense of duty. A time for courage.

Ruthlessly ambitious Ambrose Constantine is determined that his daughter Annabel shall marry into nobility. A fish merchant and self-made man, he has only his wealth to buy his way into society.

When Annabel's secret meetings with Gilbert, a young man employed at her father's offices, stop suddenly, she learns that he has mysteriously disappeared. Heartbroken, she finds solace with her grandparents on their Lincolnshire farm, but her father will not allow her to hide herself in the countryside and enlists the help of a business connection to launch his daughter into society.

During the London Season, Annabel is courted by James Lyndon, the Earl of Fairfield, whose country estate is only a few miles from her grandfather's farm. Believing herself truly loved at last, Annabel accepts his offer of marriage. It is only when she arrives at Fairfield Hall that she realizes the true reason behind James's proposal and the part her scheming father has played.

Throughout the years that follow, Annabel experiences both heartache and joy, and the birth of her son should finally secure the future of the Fairfield Estate. But there are others who lay claim to the inheritance, igniting a feud that will only reach its resolution in the trenches of the First World War.

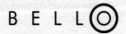

FOR MORE ON

MARGARET DICKINSON

sign up to receive our

SAGA NEWSLETTER

Packed with **features, competitions, authors'
and readers' letters** and **news of exclusive events,**
it's a 'must-read' for every Margaret Dickinson fan!

Simply fill in your details below and tick to confirm that you would
like to receive saga-related news and promotions and return to us at
Pan Macmillan, Saga Newsletter, 20 New Wharf Road, London, N1 9RR.

NAME

ADDRESS

POSTCODE

EMAIL

☐ *I would like to receive saga-related news and promotions (please tick)*

*You can unsubscribe at any time in writing or through our website where you can also see
our privacy policy which explains how we will store and use your data.*